CORRUPTION

THE CORRUPTION CYCLE
BOOK ONE

BY
ADAM VINE

COPYRIGHT 2017 ADAM CHRISTOPHER KENNEDY

This work is licensed under a Creative Commons Attribution-Noncommercial-No Derivative Works 3.0 Unported License.

Attribution — You must attribute the work in the manner specified by the author or licensor (but not in any way that suggests that they endorse you or your use of the work).
Noncommercial — You may not use this work for commercial purposes.
No Derivative Works — You may not alter, transform, or build upon this work.

Inquiries about additional permissions should be directed to: theadamvine@gmail.com

Cover Design by J. Caleb Clark

This is a work of fiction. Names, characters, places, brands, media, and incidents are either the product of the author's imagination or are used fictitiously. Any resemblance to similarly named places or to persons living or deceased is unintentional.

PRINT ISBN 978-1541022140

For Hannah, ever my light in the darkness.

Through me you go to the grief-wracked city.
Through me you go to everlasting pain.
Through me you go and pass among lost souls.
       -    Dante, *The Inferno*

PROLOGUE

ONE BY ONE the old bricks fell. "Almost got it," Katherine said, pushing hard into the broken wall until her arm slid through. The hiss and splash of bricks falling into water whispered through the ancient tunnels. "You owe me a bottle of good vodka," she told the one-eyed man watching from the shadows.

Vojciek attempted to scowl, but the cracked dolomite of his face betrayed a quiet satisfaction. "Ho-hoo! One bottle? Make it three. You've done well today, Kat."

Katherine's nickname among her fellow Vermin was Meerkat – often shortened to Little Kat, or just Kat. Meerkats were burrowing rodents supposed to have lived on the Surface before the Last Day of Sun. Bookmother had read her a story about them once. Since she was a little girl falling over on Vojciek's mats, Katherine had tried to emulate how she imagined such small, springy creatures must have fought, all sniping limbs and devious balance.

She raised her heel and kicked the broken wall, once, twice, then three times, the old stones spilling from their dusty crypts until the hole was wide enough for her and the old man to fit through.

"Let me guess. I'm taking point?" Katherine said.

Vojciek poked his torch through the hole, his white, bottlebrush eyebrows folding down into a hard squint. The light shied beyond the broken bulwark of the wall, where a few scattered glimmers revealed a canal snaking away into the darkness. A rank cloud enveloped them as the old, unseen bowels of the Night City breathed once more.

Katherine had always imagined such a discovery would be exciting, but all she could think about was the smell.

"That is a good guess," her teacher said.

The old man stopped her as she was sliding her foot through the jagged bricks. He offered her the torch. "We're just little Vermin sneaking through his halls, trying to steal a bite of cheese. And we know his cure for little Vermin. But though Vermin we may be, we are also the fire. No matter what awaits us in there…" Vojciek said.

"We know what awaits us in there," Katherine said, taking the torch.

Vojciek drew a deep breath, pulled his shawl up over his nose, and nodded for her to move. Katherine mounted the broken wall and vaulted into the darkness.

Her legs splashed into cold, oily water. The shadows retreated and advanced from the flickering nimbus of her torchlight like unsure combatants. Black islands of questionable composition floated by her in the gloom.

"Look what we've found! Another tunnel!" Vojciek said. "What a strange and mystical thing to find hidden a kilometer beneath the Surface! Ho-hoo! Is something wrong, Kat? Worried we might wake up some ancient, eldritch thing set down here to guard our Beloved Ruler's secrets? Feel any tentacles brush against your leg yet?"

"No. Can't say that I did."

"You never know down here. Better stay on your toes…"

"Ugh."

Katherine paused, holding the torch close to the tunnel's low, curving wall. Unlike the other passages, this one wasn't made of brick, but carved straight from the slick, pale rock. "Have you noticed the walls?" she said.

CORRUPTION

"Aye. Either we're standing in a very shoddily-delved mineshaft, or whoever built this passage did so in a hurry," Vojciek said.

The tunnel branched every twenty or thirty steps, a spider-web network of yawning, black mouths all waiting to devour the scarce light of Katherine's torch. They were all dead ends, Katherine knew. She had studied the manuscripts in Bookmother's library enough to know that once they passed the false wall, it was a straight shot to the cavern. The other passages were blinds meant to mislead potential grave robbers.

The tunnel ended abruptly around the next bend, and the two of them stepped into a cavern so large Katherine's torchlight barely touched the ceiling.

They were standing on a slender crescent of beach winding around the shores of a vast subterranean lake. There was an island rising in the distance, upon which stood the largest building Katherine had ever seen.

It was a great cathedral, all wrought from red brick and white marble. Its shadow-shrouded spires were so tall they interlocked with the gargantuan dripstones of the cave ceiling like twisted puzzle pieces. Katherine had to crane her neck to take in its full, nauseating height.

Her pulse quickened as the realization sank in. *The Lost Cathedral of Saint Aram. It actually exists.*

"Ho-hoo! Three bottles of vodka, indeed. Your mother would be proud, Kat. I wish she was here," Vojciek said.

"It's hard to believe I'm finally looking at it," Katherine said. "Feels a bit surreal."

"On that note..." The old man pulled a leather flask out of a secret pocket stitched into the lining of his coat, took a deep swig, and offered it to Katherine. "Distilled it myself, you know."

She took a drink and gave it back.

Vojciek put the flask away, unslung his Wyvernwood spear from where it rested on his shoulder. "Since this is your show, I trust you know how we're getting across that." He pointed his spear across the lake.

The serene, midnight water ran far past the tiny halo of her torchlight, as motionless as black stained glass. They could swim, but the lake was deep, and icy cold. *It's too warm this far down to freeze. Too bad. Some thick ice would have helped.*

"I have a plan," she said.

The old man gestured for her to demonstrate. Katherine raised her hand and released the ghost from where it rested in the casket embedded within her palm. The world gave a little scream, and a crushing pressure enveloped her. A black, shivering line bloomed from her fist. She aimed it at one of the giant stalagmites growing from the cave floor.

Katherine flicked her wrist, slicing the monstrous stone pillar from its base. The upper segment began to slide, down, down, down, until it toppled. She made another quick slash, and another, slicing angled portions from the base. The pillar rolled into the frigid water with barely more than a splash. A maze of ripples cascaded across the lake, lapping the shore with a gentle elegy of waves.

The pillar had fallen to form a natural bridge between the beach and the island that they could easily wade across. Only after did Katherine wonder if the sound could have been heard up on the Surface.

The old man frowned at her.

"We're deep enough," Katherine said.

"That was thoughtless," Vojciek said.

Katherine bedded the ghost in her palm and started across the beach. "We can handle a few shells, master. Besides, we'll be gone before they ever know we were here."

Vojciek shook his head. "It's not shells we need to worry about. They won't send a purging party. Not down here."

Katherine's eyes drifted to the empty socket where her master's eye had been, hidden under a ragged leather eye patch. The ghost shot a knife of pain up her arm at the thought. "If we're on borrowed time, then we'd best hurry."

The old man stroked his mustache. "We're all on borrowed time, Kat. One of the great secrets of life is that it can end at any instant. Realizing that will both free and condemn you. But no matter what chains the Oppressor may put on us, he cannot take away our fate."

"I thought you said fate was a choice."

"Precisely my point. Now, before we go on, I can see the ghost is giving you some discomfort. It is reacting to your fear. The People of the Sun were masterful architects, most of all when it came to weaponry. It's one of the reasons they're not here anymore. I thought you were better prepared for this. Remember your drills. You must empty your mind to avoid being stung. You must *become the fire*. Kat…?"

She stepped out onto the pillar, walking on the balls of her feet so she wouldn't slip and fall in. It was no different than walking on the balance beam in the mat room back at the Last Station, something she'd done a thousand times since she was a child.

Far beneath the surface of the lake, the shelf of the shore dropped away to limitless depths of black. Katherine's reflection on that mirrored surface was one she hardly recognized. Her once-smooth, pale skin was now yellow from malnutrition. Her close-cropped hair was spotting white. Her cheeks looked sunken, and there were deep circles under her eyes from camping in the Undersprawl for more than a week.

Yet even living the hard, likely short life of a Vermin, she was far more fortunate than most girls her age in the Burrow, already married and bearing children before their eighteenth birthdays.

So many lives I'll never live. But I chose this, didn't I? I knew what I was giving up, just like mom did.

Vojciek whistled as he set foot on the rocky shore of the island. They both took a moment to soak in the magnificent sight of the Lost Cathedral up close.

Its brick-and-marble façade rose in layers, reminding Katherine of an enormous gingerbread palace. Each of its twin bell towers was topped with a giant gumdrop of verdant bronze. The main door was carved from a single slab of pure amber, the frame adorned with hundreds of life-sized marble statues depicting choirs of angels singing and marching to war. Most other churches in the Night City had long since fallen to ruin, their statues and marble dressings stolen by time. But this cathedral was perfectly intact.

The people of the Twilight Age built this. It's like a window into another world.

"Ho-hoo! Almost makes an old atheist want to believe again," the old man said.

Katherine felt it, too, though she did not share her master's skepticism. "How old do you think it is?"

"If the legends are true, older than anything still standing on the Surface." A hint of sadness tinged the old man's voice. "But I'm still not entirely convinced they are."

"What would convince you?" Katherine said, gazing up at the cathedral's bulbous, twinkling spires. "Do you not think this is Saint Aram's?" She wanted to say, *are you mad?* But kept the thought to herself.

CORRUPTION

Vojciek picked something from his mustache and flung it off into the darkness. "It would be nice, wouldn't it? If we found the church where our Oppressor lived before his rise to power, when he was merely an acolyte; if we found his diary, that terrible trove of secrets so powerful it could undermine his rule, even make the Amber City fall...

"We have found a real, physical structure, which someone really hid – or *built* - a kilometer underground. Does that mean it was moved here by magic, or that the Crippled King was the one who did the moving, like the stories say? Or that this discovery will win us the war, and herald a glorious new age of daylight?"

The old man didn't wait for her to answer. "Now, I don't know much about any of that, but here's what I've observed in my six decades on this iceberg. Myths are always about what we want to believe, and never about what *is*. Suppose we discover some proof the Crippled King is not who he claims. Will our position have improved? Will it stop the Amber City from hunting us down like little rats? No. We'll still be Vermin to them. We will *always* be Vermin to them. Hate doesn't need a reason."

"I see," Katherine said.

The old man spat. "Oh, don't give me that face. You've found something incredible, Kat. I give you all the credit. I certainly don't want any. Fame would go right to my head. Can you imagine? I'd become as insufferable as a full bladder multiplied by a hangnail. Ho-hoo!"

She forced a smile.

Vojciek took another swig from his flask, wiped his mouth with his sleeve, and casually extended a long, bony finger toward the door of the cathedral. "But don't take my word for it. Open it. That way, when you prove me wrong and win this war, you can look back on this moment and say, *I told that old fool. I always knew I'd surpass him. What's that old saying again? To the master goes the blade?"*

Katherine took a deep breath and placed her hand on the door. There was no handle. She merely had to press her fingertips to the cool, smooth amber and a crack opened in its center. The door swung inward.

The old man's cackle echoed through the cathedral's dark, voluminous innards. "Ho-hoo!"

Katherine stepped inside and gasped.

She was washed in blinding light, then the resounding boom of organ music. A hundred airborne lamps flickered to life all floating between dozens of ornate pillars, which held aloft a great domed ceiling swathed with paintings of the saints and their sacred stories from the Sol Firma. The walls were a robber's trove of countless golden statues and icons gazing out at her from every nook and sepulcher.

Most of the vast interior of the church was occupied by a colossal black ship resting on a crystal bier, like some behemoth display in a museum built for giants. It reminded Katherine of the stories she'd heard as a child of the Twilight Age, when brave men and women still sailed the unfrozen seas all the way to the edges of the world. From a distance, the shining, ebony hull appeared mirror-smooth, but up close it was covered with thousands of tiny pockmarks.

The music thundered its final note, dwindled, and started over from the beginning. The song was a military march played in a major key. She'd heard it before, but couldn't remember when.

"The Battle Hymn of the New Republic," Vojciek shouted over the din. "One of my favorite tunes. The title refers to the new New Republic, not the old New Republic, or the old Old Republic, or the Great Old Republic, or the Grand Old Republic, or the Federation, or the Paradigm, or the republic that called itself a republic but was actually a fascist empire. No, no, the one to which this song refers is the one our Beloved Ruler usurped on the Last Day of Sun, before the fall of the True Night…"

"Master."

"Sorry. I'm rambling again. Piss on it. The point was – and I did have a point – I haven't heard this tune in decades. I still remember some of the lyrics."

The old man conducted an invisible choir with one hand as he sang:

"Mine eyes have seen the glory of the coming of the Lord…

"He is knocking down the silos where the grains of wrath are stored…

"Doot doot doot doot doot doot doot doot, I can't recall the words…

"…His day is marching on."

The old man's voice trembled and quieted, leaving only the heart-pounding percussion of the organ, then he said, "Your mother used to hum it to you. That's why you remember it. It was the only way to get you to fall asleep so she and I could train. But I doubt you've heard it since. This piece of music was banned a hundred years before you were born."

"We should turn it off," Katherine said.

Vojciek struck the ground twice with the butt of his spear. The music ceased. The old master gave Katherine a gap-ridden smirk. "Most buildings from the Twilight Age were fully automated. Some call it magic. I call it sound engineering."

"What's that?" Katherine said, venturing closer to the altar.

"Well, well. Now that is a pretty thing," Vojciek said.

He followed her up the marble dais to where a huge statue of a faceless man in white robes levitated with one palm outraised, the universal symbol of the Wanderer.

The statue was four times as tall as a man, all grown from a single vein of solarite crystal. The artist had left the face blank, but had covered the Wanderer's arms and legs with intricate spirals where they poked from beneath his tunic.

"The Wanderer, memory be upon him," Katherine whispered. She knelt and touched the tip of her thumb to her forehead, ears, and mouth. Vojciek remained silently on his feet, glowering until she stood.

"Yes, yes. Son of the Spiral, Sower of Seeds, the Gardener of Worlds, the source of as many unutterable curses as revelatory visions. Legend tells that the People of the Sun used to make these statues from solid gold. Solarite would've been a more decadent option. Gods always mirror the societies who create them."

Katherine had no desire to debate the flaws and virtues of organized religion with the old man here.

She climbed the dais and ran her fingers along the fat, smooth nodules of the statue's toes. They were surprisingly warm. "It's magnificent."

Vojciek uncapped his flask and drank. "Suppose so. Suppose not. Boo. I suppose nothing matters less than an old man's sorrow."

Katherine turned. "What?"

Her master's voice fell to a crack. "I may not get another chance to say this, Kat. S-something… I've been meaning to tell you for a long time."

"Yes, Master? What is it?"

"That I'm proud of you. The Vermin fight because we must, not because we wish to be honored. But don't think I don't see you, Katherine. The highest reward for a teacher is to watch a student reach their potential. And I know you will succeed where I failed. Because you are the fire."

The old man's lips quivered. "When the Oppressor's Dog stole your mother, I tried to get her back. She was my best student. How could I not? I climbed up the Echelon. Even got as far as the Palace of

Dolls. It was the best I ever fought. He... was there. I fought him, Kat."

Her master motioned to his missing eye. "You never asked me how I got this. Thank you for that. Now, you shall never need to. He... defeated me. But he let me live, to shame me. To send a message to any other little Vermin who might get a big idea. To remind me of that day and what he, and the regime, were capable of. And to remind me of your mother."

An old ache stabbed in Katherine's heart. She thought she might burst into tears, so she turned her face away and gazed up at the statue of her Prophet.

A muffled crash drew her eyes back to the altar in time to see the old man ram it again, shoulder down with all his bodyweight. His claw-toed boots scrambled for purchase on the slick tiles of the floor.

"Now help me... (huff)... move this... stupid... (puff)... eldritch... thing..."

"Why?" she said.

"Because if there's treasure... (huff)... hidden in this... (puff)... church, (wheeze)... it will be buried here."

But even with both of them pushing, the altar wouldn't move. When Katherine's muscles were nearly spent, she muttered "Piss on it," and used the ghost to slash a tiny wedge from the altar's base. The heavy marble box groaned and gave easily with the next concerted push, revealing a deep hole falling away to blackness beneath the chapel floor.

"Ho-hoo!"

Voyciek lowered the torch, then threw it down. He followed it in, landing six feet below on the lid of the slender crystal box lying half-buried at the bottom. No, not a box. A coffin.

A grave, Katherine realized. Someone was buried under the altar.

The death mask painted on the coffin's lid in ripples of brilliant, dancing light depicted a man with a long, plain face. There were dreadlocks in his hair and beard, and his robes were simple, but there was a penetrating humility to his face that caught Katherine off guard.

The People of the Sun buried their kings and queens in grand crypts full of riches and splendor, and their priests in the walls of their churches. Why would they bury this man somewhere no one could honor him, without so much as a grave marker, or even a name?

Vojciek knocked the loose dirt off the sarcophagus with the butt of his spear. "They grew these caskets from solarite crystal, you know. Grave robbing was considered a penultimate sin back then. You can tell from the death mask that this man had rich friends. Thankfully..." The old man slammed the blade of his spear down through the lid of the coffin. "...Wyvernwood was invented to beat solarite, so open sesame."

Katherine's excitement turned to ash as the quincunx of cracks oozed down the crystalline surface, and Vojciek gave one last, powerful jerk to pry the lid free. The top half slid away, revealing the raggedy grin and dust-eaten cloth of the corpse inside.

No buried treasure. No great secret that will win the war. There's nothing here but bones.

"Who was he?" Katherine said, trying to hide her discontent.

The old man shrugged. "No idea."

For the first time since setting foot in the cathedral, Katherine felt tired. Her eyelids grew heavy and hunger raked her insides. "Is that it? Is this what we came here for? These... bones?"

Vojciek hopped out of the grave, using his spear to vault himself up, then stood next to her, brushing himself off. "Bones are bones are bones, Kat. They can mean nothing, or everything in the world."

"Master," Katherine started to say, but was cut off by the echo of a door slamming somewhere else in the church.

The ghost stung the inside of her palm. Katherine gasped and clenched her teeth shut to keep from crying out.

"Hide," Vojciek said.

They both scrambled down behind the ruined altar.

The view of the main door was blocked by the looming black mass of the ship, but there was a gap under it where Katherine could almost see who had come inside. There were no footsteps, only a soft, golden light slowly making its way across the floor toward where they were hiding.

Shells, maybe, or the Amber Guard... she tried to convince herself. But there were no sirens. No floodlights. No screaming spears of blue flame to root them out. There was only one creature in the service of the Crippled King who hunted his Vermin alone.

A dizzying chill spread through her as she heard the *clink, clink, clink* of a heavy chain echo from the other side of the ship.

A flood of terrified memories came rushing back to her all at once, some from the earliest moments of her childhood; memories of her mother, of losing sleep over stories of the man with the lamp and the iron chain, a monster who couldn't be hit or killed, whose only joy in life was to take little Vermin like her to the Amber City so they could be turned into dolls.

The old man rapped her on the shoulder, mouthing the words, "Go, Kat. You need to run. Use the ship. Not the door."

He pointed to the vast, black vessel on display in the center of the cathedral, so tall its masts nearly scraped the inside of the dome. "Climb up and find the stairs to the bell tower. Then rappel down the outside. Stay hidden. He cannot know you're here. You must tell them what you found. And whatever happens, *do not gaze into his lamp.*"

Katherine broke cover and sprinted, only stopping once she reached the nearest of the huge, crystal columns that held the ship aloft to try and catch a glimpse of their pursuer.

Wait, where's Voyciek? Then it hit her. The old fool meant to stay and fight.

That hideous, golden glow was almost to her side of the ship now. She could see the tip of his chain, a horrid, bladed beak that snapped with each *clinking* bounce upon the floor. His boots were divided at the toe to hide the sound of his footfalls. His robe was a swirling nimbus of the color deeper than black.

She couldn't see his mask, but she didn't need to. For to gaze into the Ratkeeper's mask meant a fate worse than death. His mask was what hypnotized you. Then his lamp would trap you with its terrible light, and your soul - your life as a free individual capable of thinking and making choices - was gone forever.

The Ratkeeper. I've dreamt of this moment for so many years. But I can't stop shaking. I need to run, live to fight another day-

I'm not the fire at all. I'm nothing but a scared, little coward. Pathetic. What would mom think?

She'd tell me to escape. To make the old man's choice matter. To tell them what I found.

Katherine climbed up through a jagged wound in the ship's hull into the shadows of the lower deck. She stumbled through piles of char and the remnants of cargo whose contents had long since turned to ash to the tiny light of a porthole, where she pressed her eye against the murky glass and readied the ghost to fire.

Despite its fogginess, the window gave a good view of the altar. She had barely settled when Voyciek's slender shape stood from behind it and planted his Wyvernwood spear in the ground.

CORRUPTION

"Remember me?" his voice drifted distantly through the glass. "I thought we might run into each other again here. I've found your beloved sovereign's great secret, dog."

Another shape entered Katherine's vision. The Ratkeeper advanced, seemingly unmoved by her master's speech.

The old man retreated up the dais, keeping just enough distance to stay out of reach of his enemy's slowly twirling chain, until his back nearly touched the statue's huge, crystal toes.

"I know the terrible things he was trying to hide, the truth that will bring down your unholy regime."

He's grandstanding. Letting his enemy get close before springing the trap. Classic Voyciek. But will it work? And where is the trap...?

"Come now. Try to take it from me, then. Before I scamper off and tell the whole world. Then you'll be in a pickle, won't you? Because you fear Him far more than we shall ever fear you."

Close enough. The old man ducked and the red tip of his spear slashed back in a wide arc as the Ratkeeper's chain smashed into the wall where he'd been standing. The old man's cut took the statue off at the knees. Voyciek tucked and rolled as the huge crystal statue crashed down on top of his enemy, filling the cathedral with billowing motes of dust and ruin that swallowed master, monster, and all.

But that was only the start of it.

Before the old man was back on his feet, the Ratkeeper reappeared next to him and struck. Voyciek was ready for it, and spear met chain with a harsh cry that raised discordant echoes through the dusty shadows.

Pain lanced inside Katherine's palm. The ghost begged her for release.

Impossible. How could he-

I saw it crush him-

There's no way he could-

She couldn't fire until she had a clear shot. But a clear shot never came.

The old man cackled as the two combatants entered their death-dance and began circling crab-wise, spiraling ever closer as they checked and dodged each other's blows. "Ho-hoo! You made an error letting me live. You of all people should know the way to hunt Vermin is to stamp them out with one, quick stroke. Let us linger, and we grow stronger, faster, until one day you are overrun."

The old man was fast, the blade and butt of his spear forming a blur of sanguine red. But his enemy moved like nothing Katherine had ever seen.

At first she thought it was only a trick of the glass, but the longer she watched, the more convinced she became that it was no illusion.

When the Ratkeeper dodged, he didn't simply evade the old man's attacks. He vanished and reappeared somewhere else, moving like something shuttering and demonic, something wholly unnatural.

Try as he could, the old man couldn't hit his target. Suddenly the sag of an arm. The old man was getting tired. The flashing guard of his spear dropped an inch.

The Ratkeeper's chain grabbed the old man's spear and yanked it away. His lamp brightened and Voyciek froze. Even through the ruddy filter of the porthole, Katherine could see golden light blooming in her master's eye. The old man's hands went limp, and he said a name.

Everything was sick, and slow, and wrong. The old man wasn't supposed to lose. Katherine whimpered.

The Ratkeeper stopped his advance and looked up toward the porthole. Katherine ducked, praying he hadn't seen her.

I need to run. Mourn him later. Live now. Tell them. I am the fire.

CORRUPTION

Katherine was already at the first landing of the stairs when she heard the scream. She paused, wiped the tears from her eyes and put her other hand out to steady herself. The walls of the ship were cold, full of crevices and forgotten, ancient knowledge. He should have been there with her. No. No time to think. She had to be fast. She had to be quiet.

She took the stairs three at a time, the remains of the ship settling, creaking, and resettling with every step. She was almost at the airlock that led out to the main deck when she heard a voice calling to her from deep within the bowels of the ship.

"Come out now, Kat. I slew the Oppressor's Dog. We're safe, dear Brave One. We can go home. Call to me so I know where you are."

The old man's voice had none of its usual candor. It was flat, lifeless, ragged, like tearing cloth.

That's not him. That's not Voyciek.

The old man's calls echoed through the ship. "Don't you want to feast on roasted meat and drink vodka next to the fire? Come out now, so we can go home…"

No. Voyciek is gone. That thing is using his voice. Trying to lure me out.

She tried opening the airlock, but her hands were trembling so violently she could barely grip the wheel, and the rusty, stubborn metal was not wont to move after ages of being sealed.

The blood pounded in her chest and skull with each booming summon. He was getting closer. "I owe you a bottle, don't I? Distilled it myself, you know…"

I must run. I must tell them what I found.

A creak, nearby. Someone was coming up the stairs. A voice like needles in the darkness. "Found you, Little Kat."

Katherine spun and fired the ghost into the black maw of the stairwell. The walls split like pieces of a cloven fruit. In the scattered matrix of light that fell through the perforations, she saw him step onto the landing beneath her.

The Ratkeeper was using her master's body as a lampshade. The old man had been draped over the lantern to hide its light. He didn't move, only watched limp and lifeless from his perch with buried candles for his eyes.

Katherine screamed and cut a long, vertical line down through the ship's hull, reached back with her other hand, and pulled the airlock open.

She exited onto the main deck as the two halves of the ship were beginning to split and fall away, scrambled up the nearest mast to the crow's nest, which cracked and fell as the ship at last gave to the damage of her cut and collapsed.

She rode the falling mast over to the inside of the dome, leapt and grabbed onto the lowest protruding ledge. Her feet kicked through empty air as they struggled to find purchase. They did, and she pulled herself up onto the dusty rim.

She sat there, torn, bloody, and heaving. The dome's interior had no doorway that she could see, only the bright falsity of the circling, painted heavens.

I'll need to cut a hole. But what if he follows me, and being trapped inside that wreckage didn't kill him?

Weren't the ceilings of these old churches all made of plaster? Hadn't one of Bookmother's tomes said that?

She let the ghost guide her hand in a 360-degree cut, taking the dome down in a deluge of priceless art that rained slow, pale ruin over the vastness of the church. That way, even if the Ratkeeper was still alive, he wouldn't have the advantage of his vanishing trick. She'd be able to track his movements, to see him coming before he saw her. Katherine braced herself against the ledge and waited for the storm to pass.

When the air was clear, she stood and brushed herself off, then hurried to the corkscrew stair winding up the inside of the tower. She half expected the Ratkeeper to be waiting for her at the top, but the cathedral was silent above as it was again below.

Five hundred steps later, she entered the belfry.

The belfry was a tiny room, empty save for two giant ropes and an ancient mattress. In the old churches, this was where the Acolytes slept, as it was their duty to ring the bells.

Her first task was to get the window open. She didn't try to find the latch, instead cutting a square portion large enough for her to crawl out of from the huge panels of stained glass. A burst of cold air rushed in, nearly knocking her to the floor.

Why is it so cold? And where is this wind coming from? I'm a kilometer underground.

Puzzled, Katherine poked her head out and looked down. Her heart sank to see a thick sheen of ice covering the outer façade of the church. In the short time she and her master had been inside, the entire exterior had been encased in frost.

It would be impossible for her to climb down.

Katherine shivered and sat down on the bed. *He sealed us in a cage of ice.* A maddened giggle escaped her lips. *A cage of ice for little mice.*

He survived. Oh, he survived, all right. He foresaw our every move. He's taking his time. Playing with me. It'll be any moment, now.

She decided she would commit suicide rather than be turned into a doll.

She wanted the moment of her death to be peaceful, so she could ascend the Spiral without the baggage of hate. But she couldn't get comfortable. Not only that, there was something hard poking her through the cloth. Something hidden.

Katherine gasped and tore open the threadbare sheet, her pulse racing with newfound possibility. Could this be…?

Yes. Her fingers found four distinct edges buried deep inside the rotten slag of the mattress. A book. She pulled it out and gently set it in her lap.

The book was a mountain of thick vellum all bound carefully in stained glass. It was made by hand. The cover illustration showed twin crescent moons setting over a triangular plane. The vermillion pages cracked and whispered as she leafed through them. She was careful not to damage the delicate calfskin as she read-

Or rather, *tried* to read. The book was written entirely in Old Ithic.

Len could read this, she thought. *I couldn't translate a text this size even if I had time.*

Microscopic handwriting ran to the edge of every page, hundreds of thousands of words written in the forgotten language of the People of the Sun. There were countless diagrams and schematics depicting the stars and the mechanics of motion.

Someone went to great lengths to keep this a secret, even before the Last Day of Sun, when the church was buried, and…

This is it. Wanderer's wisdom. This is his diary. This is the Crippled King's dia-

There was a *clink, clink, clink* outside the belfry door.

Katherine closed the book and rose. The ghost burned agonizing spirals up her arm, tasting her fear and her hunger for vengeance. She held her palm to her forehead and prepared to fire. Then she realized how stupid that was. This was her chance. She could avenge the old man, avenge her mother, and all the other Vermin this butcher had killed.

CORRUPTION

You can hit him. You can track him. Remember your training. You are the fire.

Clink. Clink.

Clink.

The belfry door opened.

Her cut bisected the door and some of the wall beyond at a perfect diagonal. Massive chunks of wood and stone slid away and the cold wind howled in. But the Ratkeeper wasn't there.

Before she knew what was happening, the wall was already on top of her.

Crushing pressure. Blackness. A collapsing tunnel of red. Katherine tried to scream, but couldn't. The thing biting her legs was too heavy to move. She couldn't breathe. Couldn't think. There was only the pressure, and the sick, sick red.

She opened her eyes to an enormous pile of bricks swallowing her legs, hips, and stomach. The Ratkeeper had jumped into the room somehow, pulled one of the walls down on top of her. It didn't hurt, but the pressure – oh, Wanderer, the *pressure* – it felt like half her body was trapped in a vise.

She couldn't move.

Her enemy stepped over her casually, raising his lamp so it shined in her face. Katherine tried to look away, but he was everywhere, even when she closed her eyes.

That mask. There it was. That hideous mask. A pale circle of glazed and fired clay bearing the image of an endless spiral. There were no eyeholes, because he had no eyes.

It couldn't end like this. Not for her. She was the fire. She couldn't be beaten so easily, by some mask, or some lamp, or…

The cloaked figure standing over her faded into the shadows of the background as Katherine's ears filled with sound and with it, a pleasant warmth that brought tingles to her skin. The cold and darkness evaporated with every word they spoke, thousands of voices, then hundreds, then one.

Oh, my sweet baby girl. I love you so much. Open your eyes, honey. It's all right.

She hadn't heard that voice in years. But she knew it, didn't she? It was still there like a splinter buried deep in her heart.

My strong baby girl. You're the bravest of the brave. Braver than I ever was, her mother said.

Suddenly all she wanted was to listen, and greedily suck up every last drop of that warmth. It was as sweet as fabled sunlight.

C'mon, Kitty-Kat. Time to come home. Say yes, baby, and come home.

Katherine opened her eyes.

I

I am the tremble of the string,
Whom glory's greatness once did sing.
I am glory faded, ill with age,
Withered by each turning page.

Arkadius was a good knight
Known to never steal or lie.
A minor lord with great ambition,
He brought his lands untold fruition.

But the king was a tyrant, cruel
He murdered those he swore to rule,
Raped women he wanted to at will,
Taxed bare pockets so his stayed full.

In wine's grasp, Arkadius dream't
Of an angel, who for Country wept,
Who pled the knight: "Kill the tyrant!
And rule Country, benevolent!"

Arkadius defied the king,
To end his people's suffering,
To fell a tall and fading thing,
To tremble glory's sweetest string.

For everything must fade and stall,
'Tis God and Nature's only law,
He who hears power's siren call
In rising dooms himself to fall.

-from Arkadius: The Definitive Edition
Translated by Daniel D. Harper
Publication forthcoming

THE AIRPORT

WHEN I MOVED to Eastern Europe I was a leaf without wind. I had nothing but a suitcase full of collared shirts, cheap blazers, and a little of my parents' money. There was easy work for native English speakers in the poorer countries of the Former Soviet Union. I was fortunate enough to receive a job offer while I was still living at home, back in the United States.

The job wasn't teaching English at a language school or anything like that, which is what most directionless young Americans my age who went abroad were doing, but translating manuscripts at a book publisher that offered to pay me an "American Salary" in a country where my money was worth four times what it was back home.

I packed my bags, my parents drove me to the airport, and off I went. My old man had tears in his eyes when we said goodbye. I never thought I'd live to see that. My dad was the kind of good man I knew I could never be.

"Got your kendo stuff?" he said, even though he'd watched me pack.

I kicked the long side of my suitcase and said, "Yup. Maybe once I get settled down over there, I'll try to find a good school."

"I hope so," my dad said, and hugged me goodbye.

"Bye, Danny," my mom said with a hug and a big, wet kiss.

A fleeting thought passed through my mind as the requiem of the landing gears folding under the airplane pulled my concentration from the page of the book I was reading, and the

Boeing 757 slid from the ground into the dawn-slashed San Francisco morning. I was leaving behind everything I had ever known and everyone I had ever loved. Mom, Dad, Delia and Nick, their little girl, all the guy friends I would take a bullet for, all the girls I had ever imagined lying naked in the sunshine.

Most people reach a tipping point at some time in their lives, a moment when the song changes, and the next one begins. But usually, they can go home. They can push repeat. They can *disappear*, but they don't have to *leave*. I did.

I spent most of the thirty-hour flight to Country getting drunk and sleeping. Lufthansa provided unlimited free booze to its passengers on all their international flights, so I drank as many finger bottles of Jack Daniels as I could before dozing off to the Cthulu-esque howl of the engines. The few times I woke up, I tried to get a head start on the epic poem I was supposed to be translating for work under the dim glow of my seat's overhead reading light.

The poem was titled *Arkadius*. It was written in the 13th century by an unknown author, and remains the single greatest piece of epic literature ever produced by the Country I was moving to. It was about a good knight who becomes evil after he overthrows a tyrannical king and then fails to use his newfound power for good.

(Yes, the Country has a name, but I think it's better if I don't mention it here, since it could get the friends I have still living there in trouble, not to mention Kashka… sweet, crazy, beautiful, horrible Kashka. But I'll get to her later.)

The translation of the poem was in Russian, since there wasn't one available in English yet. I'd printed out a rough one from Google Translate that served me well enough to glean a basic understanding of the story. My edition was an antique, probably close to eighty years old, and was a gift from my new boss to celebrate the signing of my contract a few months ago at BookCon in L.A. It was bound in cracked, red leather and had full-color illustrations pressed in gold leaf.

I'd only seen pictures of the City I was moving to, but I'd read about it until my eyes had bled on websites like Wikipedia and Reddit. The City was located on the border of two countries that used to be one. Twenty years ago, it was deep behind the Iron Curtain, but today it was a pleasant enough place, with a booming economy and world-famous nightlife, a playground for British stag parties, American pick-up artists, tour groups full of old people wearing their passports on lanyards around their necks, and Erasmus exchange students from every sex-starved corner of Europe.

The City lay in the heart of a smoggy valley split through the middle by a rust-brown river thick with industrial pollution. There were mountains to the south, coalmines to the west, small towns and villages to the north and east. The City's nickname was "The City of Churches," because it had over three hundred of them, most from the gothic and baroque periods, with a few dating back to the City's founding in the year 1000 AD. There was a touristy Old Town with a medieval brick castle and a curtain wall full of watchtowers and murder holes. And of course, one couldn't mention City without thinking of the crown jewel of its skyline, the gargantuan gingerbread church with its iconic gumdrop towers, the Basilica of Saint Mary.

As dawn's pale blaze reared over the curve of the world and I awoke to see the City for the first time outside of a computer screen, all painted and miniature through the Dreamliner's tiny portside window, I expected to be overwhelmed, like I was a dribble of ink balanced on the edge of a page that was turning, ready to fall and leave all that I could not change behind me to spill down into a realm of infinite possibility. Instead, I felt the same emptiness, exhaustion, and loneliness I'd felt for the past two years since the accident.

Two years, I thought. *Christ, what a dry spell. I've finally got the chance to do it over and start with a clean slate. Who ever actually gets a clean slate? If this is what it takes, then it's what I have to do.*

When I made the decision to leave America I was determined to make a new life in City, and to make myself a new man. But people cannot change completely. We can only become better or worse versions of ourselves, and we always carry our memories with us, no matter how fast, or far, we try to run.

THE CITY

FROM THE LOOK of things on the taxi ride from City's tiny, bucolic airport, communism hadn't done the people of Country any favors, despite having ended over twenty years ago. The outskirts were downright depressing, with so many abandoned buildings that I was surprised anyone would want to live in the ones that were still habitable. Then I realized they probably didn't have a choice.

There was a techno version of the Russian national anthem thump-thumping through the old Mercedes Benz's AM/FM radio. The taxi driver muttered something and flicked it off. Noticing I didn't speak the language, he said again in broken English, "Russian trash."

I'd read about how the people in Country hated Russia. Even before the communist years, they had suffered centuries of brutality under Russian imperialism. The Country's geographical position, smashed smack-dab in the middle of Europe and Russia, had made it the unfortunate historical middle ground for the eternal tug-of-war between those two superpowers, and the cost its people had paid was their blood. Invasion, occupation, genocide, mass rape, racism, economic and cultural erasure, these people had seen it all. It was far from ancient history to them; many of the survivors were still around, walking down the same streets now passing outside my taxi window in a gray-on-gray blur.

No grayer than Arcata, I told myself.

I sat in uncomfortable silence and watched my new home slide by under a sky of polished stone. A concrete sprawl of ugly apartment buildings and half-assed skyscrapers ran for miles from the City's edge toward its center. But as we drove on, I was surprised at how modern the City became. The trams were new and fast. No donkeys pulling carts. Nice cafes lined the main avenues, full of young professionals and well-dressed couples on dates. There were beauty salons, shopping malls, department stores with names I recognized. I even saw a McDonald's.

And, my God, the *women*. The average Countryish girl was thinner and more beautiful than the best-looking girls I knew back home.

My taxi driver, whose name I learned from looking at his taxi driver's license was Krzysztof, noticed me craning my neck to look out the window and said, "Yes. We have nice girls."

"No kidding," I said. I didn't know what else to say on the subject, so I asked, "Say, I'm pretty hungry – can you suggest somewhere good to eat?"

"Dumplings," Krzysztof said.

"Okay, sure. I like dumplings. What kind do you recommend?"

"Dumplings, yes. Dumplings!" Krzysztof nodded. "Dumplings, very good. But not as nice as girls."

I wondered exactly what kind of place I had come to where the first selling point out of my taxi driver's mouth wasn't some tourist trap, or the beautiful architecture, or for that matter even the very good dumplings, but the flesh.

"Maybe I take you to girls?" the cab driver said. "I know nice place."

Hungry and sleep-deprived as I was, the offer caught me off guard. "Uh, what?"

"Sex club," Krzysztof said without hesitation, like I was some kind of moron for not picking up the hint he was putting down. With extra emphasis on the *sex*, he added, "Maybe sex club for you?"

"No thanks," I said. Suddenly I wanted nothing more than to be swallowed up whole by the cracked, broken leather of my seat. I tried to play it cool and said with a casual wave, "No, sorry. Not really my thing."

Krzysztof shrugged and turned his eyes back to the road.

Sure, I had fantasized about meeting a nice traditional girl to marry and make dozens of beautiful half-Slavic babies with, but it was only a fantasy. I didn't think I was ready to talk to another girl yet. Every time I'd tried since the accident, I ejected early and went home alone, because they all reminded me of Carly.

Besides, if anyone ever saw me stepping foot in a brothel, I was bound to get fired. Then I wouldn't just be out of a job, I'd be alone in a poor foreign country with no one to lean on. I could always call my parents if I ran out of money, but I was twenty-six years old. It was time to get on my own two feet.

After all my colossal failures back home, this was my last chance to make myself and become the man I wanted to be, this kingdom of sorrow and gray concrete buildings, of good dumplings and nice girls. This was my lifeline.

THE CITY

MY APARTMENT was in the city center, a thirty-minute walk from the Old Town. It was in the only renovated building on a busy avenue of turn-of-the-century tenements whose ashen facades were streaked with smoke and grime, their brick underwear peeking through giant, weeping wounds where the plaster had fallen away. My building was number forty-six.

I buzzed the number my landlord had emailed me. A small Countryish man and his wife met me at the front door. He introduced himself as Marcin, the son of the building's owner, and his wife as Julia. Marcin was a young, short man with brown hair stricken by pattern baldness, and sharp eyes that looked like they were evaluating a handful of diamonds. His t-shirt and jeans looked like they were from the Goodwill. His wife was slender and pretty, but I suspected the blonde in her hair came out of a bottle, and when she smiled at me I noticed her teeth were stained the color of used dishwater.

Our conversation was short, since neither spoke English well. They told me they lived in apartment number thirty-four, and I shouldn't hesitate to ask if I needed anything. They showed me how to get in, gave me my keys, and then led me upstairs to my new place.

My apartment, which I guessed I was supposed to call a flat, like the Europeans did, was number forty-two. Marcin offered to help me carry my bags. The unit had hardwood floors, big, old-fashioned windows looking out over a tiny metal balcony and a mess of spindly black autumn trees. There was a Finnish washing machine in the bathroom, a science fiction-looking capsule shower, and a box-top toilet that had two buttons for flushing.

 The secretary from my company had left a note on the kitchen table with basic directions about how to get to the Old Town and various attractions around the Market Square, how to order takeout from the Chinese restaurant down the street, and how to log on to the Wi-Fi. She had signed her name, Sabina, with a heart next to a bolded and underlined, "Welcome!!!" The note was tucked under a Christmas ornament, a red glass ball with the company's name, Bookworx painted in white glitter, even though it was early October.

 I dropped my bags on the IKEA bed and went downstairs to the liquor store across the street, where I bought a bottle of vodka. *When in Rome, right?* I convinced myself it wasn't abnormal to get drunk before I found something to eat or unpacked my luggage. My body was wrecked from the jetlag, but my buzz from the free booze on my flight had long since worn off, and I was starting to get a headache. A half-liter of Countryish vodka cost three dollars. I drank it straight out of the bottle without a chaser, rinsing my mouth out with tap water every couple of swigs. I figured the alcohol would kill any nasty critters if the water wasn't safe to drink.

 I laid in bed, tossing and turning in the dark, unable to fall asleep, partly due to the alcohol, and partly to the new environment. The slatted, golden glow of city lights filtered through the cheap plastic blinds. A Doppler rush of cars passed outside my window in arrhythmic *whooshes*. Someone's feet wrecked Kaiju thunder through the ceiling above.

 The Country was nine hours ahead of California. My parents would just be getting home from work or sitting down to eat dinner.

I texted them, *The eagle has landed. New place is pretty cool. Also, this city is unreal.*

Great! Can't wait to see lots of pictures. We miss you so much, my mom replied.

And my dad, *Cool, dude.*

I went against my better judgment and wrote a message to my best friend, Evan, too. I'd deleted our old thread after he and his wife had decided they couldn't make time to grab a beer with me before I left. *Sorry we missed you. Crazy last couple of months getting ready for the baby,* Ev's last, and only message read, an hour after I'd left for the airport.

I drafted a few passive aggressive greetings, finally settling on a simple *Got here safe. Miss you, man.*

Evan never responded.

THE CITY

"GOOD TO SEE YOU, DANIEL," my boss said, reaching over his desk to shake my hand. It was eleven A.M. my first day of work. My boss, Filip, had summoned me up to his office to discuss my first project. It was the second time I'd met him. The first had been at BookCon in L.A. a few months earlier, when he'd offered me my job.

Filip spoke English better than most of the native speakers I knew back home. The guy was a self-confessed anglophile. He'd studied the language at university, and had earned one of his four master's degrees in it. His current goal at BookWorx was to move the company into the American and British markets by providing new translations of Country's most famous sci fi and fantasy works, which were still mostly unheard of in the English-speaking world. My project, translating the medieval epic poem, *Arkadius,* may not have been the sexiest book ever published, but it was certain to be a cash cow sold in every airport and university bookstore on the planet.

"Good morning, Filip," I said.

"Please, have a seat."

Filip was a small man with a large presence. He was clean-shaved, and had gray eyes and a full head of salt-and-pepper hair. He was about a decade older than me, closer to forty than thirty. He'd started the company, which was the most successful publisher of sci fi and fantasy in Country, from scratch with his brother Jan fifteen years ago, and had all the easy confidence of a self-made man.

His gaze made you check your body language. His smile was that of a gentle patriarch whose validation you never hoped to lose.

His office was a cramped penthouse full of dust and wandering papers, dim with morning gloom despite the panoramic windows painting the walls with City's pale skyline.

"How is your first day going?" Filip said.

"Can't complain," I said.

"And how are you liking Country so far?"

"Love it."

"Are you still very tired from travelling?"

"I had long layovers," I explained. "So I slept a lot at the airport. Only since this morning have I started to feel human again."

"And have you settled into your flat?" Filip said.

"Still getting settled. Mostly, I've just been getting drunk."

Filip nodded. "The Old Town has many fun parties."

"I actually haven't been there yet, except during the daytime. But I'll check it out. I didn't realize City would be so full of Brits. Even at the supermarket, I heard so many people with British accents, I felt like I was in London."

Filip chuckled. "It's quite common in the summer and fall. Guys from the U.K. come here for stag parties. They like it here because it's cheap and they like our girls."

"The girls are very pretty here," I said.

"Maybe while you are here you will find a Countryish wife," my boss said.

It was my turn to chuckle. "Anything's possible."

Filip shrugged. "As for English stag parties. Fortunately, they seem to prefer Country in the warm weather, so around this time of year they usually stop visiting," Filip said.

"Great. I'll have the whole place to myself."

Sabina, the dark-haired secretary who had booked all my flights and found my apartment, came into the office carrying a platter of coffees.

Filip leaned forward, clasping his hands and rounding his back. "So, let's talk about your project, *Arkadius*. It is considered a very important work here, perhaps our most important. We read it in school. But there is no good version in English yet, so it is not widely read in your part of the world. There is one, but it is very old, and was translated from Russian, not the original language. I think it was published in 1903."

"Jeez," I said. "The version I read was translated by Google."

"It was probably better. Have you finished it?" Filip said.

I shook my head. "No. I mostly read it on my flight over. I'm about halfway through."

"Have you read enough to glean what it's about?"

"It was written in the thirteenth century, by an unknown author, and is about a knight named Arkadius, who has the reputation of being honest and good. Arkadius has a dream where an angel visits him and commands him to kill the king, who is an oppressive tyrant, in order to save his people. Arkadius raises an army, goes to war with the king, and Arkadius wins, killing the king and taking the crown for himself.

"But once he's in power, Arkadius realizes that the king's brutal rule was the only thing holding the kingdom together. He's forced to become a tyrant himself to keep his homeland from falling apart. He has a long, bloody rule, and becomes even more brutal and evil than his predecessor was.

"Finally, when King Arkadius is old and his power is fading, a good young knight – I forget his name - shows up at Arkadius's castle at the head of a vast army, claiming Arkadius must die for the kingdom to be saved."

"His name is Josef," Filip said. "It sounds like you read much further than halfway."

"The rest I got off Wikipedia."

"Do you remember how it ends?" Filip said.

I nodded. "Josef kills Arkadius, takes the crown, and the cycle continues. The moral of the story is that even a good man can be corrupted if the circumstances don't allow him to use his power for good."

Filip smiled. "I see you did your homework. That's a better rundown than I could give. However, I disagree about the moral of the story. It probably doesn't come across very well in a short synopsis, but *Arkadius* is about a man who loses sight of what it means *to be good*. It's about how power changes people. Anyway, it's not important right now. By the time this project is finished, you will be a true *Arkadius* scholar. You'll also have some side projects to work on, which are not similar, but may give you a lot of great insight into some of Country's other famous writers who haven't been discovered by the West."

"That's what you said over Skype," I said.

"So, we should start with those. It's better if you have a small project first, before tackling the big one. Our government really wants this translation to be great, and invested some money in bringing you over here."

"The government?" I said. *I didn't know that.*

"Don't worry. They work for the university system. They don't think you're a spy or anything."

"Maybe I am."

Filip smirked. "I know these smaller projects are not glamorous work, they might even be a bit boring. But they're very important to the company."

I put my best professional face on. "So, will these poems have artwork? You said the new edition of *Arkadius* was going to be fully illustrated."

Filip gave me a boyish grin. "Our best artist will be working with you on all projects. His name is Karol. We call him Lolek. Really, really talented guy. The first time I saw his art I was like, Wow, man, this guy is good."

"I can't wait to meet him. Anyway, I don't think I've taken the time to properly thank you yet for giving me this opportunity, Filip. There aren't that many jobs out there for unemployed poets."

My boss's grin stayed, but the twinkle in his eye faded. "Daniel, let me be clear. You are the first foreign employee we've had. I think it will not make any problems. But I am sure that in the long-term, the language barrier will prove difficult."

"Why? Everyone here seems to speak good English. They're a little bit reserved…"

"Cold," Filip cut in. "Yes. It's a problem here."

"I'll just chalk it up to shyness. Plus, I want to learn to speak Countryish, anyway," I said.

Filip sighed. "Countryish is very difficult for English speakers to learn. If you stay here for a few years, I guess it is certainly possible. But I want to treat these first projects as a sort of trial, to see if you really like it here, and, if you're a good fit."

Seeing the look on my face, he put out a hand to reassure me. "We already know we want you here, Daniel. Your credentials are great. You have a true passion for your work. I just want to make sure this is a good fit for *you*."

He seems sincere enough. He's never struck me as anything else.

"I'm sure it will be," I said. "I do want one clarification though. When the work on *Arkadius* is finished, will I be credited as the poem's translator?"

"Don't worry. Your name will be on the cover. I'm sure we can even give you some nice bonuses, since I'm pretty sure it will be a best-seller," Filip said.

As I was getting up to leave, my boss said, "One more thing, Daniel. Do you have plans yet for Christmas?"

"Not yet," I said.

"I know it's early. But if you want, I'd like to invite you to Christmas with my family. Christmas is a big holiday here, and I don't want you to be alone."

"That's very kind of you," I said.

"We will be eating and drinking for two days, opening some presents, and singing carols. All in Countryish, unfortunately."

"I won't mind," I said.

"It won't be at my place, but my parents'. Well, they live across the street from me. And my brother, he lives next door."

"I'll be there. What are we eating?"

Filip's eyes tracked up and away as he imagined the foregone deliciousness. "Dumplings, fish, pork steaks, cabbage stew, cakes, ice cream, and more. Ice cream is my son's favorite. I have a three year-old son. He's already beating me at video games."

We both laughed.

"And of course, there will be plenty of vodka," Filip said.

"Count me in."

I went back to my desk to stare at the blank excel sheet blinking on my old LCD monitor. I looked up local kendo schools online, and found one on the outskirts of City that looked to have reasonable prices, but it was an hour and a half walk from my flat, and I didn't know yet how to use the trams. I disappointedly accepted the fact that, for the time being, my training would remain on hold. *What's the big deal?* I thought. *I've already missed two years. What's one more?*

CORRUPTION

By the end of the day, my co-workers were still as cold to me as the bare concrete walls of our *biuro,* as they called office buildings in Country. I caught a few staring at me and snickering behind shielding hands, but I tried to ignore it. Dad always said I needed to have thicker skin.

THE CITY

I WENT OUT after dinner around nine PM, wearing my old black suit, the nicest outfit I'd brought with me to Country. The seams of the pants were running and they didn't quite stay up even with my shirt tucked in. I'd owned the jacket since high school. I wore it with a striped red tie and tan leather shoes, freshly polished. I combed my hair, which was almost past my ears, and put two condoms and a fresh pack of gum in my pocket.

It had been two years since the accident. Two years of living in a hole, unable to socialize and enjoy life. I'd been wrong in the cab. I was ready for a change, and I would never have a better opportunity.

A twenty-minute walk led me to the edge of the Old Town, where the medieval towers of brick and green bronze began to rise above the twilight. The gray avenues with their bare autumn trees became narrow, crooked mazes paved with cobblestones, the churches with their eternally burning candles standing sentinel at every corner.

Soon the bright lights of the Main Square permeated under the dying red and lavender sky, and I found myself guided to that beating center of gravity like a moth to its death-flame. I could taste the smoke of grilled sausage and dumplings from the Solstice Market in my nose, and the vodka I was about to consume in the thirsty, nervous clicking of my tongue.

CORRUPTION

There were dozens, maybe even hundreds of bars, clubs, and strip joints hidden away in the secret folds of that thousand year-old time capsule. There were jazz clubs in subterranean brick cellars that had once been used to store grain. There were rooftop beer gardens with creeping ivy walls and rusty iron tables that looked like they'd been there rain or shine since World War II. There were full-nude strip clubs with secret doors where any rich foreigner with enough cash and good negotiation skills could bargain for something more.

I made the boring choice, and started at a café bar obviously catering to foreigners, creatively named *Drinks Bar*, with a dancing neon martini sign over the door. I gave a nod to the three guys sitting at one of the outside patio tables, which they didn't return, then descended a winding brick staircase down two floors to the dimly-lit underground bar.

The bar was mostly empty. It was built into a cavernous old brick cellar with vaulted ceilings, renovated with track lighting and a barely-visible modern speaker system. The disco balls throwing their slow rainstorms of light over the empty dance floor made the place feel quaintly outdated. A handful of quiet drunks occupied one of the tables next to the bar, while a bald fat man stood talking loudly in Countryish with the cute bartender, a petite girl with dyed-red hair, facial piercings and tattooed sleeves.

Their conversation halted as I approached the bar to order. The bartender looked at me expectantly.

"Is English okay?" I said.

She rolled her eyes. "Sure."

"I'll have a shot of vodka," I said.

"Which kind?"

I noticed the bald man was giving me a wolf stare out of the corner of his eyes. I smiled at him and turned my attention back to the bartender. "I'd like to try a good Countryish vodka. What do you recommend?"

The bartender pulled a clear glass bottle down from the middle shelf, bearing what looked like a sleeping princess on the label. She poured me a shot in a miniature, chilled glass. "This is Ice Princess. Very good Countryish vodka."

I picked up the glass. "Do you usually drink it straight?"

"Sometimes with apple juice."

"I'll pass on the apple juice," I said. "Last question. How do you say *cheers* in Countryish?"

The bartender smiled the dull smile of someone who has tiredly recited the same answer to a thousand other clueless foreigners, and said, "*Na zdrovie.*"

"One more time?" I asked, leaning over the bar with my left ear.

She spoke slower, with a patient smile, emphasizing the syllables. "*Na. Zdro. Via.*"

I raised my glass to her, then to the bald guy next to me, and tried my best not to butcher my first phrase in Countryish. "*Na zdrovie,*" I said.

The bald man raised his beer. "*Na zdrovie,*" he said. We clinked glasses, and I drank fire. The vodka in Country isn't like vodka in the U.S. For one thing, it's smooth. You don't get the caustic feeling in your throat like you just swallowed rubbing alcohol. With Countryish vodka, the burn doesn't come until it reaches your stomach, where it feels more like a pleasant ember.

I was about to leave to go to a different bar when I heard a man shout in English from the back room. Another man responded in English, and the two of them laughed. They were just far away enough that I couldn't make out exactly what they were saying, but they sounded American.

CORRUPTION

The back room was filled with people watching sports on a big screen TV. They were watching men's volleyball. The crowd cheered as I poked my head around the corner. One of the teams had scored a point.

The back room was small, with only four tables. Two tables were filled with Countryish guys, and one with Countryish girls. The English-speaking guys I'd heard from across the bar were seated at the back-corner table furthest from the TV, huddled over half-eaten bowls of soup with huge metal spoons and a dozen empty glasses of beer. They were both wasted.

"So, did you bang her?" the Englishman was saying.

"Which one?" the American said.

"Fake blondie with the fat tets and the plump arse I saw you neckin' with outside that disco. Looked like she could suck the smog right out o' the air."

"Ah. At Samba Club. Yes. She can," the American said.

English laughed. "Christ. Tell me you used protection, Ink."

The American hung his head. "Well... the first time. But I only had one condom."

The Englishman dipped his chin, nearly face-planting into his soup. "You gotta stop raw-doggin' these girls, mate. Don't you get scared? If I get so much as a blowie from these birds, I spend the next month checkin' my nuts for hitchhikin' critters."

"No you don't," the American said.

The Englishman shook his head and shrugged. "No. I don't."

Both men laughed and toasted each other, splattering beer onto my old leather shoes.

The American looked different than I'd imagined from hearing his voice echo across the bar. He was tall and lean, with broad shoulders and an oversized head crowned with a black tumbleweed of hair falling down over his ears, slender but strong praying mantis limbs, and an ageless boyishness in the way he spoke. He had a long, hooked nose and cerulean blue eyes, a dimpled chin and neatly-trimmed beard. Dense, black body hair flowed from under the sleeves of his champagne blazer and over the neck of his shirt. I guessed he was in his early thirties.

The Englishman, who I later learned was named Big Ben, was the American's exact physical opposite. He was bald, short and barrel-shaped, and had a gigantic belly that shook when he laughed. His style was forgettable and he spoke too fast, with a heavy northern English accent. But his arms were huge, his comic book-sized muscles bulging under his rolled up sleeves, and his neck stood out with finger-thick veins.

They were both talking in loud, slurred voices, seemingly indifferent to the fact the whole bar could hear them over the roar of the game. I noticed one table of Countryish guys giving them dirty looks.

I edged a little closer. The American was already in the middle of another story:

"Her pussy was so wet, I had to use a piece of bread to sop up all the juices. I stuck my face in it and howled. And the strangest thing happened." He paused, cupping his hands behind his ears as if listening for something, and said, "*howl... howl.... howl...*"

English cracked up, nearly falling out of his chair.

I leaned over and tapped their table with two fingers.

"Excuse me," I said. "Sorry for eavesdropping on you, but are you guys American?"

"English," English said.

American stared. His left eye drifted when he looked straight at me. Without a smile, he said, "Actually, this is just one of the many thousands of tongues I've mastered. I'm a traveler. A traveler... above time and space."

English choked hard on a laugh, spewing his beer.

American illustrated with his hands. "My ship uses sequences of wormholes to jump from one part of the galaxy to the other. As I propel myself around the galactic center,"

English interrupted him. "The Galactic Bulge."

"Right," American said, "As I propel myself around the Galactic Bulge, time slows and I'm able to travel without moving. I can see the whole universe. It's far out, man."

English buried his face in his hands.

A little heckling should have rolled right off, but it didn't. "Yeah, all right," I said. "I get it. Let's all make fun of the new guy. Sorry to bother you."

"Aw, c'mon," English said. "Don't be such an uptight cunt."

My hand fell from the tabletop and balled into a fist. "What did you say?"

American put a hand on English's chest to prevent him from standing up, told me, "Relax. What this obnoxious, bald, incredibly ineloquent Island Monkey means to say is: we're just having a go at you, man."

My fist relaxed. "I know. Just curious. But where in the U.S. are you from?"

"And why exactly do you want to know where he's from?" English said.

"Mostly because I'm trying to be social, and have a conversation with someone who speaks more than two words of my language, but also because I've only been in this country a few days. Correct me if I'm wrong, but I get the impression you guys have both been here a lot longer than I have, so I was hoping I could pick your brains a little bit about what I should do and see while I'm here. Or at least, where the cheapest place is to get drunk."

American studied me with newfound interest. "Maybe we have. Maybe we haven't. You're from California, right?"

"I am."

"Up north?"

I nodded.

"San Francisco?"

"Close enough. Arcata."

The American sipped his beer. "Passed through there once. Anyway, pleasure to meet you, San Francisco. I'm Ink. This is England, but you can call him Big Ben."

"I'm tellin' ya," English said. "Knock that fookin' shit off right now. I don't have time fer it."

American grinned at me. "You know why we call him Big Ben?"

I shook my head.

"Of course you don't. Story for another time."

Big Ben took a deep breath, rubbed his temples, and finished the dregs of his beer. "All right, Ink. I'm 'bout ready for another. Are you buyin'?"

"What are you boys drinking?" I said. "Maybe I can get this round."

"Inkie, he wants to buy you a drink. I think you found your sweetheart for the night."

"Hey, fuck off with that already," I said.

Big Ben shrugged.

The American said, "Sure, you can buy us a drink. Then you can tell us your life story. I want to know something about the guy who just wasted five minutes of my time."

I returned to their table with a tray of Countryish vodka. There was a promotion at the bar, ten shots for fifteen crowns, about five dollars. That was only fifty cents per shot.

Big Ben's eyes went wide when I set the tray down in front of him. American's remained obstinate.

"You planning to drink all of that yourself, SF?" American said.

"You accepted me at your table," I said, sitting down with them. "So, the way I see it, it's only fair you accept my challenge, as well."

I divvied up the shots so each of us had three, putting the last one in the middle. "Last one to finish their three shots has to drink."

"What kinda fookin stupid game is that?" Big Ben said.

"You're just worried you'll lose," the American said.

I chuckled. Big Ben gave me the stink eye.

"You boys ready?" I said.

And the American, "Bottoms up."

I'd finished all three of my shots by the time Big Ben got to his second. The American finished next, Big Ben coming in a distant third. He sighed and grabbed for his punishment, but in his haste accidentally swiped the final shot off the table, sending the full shot glass clattering to the floor and spraying vodka on the feet of one of the Countryish guys sitting at the table next to us.

"Oi. Sorry mate," Big Ben said. "Did I get some of that on your shoes?"

"Yes," the Countryish guy said. He was huge.

"Ey, 's all right. Accidents happen," Big Ben said, bending over to pick up the fallen glass.

Their whole table was staring at us. Big Ben turned back to me and grinned. "*Na zdrovie!*" he said.

American leaned back in his chair. "So, what's a Northern Cali boy doing in Country?"

"Fast alcohol and cheap women," I said.

Big Ben scratched his head, but the American gave me the smallest nod of approval.

My tone remained deadpan. "No, I moved here for work. What about you guys?"

American and Big Ben exchanged a look, as if the answer should have been obvious. "Girls," American said.

Big Ben nodded. "The women in this country are fookin' incredible. They're beautiful, thin, sweet, and they've got these great plump arses you can just dive into like you're jumpin' into a nice, warm pool..."

"And they like American guys?" I said.

The American shook his head. "You're not going to point at a girl on the street, and zap her panties off, just for having a blue passport. It's not that easy. But it kind of is."

"Aye," Big Ben, shaking his head into his drink. "It definitely is, you Yankee Doodle son of a bitch."

The American studied me. "You walk with a little bit of a slouch, and your shoes are old. Get some new clothes, stand up straight, and girls will be eye-fucking you left and right, because you're more interesting than the potato-looking boyfriend she has at home. Use that to your advantage. Don't try to fit in"

"I had no idea," I said.

The American swirled his beer and continued. "Girls here don't enjoy shooting men down here like they do back in the States. You won't encounter the mean, hostile attitudes or get cock-blocked by the bitter fat friend playing mother hen. Short hair and tattoos are extremely uncommon here. Countyrish girls are nice girls... most of them. They're feminine. Nurturing. They take care of themselves. And they enjoy treating you like a man."

"Wow," I said, staring at my shoes. The leather *did* look exhausted. "I just sort of assumed, since so many of them look like models, they wouldn't..."

"Want anything to do with you?" the American cut me off. "No. You're right. They don't. So keep getting drunk by yourself in your apartment. Your time here in Country will be very fulfilling."

I didn't say anything about getting drunk at my apartment, I thought, but was already too drunk to think much of it.

Big Ben chuckled and slapped me on the shoulder. "Mate, you gotta believe in yourself. Good lookin' lad like you? If I'da known what I know now, when I was your age, and I was here, I would've been pillaging so much arse, they would've thrown me in jail. Look at Ink. He should be deported. Just this week, I've seen him with three different girls. Not ugly ones, neither, nines and tens."

"Tens don't exist," the American called Ink said.

"That's not the point. The point is, well, I lost the point. But that wasn't it."

"Hmmm." I drummed my fingers on the tabletop. "So, how do I talk to the local girls? What do I say?"

The American leaned closer to me. "The line you use, is, *Are you French?*"

"I don't understand," I said.

"You ask them: *are you French?* Countryish people associate France with beautiful people, beaches, sex, and wine. By asking if she's French, you're complimenting her."

"Does that actually work?" I said.

American stared me in the eye, softly cracked his pinkies. "Never," he said.

I couldn't tell if these guys were having another go at me, or not. I decided to play it neutral. "So, how long have you both been here?" I said. "Am I right that it's been a while? That you all flew the coop, got the hell out of Dodge?"

"I'm from Blackburn. Where the fook is Dodge?" Big Ben said.

The American tapped Big Ben's arm. "It's an idiom."

"Oh." Big Ben said. "Ink lives here, but I'm only here four days, maybe five. Sixteen times I've been in Country. Every time gets better."

"Sixteen," I said. "That's a lot."

A dour look crept onto the Englishman's face. "Or maybe it's not enough. It's bloody cheap to come here for us. Get drunk. Stay in a nice apartment. If you earn pounds, the money here isn't even real. It's like play money." He took out a silver money clip shaped like a naked woman from his pants pocket and tossed a few twenty-crown notes onto the table. "Shhhh-it. Fook. I think I need another drink."

The American grinned. "Thought we were on good behavior tonight, Benny."

"Do what you want. I'm on the righteous path."

"In that case, why don't you go get us all one more, so we don't stray from it."

Grumbling, Big Ben got up and went to the bar.

"So, how long have you lived here?" I said.

"Four years. Before that, I was in Thailand. Haven't been to the U.S. in six," Ink said.

"Do you see yourself ever going back?"

"No."

The TV blared as Russia scored a point and raucous shouts and booing filled the bar.

When the noise died down, the American stroked his beard and said, "I think you'll find during your time here, that this place is not really what you expect. You'll find it gets harder and harder to go back to what you were, until you reach a point where it becomes impossible."

Big Ben returned with three beers, set them down in front of us.

Ink raised his glass. "Fuck England."

Big Ben toasted him. "Fuck America."

CORRUPTION

We all clinked glasses and drank.

Our conversation died as a pretty red-haired girl in a black dress and candy-apple high heels entered the room. We all watched as she weaved gracefully through the tangle of high-backed chairs and shaved heads toward her friends, two attractive girls sitting at the table under the TV. She was tall and thin, the cookies-and-cream of her slender legs elegantly concealed in warm winter tights, her ridiculous neck holding up a delicate skull wrapped in freckled white paper.

She held the attention of every man in that room, my new friends and I included, as she joined her friends at their table and they all hugged, delightfully greeting each other with a word that sounded like the English word *chest*. She sat down, and the volume level of the bar slowly rose back to normal, as everyone except the American stopped staring and went back to their business.

Ink didn't move or adjust his appearance. He watched her through a gap in the chairs and waited, sipping the foam off his beer. He absent-mindedly picked up the metal spoon from his soup, licked it, and began lacing it through his fingers like a casino dealer would a poker chip.

Across the room, the pretty redhead caught his stare and blushed.

"Excuse me," Ink said, standing up.

He went over to the table of Countryish girls and asked if they were French. I couldn't hear what he said over the din, but I knew from his body language, cool and relaxed, drawing the three of them up into his field of gravity where he towered over their table, that was what he said, or something like it. The girls took the bait, and within an instant they were all laughing and smiling at his jokes.

"That's why we call him Ink," Big Ben said to me.

"Why?" I said.

"Because he's a dark cloud, fast-moving, who stains anything he touches."

Before I knew it, Ink had the girls rising from their chairs, beer glasses in hand to come over and join us at our table. Big Ben and I had to shuffle the chairs to make room. There weren't enough seats, so Ink grabbed a spare chair from one of the tables next to us. The dirty looks from the Countryish guys sitting there went from bad to worse.

"These are my friends," Ink said, introducing us, with a hand already on the small of the pretty redhead girl's back. "This is Big Ben," he pointed to Big Ben. "And this is Frisco. He's from California."

I smiled and tipped my glass.

The other two girls, a blonde girl in a modest green wool sweater-dress, and a black-haired girl in a short skirt and nude-colored tights, sat down between Ink and Big Ben, leaving me alone on the opposite side of the table.

"Nice to meet you. I am Agnieszka," the pretty redhead introduced herself.

The girl in the green dress said, "I am Gosia."

"Hello. Jadviga," the black-haired girl said.

"This is Ink," Big Ben said, waving his thumb in Ink's direction.

"We know," Gosia said. "We already met."

"You know why they call him Ink?"

Ink threw his hands up in the air in mock exasperation. "They don't want to hear that story, Ben."

"Sure they do," Big Ben said. "Look at their faces. If I don't tell 'em now, they'll be disappointed."

"Tell us!" Agnieszka said.

And Gosia, "Come on."

Ink rolled his eyes. "Fine. Ben can tell you. But you have to promise never to let this story leave this table. It could hurt my image if the wrong people hear."

Agnieszka put a hand on his chest. "We promise."

Ink winked at Big Ben, an obvious gesture to proceed with the routine.

Big Ben cracked his knuckles and started:

"Ink's not his real name."

"We know," the Countryish girls said.

"We call him that because, when we was in the Army, in Afghanistan – that's how we know each-other – Ink was a journalist. He wrote famous articles for the other soldiers about killing the Taliban. And every-fookin-where we went, the little Afghani children would run up to him and ask him for a pen."

"A pen?" Gosia said. "Why a pen?"

"Fook if I know," Big Ben said. "Pardon me, girls, but I swear like a sailor."

"We don't care," Jadviga said.

"All right. Wonderful. Wonderful. Anyway, these little kids would always run up to us and ask Ink here for a pen. And Ink, being the wonderfully nice guy he is, always brought extra pens so he could give one to every kid who asked. Then, one day, the enemy caught us while we were sweeping a mountain pass for IEDs. We were under heavy fire, with no radio to call in air support. Every man in our squad thought for sure we'd be killed. I never wrote down me last wishes, you know – give me love to mum, and me Xbox to me little brother, and so on."

The girls smiled.

Big Ben cleared his throat and continued. "So I asked Ink to write them down for me. But he'd given all his pens to the little Afghani children. The only one he had left, he hadn't given away, because it was broken. Damn thing couldn't write a word. So he snapped it in two, like this."

Big Ben illustrated by breaking an invisible pen with his hands. "He wrote down me message with the broken halves, even though there were bullets flyin' at us, and rocket-propelled grenades goin' off over our heads. He risked his life to write me last wishes with a broken pen."

"So... that's it?" Agnieszka said. Her hand was on Ink's now, stroking his black hair.

Big Ben shrugged. "When the battle ended, we'd all somehow miraculously survived, but his face was so black from covering it with his ink-soaked hands, that we started callin' him Ink."

The girls gave each other a few impressed gazes.

"He still has the note, too," Ink said. "Framed on his mantle..."

One of the Countryish guys said something from the other table, interrupting Big Ben's story. It was directed at Agnieszka. Agnieszka's face twisted in discomfort. My perception of time slowed as I, and everyone else at our table realized the guy was talking about us, and he had said something insulting.

Agnieszka responded in Countryish. While I couldn't understand her, her tone told me everything I needed to know. The guy had implied she was a slut for hanging out with foreigners, and she had told him to piss off.

But the soccer thug-looking guy wasn't having it. He and his four friends were all bad-looking dudes with shaved heads, keg-shaped guts and big muscles, and this wasn't America. Agnieszka's comeback had caused the guy to lose face in front of his comrades, and now he was going to make us pay for it.

The guy said something else, and the three girls exchanged nervous glances.

Big Ben asked Agnieszka, "You know these guys, luv?"

Agnieszka shook her head.

Big Ben turned around and said to the provoker, "You need somethin' mate?"

The provoker looked at him, but said nothing.

Big Ben smiled a mouthful of mismatched gold teeth. "You can see we're havin' a conversation, and it's not polite to interrupt. So why don't you tell us what you need, then mind your business."

The provoker ignored him a second time.

"Hey, I'm talkin' to you, fookhead."

Then the provoker said something in Countryish to Agnieszka that scared her and her friends bad enough that they got up, took their purses, and headed for the door.

"Hey, wait, wait," Ink called after them. "You don't have to leave because of this drunk idiot."

"Sorry," Agnieszka said. "It was really nice to meet you."

And like that, they were gone.

All five of the soccer hooligans were glaring at us now. My blood was cold sludge and all I could see in my mind's eye was my face getting pummeled.

"You ever been in a fight, Frisco?" Ink asked me under his breath.

"I used to do kendo," I said. No response.

"I guess she doesn't want to talk with you, English. Big Guy," the provoker said to Big Ben, in decent English. I looked around and noticed the other tables in the bar had all cleared.

Big Ben stood up. The Countryish guy and his friends all moved in unison as if to stand up, too.

There was a sudden *whoosh,* and a zephyr flash of silver flew across the gap between our tables so fast that if I had blinked I would have missed it. The Countryish guys froze, their eyes going white as their confusion transmuted into fear.

My vision trailed to the tail end of Ink's spoon, where it stuck quivering in the wall inches above the provoker's head. Only after the fact, when I saw Ink's calmly outstretched hand – I hadn't even seen him stand up – did my brain process what happened.

The spoon was stuck a half-inch deep into the dartboard next to the soccer thugs' table. Ink had thrown the spoon dead into the center of the bull's-eye, exactly where the provoker's face would have been if he'd been a fraction of a second quicker to his feet. I'd never seen anyone throw a knife so accurately, let alone a spoon. I'd never seen anyone throw a spoon at all.

Ink dropped the blazer off his shoulders, a real knife appearing in his left hand from where it had been stashed up his sleeve.

A panoply of colors filled my vision as I beheld Ink's bare arms. They were covered by full-sleeve tattoos so bright and strange they seemed not of this world, dancing and swaying in the dim light of the bar like a thousand tiny previews of a thousand silent films. There were nude women, golden cities, holy mountains, and alien gods.

I thought I was hallucinating, but for a split second as Ink closed the distance between the tables and chucked the knife up into the air, I thought I saw a ring of golden light flash inside his eye.

Not a ring, I thought. *A spiral.*

The knife rose one or two feet above his head, then began to fall. Ink's face was calm. A second knife appeared in his left hand, and he started to juggle. A third knife came out of a hidden pocket in his jeans as the first knife returned to the hand that had thrown it. Ink caught it, threw the third, caught the second, threw the first, and threw the second, all while staring his opponents dead in the eye, a well-trained circus monkey juggling three killer apples.

Ink juggled his knives, and our enemies ran.

THE CITY

WE GOT HAMMERED. The night fractured into a kaleidoscope of vodka shots, bar-hopping, and a slew of offensive jokes that would have had us thrown out with an ass-kicking anywhere back in the U.S. At one point, Big Ben wrestled both me and Ink under his arms and knuckled our hair like we were his little brothers.

After we left Drinks Bar we made the rounds to at least five other bars and music clubs, unsure if we'd get jumped as soon as we stepped out into the six-degree Celsius night. But every bar was empty except for pockets of other foreigners and the occasional Countryish soccer thugs.

Most of the other foreign guys I saw had dark complexions; brown Mediterranean skin and eyes, like Ink's, rather than the light brown or blonde that was more common in Country. Ink told me they were probably Turkish or Greek if they were older than thirty, because they came here to work, or Spanish if they looked younger, because they came over here on student exchange to study on the cheap and chase girls.

"Countryish girls love guys who look Latino," Ink said.

"Why?" I said. Big Ben snorted with disapproval.

"Because they're exotic. Anywhere you go where you stand out from the average, you boost your attractiveness by at least two points," Ink explained.

"Points?" I said. "I didn't realize anyone was keeping score."

"Simmer down. It's just how we talk, mate," Big Ben said. "Makes bird behavior a bit easier to understand."

"When was the last time you got laid?" Ink asked me. "Truthfully."

I had to think about it. "I guess it's been about two years."

"Two *years*? Jesus fookin Christ," Big Ben muttered.

"Exactly," Ink said. "Take me, for example. I don't look Caucasian. In Greece or Turkey, that wouldn't help me with the women, because I look like every other horny guy who tries to talk to them. But thanks to my dark hair and eyes, I have a Mediterranean look that the girls *here* like, because all the other guys are grimy potatoes. No offense."

"True, that. These Countryish lads don't know how to dress or be polite. They think the game is telling a bird she has a nice ass on the dance floor at two-thirty in the morning," Big Ben said.

"Hey, if it works, it works. Sexual strategy, buddy. You do what you gotta do." Ink said.

As repulsed as I was, I found myself intrigued. I hadn't been doing much of anything since the accident. I certainly hadn't met anyone new. "Is that why you learned to juggle knives? Sexual strategy?" I said.

A small smile curled up the corner of Ink's cheek. "I'm a street magician. It's one of my sources of income." Ink pulled the knives out of his sleeves and handed one to me. "These are show knives. Blunted. Couldn't cut your grandma's meatloaf."

"I'll be honest. I didn't know it was possible to throw a spoon," I said, handing the knife back.

Ink combed his hair with his fingers. "You can throw any balanced piece of metal with enough practice."

"How long did it take you to learn?"

"Long enough," Ink said.

Big Ben sighed. "Oi. We woulda been right fooked if those piddly-winkin mum-jammers called your bluff."

I didn't know what a piddly-winking mum-jammer was, but I kept that to myself.

"We're lucky they didn't," Ink said.

"Ah, we coulda taken 'em. Countryish buggers donno how to throw a good poonch."

"Benny, I've boxed you, and I know you could've taken any one, or two of those guys. But five-to-two? Would you put money on those odds?"

Big Ben pursed his lips and muttered.

"Five to three," I said.

They both looked at me strange.

"If either of them had actually put a hand on you, I'd have picked up a bar stool and bashed their brains out," I said.

Big Ben hooted. "Listen to Jack and the Beanstalk over here, talkin' about how he wants to make Country fear the Reaper. Those chairs in Drinks Bar are pretty heavy, mate. Trust me, I've tried."

"While I appreciate your enthusiasm, violence only leads to one thing – the pussy leaving, as you saw tonight," Ink said. "But, y'know, Frisco? You're okay. I had my doubts, but you're all right."

"Th-thanks," I said.

We took another round of shots at a bar I don't remember the name of, then wandered the shivering streets until we were the only souls in sight save for the strip club promoters who loitered around the Main Square trying to lure drunk men to overpriced beers and lap dances. The promoters swarmed us as we made our way through the Square, a horde of mostly cute, bored college girls carrying pink umbrellas who asked us:

"Hello, where are you going?"

"Maybe some strip club?"

"Strip club for you?"

"Want to go to party?"

"Hello, thirty beautiful naked girls…"

Eventually Ink had us take a side street so they'd stop approaching us. "Most of them are nice village girls just trying to make a little money," Ink said. "But some are actually semi-pros out looking for sponsors."

"What's a sponsor?" I said.

"Sponsors are rich older men, who pay a pretty young girls' school or living expenses in exchange for sex," Ink said.

"How is that any different than prostitution?"

"Well, it's not."

"Have you ever… y'know… paid one?"

Ink narrowed his eyes and shook his head. "I don't pay to play." That was the last we said on the subject.

It was past three in the morning when we stopped to get a kebab from a dingy stand on St. Mary's Street, the main tourist drag that bisected the Old Town from the Basilica on the Main Square to the medieval fortification known as the King's Gate. The guy who made our food was a cornrowed Greek in his late fifties, who saw my American passport (where I kept my cash) and said in broken English, "You are from America? You get nice bitch here. Too many bitch for you, here."

We ate our kebabs at a bench on a nearby street corner. I was halfway through mine when two drunk girls stumbled around the corner onto St. Mary's from the Square. They were holding eachother up and tottering perilously on the cobblestones in their ten-centimeter high heels, spider-slim legs spilling out of black dresses so short I could almost see the tops of their dark winter tights.

Ink got up, tossing the unfinished half of his kebab in the trash, and went over to them.

I got up to go with him, but Big Ben held me back with a hand on my arm. "Don't," he said. "Ink opened the set. He gets to pick the girl he wants. If we all go over there together, we might scare 'em off. A good wingman never hurts his friend's chances of stickin' his sword in the stone. Understand?"

I nodded.

Ink returned two minutes later. The girls stayed where they were. "After-party at their place," he said to Big Ben. "I told you. That's the opener to use for street approaches this late. Works like a bullet."

"And?"

"I'd invite you guys to come, but they said their place is too small. I'm going to try to pull the threesome, but I think black hair is more down for it than she of the flaxen."

"Good luck, mate."

"You too, buddy."

"Frisco." Ink extended his hand. I shook it. His skin was cold and his grip too strong. The handshake lasted a few seconds longer than I was comfortable with. Then Ink and the drunk girls disappeared under the colossal shadow of the cathedral.

When they were gone, Big Ben and I finished our kebabs in silence, until he said, "So, do you think he asked them if they were French?"

I chuckled and picked at the pita bread at the bottom of my paper cup, dabbing up the last smears of sauce. "Man, that guy."

"Aye. He knows what he wants, our Ink."

"How does he do it?" I said.

Big Ben blew a raucous burp at the moon and shrugged. "After watchin' Ink in action for many years, I can tell you 100%, the keys to his success are: practice, persistence, and not givin a fook if he fails."

Failure. My greatest fear, my oldest friend. #41's *shinai* crashed toward me in my mind's eye. The crowd roared, but my ears heard only silence. I should have given Evan the keys.

Big Ben sensed something was wrong and tapped my shoulder with the side of his finger. "So, you used to do, what was it, karate?"

"Kendo. Japanese fencing. Think two dudes dressed in black robes and full-face mesh masks trying to hit each other with samurai swords. Except we used wrapped-up bundles of sticks, not real *katanas*," I said.

"Oh, I've seen that on YouTube. Big masks and black capes, is it?"

"Yep."

"Were you any good?"

"I was state champion six years in a row. But that's not saying much. There were only about five other guys in my state who were any good. My girlfriend... I mean, my ex-girlfriend, she was the really talented one."

"What happened? She cheat on you, or somethin'?" Big Ben said.

"Nope."

"Well, what was it, then?"

"She died." It was the first time I had said those words out loud.

Big Ben slapped me on the shoulder. "Oh. I'm sorry to hear that, mate."

"It's all right. It was two years ago."

"Damn. Two years. I understand why you've been celibate. But still, mate. You've gotta get back out there. You can't let your whole life pass you by bein' sad."

"I guess not," I said.

"Oi, bruv. How 'bout we get another drink, then? One more, then let's call it a night?"

"Sure. One more," I said.

We were walking back across the Square when a slender, homely blonde girl with braces approached us. "Hello, maybe some strip club for you tonight? Great party. Beautiful naked girls."

"Will you give us free beer?" Big Ben said, putting his arm around her. She didn't flinch, but I could tell her smile was only to be polite.

"Yes, of course. You get free beer with entrance."

"How much?"

"Twenty crowns."

I ran the math through the clogged pipes in my head. Eighteen crowns was about five dollars. Before I could say anything, Big Ben gave the promoter a kiss on the cheek and said, "All right, luv. That's grand. We'll go to your club. Show us the way."

The club was in a crooked alley a few blocks off the square, through a spiked metal door under a flickering neon sign. My heart hammered as we navigated down a maze of brick cellar stairs and narrow hallways lined with dimly-lit VIP rooms, stained couches and floor-to-ceiling mirrors peeking from behind their half-open velvet curtains.

All I could think about was Carly. My mirror images all sliding by in seemingly endless repetition looked like haggard, beckoning imps who told me to take what little money I had and spend it on a few short minutes of forgetting. But could I forget, even with another girl's hair and flesh under my fingers, another's scent in my nose? Could I ever outrun this beautiful ghost? If not, could I at least fake it for the duration of one bad techno song?

Big Ben and I drank and watched the girls buck and writhe onstage until we both ran out of stories to tell each other. Daylight and the office I had to be at in a few short hours became a hand slowly tugging me back to reality. But I didn't want to go home yet. I needed human contact, needed to get laid, needed something, anything that was warmer than being alone.

"Was all of that true, what you said about you and Ink in Afghanistan? Were you two actually in the army together?" I asked Big Ben.

Big Ben drained his beer in one gulp and smiled. "No."

A minute or so later two mean-looking strippers approached us and sat down at our table. Each made a pitch about going with them for a private dance. I asked my girl if she was French. She handed me a menu. The waitress came over to ask if I wanted to buy the stripper a "girl drink." The cheapest one was fifty U.S. dollars. I said no.

The stripper called me a selfish bastard and left.

BENEATH THE MASK

HE WAS BORN on a distant world now lost to the turning of the Great Spiral. His mother named him Hyro. His friends called him the Black Ward, for the midnight temper of his skin. He always hated that name. The color of his skin didn't make him faster or stronger when they sparred, nor did it make him weaker. It was his colors inside that won battles, both real and in the practice yard, and it was those that would eventually reveal and define him, not the other way around.

These memories were vague, fragments of dreams of dreams, but when did he not dream? The Blot had taken his ability to wake.

The girl under his arm moaned and stirred restlessly. She would live to meet his master. The other, the old man, wouldn't without certain operations. Both were broken, the girl less so than her old, brittle counterpart. The slithering bastard had nearly nicked his mask with that flashing, sanguine spear, but Hyro had learned early in life never to underestimate a crippled man, for it was often the most broken men who fought hardest and purest of all.

Where had he learned that? From which teacher? He couldn't recall. He only knew it was many centuries, perhaps millennia, before his enemies began calling him Ratkeeper.

And the book, yes. He needed a place to hide it, where it could be safe, where his Little Lord Master and his shell-troops and mutated, Surface-scouring crustaceans would never find it.

He would need to stop at Ganhiem to fix the old man's spine, as well as the girl's shattered legs, both crushed by different falling sections of the Cathedral... another secret he must keep from his master. There could be other books there. Other books, other secrets, and he wanted to plumb them all, someday he would go back and plumb them all... when he had time...

But when do slaves ever have time?

He found Ganhiem empty, save a few scattered patrols leaning against the cold on their bows above the walls of the courtyard. His hideous little children. The gets of his experiments. The closest thing to sons this Black Ward would ever have, their skin as pale and scar-mottled as carved up old bone.

A vision came to him as he was crossing that cracked, frosted common, the frigid wind tearing at the edges of his fuliginous cloak like hungry fingers. The memory was nothing more than a jagged-edged shard bubbling up through the deepest oils of the Blot, like all the others, but this one was special, and made him pause momentarily before stepping through the great amber door of the main hall.

It was from a time when this place was still a school, in his old life as Hyro, long before the Last Day of Sun. There were no prison barracks or high, spiked walls, no flat and frozen ground where his Snowmen patrolled bored and high as sin on their own stupidity; only rolling, open fields of tawny grass speckled with red patches of wildflowers baking in the midday sun, all framed under the blue-white arrowhead of Mount Bagra. The laughter of children drifted on warm air – gods, had it been warm. Somewhere else, the whistle of the junior cadets drilling sliced through the afternoon calm. There were Yesaedan flags crackling in the breeze. A birdsong sounded, unafraid-

The memory faded. The facility, and the world, grew cold once more.

He found the main tower abandoned, as well. Once the halls of a glorious old academy, the crown jewel of the Yesaedan Peacekeeping Force, now a sepulcher of gray dust and black ruin. He made his way to the lowest basement floor, where the water drip-dripped through the hidden cracks, to his laboratory, and set the girl and the old man down on the operating tables. The docile prisoners would remain there until he willed otherwise. That was the power of the lamp, and of the mask. His power, and his bondage.

It was better to be a king in Hell than a slave in Heaven. Hadn't someone told him that, once?

It was his Little Lord Master who had told him that. Before the binding. Before the Long Fall into Darkness. Before this world saw its Last Day of Sun.

But which was Hyro? The king, or the slave? Was it possible you could be both simultaneously?

That he could even have such doubts of his master's authority at all was a sign the mask was weakening.

He had felt it when the girl gazed into his lamp. She had almost looked away. Almost. Part of him wanted her to, to wake and give him his freedom at last. But he wasn't strong enough to tempt her out of her burning, blissful vision. She wouldn't be the one to kill him and set him free to travel up the Spiral unbound. That was the role of another. It was the Spiral's will. He could feel it pulsing through the Blot, like ripples through black water breaking on shores unseen. As his connection to that intangible power grew, so did the power of the mask wane, and his master's grip on him wither.

Perhaps that was the way it had always been. Perhaps this, too, was only the Spiral's turning.

He made his way to the Archives, deep in the caves under Mount Bagra, to the darkest corner of the Vault, where he removed the Glass Book from his tunic and carefully weighed the object in his hands. It was splendid to behold. A book wrought from stained glass and vellum paper, like the ancient books he used to read back on Home, ages ago in the half-forgotten shards of his past. It held a curious ache, a psychic begging as his fingers traveled over the ridges of its cover, yearning for him to open it and read, to learn his master's secrets.

Later. There was no time now. The mask thrummed, new orders bubbling to him through the Blot. These direct from the Amber City: *bring them here when they are ready. Do not allow them to wake. If their injuries prevent safe passage, destroy them.*

Such empty, fleeing joy, killing and capturing brave little vermin. And apparently, the only duties for which a Blotling like he was suited.

He had all the time in the world for reading. A thousand lifetimes were behind him. Why not a thousand more ahead? A thousand lives to study and dwell on what the Little Lord Master had done, a thousand lives to plan, and scheme, and perhaps, escape.

No. The Glass Book was his. His secret. His burden. His key. His benediction. No. He would never, ever tell.

THE CITY

THE ONLY PERSON at work who showed me any degree of warmth for the rest of that first week was the secretary, Sabina. On Friday, I walked by Sabina's desk and she gave me a big smile, so I stopped to chat with her for a minute. The thought of going my whole first week at my new job without chatting with anyone other than my boss seemed just... *wrong.*

"Are you French?" I asked Sabina.

The secretary gave me a cocked eyebrow and a sterile smile and said, "No. I have never been there. I hear it is very warm."

She was older than the other employees, in her late thirties, but still rake-thin and eye-catchingly attractive. I could tell she'd been a knockout ten or fifteen years ago. She was too old for me, but I made a point to flirt with her, anyway; both because of what Big Ben had said, and because I felt like I might be looking down the barrel of the next forever trapped in a concrete office building with no real human interaction during the daylight hours.

"You know of a good place where I can get some lunch?" I said. "All I've been eating since I got here is kebabs."

"This is bad. You should not eat it. But lunch, yes, I go with you. I know a good place," Sabina said.

"Great," I said. "What kind of food is it?"

"Kebab."

I pursed my lips. Sabina laughed.

"All right. You got me. When should we go?"

"One moment. I need my jacket."

We sat at a small Countryish restaurant around the corner, where I ate fried dumplings and soggy cabbage salad. Sabina ordered sparkling water and a white coffee. I didn't realize until our waiter came back with Sabina's drinks that white coffee just meant coffee with milk.

"So, how do you like living here?" Sabina said.

"I love it. Good food. Nice people. The girls are pretty," I said.

"Do you have a girlfriend?"

"No. It's only my first week."

"It was joke. All my friends are too old for you. I have one daughter, but she's too young. She is sixteen next month."

"Do I need to be dating somebody? I thought I would just try to stay single for a while. Play the field," I said.

Sabina considered it. "You could. Maybe for a few months. But most people your age here are already married."

I smiled and finished my meal.

As we were walking back to work, I saw Ink from across the street walking with his arm around a pretty Countryish girl. The girl wasn't one of the two he'd gone home with the night I got drunk with him and Big Ben.

Already? I thought. I kept my head low and pretended I didn't see him.

THE CITY

I WENT OUT that night around ten after drinking half a bottle of vodka alone in my flat. I drank it with crushed lemons to make it taste better. Lemons were the only fruit I had seen at the corner shop across the street that looked fresh. Everything else looked minutes from rotten.

By the time I was buttoning my old black coat and walking out the door, I had a good buzz that made the long walk to the Main Square seem short. I said hello to a slim, mouse-faced girl with a plant of curly, sand-blonde hair walking the opposite direction, but she only smiled politely and averted her eyes. I thought about turning around and following her to ask if she was French, but she quickened her step and disappeared into the chilly October night.

I ventured into the Old Town through a twilight of blue shadows and the smell of fallen leaves. The Old Town became a madhouse on Friday nights. It was a different world than what I'd seen the night I met Ink. Everything was alive, the cathedral lit by floodlights that painted its red bricks and gothic spires bright against the bauble of the silver moon.

There were people everywhere, Countryish and Spanish and Germans and British, even some Russians and probably a few other Americans. Street musicians played on every street corner and restaurant patio, hats held out for coins in the interims when the music stopped. Horse-drawn carriages decked in white and red velvet rattled by on the old cobblestones. Pairs of porcelain girls strolled arm-in-arm, heads held high and backs stiff, the *clop clop clop* of their high heels sounding out the silent heartbeat of the city. Gangs of drunken Englishmen on stag parties roamed the crooked streets, screaming indecipherable curses and singing football songs so loud you could hear them from blocks away. The grooms-to-be wore dresses and women's makeup.

My first stop was Drinks Bar, where I hoped I might run into Ink or Big Ben again. But they weren't there. I ordered two shots of Ice Princess and left.

At a different bar called *The Dragon's Cave,* I ordered another shot of vodka and tried talking to the pair of cute blonde girls sitting at the table next to me. "Excuse me, are you French?" I said.

"We don't speak English," one of them said to me, in perfect English.

I stumbled around the square for an hour or two, kicking trash and working up my courage. I hadn't expected such a harsh rejection on my first try. I was supposed to be exotic here, wasn't I?

I stopped to fix my tie in a jewelry store window halfway up St. Mary's Street. I realized my posture was bad and I was frowning, so I straightened up and took a few deep breaths to clear my mind.

I headed down St. Mary's with an easy gait, focusing on keeping my hips forward and my shoulders back, checking myself out in the store windows every few steps to make sure I wasn't slouching. The baroque street was a light parade of dance clubs, kebab stands, novelty shops, and strip joints, the clear majority of the crowd consisting of tourists. At this hour, practically everyone was wasted.

I was almost to the end of the street, when I saw a pair of girls talking under the bright neon sign of a strip club. One of them made eye contact with me and stared. She was sitting in the window on the wide stone sill, wearing a traditional red and white floral printed dress, a white knit shawl, and black leather shoes.

I smiled at her. The girl on the windowsill started laughing.

Before I could approach the Laughing Girl and say hello, her friend intercepted me and said, "Hello, maybe strip club?"

I broke eye contact with the Laughing Girl and saw her friend was trying to give me a glossy paper flier. "You get free entrance. Thirty beautiful naked girls. What do you think?"

"No, he's too handsome. But maybe he wants to buy a flower for a pretty girl," Laughing Girl said.

What would Ink do? I leaned back on my heels and said, "I'll buy a flower for you."

Laughing Girl slid down from the windowsill and walked over to me, putting the tips of her toes against mine. Strip Club Girl left. In the Laughing Girl's hands was a bundle of roses.

She's selling them, I realized. I should've known she was a flower girl from her costume. I'd seen old women selling roses at the Main Square wearing the same traditional dress, but never one so young or attractive.

"You can't buy me my own flowers. But maybe a beer. It depends," Laughing Girl said.

"Depends on what?" I said.

"Where are you from?"

"Where do think I'm from?"

"Hmmm…. U.S.!" Laughing Girl said, with a grin that conveyed she didn't need to guess.

"I'm from California," I said.

"I've never been."

"You should go. You'd do well there."

She giggled. "Take me."

"Sure thing. Pack your bags. We'll get on the first flight tomorrow."

Laughing Girl wrinkled her nose. "What is your name?"

"I'm Dan," I said, extending my hand.

The Laughing Girl shook it. "Kashka."

"Is that short for something?"

"Yes. Katarzyna."

"I thought the diminutive form of Katarzyna was Kasia."

Kashka raised her eyebrow, impressed. "It usually is. But I wanted to be different. So, everyone calls me Kashka."

Our hands parted as two huge bouncers stepped out of the door of the strip club and glared at us. I realized the bouncers probably didn't want random guys hanging around outside their strip club if they weren't going to come in.

"Well, Kashka. How about that beer?"

Kashka *hummed*. "I have a break in ten minutes."

"Where should we meet?" I said.

"Over there, on the corner." She pointed. "You say on?"

"That's right. Very good. Okay, I'll see you in ten minutes."

I walked away and didn't look back.

THE CITY

WE SAT in the window at a pub around the corner from the cathedral called *Castle of Beer*, neither of us talking nor wanting to be the first one to break the ice.

At last I said, "Na zdrovie."

"Na zdrovie," Kashka replied. We clinked glasses and drank.

I leaned back in my rickety chair and slicked the water from my hair. "Does it rain a lot here?" I said. It had started to rain outside, and my shirt was patterned with spots of wet and cold. I'd given Kashka my blazer, but there were droplets of rain in her hair, and mine was downright soaked.

"Yes, from now on, it will. This is the start of the rainy season," Kashka said.

"Weird. Earlier today I could swear it still felt like summer."

"It's a land of extremes. We have very short fall season, usually less than one month. I think we will still have a few more weeks of warm weather, but it changes very fast."

"Say, I've been meaning to ask you. Are you French?" I said.

Kashka tilted her head. "No. Why?"

"Because you look a little French."

She playfully batted her eyes. "Does that mean you think I'm beautiful?"

"Maybe."

"We have a saying here that maybe is deep and wide," Kashka said.

"I don't get it," I said.

"In Countryish language, the words for *maybe* and *ocean* are the same. It's... how you call it? Play on words?" Kashka said.

"Oh. Right. Maybe is deep and wide. That's good. Anyway, to answer your question, I think you are very pretty, and I also think I'm not the first foreign guy to tell you that."

"Maybe," Kashka said.

It was my turn to laugh.

Kashka's English wasn't perfect, but when she spoke, her accent didn't detract from my understanding of her, instead giving her words a pleasing depth the way harmony does to music.

I liked listening to her speak, liked watching her as she spoke and giggled and trolled me for a grin. She had green eyes the color of burnished jade and long, crow-black hair that fell almost to her waist. Her face was a pale jewel, what poets and prose authors meant when they described a woman's face as being heart-shaped. It actually did look a little like a heart, soft and round, with a tapered chin that shifted upward when she smiled.

She wasn't beautiful the way Carly had been, but that didn't change the fact that I was insanely attracted to her. Besides, Carly had never known it, and Kashka did. Her confidence both allured and intimidated me.

"So, you sell flowers to handsome foreign guys. Do you like this job?" I said.

"Yes." She nodded vigorously. "I get to meet many people. I met you. I picked you up." She giggled into her beer.

Is she for real, or is this just an act? I wondered. *I can't be the first foreign guy she's met. She didn't even try to shoot that down when I mentioned it.*

It was hard not to fold into her pulling stare and half-holstered grin. "Maybe that's what I want you to think," I said. "But thank you. I heard Countryish girls were sweet."

"We are."

"Are you a student?"

"Not anymore. I graduated several years ago. I earned my, how do you call it? Master's degree? No. PhD."

"In what?"

"In astronomy. I also studied Russian for many years."

"Wow, smarty-pants. I've always wanted to learn Russian. But I've heard it's hard."

"We say you should learn the language of your friends, and of your enemies," Kashka said.

"You have a lot of sayings."

"We don't like Russian people here. We say they are impertinent."

"What does that mean?"

Kashka weaved her hands, thinking. "It means they do not think before they act."

"And you do?"

Kashka leaned forward and pursed her lips. "Maybe." I'd kissed enough girls to know when a girl wanted me to kiss her. But it was too soon – we'd barely had time to get our drinks and sit down. Part of me didn't believe it was real. Was I misinterpreting her signals? I'd never kissed a Countryish girl before. Maybe I was getting it wrong, and if I messed up our first kiss, I was sure I'd never see her again.

One thing was certain. She'd definitely been open to meeting someone tonight. If it hadn't been me, would it have been someone else? Or anyone?

I took her hand and kissed it. That could have come across as creepy back in the States, but Kashka seemed to like it. She blushed and gave me a look that made my pulse quicken.

"Have you dated many foreign guys before?" I said.

"Yes. A few. My last boyfriend," Kashka said, retracting her hand. "They all ask to buy me a flower."

"I'm sure," I said.

She tried to wink, but couldn't, and ended up closing both her eyes instead. We both laughed. "See? Of course guys like me. I'm funny."

"How do you say *you're pretty* in Countryish?"

"*Jestes piekna*."

"Jestes piekna, Kashka," I said.

"Thank you. I know."

"I think we found the real reason you like your job so much. You get to meet foreign guys who tell you you're pretty and buy you beer."

"It's a nice perk."

Kashka's phone buzzed in her purse, letting out an obnoxious dancehall ringtone. "It's my mom," she said, glancing at the screen. I waited while she answered, "Czesc," then mechanically sipped my beer for the next five minutes while she rattled on in Countryish, voice wavering between delighted sweetness and grim concern. Finally she said, "Okay. Okay," I guess *okay* was the same as in English, then said, "Pa, pa," and hung up.

"Sorry," Kashka said, shoving her phone back into her purse. "She is really worried."

"About what?" I reached to take a swig of my beer and found it was empty, but I didn't want to get up for another one yet.

"She heard a story about Russia on the news. They are threatening us."

"As in, Russia, Russia? The government? What did they say?"

"The president's cabinet member said he wants to nuke us. To send a message," Kashka said.

I swirled the dregs at the bottom of my glass. "Jesus."

"Yes, they say stupid things. We have been in the European Union for more than twenty years. But because we were part of the Soviet Union before, they still think they have influence here. Maybe they do, I don't know." Her dour tone brightened, and she smiled. "I'm sure it will be fine. This is old news. How do you call it? The story of our lives," Kashka said.

I shook my head, unable to wrap my brain around the possibility that Russia, a leading member of the U.N., could threaten another nation with open war in this day and age. But I remembered how everyone thought the same thing about Ukraine a few years earlier, and we all saw how that turned out.

"Are you all right?" I said, taking her hand.

"Yes, I'm okay. I just remember how it was before. Life was very hard for people," Kashka said.

"Wait, you were alive during the communist times?"

"Yes. I was only a little girl, but I remember it." Kashka gave me that sympathetic half-smile that said *you wouldn't understand*, but also, *you're lucky you don't*.

My eyes narrowed. "How old are you?"

Her playful, singsong tone returned. "How old do you think I am?"

"I hate this game."

"Guess."

That's something Ink would say, I thought. *The girl is good.* "Fine. Twenty-two," I said.

Kashka shook her head.

"Twenty."

Wrong again.

"Nineteen."

She smacked my hand. "Don't lie."

"You win, all right? Just tell me."

"I'm twenty-seven."

"You're kidding," I said.

"No, I'm not. My birthday is first of January."

"You're about ten years older than you look."

"My mom also looks young. When she was fifty, she looked thirty-five. My dad was a happy man," Kashka said.

"You must have good genes," I said.

Kashka paused, drawing circles in the foam of her beer with the tip of her pinky. "I am curious. How long will you stay in Country? Are you only here for weekend?"

"No. I live here now. I got offered a job. So, I plan to stay for at least a year, but it could be longer. Depends." I didn't tell her I was thinking about staying indefinitely.

"On what?"

"If I want to or not. You know, you never asked what I studied," I said, changing the subject.

"Are you going to tell me, or just play games?" Kashka said.

"I'm not playing games. I studied poetry."

"And you got a job here, doing what?"

"I'm supposed to be translating *Arkadius*," I said.

"A-ha. Yes, the epic poem. We read it in school. There is not already an English version?" Kashka said.

"Not yet. So, I want to know more about you, Kashka. Where are you from? Did you grow up in City?"

"No," she shook her head. "I grew up in small village about eighty kilometers from here. I moved to City when I was fourteen, for high school."

"Do your parents own a farm?"

I was just teasing, but she said, "Yes. We had a cow. Chickens. Sheeps. There is a forest where we pick mushrooms behind my house. My grandfather built it, before Second War."

"Can I see it sometime?" I said.

"Okay. Let's go." Kashka grinned.

"Everything is so different here," I said.

"What do you mean?" Kashka said.

"People seem to value each other more. They're polite. You have traditions. Even the beer tastes better."

Kashka raised her eyebrows. "Really? I think Countryish people are very rude. But you probably don't see it. You're American."

That was probably true. Country was the United States' most valuable ally in Eastern Europe, due to its geographical position as a buffer zone between Western Europe and Russia. Most of the people in Country saw the United States as a protective older brother; an asshole older brother maybe, but ultimately one that had their back if the shit ever really hit the fan.

"Is that why you agreed to go out with me? Because I'm American?" I said.

Kashka rolled her eyes. "Oh yes, all Countryish girls love American guys. We think all of you are Brad Pitt."

"Hey, 1995 just called. They want their joke back. By the way, how long is your break?"

Kashka checked her phone. "I have five more minutes."

"When will I see you again?"

A sly glimmer radiated in her eyes. "Are you asking for my number?"

I shook my head, leaning back in my chair with one arm over the back, the way I thought Ink would. "No, I'm not," I said.

Kashka's playful smile fell to a confused frown. "But, I thought…"

I leaned back across the table and grasped both her hands. "Relax. I don't have a phone that can make calls here yet. Why don't we just meet tomorrow at the Square? Say, at nine o'clock, on the corner of St. John's Street."

Kashka pursed her lips hard, studying me. "In Country, when a guy tells a girl he doesn't want to take her number, it usually means he doesn't want to see her again."

"You know I want to see you again," I said.

Kashka folded her arms over her chest. "No, I don't."

"Yes you do," I said. "Will you be there or not?"

The tension in her face relaxed a little, and the sly smile slowly crept back up her lips. "Okay. Yes, I believe you. We can meet at St. John's Street at nine tomorrow."

As we were leaving, I pushed Kashka against a wall outside the door and kissed her in the rain. Her arms slid under mine and I cradled her head so she wouldn't bump it on the rough, wet stone. No woman had ever kissed me so passionately in my life. Her lips, her scent, the warmth of her sides and lower back where my fingertips stroked her were soft and magnetic, drawing me toward a light that hadn't shined on me since Carly died.

For that moment, I was happy.

THE CITY

I WAS DRUNK again by the time I got home. That last beer had really put me over the edge. I barely managed to slither out of my blazer and shoes before stumbling into bed.

The wind howled outside, a deafening caterwaul that shook the trees so hard they snapped and struck at the sides of my balcony and windows. It wasn't raining anymore, but the weather was still hostile, only one or two degrees above freezing. I had only shut the curtains halfway before getting into bed, and the bare, black branches extended and contracted like the twitching fingers of the dead, all whispering, *Come and join us, come and join us.*

The heater cycled on and blew a gust of hot air up next to the door, stirring the curtains. As the cheap cloth danced in that spiraling updraft, I saw a golden light glimmer just outside my window, a dim, but visible pattern that was at once both familiar and terrifying: it was a golden spiral.

The light vanished as fast as it had appeared. But where it had been, the dark, looming silhouette of a man stood blackened against the paler shadows of the storm, gazing into my window.

There's someone outside, I thought, my mind a twisted labyrinth of alcohol and sudden adrenaline. *He's right there. I can see him. Is that... Ink?*

The featureless shadow stared, unmoving, from my rain-slicked balcony. I sat up slowly, grabbing for the cheap pocket knife I kept on my nightstand. Was I just drunk and seeing things? The more I stared, the more the shadow looked like a frightening coincidence than a person looking in my window. How would Ink even know where I lived, anyway? Why the fuck would he be peeping into my apartment? From what I could tell, the guy didn't even like me that much. Who could climb up to a third-floor balcony in the freezing rain?

I fumbled the knife as I was folding it open, and it fell, clattering to the floor. By the time I reached down to grab it, the curtain had returned to its original position, blocking the shape that I'd seen outside. Blood thundered through my veins as I rose, quiet and silently as I could, crept out of bed, across my apartment, and pushed the blinds all the way open.

There was no one there. The balcony was empty save a few scattered pools of rain, and the ceaseless elegy of the wind battering the trees. *I imagined the whole thing.* Breathing a sigh of relief rank with vodka and exhaustion, I crawled back into bed and fell asleep as soon as I closed my eyes.

I dreamt I was running through endless, ancient tunnels. The lightless brick corridors stretched infinitely, every turn bending back on itself like thread caught in some nightmarish loom. Permafrost crusted the stones of the floor, and my breath made pale clouds in front of me as I ran. The perpetual torches were housed in sepulchers of stained glass that cast the tunnels in myriad colors of crimson, violet, indigo, and amber light.

A girl's screams echoed somewhere nearby, her excruciating cries drawing me reluctantly forward. I was almost to her when the dream abruptly ended and I awoke to the gray ghost light of dawn filtering through my curtains.

I don't know if that was my first visit to the Night Country, or if my dream was only some rare coincidence. I believe it was a premonition of events to come, a calling across time and space, drawing me to the place I would eventually belong. But I have no evidence that it was anything more than a dream brought on by the brutal cocktail of stress from moving overseas, drunkenness, and sleep deprivation, and that I didn't truly enter that other world until I contracted the Blot.

I suppose I'll never know for sure.

Later that morning, while I was drinking my morning coffee and eating runny scrambled eggs fried with pickled mushrooms and smoked sausage, I noticed something strange on the window leading out to my balcony. Someone had drawn a spiral on the dirty pane of glass.

I tried wiping it away, wondering if I'd made a thoughtless swirl in the dust with my own fingertip the night before while I was drunk and half-asleep, but the spiral was on the outside of the window.

THE CITY

"HI, MOM."

"Hi sweetie! How are you?"

"Doing okay. Hey, dad."

"Hey there, weary wanderer."

"Can you guys hear me okay?"

"Yeah. Can you hear us?"

"You're cutting out a little. My internet sucks here." The Skype connection skipped and tore my parents' faces into jagged asymmetry. "Hold on. You there?"

A moment later the audio resumed, crackling like a machine gun. "Danny? Sweetheart? I think we lost you." My mom's voice said from the still image.

The video stabilized and resumed. "Nope. I'm here," I said. "We might have to make this fast. I think next time I'll have to call you from a coffee shop or something."

"So, you gonna show us your new pad?" my dad said.

"For sure. I'll give you guys the grand tour."

I carried my phone with the camera facing away from me and took a couple paces around my flat. "Not much to see," I said. "Kinda small, but, new building, right?"

"Oh, it's so cute!" my mom's voice echoed from the speaker.

And my dad's, "That bathroom looks far out."

"I couldn't figure out how anything worked for like, two days," I said, sitting down at my tiny kitchen table.

"Couldn't flush the toilet?"

I blew a raspberry at my dad and shrugged.

"We miss you," my mom said.

"I miss you guys, too. How are Dee and the baby?"

My mom frowned sympathetically. "They're good. She's bummed they couldn't come over and talk to you. She's working the double shift today. You feeling okay, honey? You look a bit pale."

My dad cleared his throat and gave her a look like she was on something. "Jeannie, it's Saturday morning."

"So? I'm asking if he's sick."

"I'm fine, mom. Just overdid it a little last night. That's all."

My dad grinned at me through the phone screen. "Nightlife pretty fun there, huh?"

"It's crazy. The bars don't close until seven in the morning. And even then, people don't stop partying. They just take it home. Or to the street."

A worried frown seized my mom's face. "Make sure you're not drinking the hard alcohol, Dan. Wine and beer, okay?"

"Jeannie," my dad tried to interrupt, but she cut him off.

"He shouldn't be drinking that stuff."

"Jeannie, he's twenty-six years old."

"It's not about his age, Tim."

I raised my voice over both of them. "Mom, relax. It's not like I'm driving anywhere. I don't even know anyone who has a car. Everything's in walking distance of my house. Okay? Stop worrying. I'll be fine."

Simmering, my mom shook her head, smoothed her shirt, and gave me her best: *This is me choosing not to give you a big fat piece of my mind, for your own sake,* smile. "So what else is new?" she said.

"I met a girl," I said.

My dad chuckled. "That was fast."

I crossed my arms over my chest without thinking, then, realizing how defensive I looked in the tiny image where my own picture showed up in the corner of the screen, unfolded them and said, "Well, it's been two years since I've dated anyone, and I like her, so, I'd call it good timing."

"And what's her name?" my mom said.

"Kashka."

"Is she Countryish?"

"Yup. From a village about eighty kilometers north of here. She's smart. Has a PhD in astronomy."

"Uh huh. Well, that's nice."

"How did you meet?" my dad said.

"She sells flowers at the Main Square. We started talking, I thought she was cute, so I asked her to go for a beer, and she said yes. We're supposed to meet up again tonight. Thinking we'll check out the Jewish Quarter."

My dad's eyes wandered off screen. "A guy I work with, named Bill – big, fat guy, but he's so sweet; well he's funny, you know, but he's just got such a great spirit – his family's from City, and he said that's an absolute must-see."

"That's what I keep hearing," I said.

"Well, cool, Dan. I'm glad you're making friends."

"He said he likes this girl, Tim. That means they're more than just friends," my mom said.

And my dad, "So what?"

"Nothing. Never mind."

"No. So what."

I'd seen this fight unfold a thousand times before on a thousand different subjects, and my head and stomach hurt too much to watch it replay again from the other side of the world. "Anyway, guys. It's really great to talk to you, but I should probably get going. Got a bunch of stuff I need to pick up for my apartment. They didn't even set me up with a real cooking knife... or a spatula... or hand soap. Had to make scrambled eggs with a spoon this morning."

"Is there a grocery store nearby?" my mom said.

"There's one right downstairs, mom."

"Okay. I'm not nagging, honey, I just want to make sure you have food to eat."

"I miss you guys," I said.

"We miss you too, sweetie. Can we talk again next week?"

"Sure. Love you."

"Love you, too," my mom said.

"Miss you, man," my dad said.

I clicked end.

I had a thought about happiness while I was putting my shoes on over my mismatched socks to walk over to the mall.

Happiness can vanish from your life in an instant. But it can reappear just as fast, and it always comes in the form of a person. Now, don't get me wrong. Nobody else can give you happiness. We're all too flawed and fucked up inside, carrying patches of ugliness and misery so deep that if the rest of the world ever ripped off the Band-Aid smiles and saw them, we'd be too ashamed to live. At least, that's the way I am, but I'm pretty sure everyone else is the same way, too, sometimes.

Telling my parents about Kashka had put me on a cloud. Nobody else can give you happiness. But the idea of them can. The impression left by a stranger who you have no business knowing at all, but who stumbles wind-blown and wild into you anyway, can change your life in the blink of an eye; a thirty-minute talk in the window of a musty pub, or a joyful smile, or a kiss in the autumn drizzle, can ignite something that cancels out that old pain and renews you.

Hungover and feeling like it was suicide to walk out my front door into the cold autumn sunshine, a memory resurfaced of the records my parents used to play when I was a kid. They'd put on cheesy old love songs while they were cooking dinner and dance together in the kitchen, Richie Valens, the Beatles, and Van Morrison, then smooch and giggle to spite me when I'd run out of the room pretending to puke. They didn't act like it these days, but I knew they loved each other more than anything. My greatest fear, possibly even more than dying, was that I'd never be able to build a life like they had, that I'd lost that chance with Carly.

Years ago, when I started dating Carly, I'd put those same songs on whenever we'd drive somewhere in my car, or cook breakfast together, or make love. Music is a powerful bond. It creates an echo that carries all of another person's love, and sadness, and magic into our lives. Poetry is the same.

I always remembered Carly when I heard the golden oldies. But Kashka had that echo, too, somehow, although I'd only known her for a grand total of twelve hours. She was those forgotten melodies, remembered. But instead of bringing pain and loss, she brought a satiating numbness. I knew I'd never love Kashka the way I loved Carly. But I thought maybe, for a while, she might be able to help me forget.

BENEATH THE MASK

HE CLIMBED the Echelon under a black and crimson sky, the first frail hints of a false day drawing over the horizon. From here the world looked inverted, the ground a distant pale sea, the ice floes and their pressure ridges that moved across the harsh, apocalyptic Surface in slow, geologic marches like towering frozen tsunamis all dotted with the tiny blackcaps of skyscrapers and buildings half-encased in graves of white. Then the gravity changed around the midpoint of the ascent, and it *did* invert, as his feet anchored comfortably to the cold, smooth stone of the Secret Stair, and what was below settled above.

The girl under his arm stirred at the shift in gravity, mumbled a few words only decipherable by the characters of her dreams, and pulled at the edge of his cloak.

He wanted to warn the little Brave One that she would find no warmth in there. It had been ages since his body had produced heat, and in truth, the inside of his cloak was even colder than without. To Hyro-Now-Called-Ratkeeper, temperature was no more than a pretty way of describing the motion of some microscopically small portion of the Spiral. It meant little to one capable of viewing the greater picture.

The old Brave One slung over his shoulder did not stir. Hyro might have thought him dead, had he not been able to observe the old man's heartbeat in Slow Time. It had stalled to the pace of a hibernating animal. The surgeries had taken the old man to the precipice of death. Hyro had considered him as a candidate for Transformation, though he wouldn't have survived the experiments to his heart, throat, bladder, or lungs.

Besides, the Little Lord Master wanted famous rebels like these, the truly Brave Ones, to put on display in his Palace as spoils of war, or proof of the primacy of his regime, or propaganda that the Amber City could never fall.

But it could fall, couldn't it? Hadn't Hyro caught glimpses of those terrible, unknowable--yes, even treasonous--secrets in the Glass Book, which the Little Brave One had found in the wreckage of the Cathedral?

Had that really happened, or was it just another dream? Hyro couldn't remember. Even his most solid memories faded fast, like snowflakes, or calm moments in a storm, or - yes - like dreams. He had lost his ability to recall them at will when he'd given himself to the Blot. That, at least, he could remember. That it was a choice. That he'd paid the price willingly. That it wasn't always like this, and there was a time before.

For the people, he recalled. He'd put on the mask to serve the people. Then he forgot again.

At the top of the Secret Stair, he gave the Sign of Passage to the Watchman, who summoned the lift that would take Hyro and his charges to the Amber City. There were new bones there, which completed the picture Hyro's imagination had drawn when he'd come across the remains of a campfire some hours earlier, secreted in the shifting masses of stone and black, twisted metal. Another little vermin with a big idea. Unfortunate, but sadly not uncommon.

Contrary to what his enemies said about him, Hyro - unlike his Lord Master - did not enjoy the death of those little vermin. There was a certain thrill to killing - yes, of freezing their bones and shattering them like icicles, or slashing them to pieces with his chain, but there were so few worthy adversaries left in this waning world, and eternity is not what it looks like from outside. Eternity is tedious. Boring. Full of doubts and bubbling dreams. Eternity doesn't merely want for noble enemies. It requires them.

The lift arrived, and they went up.

Hyro took the secret way out of the lift, exiting into the outermost of the city's nine concentric rings, the sprawling public garden known as the Arboretum. The towering redwood trees and dense ferns of the forest floor provided easy cover from the milling throngs of students and lovers meandering along the main paths. Hyro would take his charges to the Palace via the Skyline, so as not to arouse a public stir. This was protocol.

The camouflaged transport arrived at the hidden station, high above the pyramid-like tips of the redwood trees, an invisible, one-lane fast-track to the Palace built only for him. As they skimmed soundlessly above the crimson-verdant forest, over the universities of the Eighth Ring and then the dive bars, taverns, and dance clubs of the Seventh, a fragmented memory effervesced from the darkness of the Blot, of the time long ago when this forest had been a broad, open plain, an endless ark of grassland where multitudes of species grazed and galloped between the impossibly-spaced campsites of the research teams. Portions of that biome remained in certain places along the outer ring, but they were like all things preserved after their time has passed: tired, small, and growing ever smaller.

When the Little Lord Master had begun the current phase of the Biome Plan, he'd filled those plains with seeds of myriad trees and the things that grew under them. The memory gave Hyro a strange sensation, an old one that had lingered in his mind for days, then months, then years after the Great Planting. A secondary memory arose, that he'd recalled the first time many times before, every time he rode the Skyline to the Palace and looked down on the tops of those towering trees that had replaced his beloved open hills. What he felt was not sorrow, or regret, or joy. Those were empty vessels. This was something deeper, an infection of the soul rather than the body.

What Hyro felt was loss. Those wild hills of the old grassland were the only place he had ever found where the memories had stayed gone.

They passed into the Sixth Ring, where the city's middle income housing was - there was no such thing as "low income" in the Amber City - then the Fifth, the market district and the boundary delineating the start of the City Arcanum. The Fourth Ring was the fashion district, with its panoply of bright, modern loft houses and aesthetic high rises; the Third, the memorial district, a floating garden of clean urban parks full of looming statues, garish murals, and carefully-curated government museums to remind the people of the world that was lost; the Second Ring was the waterfront district, where the grand estates of the Amber City's richest and most important citizens marched alongside the beautiful promenade of the Amber River.

At last they came to the Priorion, the First Ring, where the Palace jutted like a gargantuan hand carved from pure, glittering amber raised palm-out over the vastness of the city. Within the walls, the lush hanging gardens of the Little Lord Master's estates stood out like pieces of floating jade. Busy lines of air trains and military cars drifted in and out of the thin gray clouds. There were an unusual number of soldiers about the Palace, companies of them upon companies marching and drilling all in their shining solarite crystal armor.

Hyro paused the tram to take a closer look. He held the controls so the Skytrain wouldn't start again before he was ready. It wasn't just an unusually high number of soldiers gathered at the Palace; it was a veritable army.

Typically, the Palace of Dolls kept several specially-trained units of the Amber Guard to act as the Lord Master's bodyguards - not that he needed any - and to protect the grounds from thieves, horny teenagers looking for a secret place to explore each other, and the occasional political malcontent. Yet today there were so many that the usually vast, open walkways were barely visible beneath the armored boots and bodies marching in perfect synchronicity.

There were troop transports, as well. Practically a fleet of them, their light-slowing cloaks already active, drifting in and out of the motes of light that fell through the Palace's outstretched amber fingers like ghost machines built of prismatic ether. The traffic had seemed abnormal, yes.

Yes, they were definitely planning something. An operation. Perhaps the final operation, yes. But why had Hyro not been made aware of it? He'd received no orders for a purging. Had barely felt the mask thrum at all since he'd left the Surface.

He released the Skytrain controls, and the panel fell from the wall in a flurry of frost and shattering, frozen metal.

He found the Lord Master kneeling in a pool of his own magnificent prayer robes on the Palace's observatory deck, meditating as he did above the skyline and the trees and even the city's second sun, which burned several meters lower than the rooftop's terminus. The Lord Master had lowered the shade, blacking out that brilliant ball of storming gold to a thin red line, so that the stars could shine in all their infinite, terrible splendor.

There was nothing the Lord Master loved more than thinking under the stars. "The Pale Vertigo," he called it, that feeling of falling upward into the heavens.

"Wait," the Lord Master said to him as Hyro crossed the threshold. Hyro waited. The ageless man did not rise. He finished his contemplation, made the Sign of Rendition, but remained kneeling on his little lordly pillow, preferring to speak over his shoulder instead. His voice had a lute-like quality, soft and elegiac, kind perhaps, but not gentle.

"Enter, old friend. Noble servant. Loyal Knight of the Last Republic. The honorable Ratkeeper. Show me what spoils you've brought me."

Ratkeeper. There it was again, that name. That was what his enemies called him. Hyro did not consider it an honor to be a keeper of rats.

Hyro set the Brave Ones down on the observatory floor. They did not stir as the Lord Master rose and examined them. The ageless, hairless man was wearing the face that looked like the Prophet today, though Hyro would never be fooled by it, and they both knew it. Did that make him a danger to the Master?

The Lord Master bent down and stroked the shaved remnants of the little Brave One's hair with his good arm. The lamp had done its work to put the girl's mind at ease (the old man's, too), to give them the peace required to become fixtures in the Master's garden. For an instant, Hyro wondered why he'd done it.

The Lord Master lowered his voice almost to a whisper. "They're still having problems with lice down in the Burrow. Those poor people. Of all the indignities man and womankind were not meant to suffer, insects of the scalp would be chief among them. Someday, my friend. When they are tired, and sad, and weary, and have no more tolerance for the cold and the endless hunger, they will come to us and end this idiotic rebellion. Maybe then, we will know peace, eh, old friend?

"These are good, brave warriors. But they are not strong. Look who they make to fight their war for them. A one-eyed old man and a teenage girl. They even gave her the responsibility of carrying a ghost. Despicable."

The Lord Master pressed the palm of his good hand against the Little Brave One's and withdrew the ancient weapon with a silent shivering. Then the ageless man raised a hypnotically garmented arm toward the door.

"People like these should be innocent. They should not be forced to carry the burdens of this sick, corrupted world. We will give them the highest places of honor in the Garden. I want them to enjoy their new lives here, to spend the remainder of their days without a shred of pain or worry. I want the public to know at last what our enemy is capable of, what the Burrow does to old people and children. Can your magic lamp do that for me, Good Sir Knight?"

Hyro nodded.

"Splendid."

Hyro knelt, scooped the Brave Ones up from the floor, then waited to receive the Master's blessing. But the Master did not give it. Instead, the ageless man began to pace, his mesmeric robes drifting in the low gravity of the observatory deck to mirror the sun-strewn curtain of the stairs.

"I didn't tell you we are ramping up preparations. I apologize. I don't want you to think I was hiding it from you. There are no secrets between us, old friend. I simply wanted you to keep your mind on the task at hand, and the one to come. Everything for its proper time and place, right? Wasn't that one of your favorite sayings, back before all this?"

That seemed right, yes.

"When the moment comes for us to strike, and to kill those little rats who do such vile things as conscripting innocent old men and teenage girls to war, I promise that you, my Ratkeeper, will lead the charge. But first, we must prepare. Make your enemy underestimate you, and victory is yours - another of your favorite sayings, was it not, comrade? I will not make the same mistake again. We will bait them into the open. Make them show their hand. Expose their weak points. Then, and only then, will we do what we must to end this madness. To win the game of war, you must think five steps ahead of your opponent. Didn't you tell me that, too? Way back in the childhood of our souls? And I never forgot it."

Hyro couldn't remember if he had or hadn't.

The Lord Master went back to the edge of the rooftop and knelt once more, tucking his good right arm back inside his robes to match the lame one resting in the makeshift sling of his lapel. It was always strange to Hyro that the Master could wear so many different faces without ever changing such a simple thing as a lame left arm. The Master had not *needed* to suffer his disability since his birth-face, and yet, he did. The Master was crippled *by choice.*

Why? Did he cling to his inadequacy? Was it out of superstition? Or was it out of some sense of duty to the people, who had grown to expect it? Was it for the same reason Hyro had chosen to wear the mask? If all we are is a story, then which version is true - the story we tell ourselves, or the one other people tell about us after we are gone?

The Lord Master settled back on his heels for a deep, long kneel and cleared his throat. "But this war is *not* over, as you know better than anyone else, old friend. The Vermins' Rebellion is far from broken. They will send us more old men and child warriors until they have sent them all, if I allow it. But I will not. I am still their sovereign, whether they choose to accept my divinity or they deny it. I have a duty to protect them, even from themselves... most of all from the radicals among them, those dishonorable and extreme enough to terrorize, kidnap, and brainwash the innocent into fighting.

"Fire and shadow create balance. When one grows too bold, the other retreats, so it can lash back stronger and more efficient to regain equilibrium. When our enemies turn to using our own fears against us, we must become the most terrifying thing of all to stop the escalation. Didn't you tell me that once, Hyro?"

Hyro couldn't recall, but was almost certain he had. In the fragments of memories that the Blot gave him he'd been a foolish, violent young man, a single atom on the Spiral made of balls and fear and hate, and - yes - brutal talent, whose errors should've been erased ages ago by the Spiral's spinning. But they never would be now, would they? No, not until...

Not unless he...

No. Such thoughts were forbidden.

But what if...

No.

But it was only a mask...

Never. To imagine such things was...

Inside him, the coldness thickened.

Hyro's thoughts jumped to the Glass Book. Part of him demanded that he confess to the Little Lord Master he'd found it, that he'd almost hidden it away and committed an unthinkable crime against the regime. But a deeper part, the part upon which the mask's control was slipping, told him wait, read, learn. Everything for its proper place and time.

When the Little Lord Master spoke again, his voice had lost all its music, and had taken a metallic quality, still smooth, but hard where it had been kind. "I want to tell you this in person, so you understand the importance of this charge. Intelligence has located a village deep within the settled region of the Undersprawl, in the ruins of an ancient cistern that now provides key ventilation to the network of tunnels our enemies call the Burrow. They believe this village has strong blood and military ties with the top leaders of the rebellion."

Hyro drifted as the dream of a dingy village nestled between towering stone pillars and gentle winds blowing deep underground came to him through the mask.

"You will cleanse this village of every man, woman, and child," the Lord Master said. "Take any able-bodied prisoners you find to Ganheim. Pacify those too weak to survive the harsh climate of the Surface. Destroy any human remains or signs of a slaughter. Uncertainty will be *our* weapon. We will not give them the courtesy of knowing. Their loved ones shall not sleep, shall not mourn. Leave nothing but silence and ruin. Do you understand these orders?"

The Ratkeeper bowed.

"Good. One more thing," his Lord Master said. "There comes a Visitor, and with him a time of unbalancing to the Great Spiral. I do not wish for you to interfere, yet. I see potential for this Visitor to serve our holy cause... even if he joins our enemies."

That wasn't all of it, though. There was something else the Lord Master wasn't telling him, would not tell him until the time was convenient. Something powerful, a game-changer. Hyro knew his Lord Master well enough to know when he was emotionally affected, and he had not seen this much of a tremble in the last joint of the ageless man's middle finger in a very long time. This had nothing to do with Visitors or vague, eschatological prophecies. But it was not his place to ask. He couldn't, even if he wanted to. The mask did not permit Hyro to question.

No secrets between old friends, indeed.

The Lord Master raised his palm in the Sign of the Wanderer. "Go now, in providential service of this republic."

CORRUPTION

The Ratkeeper took his blessing and went.

THE CITY

I THOUGHT about her almost every second until I saw her again.

I spent the afternoon drinking alone at my apartment, then waited for Kashka at the corner of St. John's Street, leaning against a lamp post in a way I thought looked cool. The air was chilly, the first night of autumn that was supposed to fall below freezing.

I scanned the crowds of strolling people - much thinner than the night before, I guessed because of the weather – until I saw her walking toward me, bundled in a red pea coat, her pale face bobbing with a huge, toothy smile. There was that awkward pause when you see someone you know from a distance, and they're still too close for you to pretend you don't see them, but too far to say anything.

When Kasha got close enough, she said, "Hey, babe."

I took her in my arms and kissed her. Her chin tilted up and her mouth opened to mine. We kissed for ten or fifteen seconds before our lips parted.

"You look like Little Red Riding Hood," I said.

"Who?"

"You know, the fairy tale. About a girl with a red coat who goes to her grandmother's house, but her grandmother has been eaten by a wolf."

"Oh!" Kashka nodded. "We call it different, here. In Countryish, it calls *Little Red Coat*."

"And what do you call the Big Bad Wolf?" I said.

"Big Bad Wolf is the same. Where are we going?"

"I was thinking the Jewish Quarter," I said.

Kashka's face lit. She linked her arm into mine and said, "Yes! Jewish. It's my favorite place in City."

We walked into the sideways pillars of mist that had fallen after the rain abated, heading south from the Market Square into a world of shadows, the glowing islands of the streetlamps guiding us through empty, narrow streets.

The Jewish Quarter was a twenty-minute walk from the Main Square. It was a UNESCO World Heritage site, and unlike that far more touristy attraction, the smog-blackened tenements and brick synagogues of the Jewish Quarter hadn't seen a fresh coat of paint or plaster since the 1920's.

The Quarter was settled in the thirteenth century as a separate town where the Jews could live in peace and privacy, and spent most of its history as a suburb of the City, until the City grew and swallowed it up. When the Nazis came in the 1940s, they transformed the place into a ghetto where the Jews were held prisoner before being shipped off to the death camps.

I was surprised to see that old hate was still alive. Graffiti covered the grimy walls, slurs like "Gay Jews" or giant swastikas. The slick cobblestones pleaded for remembrance with every footstep, but their whispers were as thin as the bare branches we passed under. Kashka was so quiet on my arm that I briefly wondered if she was having second thoughts.

But once we got deeper into the quarter, I saw that behind the sloughed-off patches of broken plaster and their inherent ghosts, there were worlds blooming. Pubs and restaurants full of laughter and light; hawkers selling antique jewelry, knives, and hot chestnuts; old cemeteries where the grass grew unabashedly across the time-smoothed graves, as if to say, *You belong to us now, welcome home.*

"So, what's the best spot around here?" I said.

Kashka looked at me quizzically. "A spot? Where is a spot?"

"A bar or a place we can get a drink."

"Oh. Yes. I will show you."

We arrived at the Jewish Quarter's small market square, dominated by a huge gothic brick building that I had read on Wikipedia was the Old Slaughterhouse, now home to a row of café bars and music clubs. The outside tables were all full, despite the cold, and the crowd was raging.

"Looks like we found the party," I said.

Kashka nodded. "This quarter is better than Main Square. It's cheap here, and there are more locals than tourists."

"Looks authentic," I said.

"We have a saying: you can only find authenticity by accident," Kashka said.

"Oh, yeah? What's the rest of it? That can't be the whole thing."

"You can only find authenticity by accident, because in searching for authenticity, you destroy it. Here," Kashka said, and pulled me by the hand down a hidden alley. I couldn't see anything except for the dim yellow glow of a flickering lamp at the end of the tunnel, under which we found a second tunnel, which opened to a dimly-lit courtyard overgrown with unkempt weeds and ivy. The only sign that there was any kind of establishment was a handwritten chalk sign that read (in Countryish): *Local beer – 3.5 crowns.*

"This is my favorite place. It is called *Magika*," Kashka said, as she pushed open a heavy wooden door and laughter and music suddenly filled the abandoned courtyard.

We stepped into a bar no bigger than my apartment. Beyond the iron-braced double doors was a candlelit parlor decorated to look like a magician's study, complete with an alchemy lab, huge black candles, and an assortment of stuffed dead reptiles hanging over the bar from copper wires.

I knew from the name of the place that it was based on the poem I was translating, *Arkadius*. *Magika* was the name of the force the evil forest spirits who were loyal to the king used to repel Arkadius and his army so they couldn't march on the royal castle.

And it was packed. Kashka led me by the hand through a secret door behind the bookcase on the back wall that led to a room decorated like the great hall of a castle, filled with communal tables. There was even a suit of armor. The armor looked real, but I noticed a conspicuous lack of weaponry.

We found the last two open seats and took our jackets off. Kashka sat down. "I'm going to go get us some drinks," I said.

When I returned with our beers, Kashka was busy checking her makeup in a small handheld vanity mirror shaped like a half-opened bar of chocolate. "You look beautiful," I said off-handedly.

She must have thought I was being serious. "You say this to every girl."

"Yeah, I do." I thought that was what Ink would say, but she didn't smile. I quickly changed the subject. "I think we're the only people in here speaking English."

"Can you not speak any Countryish?"

I shook my head *no*. "The only words I know are yes and no, which I learned from Google."

"And what are the words for *yes* and *no* in Countryish?" Kashka said.

"Yes is *tak*. No is *nie*. Ask me a question."

"Any question?"

"Tak."

"All right. Do you like me?"

"Tak," I said.

"Now it's your turn," she said.

"Okay, Kashka. Do you enjoy listening to Gangster rap?"

"Tak. It's okay. What do you call them? Sweaty pants?"

I chuckled. "Track suits."

"Tak. I like them. They are nice."

"Do you own a track suit, Kashka?"

"Nie."

"Me neither."

The conversation fizzled. I was about to get up and order another one when someone tapped me on the shoulder.

It was an old woman. She was wearing the same traditional flower-print dress Kashka had worn the night we met, and was offering me a bundle of red roses. Her head was covered in a shawl, and her upper lip was thick with a carpet of gray hair capped by a huge black wart.

The flower lady raised the flowers so I could look at them, repeating the Countryish word for please: *"Prosze. Prosze."*

Kashka said something snappy to her and the old woman scowled. I didn't understand what she said, but I was certain it equated to *scram* or *get lost*.

The flower lady cursed at Kashka and brushed me on the shoulder with an old, warty hand. Kashka said something meaner, but the old woman wouldn't go away. She stared at me with the saddest puppy dog eyes I'd ever seen. Finally, she muttered something scathing and moved onto the next table.

"What did you tell her?" I said when the flower woman was gone.

Kashka lowered her voice. "She is a gypsy. She says she has no food and cannot eat unless we buy her flowers. She says I have a rich man, she is a poor old woman, and she will starve if we don't help her."

"Jesus," I said, reaching for my pocket.

"Stop. Don't give her anything," Kashka said. "I know this woman. She is always going up to people at the Square pretending to sell them flowers. She steals from them. She makes all of us other flower girls look bad. Plus, she is old. Do not let her touch you. She will curse you."

You've gotta be kidding me, I thought.

"It's cool. No worries," I said. "I won't buy you a flower from her, then. But, listen, Kashka... are you all right? You seem a little out of it tonight."

After a long silence, Kashka said, "Yes, Dan. I'm okay. I am just tired. I haven't slept."

"Since when?" I said.

"Since last night," Kashka said.

"You haven't slept in twenty-four hours?"

"Nie."

"Why?"

"I never sleep. It's because I don't eat, and I have bad dreams," Kashka said.

Red flag number two, I thought. "Jesus. What are you doing here? You should be at home, sleeping."

"I wanted to meet with you."

I smiled uncomfortably. "That's very kind of you. But, you should take better care of yourself."

"You sound like my mom," Kashka said.

"Maybe you should listen to her," I said. I didn't want to belabor the point. "What were we talking about, again?"

"So what do you do with your free time?" Kashka said.

"Mostly drink. I used to do martial arts," I said.

Kashka looked confused. "Uh huh. Okay. Which martial arts?" I don't think she knew what the term *martial arts* meant in English, and was trying to glean it from context.

I played along. "I did Kendo for about fifteen years. I was state champion. Six times." I held up six fingers to demonstrate.

"So, does that mean you will protect me?" Kashka said, taking my hand.

Jeez, does this girl not know how clingy she sounds? Maybe it's different here. "Protect you from what?" I said.

She got quiet, and suddenly I could see she wasn't kidding. "I don't know. Guys."

"Who?"

"Different ones."

"Bullshit. Is someone bothering you?"

"Well, to be honest, it's my ex-boyfriend. He is still angry at me. You say at me?"

"Yes."

"Why not with me?"

"You can say both. Don't avoid the question. How long ago did you break up with this guy?" I said.

Kashka thought about it. "Seven years ago," she said.

I choked mid-sip. "Seems like a long time to hold a grudge. What did you do to the guy?"

Kashka gazed at the wall, her eyes blanking like a doll. "We were together for many years. He was my first boyfriend. I was planning to marry him. But he cheated on me. So I left him. Not at first. We had many fights. But then I did not want him anymore. He was a bad man."

I cleared my throat. "I mean, that's not *so* bad."

"It is here," Kashka said.

I took her hand. "Kashka, nobody is going to mess with you while you're with me, understand?" I only half-believed myself when I said it.

Kashka gave me a sweet, obviously rehearsed smile. "Thank you. But I can take care of myself. Yes, Maciek hates me, but we will never run into him. And if we do, he will not say anything."

I tapped her glass and said, "In that case. Ready for another?"

Kashka hopped in her seat. "Tak!"

An hour and three rounds later, we were stumbling through Slaughterhouse Square, arms and waists entwined. Kashka took me to a music club called Fetish in a deep brick cellar underneath an old tenement building. We stood at the bar and Kashka ordered us a tray of vodka shots. My head reeled at the sight of the twelve little glasses in front of me. *I'm already shitfaced. Red flag one million.*

"Drink," she said. "I want to dance with you."

We took our shots, danced, drank, and danced. I was drunk enough that I didn't give a damn if I had two left feet. Our dancing mostly consisted of Kashka rubbing her ass on me and then turning around so we could make out. At one point, she stuck her hands down my pants right there on the dance floor. I got embarrassed, so I backed away, gave her my best Steve McQueen impression – I'd watched hours of clips of his old movies on YouTube earlier that afternoon – and said, "You wanna get out of here?"

We were walking back toward my place through the gloomy, tangled streets of the Old City, when Kashka stopped me and said with a low quiver in her voice, "Dan, this is the last time we will see each other."

I smirked. "What are you talking about?"

"I'm going to Italy on Wednesday," Kashka said.

"You're telling me this now?"

She shrugged. "I'm sorry. I made this plan many months ago."

"Are you coming back?" I said.

She shook her head. "I don't know."

My mind and heart fell simultaneously. "I don't want you to go, and if you don't want to tell me why you're going, that's fine. I'll survive. But I don't want this to be the last time I see you. Will you call me if you come back?"

"You didn't give me your phone number," Kashka said. "Why not?"

"I already told you. I don't have a phone here yet."

Kashka sighed. "A-ha. Okay. I thought you just didn't want to. In Country, when a guy doesn't ask a woman for her phone number, and tells her to meet him someplace, it means he won't be there."

"But I was there," I said.

Kashka didn't listen. "Usually it means he doesn't want to see her again. Maybe you thought, who is this slutty Countryish girl? Maybe you only wanted to have sex with me, or see me once or twice, and then you would find new girl. Or maybe you have a girlfriend back at home, in the States. This is what I thought."

Christ, this girl has issues. What happened to the giggly girl who practically ate my face off last night outside Castle of Beer? And at what point did she get replaced by Wednesday Addams? I guess I'm not one to judge, though. I've got plenty of baggage myself.

I put my hand over her lips. "Stop it," I said. "I'm here, with you, because I want to be. That's the only reason. How about this - I'll give you my email address and Facebook. That way you can look me up and know I'm exactly who I say I am."

She put her arms around my neck and kissed me. "Deal."

"Are you still going to Italy?"

"No."

It was my turn to sigh. "This was all some kind of test, wasn't it."

"Yes. It was," Kashka said.

"Did I pass?"

"You did."

"You are fucking impossible," I told her.

She started laughing. "I know."

Kashka turned the light off as soon as we got through my front door, self-consciously clutching her breasts as I took her shirt off and we made out on my bed. She had a tiny porcelain belly and the skin of her back and shoulders was polka-dotted with moles.

We didn't have sex that night, but I woke up at dawn to feel Kashka's lips kissing their way down under the elastic band of my boxers. We didn't go all the way, only to Third Base. Still, she was the only girl I'd gone that far with other than Carly.

To be honest, it seemed somewhat cold and mechanical.

When I woke up again, she was putting on her clothes. "I'm supposed to go to the village to see my mom today. I can bring you fresh eggs and jam," Kashka said.

"Sure."

As I was putting my own clothes on, Kashka touched the obsidian arrowhead I wore around my neck, the one Carly had given me the day of the West Coast Invitational. "I like your necklace. What is it?" Kashka said.

"It's a Native American arrowhead. Made from obsidian."

"What is obsidian?"

"Volcanic glass."

"I don't understand. Please explain?"

"It's lava that froze and hardened into stone."

"A-ha. Okay. I didn't know the word," Kashka said. "Who gave it to you?"

I pulled my shirt over my head, making sure the necklace was tucked out of sight. "I don't remember. I've had it forever."

I pulled her to the side of the bed and kissed her on the stomach. "When will I see you again?"

"I don't know," she said. "I will email you."

I wrote my email address on a scrap of paper, and she wrote her phone number down for me.

I knew I could sleep with Kashka if I wanted to, either on our next date or the one after, but despite my two-year dry spell, something wasn't right. What had at first come across as intriguing personality quirks now belied deep emotional scarring that I wasn't sure I could deal with without hurting her. Plus, I'd been in a relationship for almost ten years before losing Carly, and had never had a one-night stand. As cute as Kashka was, and as much as I wanted to be like Ink, I didn't think I could just *use* somebody like that, especially someone who was so obviously troubled.

I made up my mind that I wasn't going to see Kashka again.

THE CITY

I WAS OUT on my lunch break strolling through the Old Town, lost in my own head and attempting to hold eye contact with every pretty girl I saw, when I came upon a crowd of people gathered at the corner of St. John's Street. Curious, I edged my way to the front, curious to see what all the fuss was about, and stood next to a group of fawning teenage girls. It was a magic show. The magician was Ink.

I almost didn't recognize him. Ink was wearing a blue suit with a white shirt, a skinny wool tie, a silk pocket square, and gold cufflinks. His wild midnight hair was tied up in a top-knot.

He was juggling a deck of playing cards, shuffling them through the air and rolling individual cards down his arms and hands to fall seamlessly back into the ceaseless flow circulating through the air. There was a small radio next to him playing 1920s American jazz.

Ink saw me and winked, but stayed in character as the song changed to a slower tempo minor swing. Ink let the playing cards fall to rest in a neatly stacked deck in the palm of his right hand.
The audience applauded.

Ink took the top four cards and put the others away. He held them up so the audience could see them: ten of hearts, ace of clubs, two of diamonds, and the king of hearts. Ripping the cards in half, Ink approached four teenage girls standing at the front of the little crowd and gave each girl half a card, folding the remaining halves in his pocket square and tucking them inside the breast pocket of his coat.

The first girl gave Ink her hand and he closed it around the torn ten of hearts with great flourish, kissed her fingers, whispered an unheard spell, and pulled the same, un-torn card from the folds of her scarf. The girl gasped and covered her mouth.

When Ink opened her still-clasped hand, it was empty. The only ten of hearts was the whole, pristine card Ink was holding. *That's easy to explain,* I thought. *She's in on it. Or maybe he hid a spare card there while he distracted the audience by giving her the other half.*

Ink moved on to the next girl, took her torn-in-half card, the ace of clubs, put the card half in his mouth and swallowed it. Ink opened his mouth to show the audience there was nothing inside. He cupped the girl's cheek softly with his hand, staring into her eyes. She looked flattered, but a bit uncomfortable, and for a second I wondered if an angry father was about to fall out of the crowd and land with his fist on Ink's face. Instead, Ink stroked the girl's hair. She smiled nervously. With a sudden flick of his wrist, he pulled the ace of clubs – complete and untorn - from behind her ear.

The audience cheered. The four girls giggled to each other.

Okay, that was a good trick, I thought. *But it's still not magic. He had a double of the same card hidden up his sleeve. And I'm sure the girls are in on it now.*

Ink approached the third girl and motioned for her to hold her card half, the two of diamonds, up high where everyone could see. Ink tapped the card with his pinky, then closed the girl's fingers around it and breathed into her palm. When he motioned for her to unclench her fist, there were two cards there: both the two of diamonds.

I have no idea how he did that.

The audience started to applaud, but Ink held up a patient hand, telling them to wait. The trick wasn't over. He gestured for the girl to throw her cards up in the air, gave her an example of how to flick her wrist so they would fly straight. She looked terrified that she was going to mess up his show, but Ink put a reassuring hand on the small of her back and nodded.

The girl threw the cards quickly, one after the other. Both cards sprouted throwing knives mid-flight. Ink's knives found their targets perfectly, ripping the cardboard with a soft hiss. The audience gasped and clapped, and the knife-impaled cards twirled down to Ink's awaiting hands like bombs with paper tails.

Ink didn't acknowledge the audience's thundering applause. Without missing a beat, he moved on to the fourth and final girl, beckoning for her to present her card half, the king of hearts. She held it up high with a gleeful smile. Ink repeated the gesture of taking the girl's hand and folding her fingers around the card, as he had at the beginning of the last trick. But this time he ignored the card completely, reached down, stuck his hand up the bottom of the girl's pea coat, and pulled out a bird.

What the hell? Impossible...

I couldn't believe my eyes. There was a real, living, breathing hawk bobbing up Ink's arm, displaying its feathers and cooing; it wasn't a normal hawk, either, but an albino with snow-white feathers and eerie, amber-colored eyes.

I knew that there had to be some rational explanation for the illusion, but I had no clue what it could be. There wasn't enough room to hide a bird under the girl's coat, even if she was in on the performance. The coat was snug and form-fitting. Besides, how could anyone hide an animal under their coat for so long without it getting crazy and causing a scene?

The bird must be extremely well-trained, I thought.

Hawk-girl's eyes grew into china bowls as she turned around and saw what Ink had pulled from her coat. Gasps and cheers flooded the audience. Ink rolled a piece of sausage out of his sleeve and popped it in the hawk's mouth, then stroked behind its bulbous skull and presented it to the crowd.

Applause exploded all around me. But that wasn't the end.

Ink approached Hawk-girl again, and with his free hand, motioned for her to give him her card half. A look of confusion crossed the girl's face as she opened her palm and saw her half of the king of hearts was no longer there.

With a single flick of his wrist, Ink removed and unfolded his pocket square, raining four cards across the cobblestones: the ten of hearts, the ace of clubs, the two of diamonds, and the king of hearts; each the whole, un-ripped version, without so much as a crease to mar it.

Ink whispered something in the girl's ear. She blushed. He backed away, then smiled and bowed. It was the first time I'd seen him do either since I'd started watching the show. He held the hawk aloft so it might get its fair share of the applause, too, and they both took a bow. The hawk gave a theatrical flourish of its wings.

I expected the crowd to dissolve once the show was over, and Ink to begin asking those who remained for money, but he didn't. The lingerers seemed disappointed it was finished. The four teenage girls seemed especially sad, frowning to one another before slowly drifting away. The one in the pea coat blew Ink a kiss and waved.

Ink pretended not to hear the clink of coins as they fell into his upturned top hat, tending to his bird instead. He didn't seem to see me approach, but as soon as I got close enough, Ink said, "How ya doin', Frisco? You enjoy the show?"

"That was awesome," I said.

"Awe is what keeps me gainfully employed. Man, you look like shit," Ink said.

"I know. I haven't been getting enough sleep. Drinking too much," I said.

"Running the Gameboy on both batteries, huh?" Ink stroked the hawk behind its neck. "You see that brunette? She was something, wasn't she?"

"Hawk-girl? Yeah, she was pretty. It's like every other girl I see here could be a model. Hey, doesn't it hurt when he claws your arm like that?" I said.

Ink glanced away to see if the crowd had dissipated. It had. He rolled up the corner of his sleeve to show me he was wearing a leather armguard to protect his skin from the hawk's talons. "Did you think me and Ben were lying? Anyway, as long as Mr. Snow here doesn't touch my hand, no, it doesn't hurt. Sometimes he gets a little... *ambitious*, and I just have to think: Mom's meatloaf, granny panties, the quick brown fox jumps over the lazy Countryish man's back."

I chuckled. "He's a beautiful bird. Can I touch him?"

Ink recoiled. "No. Mr. Snow and I have been training together for years, so he's used to me. He doesn't like when strangers touch him."

"Oh. All right. It's cool. So, how's the nightlife been treating you?"

Ink's mouth remained a level line. "Better than it's been treating you, from the look of things. Why don't you come out with us sometime?"

I remembered the spiral scrawled in the dirt outside my window and the shape I thought I'd seen watching me sleep from the balcony of my apartment.

"You sure?" I said.

"Yeah. Listen, I need to get going. Mr. Snow doesn't like being in public for too long after a show." The hawk stared at me with huge, amber eyes. "We'll be at Drinks Bar tonight. Come have a beer," Ink said.

"I'll be there," I said.
"Uh huh."

THE CITY

I MET UP with them a little before ten, wearing the same outfit I'd worn every other night I'd gone out in City, my frayed black blazer over a faded button-up, slacks, and busted leather shoes.

Taking a bathroom selfie before I left my apartment to post on Instagram had produced mixed results. I'd always considered these my best clothes, but now they looked old, ratty, in dire need of an upgrade.

I did, too. In the picture, my face was sunken and pale, and no amount of filtering or adjusting the saturation helped. Dark circles ringed my reddened eyes. My hair was an overturned nest of ginger straw. I hadn't had it cut in months. I was hunched over, wiry, and had lost most of my body fat from not eating. An overgrown, sandpapery beard sprouted from my cheeks and neck.

Evan was one of the first people to like my photo.

When I got to Drinks Bar, Big Ben asked me with his trademark North English twang, "So, Frisco, you find yourself a girlfriend yet?" Ten minutes after my arrival our small, back-corner table was already half-covered with empty pint glasses.

"Actually, I did meet one girl," I said, getting nervous when Ink and Ben exchanged a guffaw. "But we didn't go all the way. And she's got issues."

"You know any women who don't have issues?" Big Ben said.

I thought about it. "Uh... my mom?"

"His mom!" Big Ben howled. He stood and tapped the table with his ring finger. "Fook me. That's good."

"I'm interested to hear how this relationship started," Ink said, ignoring him. "Did you use the material I told you to?" He folded his arms and leaned over the table eagerly to hear me above the music blaring from the digital jukebox. It was playing Ink's playlist, currently cycling through sixties pop. The song was Doc Watson's *Walk On Boy*. The bar was empty because it was a weeknight. Ink had turned the music up to full volume. Curiously, I noticed Ink was wearing flesh-colored earplugs.

I considered how best to answer his question. "I did, but not exactly the way you described. I asked her if she was French, but it was about half an hour into our first date."

Ink's eyes glimmered eagerly. I held his gaze to see if I could catch a glimpse of that strange, golden spiral again. No such luck.

"And? What did she say?" Ink said.

I wobbled my hand. "She *seemed* flattered. I mean, I don't know if she actually was."

"Of course she was," Ink muttered, more to himself than to me. His gaze wandered to Big Ben, currently standing a few paces from our table, where he was pulling darts off the dartboard to start a new game with himself. "Hear that, you moist towel? Frisco used the French opener and he was successful on his first try. You owe me a round."

"It wasn't his first try," Big Ben protested. "He said it to a stripper. She called the poor lad a selfish bastard because he wouldn't buy her a lady drink."

Ink turned back to me. "Is that true?"

My eyes fell into my beer. "Yup."

Ink pursed his lips. "Hmm. Interesting. Very interesting."

"Oh, don't get upset, you wee cunt. She was only after your wallet. Dated a stripper once. No, twice. Worst mistakes I ever made. One was like dating Stalin. The other was Pol Pot," Big Ben said, launching his first dart. It sank into the wooden housing of the dartboard, nearly a foot wide of its target. Big Ben hissed.

"So, what's this girl's name?" Ink asked me.

"Kashka," I said.

Ink took a swig from his glass. "Well, she's definitely Countryish."

"Yeah. I was really into her at first, but I don't think I'm going to see her again. She's too crazy. Almost like she's bipolar," I said.

Ink shrugged. "So bang her and fade out. Just wrap up before she backs up. You don't want to catch the Blot, man. It'll rot your brain. A buddy of mine got it from a girl he was sleeping with. Poor guy lost his mind. I watched him go from zero to crazy in a matter of months. One day he was fine, drinking beer with me and pulling girls off the street. The next, he looked like he hadn't slept in weeks, and was babbling on like a madman about frozen night countries, floating cities, snow cannibals, and crippled kings."

"Huh? I've never heard of an STD like that before. You said it's called the Blot?" I said.

"STD. Sexual curse. Same difference, right? You don't want to know, Frisco. Let's leave it at: you don't want to know. Still, possible negative mementos aside, I fail to see the problem in you sleeping with this girl," Ink said.

I shook my head, gazing into the bowels of my glass. "I dunno, man. If I do that, she might explode."

Ink raised a quizzical eyebrow. "Dude, were you a Boy Scout or something?"

"Actually I was. I stopped when I earned my Eagle Scout."

Ink shook his head, massaging his forehead with a gun barrel made of two fingers. "I'm not calling you Frisco anymore. From now on you're Boy Scout, until you spit out whatever pill you swallowed that told you sex with pretty girls is wrong. *That* shit is what's unhealthy. How long did you say it's been?"

I cleared my throat. "Uh... about two years."

Ink leaned in closer. "And does she like you?"

"I think so," I said.

He leaned back again, clapping his hands on the table. "Great. Your giant moral conundrum just solved itself." His phone buzzed. He answered, said something in Countryish, and hung up. "Apologies. Speak of the devil and she shall appear."

"Do you have a date tonight?" I said.

Ink finished his beer, stretched, and yawned into the back of his hand. "No. The date was earlier. This is the vetting. You and Bennie over there are going to help me decide if this is gonna be the one I put a baby in. Just kidding. Maybe."

It was my turn to raise an eyebrow. "You can't decide that on your own?"

Ink fixed me with a lion's gaze, folded his hands on the table and said, "That's really the million-crown question, isn't it, Mr. Eagle Scout. A man alone is blind. He has biases, weaknesses, overlooks things that are right in front of his face, things his friends might have seen immediately and warned him about, if he had been wise enough to ask for their counsel. Then again, not all counsel is created equal. This girl could be a ticking time bomb, and you could still be the idiot who tells me to just man up and put a ring on it. Are you that guy, Frisco?"

I shook my head, "No," simultaneously thinking, *Maybe Kashka's not the only one who's got issues.*

Ink smiled. "Good. In that case... you ready for another?"

Ten minutes later, an attractive brunette girl walked into the bar and gave Ink a hug. I recognized her instantly. She was the Hawk-girl from Ink's magic show. She was wearing the same pea coat she had been at the show, but the hood was drawn, framing her blue eyes, pearl-white skin, and slender, bow-shaped lips in a halo of fur. She barely looked old enough to be in a bar, even in Country, where the drinking age was eighteen.

Hawk-girl gave me a studying second look. I thought she recognized me too, so I said "Hello."

"Hey," Hawk-girl said. Her smile was shy and innocent.

"This is Dan," Ink said. "He's from California."

We shook hands. "I'm Iza," Hawk-girl said.

"Pleasure to meet you, Iza," I said, then in Countryish, "*Milo mi cie poznac.*" It was the only thing I knew how to say in Countryish other than "Cheers" and "Thank you."

Iza gave a nervous giggle. "Me, too."

"You want a drink?" Ink asked her.

Ink got him and me vodka shots from the bar. Iza ordered "*herbatka.*" Ink shrugged and clinked my glass. We drank. A moment later, the bartender handed Iza a steaming mug of Lipton black tea, complete with a lemon slice. We went back to the table, where I sat while Iza and Big Ben made introductions.

Over the next hour I caught Iza stealing glances at me more than once. I smiled, and she quickly looked away. Her English was good, but she didn't speak much, except when Ink asked her something. Mostly, the conversation consisted of Ink and Ben regaling her with stories, which I now knew to be meticulously planned and rehearsed: the pen in Afghanistan, Ink throwing the spoon, the stripper calling me a selfish bastard when I asked her if she was French.

I laughed and played along, all the while wondering if the reason Ink's date kept staring at me wasn't because of how much younger I was than him. He had to be twice her age, which, granted, wasn't that unusual to see in Country, but the more I watched her, the more I witnessed her immature mannerisms and the gullible way she gulped down Ink's blatantly obvious routines like she was the first girl to ever hear them.

"Hey, can I bum a smoke?" Ink asked Iza. She nodded, reaching for her purse. "You coming, Boy Scout?"

"Sure," I said.

Big Ben stayed inside to play darts.

We went upstairs and stood huddled under the dancing neon martini sign. There had been a score of tables on the patio just a few nights ago, now bare flagstones riddled with fallen leaves. It had grown brutally cold, and frozen blades of wind tore through the thin fabric of my blazer. Within seconds of stepping outside my teeth were chattering and pale clouds of breath clotted the air in front of me.

Ink, who wasn't wearing a heavy jacket either, didn't seem affected by the temperature. Iza tucked her arms under his, and didn't make any effort to appear comfortable.

"So, Iza. Didn't I see you at the magic show earlier?" I said.

"Yes, that was me," she said.

Ink lit her cigarette. "Very observant. That's where we met."

"But we went to coffee after his show," Iza added.

"I hope you don't mind me asking, but how old are you?" I didn't realize my question was rude until Ink shook his head at me in silent disbelief.

Iza wasn't offended. "I'm seventeen."

"Do you study here?" I said.

I meant at a university, but, puffing her cigarette, Iza said, "Yes. High school. I'm in my last year."

Ink reached into his pocket, took out his billfold, and handed Iza a twenty-crown note. "Hey, go inside and get yourself a drink. I'll meet you in a minute."

Iza stared sadly at her half-finished cigarette. I expected her to say something sassy or tell him to fuck off, like an American girl would have, but she only dropped her unfinished cigarette on the ground, extinguished the ember with the heel of her boot, and gave us both a pleasant smile before heading back downstairs.

When she was out of earshot, Ink put a gentle hand on my shoulder. "Everything all right with you, buddy? You seem a little bit off," Ink said.

How about the spiral you drew on my window? I thought. *How would you even know if I was off? We barely know each other, unless you've been spying on me.*

"Yeah, man," I said. "Groovy as a goose. What's up?"

Ink slowly let his hand drop from my shoulder. He vaulted his eyebrows and threw his unlit cigarette into the gutter. "Nothing. Everything's cool with me. I just want to make sure you're okay. Nothing's on your mind? There's nothing you want to talk about?"

"Nope," I said. "Uh, I mean, yeah, I do have one question. Are you sure it's legal if you, you know…?"

"If I have sex with her?" Ink said.

I nodded, breathing a hidden sigh of relief that he'd bought my ploy.

Ink took on a deliberate, professorial tone, like he was explaining what two plus two equals to the biggest idiot in the world. "The age of consent is sixteen here, Daniel. We're a long way from California. Besides, did you see her?"

"She just seems so… young. I mean, she's beautiful, but…"

"She's from Ukraine," Ink said matter-of-factly. "Ukrainian girls have classically beautiful faces. They look eighteen until they hit forty-five. A lot of them came over here during the war, because they had rich families who sent them away to school, or because they had Countryish boyfriends. Ukrainian women are the most attractive, feminine women on the planet, even better than the women here. I lived there for a while, but..." Ink laughed at some private joke I wasn't a part of. "But, the time came when I had to leave."

"Because of the war?" I said.

Ink dug his hands deep into his pockets and leaned back on his heels, eyes carving unseen reminiscences from the overcast canopy of the night. "No, man. It wasn't because of the war. You keep shivering. Are you cold?"

"You're not? It's fucking freezing," I said.

Ink shook his head. "No. This is balmy to me. T-shirt weather."

"I feel like my balls are going to climb up into my stomach," I said.

"I'm probably more adapted to it than you, but you're not exactly dressed for the occasion. Isn't the Scouts' motto to *Be Prepared*? You did realize it's going to snow tonight, right?" Ink said.

"How? It's October," I said.

Ink shrugged. "Fall is short here. And the winter is *long*. Shall we head back inside? I only came out here to let Iza know I wouldn't judge her for smoking. But those things will kill you. Great way to meet women, by the way."

"What? Cigarettes?"

Ink winked. "At least half my lays at bars and dance clubs have been from asking the girl if I could bum a cigarette. I don't even smoke."

"No shit," I said. I let a vodka-tinged cackle slip between my chattering lips.

Ink prodded me in the belly. "Ah? Ah? Ah. Come on, Boy Scout. Let's get you indoors before you lose your ability to reproduce."

We went back inside and ordered several more rounds of vodka. Ink stopped drinking after the fourth, proceeding to sit at the table and run his fingers all over Iza's thighs, neck, and hands while I watched on from the dartboard, where Big Ben and I played game after sloshing game, neither of us slowing our own rate of alcohol consumption.

Eventually Ink and Iza got up to dance. A small, midnight crowd had filtered into the bar, and a few people were milling about on the dance floor, grooving to the music, Otis Redding's *Sittin' on the Dock of the Bay*. I didn't see anyone I was interested in talking to.

The way Ink dragged her to her feet and practically threw her on the dance floor made me sick inside. I didn't know why. It was clear from watching them interact all night that she liked him. She was just so *nice*. She didn't even try to resist when he whipped her around the dance floor or grinded his crotch between her ass cheeks. I doubt she'd even tell anyone if her arms bruised the next day due to his roughness.

He's treating her like a caveman would. She's too good for him, not to mention young. She should be with a good man, like me. Well, not me, but...

Ink surprised Iza with a spin move, swooping her from one side of his body to the other, maintaining perfect time with his footwork. They both laughed and he pulled her in close, pretending to lean in for the kiss. She closed her eyes and tilted her chin up, waiting for his lips to touch hers, but he pulled away, tapping her on the nose with his finger.

Or maybe I'm just drunk and jealous there's no one here to dance with me the way she's dancing with him. Of course she likes Ink. The guy's tall, fit, good-looking, charming, and he's even a pretty good dancer. The bastard probably practices his moves in the mirror.

Jesus Christ, I am jealous. There's no way I could dance that well. It would take me years to learn how to do those moves. I wonder if he could teach me? At least I know I could beat him in a swordfight.

Big Ben's dart sailed and sunk into the ring outside the bull's eye, ending our tournament with a brutal nine-to-one streak. "Sorry, Frisco," Big Ben said. "But I don't think you're goin' to catch up to me tonight."

I blew out a nimbus of searing, vaporized vodka and hanged my head. "Yeah, I should probably head home. Thanks for the drinks, Benny-Boy."

"Who the fook you callin' boy, lad? You want to get your head smashed in?" Big Ben said.

"Maybe you should, since I can't seem to get out of it for five goddamned seconds," I said.

Big Ben sighed and shook my hand. "Lighten up, all right? For your own sake. Tonight was a slow night – it happens. Don't go freezin' to death on the way home."

I put my jacket on. "Does that actually happen?"

"Oh, all the time. People die that way every year. I think you'll be fine, since it won't drop too low below freezin'. Just don't go lyin' down on any nice, comfy snow banks."

"I won't. Goodnight, Benny."

"Oi. Goodnight, fookhead."

I stood outside the bar and emailed Kashka using the free Wi-Fi. Snow was already starting to flutter down from the fat, black-bellied clouds in scattered patches, clinging to my clothes and face.

Are you at work? I wrote.

Kashka's reply came a few minutes later. *Hi Dan. No. I am home now.*

Come over, I wrote. The gesture, a desperate, pleading hall of mirrors reflecting back into the infinite darkness of the years, hung in virtual purgatory for what seemed like hours before an unread message appeared in my inbox.

Okay. I will see you in half an hour, Kashka replied.

Great. Meet me in front of my building. I'll let you in. Half an hour was exactly how long I needed to walk home.

Kashka was waiting for me under the overhang of my building's main entrance when I got home. She was wearing her Little Red Riding Hood coat, hood drawn tight over her face to keep out the sideways-blowing snow.

"Hey, babe," she said. I kissed her and took her upstairs.

The sex we had was short and awful. Kashka screamed at the top of her lungs like it was the greatest sex of her life, gasping and squealing so loud my neighbors banged on the wall for us to shut up. I didn't believe it for a second.

II

The kingdom was patchwork at best,
Woven by blood in brutal jest,
Forty years of sorrow and war,
An endless fire forged Country's core.

When Country's tribes bickered and fought,
The king crushed them with quick onslaught,
King Mirek's only clear desire
To leave his son a vast empire.

No man, woman, or child left alive,
All burned, butchered, flayed and dried,
So those who might rebel would reason,
Their kin would perish for their treason.

Arkadius raised his force by dark,
From those who'd heard the angel's "Hark!"
Orphaned boys with nothing to yield
But blood upon the fallow field.

An old man's youth is repaid in pain,
Walls of ghosts and rust-eaten blades,
Empty halls where his demons bray
The waning echoes of his name.

The Good Knight knew the cost to fight,
But his heart was true, and pure, and right.
And so they marched 'neath Zorya's light.[1]
Redemption does not fear the night.

---

[1]*Goddess of the stars in Slavic folklore.*

???

I AWOKE in the dark and the freezing cold. I gasped, jerking up from the stinging, crunching wetness that surrounded me. *Snow? Am I outside?*

It was so cold I could barely think. It took me a moment before my thoughts collected and I could take notice of my surroundings. I was lying in a snowdrift amidst an endless, frozen field. A blistering wind howled, sending snow devils to lash across my exposed face and arms. My teeth rattled violently inside my skull. I couldn't feel my feet. *Don't go lyin' down on any snow banks,* Big Ben's voice echoed in my mind's ear. *People die that way every year.*

Where is my building? Where is City? Where the fuck am I?

I climbed haphazardly to my feet. I was lucky I'd woken up before I'd frozen to death. I couldn't have been out here more than a few minutes. It had to be at least fifty degrees below zero. I'd never felt anything so cold.

It was too dark to see anything. I picked a direction and started walking. I didn't know where I was going, only that I had to find shelter. If I didn't get indoors soon, I was going to die. I trudged across a tundra of waist-high snowdrifts, a sea of pale ghost cotton lit only by its own hideous, nascent light. My body temperature was rapidly dropping. A memory bubbled up from one of the winter trips I'd taken with the Scouts back when I was a kid. *The first sign of hypothermia is disorientation. The second is paradoxical undressing. The third is the overpowering urge to fall asleep and never wake up.*

I stumbled over hill after hill of smooth, dead white, nothing but darkness on every side of me. I was lost. I was certain I would freeze to death before I could find somewhere warm. That was when I saw lights twinkling in the distance, penetrating the deep, starless darkness of the tundra. They were miles away, tiny candles twinkling on the horizon, but if I didn't reach them I was dead.

Your dream self always knows you're dreaming as soon as you regain enough of your cognitive faculties to wonder, and I wondered. This was real. The cold was real. The painful heaving in my chest was real. And if I didn't get inside soon, my life would really end.

Yet again, I'd had too much to drink, my inner demon had won, and I'd made a catastrophic mistake that couldn't be undone with wishful thinking.

I had no clue where I was, but I guessed it was somewhere several miles outside the City. I'd wandered, ran, or maybe even stolen a car and drove, out past the City limits. I'd finally done it, strayed until I was too far gone, and now I was going to pay for it with my life. It didn't matter that I couldn't remember how or when.

At least, that's what I thought, until I saw the corpses.

I wasn't sure what I was looking at, at first. I thought the black, head-high shapes that began poking from the snow the closer I walked toward the lights were the frozen trunks of long-dead trees. They were slender and crooked, bent over as if the wind had corrupted their brittle forms.

My foot struck something half-buried in the snow and I stumbled and fell into a drift. Something hard cut my face and hands. Droplets of my blood hissed and steamed on the snow. I pulled back and my breath caught as my gaze settled on what had cut me: the gray-green of old bones poking from rotten, frozen cloth;

dark, empty sockets glaring their eternal gaze; the broken crescent of a toothless, everlasting smile.

I'd fallen into the outstretched arms of a human corpse. The bones were kept rigid by their deep blanket of frost. The corpse had been camouflaged by snow. It grinned back at me from where it lay in its tomb of hoarfrost.

All I could think was: *Dead, all of them dead, preserved by the cold. A forest of the dead. Only some of them were dead before they froze. Most were still upright and walking.*

Where the fuck am I? Where the fuck is Kashka? Where the fuck is my building?

I stumbled to get a closer look at the black stumps I had thought were the remains of trees, and found they were not trees, but corpses, frozen upright in standing or leaning positions. They were everywhere, dozens of them – hundreds, even. Most still had faces, their skulls covered in a fine layer of sallow skin and brittle hair, all wrapped in shining layers of ice. Some were old. Most were young. There were women and children.

I lurched and staggered to escape that mordant forest, the sour taste of vomit rising in my throat with every step. *Dead. All of them. This isn't real. This isn't happening. It isn't real. It isn't real...*

It wasn't long before I saw the tracks, maybe a half mile or less. The distant lights were bright enough to cast fickle shadows on the snow, and between those shadows, a trail of sunken boot prints carving its way between the corpse-trees. I momentarily considered the possibility the tracks could be mine, but I was sure I hadn't changed direction. Those far, glimmering lights were still ahead of me.

A howl echoed somewhere in the near darkness, feral but distinctly human. I held my breath, waiting for it to repeat, my fight or flight instinct dumping hot scores of adrenaline into my veins.

Something's over there. I didn't want to see what it was, prayed that it hadn't seen me, either. But I was so cold, and if there was a living thing on the other side of that hill, that meant there might be shelter, too. Sinking to my knees, then my stomach, I crawled quietly as I could up to the ridge and lay prone in the snow.

A hundred feet down the gentle slope of the valley, a cart lay waylaid under the piling drifts. Its cargo, including a dozen or so dead passengers, were scattered around it in a grim tableaux.

A bipedal shape was scouring through the wreckage. It wore a loincloth, a fur coat made of dead animals stitched together, and strange plates of mismatched translucent armor that looked like they'd been salvaged from a prism junkyard. A white shadow rising from the hoary ground, half snow, half man.

The Snowman hurdled rather than walked, was crude and ineffective in its movements as it dug and searched for potential spoils, a tight ball of pale muscle and paler hair. The long, human-looking femur it carried in its hand dragged lazily behind it in the snow.

I considered calling out to it, but something about the creature stank of hostility. I thought about retreating down my side of the hill, but I'd still be exposed. My own tracks were everywhere, and my strength was draining fast. Very soon I would stop feeling cold and start feeling tired. I'd begin to hallucinate my temperature was rising feverishly when in fact it was nearing its fatal bottom line, and strip naked before laying down to slip away into the cold sleep of death.

I had two options, neither of which involved going back. I could wait for the creature to leave, then crawl into the cart and hope its meager shelter would provide me with enough warmth to keep from freezing to death until the sunrise; or, I could try to sneak up on the creature and kill it, at least knock it unconscious, so I could take its fur jacket.

I decided it simply wasn't possible to wait. I'd either freeze to death before the creature found what it was looking for, or it would come back this way, find my tracks, and hunt me down as I grew weaker and weaker.

I had to kill the Snowman, and fast. If I didn't, I was going to die. Whatever fallout I might face, legal or otherwise, I would have to deal with later.

I descended the valley slope, careful not to make any noise. The creature moved toward the opposite side of the cart. I seized my chance and crouch-ran the rest of the way down the hill, taking cover behind one of the cart's huge, upturned wheels.

I could see the Snowman through the gaps in the cartwheel spokes. It halted next to one of the corpses, clicking its tongue with satisfaction through thick, white clouds of breath: *click, click, click, hnnnnh.*

The corpse was short, that of a small child, no older than six or seven at the time of death. One of the corpse's arms was frozen upright, eternally reaching for a pair of larger corpses lying farther out that I assumed were its parents.

Click, click click, hnnnh.

The Snowman hoisted its bone axe over its head and brought the blade down in a swift slash, hacking off the dead child's arm. Brittle, frozen flesh shattered like glass. The Snowman stepped over the severed arm, lifted its loincloth, and let loose a powerful stream of urine.

Click, click click, hnnnh.

The steaming liquid doused the frozen meat for several endless minutes. When it ceased, the creature tossed its axe aside, squatted, and started eating.

He thawed it, I realized in horror.

Gray meat separated from bone with a decrepit, audible *crunch*. Parts of the arm were still frozen, but that didn't slow the creature's appetite.

I wanted to be back home, in my bed, with Kashka's sleeping face nestled under my arm. It's amazing how quickly you can come to want something you once despised when the shit hits the fan.

I didn't see any way out but the plan I'd already made.

I grabbed one of the spokes of the broken cartwheel and started quietly working it loose. The ice had sealed the broken spoke to its splintered base, but with a little muscle, it gave. I took my time, trying not to make any noise.

Once I had it free, the wooden beam I held was as long as my arm, about the same dimensions as the wooden swords we used to practice forms with in kendo class. I held the makeshift *bokken* in a high samurai grip, and rose.

The Snowman must have heard me, because he stopped eating and turned around, intently sniffing the air. That's when I realized he was blind.

His eyes had been cut out and sewn shut. The stitches were still there, fat strips of crisscrossed leather all crusted with frost. His gray, mottled skin clung loosely to his bones. His belly was scored with deep, old scars and patches of wandering cancer. When the Snowman opened his mouth to breathe, his rotten teeth formed a string of yellow blades sprouting from black, rotten gums.

Click, click, click, hnnnnh.

The Snowman dropped the half-finished morsel and fumbled in the snow for his bone axe, touching his lips with his other hand, then stuck his fingers in his mouth and bit down hard. A big, juicy chunk of his own finger came off. Hot blood flowed down his knuckles. He chewed it, swallowed, and grunted.

CORRUPTION

Click, click, click, hnnnh.

The Snowman took another bite of his finger, and another step in my direction, as if he was trying to decide if I was prey worth pursuing, or just another random noise of the tundra. I tried my best to mute the sound of my breath and the violent shivering of my body, but the closer the Snowman got, the more impossible that became.

There were a dozen other wounds littering the skin of his hands and forearms. The patchwork sleeve of ancient scars told me he'd been eating himself for a long time.

He gave a low growl and lurched suddenly toward me, the distance between us vanishing. Time slowed. The Snowman raised the bone axe over his head to brain me, and my instincts responded. I was sure I was dead. But my hands disagreed.

I thrust the broken spoke up to deflect the Snowman's strike, and his weapon slid off it like water. Years of practice guided my hands as I followed the momentum of the block with a downward cut, smashing him on the forehead. I put all my force into the last six inches of the wood, like I'd done a thousand times in class, a textbook head strike that connected perfectly.

If I had struck him with a real sword, the Snowman would have been cut in half from forehead to aorta. As it was, the cartwheel spoke was still heavy enough to deliver a killing blow. I felt the impact travel up my arm, the makeshift sword shivering in my grasp, and a deep depression formed where the creature's forehead had been, quickly sponging with blood. He fell backwards into the snow and did not move again.

I didn't stay long enough to find out if he was truly dead. I took his bone axe and shoddy fur coat, throwing the string of rabbits, possums, and mice over my own shoulders, and ran.

Blood thundered in my brain and ears. My lungs felt like they'd been scraped raw. It had been so long since I'd been in a fight that I'd forgotten the feeling that comes after one.

West Coast Invitational. Jaime Jimenez, #41. Cast the sword like a fishing rod. Cut with the last six inches of the blade. The memories came to me jagged and divorced.

A heavy sense of guilt followed. Whatever the creature was, I'd been wrong to kill it. What if, as vile as it seemed, it had a family, children? What if it had only been trying to feed its young?

It attacked me first. I was defending myself. Oh god, Jesus, I'm sorry. I'm so, so sorry.

A howl split the air somewhere nearby in that macabre forest of human trees. *The Snowman wasn't a scavenger; he was a scout,* I realized. *A member of a hunting party. They heard me kill him, and now they're going to come for me.*

The distant gang erupted in a chorus of echoing, hollow screams that rang over the tundra like the cries of men charging to war, half a dozen, no, a dozen, no, a hundred strong. My legs felt like they would snap under me with every step, but I ran, and ran, and ran toward those distant, bobbing lights until they weren't so distant anymore.

Snow and sleet battered my face. At the top of the next ridge I dared to look back. I instantly regretted my mistake. The shallow valley was swarming with fast-moving shadows all scoring brutal spider web tracks in the ghostly canvas of the landscape. They loped on all fours in strange, snaking lines, following their noses and only changing direction when they got too close to each other. They moved erratically, full of anger and bloodlust as they scoured the snow for what or whoever had slain their comrade. Their harsh cries carried above the storm like an eldritch wind.

Blind hunters, perfectly adapted to the cold and the darkness, I thought. *I need to get the hell out of here, now.*

I was food to them, nothing but warm meat that was slightly superior to the kind they were used to eating. Wherever I was, I was no longer in Country, or any place on Earth. I didn't know how I'd gotten here, or why, only that I had to keep running.

By the next ridge, the lights were so close that I could make out the outskirts of a city bordered by a vast, frozen river. But the lights weren't static. They were moving, skimming through the pale, interstitial clouds of blizzard as if on guided tracks, occasionally disappearing behind the vague shape of a building only to reappear again a fraction of a second later.

Just need to make it across the river, I thought, beginning my descent down the mire of snowdrifts that covered the gentle slope of the riverbank. *They won't follow. Dear God, please don't let them follow. If I can get across, someone can help me. They can give me warmth, shelter, food. Need to get across. Need to...*

I dismounted the bank and set one numb, shaking foot down to test the ice. I remembered from being in the Scouts that ice needed to be at least three inches thick to support the weight of an adult human. The ice was solid from shore to shore, so I estimated it had to be at least that thick. It was risky, but falling through the ice and drowning in a frozen river seemed a lot better than whatever the Snowmen would do to me.

As soon as my foot was on the ice, black figures began swarming down the riverbank above me. I took a deep, chilly breath, said a faithless prayer, and stepped out onto the ice. I couldn't run at a full sprint, but the thin layer of snow made the ice less slippery than I anticipated, and I could move at a slow jog.

When I was halfway across, and the glimmering lights of the opposite shore were closer than the black silhouette of bluffs I'd left behind, I glanced back to see how much the Snowmen had caught up.

They were still standing on the riverbank, arguing with each other and slashing at the air with their bone-axes. Not even one had set foot on the ice. Their cries went lost in the cruel howl of the wind, but I could tell from their gesticulations they were furious that I'd escaped.

The river marks the edge of their territory, I realized. *They're scared of it, or whatever lies beyond it. I'm safe. I'm going to live.*

The ice cracked under my feet before I heard the sound. It was like missing the bottom step when you're drunk and trying to walk down a flight of stairs in the middle of the night. The world split, and black, freezing water swallowed me. Stabbing knives of ice perforated my lungs. I tried to stay calm, but the water was so cold it hurt.

Fuck shit it's cold holy shit it's cold-

Open your eyes. Swim to the surface. There's space under the ice. Air. At least half an inch. Breathe. Then find the opening you fell through and pull yourself back up.

I forced my eyes open. The water stung bitterly, but that was the only difference. I had plunged into a world of darkness absolute. I couldn't see my hands inches in front of my face. No light penetrated the ice to guide me back to the hole I'd fallen through.

I didn't know which way was down or up, left or right. As my breath expanded and my lungs began to give, I became a primal, pure state of being guided by terror and mammalian instinct. Water entered my nostrils. I spun and flailed, but my hands and feet touched nothing but a dark, empty infinity. It was in my mouth and lungs, searing my insides like frozen fire. I couldn't cough. I couldn't breathe.

Going to die going to die why Jesus why God why fuck

CORRUPTION

A periscopic filter collapsed my vision down to the head of a pin. My thrashing subsided to a defeated series of numbing twitches. In my last seconds of coherence, I thought about how I'd never see Kashka again, and would never finish translating *Arkadius*. I hated all the people who would get to do the things I wanted to, but never could.

Cold. Hurts. Lungs going to pop. Hurts. Cold. Goodbye.

A muted crack reverberated somewhere below me and a brilliant white light pierced the darkness. A hard, sharp hand snagged my foot and pulled me down, down, down toward that harsh, terrible light.

I'm dying. This is the end. I'm not ready. I don't want to go yet. Why

My feet broke through the surface of the river, followed quickly by my legs, chest, and face. I flew down toward the sky, the shattered moonscape of floodlit ice vanishing above my head. Sputtering, choking, coughing up water that spewed from my mouth and nose, I swung through the air like a crane-lifted corpse as the light examined me.

Not dead. Not heaven. Not hell. Not oblivion. Alive. Something has me. Can't let go. Can't fall. Too high up. Oh God, what the hell is that?

The light filled my inverted vision, jerking me left, then right, and finally straight up again, then spun me so I was no longer upside down. A pair of huge armored claws were wrapped around my torso, made of some clear kind of metal, all tangled and gnarled and cold, not crushing me, but still closed too tight for me to get free on my own.

The light in my eyes brightened and an air horn blasted in my face.

Saved me. Won't kill me. Can't breathe. Can't move. Not yet. Can't die now.

The spotlight suddenly shifted off me, the fleshy stalk it was attached to aiming back toward the shore. *Bioluminescence...?*

The thing carrying me was huge, terrible and old, its face a crusted chitin mask as pale as porcelain, all clothed in a suit of translucent armored shell that split the light like a prism. It had a curved, demonic beak surrounded by dozens of glowing, pinhole eyes. Its body was a naked bulb of scars and legs, twelve slender, bladed spires that moved in perfect concert, each twice the height of a man. It looked like some kind of giant, alien louse, like you'd see in a heavily magnified photograph in a biology textbook, but adapted to walk and hunt on land.

The Louse's movement was so fluid I barely felt when it turned and began to run back toward the shore. In an instant I understood that the lights I'd seen hadn't been streetlights, but a pack of these same giant Lice hunting along the fast-approaching riverbank.

The Lice's headlights bobbed together in a silent rhythm. *Waiting for me,* I thought. *Waiting for us.*

I thrashed and writhed in the Louse's grip, slamming my fists and knees into its bulky, transparent claws, but the motion only made it close its grip tighter. I choked on the breath and cold water being forced out of my lungs. My skin, nostrils, and eyes screamed in the freezing air. My soaked clothes were already stiffening with frost, making it harder and harder to move my arms and legs. A violent chill rolled through my body and I stopped fighting, too cold and sick to do anything but shiver.

I'm sorry God. I'm sorry Car. I'm sorry I wasn't a better man. I'm sorry. I'm

Something exploded less than a dozen yards away, near the cluster where the other Lice were gathered. The heart-shaking boom slithered across the ice, hitting me with a harsh blast of pressure and a stinging shrapnel rain. I screamed as tongues of smoke and flame lashed the Louse's carapace.

When I opened my eyes, the other Lice were gone, reduced to nothing but patches of gore-splattered snow. White-hot bullets of molten shell and scorched meat clung in my hair and on my skin. The smell reminded me of burned crab.

A human voice shouted from the swathes of dead brush lining the riverbank: "We've got a live one!" the woman said; then, "Vermin! Attack!"

A dozen shadows materialized out of the darkness around me. Something hissed next to my head. The Louse carrying me groaned as an arrow sprouted from one of the armpit joints in its shell. It aimed the polyps of its flame stalks at the shapes running through the murk, there was a *clunk, clunk, clunk* like an old engine starting, and twin streams of blue fire sprouted toward the running shapes, turning the night as bright as day.

But it was too late for the Louse; the arrow had found its mark and severed a nerve. The gouts of fire from its mandibles struck wide as one leg wilted under us and the Louse tilted, crumbling into a steep snowdrift, the flames carving a harmless, steaming streak from the riverbank. The Vermin were already gone, their dark shapes vanished back into the drifting pillars of smoke.

I braced myself against the Louse's claws as we toppled over. The snow was deep, so I wasn't hurt.

A tiny avalanche piled down on us from the upset drifts higher up on the bank, burying the Louse and I under several feet of snow. I fought with all the strength I had left to get free of its vice grip. I wasn't going to die now, when I was so close to being rescued. I dug a small hole above my face that broke through the fallen snow.

The Louse moved beneath me. Its claws opened a fraction of an inch, and I wiggled free, first one leg, then the other. I kicked up, pushing my head through the hole and pulling myself up onto the hillside with my arms. The snow shifted under me, swirling down into a vortex. I scurried and leapt, barely avoiding being sucked down again. The huge, crippled monstrosity of the Louse emerged behind me, scattering loose snow and smoking meat everywhere.

My limbs were numb and nearly useless, but somehow I stumbled up the bank toward the angled shadows of the nearest buildings. If I was going to die, I wanted to at least die running.

No sooner had I reached level ground, a second explosion split the night, this time to my rear. Another one of the Vermin's missiles had struck the Louse as it was climbing out of its snowy grave. Jets of melted ice and hot shrapnel descended in a caustic, violent rain around me. I looked back to see the Louse's legs crumple and fall over, free of the smoking ruin of its body.

A fanfare of the Vermin's victorious cries followed, but I couldn't see where they were, only a wall of lights approaching quickly through the storm.

The edge of the city seemed to grow up around me as I ran. The watchful ghosts of ancient buildings passed silently behind a billowing fog of snow and ash, all bombed-out shells of brick and plaster leaning steadfast over a tangle of cratered, broken streets.

Not a city, I thought. *A ruin.*

I ran until I could run no longer, and then hid under the blackened windowsill of what appeared to have once been a shop. The sign above the door was written in an alphabet I'd never seen. In my delirium, I thought it might have been Cyrillic, but the more I considered that curving, alien script, as I huddled shivering under the window and waited for the prowling searchlights to pass, I decided that was just my panicked mind trying to rationalize a situation that was inherently irrational.

Impossible as it seemed, this plane, world, dimension, or whatever the hell it was, wasn't the same as the one in which I'd fallen asleep. I'd sleepwalked or fallen through some kind of hole or doorway into another world, a night world full of darkness and cold, where terrifying abominations waited to prey on unwary wanderers like myself. As far as I could tell, this new Night Country I'd wandered into had no relation to the world I called home.

The window had been blown in long ago. I tried to build a shelter out of the snow packed under the ledge, but I was too weak to do anything but curl into a ball. I fought to stay awake, thinking of anything I could to keep my eyes open: my mom and dad, Dee, the baby, Evan, Kashka; but most of all, I thought of Carly.

There was shrapnel stuck in my shoulder. I'd been too cold, or scared, to feel it go in. The large, jagged fragment of the Louse's shell wasn't metal, but it might as well have been. The blood had frozen around the wound, and with no more adrenaline to numb it, the pain became so excruciating that I lost control of my left arm.

Crying and alone, I shivered in the rivers of my wet clothes and waited for death to take me.

THE NIGHT COUNTRY

MY EYES FLICKERED open to a brilliant nimbus of light. The nearby shriek of a siren jolted me from the half-sleep I'd slipped into under the warmth of the windowsill. The noise was so loud I had to clutch my ears just to think.

My clothes were still damp, but I was warm. I was alive. The snow I'd buried myself in as my survival shelter was now a melted pool on the floor around me. At some point, the wall under the window had grown hot. It glowed with a gentle orange radiance.

A heater. Must be automatic. It sensed me dying next to it and turned on.

The light outside the window moved. In my delirious brain fog, I somehow didn't realize it was a searchlight until it turned and shone its beam directly into the window.

I didn't think the Louse could see me. I held my breath and tried not to move.

A fleshy gray thing slid through the window. It was a long, prehensile filament with a bioluminescent lure at the end. The searchlight hung in the air a foot above my head. The siren grew oppressively loud, then fell silent. A dozen others answered in the distance.

I clutched my ears and curled into a ball, lying motionless. The spotlight scoured the ancient, crumbling walls of the shop.

CORRUPTION

Too weak to run. Didn't freeze. But still cold. Heater kept me alive. Not going to die here. Going to live. It can sense the heat. See it. How else could it hunt in this hellish place? Which means it knows I'm here.

My fingers closed around the handle of the Snowman's bone axe where it lay forgotten under the window. Somehow I'd held onto it when I fell under the ice, and while the Louse-thing was carrying me.

The searchlight, which was really more of an eyestalk than a lure now that I saw it up close, passed within inches of my face, but by some extreme luck or the Louse's negligence, stopped short of turning the full 180 degrees to search under the window where I was hiding. My breath begged to burst from my lungs.

Slowly, I hoisted the bone axe, and with a single, swift, hacking motion, drove the tip of the blade into the Louse's eye. The light flickered and died. The wounded eyestalk jerked and recoiled back through the window, its owner screaming a thunderous, piercing wail. A dozen other cries added to the cacophony outside.

I rose to my feet, and was about to duck into the nearest hallway to try and find my way to the back door, when a second stalk appeared in the window, not coming all the way in, but hovering an inch or two inside the frame. The wet clunk of flesh engines started. I dove back under the windowsill as a searing, white-hot burst washed the room in fire.

Hot hot hot hot OW HOT FUCK

I don't know how close the flames came to touching me, but my guess is within fractions of an inch. Maybe they did graze me a little, and I was only spared from being badly burned, or killed, by the dampness of my clothes. I tucked my chin and arms tight to my chest and waited for the flames to die.

A second deluge bathed the room in white. The flames did touch me, then, dancing across the wound in my shoulder. I cried out in pain and the flames suddenly stopped, aiming toward the direction of the sound with an eerily, silent twitch.

I knew I didn't have much time, seconds, or fractions of seconds, before I would be burned alive. I lashed out with the bone axe as the flame stalk was turning to aim at me, severing it at the base of its budded tip. A squirt of blue plasma spat and guttered like the last flame of a cigarette lighter, and the flame bud fell and rolled into my lap.

Second chance. I have a second chance. Need to run. Pick it up. Flammable. Could use later. Pick it up. Shit. Run

I crawled to my feet, scooped the flame bud up, and ran full speed through the smoking embers of the room and the hallway beyond. I found the back door at the opposite end of the building. The pursuing lights of countless other Lice were already bobbing on the adjacent streets outside, searching the gutters and alleys for any sign of where I'd gone. A few more flame baths washed the interior of the building, then with one huge blast shot by three or four Lice in tandem, they burned it to the ground.

I ran without hesitation or abandon, trying not to think of the pain in my shoulder. I held the severed flame bud and the Snowman's axe tight to my chest. I tripped, fell, dragged myself to my feet, tripped and fell again, picking my spoils up each time I lost them.

There was no way to hide my tracks on the thick, fresh-fallen snow. Only speed could save me. I ran through crowded alleys of roofless, bomb-bitten brick walls, the charred remains of tram cars, weeping lamp posts, and the limbless, nameless statues of heroes, all of it worn smooth by wind, frost, and time, featureless black shadows under an empty, lightless sky. I ducked and wove between the buildings, leapt fences, cut through alleyways and made switchbacks to keep my pursuers confused, but they kept coming, their blinding spotlights scouring the ruins behind me, never more than a few blocks away.

The dead once-city stretched for miles. The snow cover reflected a little bit of ambient light from some source I couldn't yet see, giving the streets a nascent, tawny glow. Whatever cataclysm had caused this mighty metropolis to fall and turned it into a frozen, war-torn waste had eradicated its human population. The guerillas who had freed me from the Louse's claws – the ones the woman with the war-paint had called the Vermin - were long gone.

Eventually, the adrenaline ceased and exhaustion began to gnaw at my muscles. I ran for as long as I could, until my legs could no longer push forward. I slowed and glanced back over my shoulder. The lights of my pursuers were still only several streets behind me. The Lice didn't get tired. They would follow my tracks until they found me, or they died.

Almost as soon as I stopped to catch my breath, the lights were scouring less than a dozen feet behind me.

Gotta run. Run. Run. But my body was too fatigued to move faster than a pathetic stumble. This was the end. They would be on me in seconds.

I rounded a corner and found myself looking down over the slope of a deep valley. I caught myself on an outcrop of broken asphalt where the road ended just as I was about to trip and plummet off the edge. The valley was hundreds of feet deep, perhaps thousands. The fall would have been certain death. A brutal wind bit my face, sending snow devils dancing up over the sheer, naked cliffs and pushing me backward onto my ass. I crawled back to the rim and looked down, my guts churning at the nauseating height.

Not a valley. A crater.

A narrow switchback descended the crater wall where the road should have been. I started to make my way down. My feet slid on the loose-packed snow. The buildings ceased to stand upright, becoming collapsed piles of ancient rubble.

I could finally see the light source that gave the snow blanketing the city streets their glow. It had been previously obscured by the crowded, broken skyline, but from the crater my view of it was clear.

There was a gargantuan black plate hanging in the sky surrounded by a halo of golden light. It broke the low, rolling cover of ebony clouds like a cliff dissipating the tide. Long, jagged shapes dripped from its starless center, huge stalactites the size of upside-down mountains made of oily stone and twisted metal.

The floating behemoth blotted out most of my view of the sky from inside the crater, but the brightness of its halo gave enough light for me to see at least a few steps ahead on my treacherous path. A silent theater of weird shadows cast in amber danced and flickered all around as the dark clouds came and went a mile overhead.

I hadn't descended more than a quarter of the crater when the searchlights rounded the ledge above me. Sirens sounded, shrieking through the vast amphitheater of the crater as if the world itself was screaming.

The Lice rappelled down the cliff face with eldritch efficiency. Their slender, bladed limbs picked claw-holds faster than I could walk, and the buffeting winds and nearly vertical incline of the slope didn't seem to slow them at all.

I lost my foothold, caught myself on a busted steel pipe hanging out of the frozen dirt, recovered and kept moving. They were so close behind me I could hear their flame buds extending out of their shells and *clunk-clunk-clunking* into position. I was certain I would be dead in seconds, tried to make peace with God, gazed longingly toward the shadow-shrouded bottom of the crater-

There was an opening in the snow. It was the entrance to a tunnel, bricks the color of old soot lining an arched, weed-bedraggled cave mouth. A few stone piles stood outside in loose, man-made shapes. Beyond the pale border of foreground where the snowfall ended, twin metal tracks ran away into the darkness.

A subway tunnel, I thought. *It's been torn open. The Lice won't fit inside.*

I didn't know how tall the Lice were, but they looked a lot taller than a subway car. Whatever impact had formed the crater had vivisected this old tunnel like some unfortunate prisoner of war, its brick and mortar guts all spilling out down the hillside. My eyes tracked up to the black disc hanging in the sky with its dancing ring of gold and dangling, inverted mountain of spires. I thought I was close enough to jump and roll inside, but the distance was hard to estimate in the dim, flickering light.

If I missed, I'd fly off the path into five or six seconds of freefall before meeting my end on the broken slope somewhere near the bottom of the crater.

I'll be dead either way.

A burst of flame lit the night, cooking the skin on the back of my neck. I screamed, sprinted and dove into that oil pit of darkness.

I had run a good fifty feet deep into the tunnel before I looked back. The Louse was still at the tunnel entrance, trying to fold its triple-jointed legs into a shape that could fit inside the narrow mouth of bricks and steel. For an instant, its floodlight swung toward me, whiting out the pale crescent moon of the entrance and the unnatural night beyond.

It can't fit.

The light swung away again and started moving frantically. It was stuck. The Louse jerked hard, trying to remove the leg that was jammed, whipped back and slammed its bulbous carapace into the curved arch of the tunnel mouth. A dread rumble rose outside, and the dim light of the opening was blotted by the Louse's body and the sudden avalanche that buried it.

It was a long time before I looked back again. When I did, the tunnel mouth was a distant pinpoint of white, a single star shining against a pitch-black sky. One of the other Lice had pulled the stuck Louse free. But they hadn't followed me in.

I exhaled and slowed my pace to a painful, gasping limp. The tunnel was noticeably warmer than outside. By the time the light of the tunnel mouth vanished behind me, I had all but forgotten about the Lice and the Snowmen.

THE NIGHT COUNTRY

I WALKED through deep silence broken only by the occasional hidden drip of water and the soft scuffle of my footsteps. The ground was smooth, polished stone.

At least, I thought it was, until a dim, yellow light flickered on beside the tracks, and I saw that the floor beneath my feet wasn't rock, but amber. The lights turned on in domino fashion, each coming to life with a sound like a match striking, a marching line of ghost lanterns stretching around the distant bend of the tunnel.

Not electric. Gas, maybe, or something else.

That's when I noticed I was covered in blood.

I stopped to check my wound. I couldn't see how deep the cut in my shoulder was, but it was agonizing just to peel aside the torn flap of my shirt. The lamps in the floor weren't bright enough for me to get a good view, but they were bright enough that I noticed something funny about the clothes I was wearing.

This isn't the shirt I wore to bed. This isn't my shirt at all. Nor are these my pants or my boots. They look homemade.

I didn't feel surprised by this discovery, only tired, a vessel of aches and pains and the perpetual, gnawing cold.

I followed the tracks until the light bloomed bright and the tunnel widened. There was a subway station a short ways ahead. I sprinted to it and mounted the platform.

It wasn't much different than a subway station back home. There were vending machines, wall-sized advertisements, trash bins, and what appeared to be newspaper stands. The subway signs were mostly still intact, all written in that strange, pseudo-Cyrillic script, but the grand, mosaicked ceiling arches were almost completely caved in.

And the floor of the platform was covered in human corpses.

They were clustered together as if they'd died sharing a group hug. Their skulls and rib cages wore dry, random patches of skin and leathery meat, their remains partially mummified by the frigid air. Their clothes, shoes, and jewelry looked upper class, not much different than one would see at rush hour in San Francisco, New York, or even the City I'd left behind. The cuts and fashions of their clothes were unfamiliar, but not alien. One mummy I found that had squeezed herself into the gap behind a device that appeared to be a vending machine was nearly perfectly intact, as was the corpse of the infant clutched to her breast beneath the fuzzy lapel of her fur coat.

Were they trying to stay warm? Or was it something else, and not the cold that killed them? Whatever it was, they look like they knew it was coming, though not for long.

I left that sallow crypt, taking the main stairs up to the station proper, a grand open arcade with a domed ceiling at least a hundred feet tall, all marble pillars and statues made of hand-carved amber. The automatic lights must have been broken, because only a few came on, too dim to reach the gloomy upper levels of the dome. Glimmering shadows danced on the ornate architecture. The stinging smells of death permeated the air.

There was a ticket counter against the back wall crowded with more rings of corpses, all sitting or lying against each other. Beyond, another stairway descended into inky blackness, framed by a golden archway watched over by the statues of two mythical, humanoid creatures that looked like angels; each had four wings instead of two. In place of human faces, they wore beaked masks. They carried flaming scepters in their hands, crossed to show guardianship over whatever lay in the tunnel beyond.

    I crossed the arcade, careful not to trip on any of the dead bodies littering the floor, and descended the stairs under that golden gateway. The stairs terminated in a dark hall. A lamp above the door switched on as I entered, casting a ricocheting beam of light that bloomed off the walls and spread down a spider web of branching tunnels. The walls were covered with twelve-foot high, floor-to-ceiling mirrors, allowing that single light source to illuminate a vast network of passages.

    I was standing in a hall of mirrors that stretched as far as the eye could see. Each adjacent passage stretched beyond the horizon of my sight. I had no idea which way to go, but I couldn't go back. This place was warm, so warm I broke a sweat walking through its passages. *Maybe the climate control is already on,* I thought. Whatever this place was, it had its own subway station, so it had to be important.

    In the end, I chose the passage immediately to my right, following the old principle I'd learned in Boy Scouts, that when lost in a maze, you can usually find your way out by simply walking forward, while keeping your right hand in contact with the right wall.

    I didn't touch the mirrors, though. There were strange illusions floating in the glass, images of men and women in regal poses with their eyes closed. Each mirror contained its own slumbering resident, most of them old, some of them young, all with beautiful, noble-looking faces, high cheekbones and sharp noses that hinted at mass quantities of wealth and importance. Their clothes were lined with fur and trimmed with golden thread, their hair perfectly brushed and their heads adorned with circlets of pure amber.

There must be hundreds of these portraits, I thought. *Maybe thousands. These tunnels look like they go on for miles.*

They look like kings, queens, or celebrities, maybe - ghosts of the rich and famous, sleeping in the glass. But they're not asleep, are they? They're dead. These aren't portraits. They're tombs, and this place is a catacombs. It's the Royal Crypts of whatever civilization once stood here... wherever here is.

There were names etched into metal plaques under each mirrored panel, but I couldn't read them. Instead, I used them as landmarks in case I needed to turn around and go back: a man, whose name looked vaguely like the English word for *Dude*, fittingly bearded; a very old woman, whose name looked like a cottage on the shores of a peaceful lake, who I called *Grandma*; a young man, whose name was a series of two-character combinations connected by dashes, who I decided to call *Dashiell*.

In the hallway beyond Dashiell's, a body was strewn across the floor. I approached slowly, careful not to disturb her. It was the corpse of a young girl who had frozen to death. She was so well-preserved I wouldn't have known she was dead if I hadn't already seen the other bodies.

The frozen girl was curled up in a fetal position, facing the dead end wall of the tunnel. Her skin was pale wax, her hair, the color of whiskey. She wore it in a long braid now brittle with frost. *Carly used to wear her hair like that before a match. It was the same color, too. Same length. She even looks a little like Carly.*

I knelt down to look closer. The girl wasn't breathing, but she didn't look dead, either, only sleeping, like the people in the mirrors. I ran a fingertip along the curve of her cheek. Her face was round, like Carly's, and she had the same wide-set eyes and tiny button nose. The longer I stared at her, the more I began to think I was looking at someone I loved very much, rather than the dead body of a stranger; someone who should've been gone, but wasn't; was here, lying on the floor in front of me.

I cupped her head behind the ear, stroked a frosted wisp of her hair with my thumb. She'd never be able to make a braid again, to sigh in frustration as she tried to catch the extraneous frizz the way Carly used to. She'd never laugh or cry again, never read, or write poetry, or fall in love again...

She's so cold. The heaters are on. How is she still so cold? Why did she come here to die, rather than stay with the others? Did someone move her...?

The dead girl trembled. I jerked back my hand and waited, motionless. *I'm seeing things. No. She definitely moved.* "Hello?" I said. "Can you hear me?"

My voice caught in my throat as a long, pale cloud hissed from her lips.

I touched her face again. It was still ice-cold.

She gasped, shivered, exhaled, gasped, shivered, and exhaled again. The rhythm of her breathing stabilized and one of her eyes flickered open, then the second, two orbs a missing shade of deepest blue.

"*Dzi...en? Dzien?*" the frozen girl said. Her voice came out a cracked whisper, so weak I could barely hear her. Her eyes lolled under half-risen lids, adjusting to the light. She muttered something I couldn't understand, that I thought was a foreign language. She stared at my face, eyes narrowing, closing, opening and focusing.

She's fighting to stay awake. I shrugged out of my fur coat and bundled her in it, cradling her in my arms. She was small, but surprisingly heavy. *All muscle,* I thought.

The girl's voice shifted as she approached full consciousness, and she said in near-perfect English, "You... not... Dzien."

"No. I'm Dan," I said. "Daniel Harper. From California."

"Daniel... from California." The frozen girl said my name like it was a bitter drink. "Nice... to meet... you, Daniel Harper... from California."

"Do you remember your name?" I said.

The frozen girl gave me a look like I was the biggest idiot in the world. She offered me a slender, delicate palm. "I'm... Zaea."

I shook her hand. She stared at me. I thought she would pass out again, but instead, she tried sitting up. There was a pool of dark water quickly gathering on the floor underneath her. I helped her sit up after her third attempt failed. She started shivering violently. I gently crossed her arms over her chest, rubbing them with my palms to help her body generate heat.

I spoke as slowly and clearly as I could. "Zaea, we need to get you warm. You're suffering from severe hypothermia. Do you understand what I'm saying?"

Shivering, Zaea nodded.

"Do you feel hot at all?"

Shivering, Zaea raised an eyebrow at me and shook her head *no*.

"Do you feel any urge to undress?"

Her hand fell to her boot, where she groped clumsily and drew out a long, skinny knife.

"No no no no," I said, leaping to grab the knife out of her hand. "Stop, stop, stop. I didn't mean *that*. *I* don't want to undress you. I'm worried you're in danger from the cold. Do you understand?"

Studying me with sleep-sick eyes, Zaea let her hand drop away from the knife, and nodded. I switched my grip to the blade and gave it back to her, offering her the handle the way they taught us in Boy Scouts. "I'm going to give this back. Please don't stab me, okay?"

Shivering, Zaea nodded. She wrapped herself in her arms again, but kept the knife wedged out of one fist, pointed at me in case I tried anything.

I held my hands out, palms up, to show her I wouldn't. "Okay. Good. You don't have to trust me. That's fine. We just need to find some blankets or something, and a way to start a fire, so we can get you warm."

I remembered the Louse's flame bud I'd absentmindedly set down on the floor next to Zaea a minute ago. I gave it to her. "I think the substance inside this is flammable. But I have no way to get it lit. We need to cut it open and find some way to light it."

I looked around, but the halls of the crypts were empty except for the ghosts floating in their graves of glass.

We're not going to find matches here. The people outside all look like they froze to death after being trapped inside this place. If there was anything in here that could light a fire, they would've found it.

Wait. The blade of the Snowman's axe. That stone might be... I tested it with my finger and breathed a sigh of relief. *Flint. Thank God.*

"F-food. P-please, food," Zaea said.

"You're hungry?"

She nodded furiously.

Shit. Is severe hunger a sign someone has hypothermia? Or a sign they don't? I couldn't remember.

"All right. Zaea, I need you to stay here, okay? I saw a vending machine outside, in the subway station. I'll be back in ten minutes. Please don't go anywhere." I didn't realize how stupid that sounded until after I said it. We were in the middle of a labyrinth of mirrored catacombs - where was she going to go?

I ran as fast as I could back to the main hall, trailing my left hand along the walls to avoid taking a wrong turn. It didn't take long to reach the big room with the domed ceiling, or the subway station beyond.

My suspicion proved accurate - the tall, rectangular box the dead woman and her baby were hiding behind was definitely a vending machine. It was made of stone rather than metal, but there was a screen on the front panel that glowed when I touched it, showing that same strange language I'd seen on the signs over the subway platform. I didn't see anywhere to put money, not that it mattered. I didn't have the time or stomach to start looting corpses.

The front window of the machine was glass, too coated with ice to see if there was still food inside. I cocked the Snowman's bone axe behind my shoulder, taking a low grip with both hands like I was holding a baseball bat, and swung it as hard as I could. The glass didn't shatter, but it cracked, and I worked to get the axe head free where it had penetrated so I could swing it again.

It took three more swings to break a hole big enough to get my arm through. I snapped the bone handle of the axe clean in half on the last swing, but the blade was still sharp enough to salvage, so I hung onto it. There was still food in the machine, too - some kind of energy bar in a translucent wrapper that looked like rice paper.

Whatever killed them, they didn't die from starvation.

I took as many as I could reach and made my way back to Zaea.

THE NIGHT COUNTRY

ZAEA WAS STILL where I'd left her curled up under the Snowman's furs. She'd cut open the flame bud and doused one half of the outer flesh with the black, oily substance inside. Her knife was sitting next to it, a clear indication that I was supposed to strike it against the blade of my axe and make fire.

I gave her an energy bar and set about trying to light our little pile of stinking Louse flesh while she sat and ate. She tore the lumpy white bar greedily from the rice paper and shoved it into her mouth, scarfing it down in two bites. She made the second bar disappear even faster.

By the time she was on her third, I'd hit a spark off the flint blade of my axe, exploding the oily flame bud in a brilliant pyre of red and green fire. I kept the other energy bars hidden in my pocket.

The initial burst of flames subsided and the fire diminished to a slow, gentle burn. When Zaea was finished eating, she warmed her hands above the flames and said, "They were royalty."

It took me a second to realize she was talking about the tombs. "Oh. Yeah. How do you know?"

"I was a princess," Zaea said, staring at the faces floating in the infinite march of the mirrors.

"Wait, did I hear that right?" I said. "Did you just say you're a *princess*? As in, the daughter of a royal family?"

She gave me that disappointed look again, like she was sad I wasn't using my intelligence. "Yes. That's what I said."

"Of where?"

"Of Neen, the City Arcanum."

I'd never heard of a city in Europe, or anywhere else, called Neen.

"Have you been here before?" I said.

Zaea's expression became forlorn. "I don't remember. I suppose I must have, since we're here now. But I can't recall how I got here. When I fell asleep, I was in my own bed. Of course, I was pretty drunk. But then the next thing I know, you were shaking me awake and talking to me about fires. Did you bring me here, Daniel Harper from California?"

Her words sent a slow tingle down the back of my neck. *She fell asleep in bed when she was piss drunk, like I did.* I shook my head. "No. I didn't. We're in the same boat."

"What?"

"We're in the same boat. It means I'm just as confused as you are."

"Oh," Zaea said. "A boat of confusion?"

"Yes." I let out a chuckle. Searing pain shot through my shoulder. I gasped and clutched it. The shrapnel piece seemed to be gone, but a huge swathe of my skin was wet and excruciatingly painful to the touch.

Zaea motioned for me to turn around so she could look. I heard her whistle behind me. "You're burned. It looks bad, but I can treat it. Doesn't seem to have gone all the way to the bone. You're lucky."

"Lucky is exactly what I feel right now." Zaea didn't pick up on my sarcasm. I knee-walked across the floor to examine my wound in the closest mirror. The looping pingback of reflections from across the hall made it easy for me to get a full view of the damage.

My left shoulder, lower neck, and the upper triceps of my left arm were an open, oozing mess of dead, cooked flesh and blackened skin. There was a small silver lining to that cloud, though; the flames had sealed shut the deep score created by the shrapnel, between the top of my left scapula and the bottom of my trapezius. At least now the cut wouldn't get infected. The burn still would if I didn't clean and bandage it, but I knew enough first aid to know that burns were easier to treat than deep cuts.

My t-shirt had disintegrated where the Louse's flame had touched me, an oblong spear rather than the formless firewall I had imagined. That made sense. The flame bud's hole was small, like the opening at the end of a gun barrel. When the flame bud primed and fired, the hottest part of the fire it shot would be something like a lance that could be aimed directionally, rather than a nebulous cloud.

"Could be worse. But we'll need to find bandages," I said.

Zaea crept up to my back, looked at my wound again, returned to the fire, and with nurturing dismissal said, "Don't worry. You'll be fine. We simply need to find an AutoLek. I might need to ask my father to link me a new bank fab. I seem to have left mine at home. Then, we can figure out where the nearest flyder station is, and when the next launch will be that can take us home. We were very drunk, that's all. We got blackout drunk and took the wrong flyder somewhere, we walked around, we got lost, and now... here we are. This looks like it might be in the QZ," the unfrozen girl gave me a reassuring smile.

"QZ?" I said.

"Quarantine Zone."

Jesus. She thinks she's still on her world, like I did, I thought. *But something deep inside me tells me that isn't how this works. Neither of us are at home any more, Zaea. Both of us are very, very far from home.*

"Um... Zaea? What exactly is an AutoLek? And a bank fab? And a flyder? I've never heard those words before," I said.

Zaea raised an eyebrow at me. "An AutoLek is a doctor's kiosk, a place for treating wounds and diseases, up to and including tier one and two cancers and basic biotechnical surgery. You can find them on any street corner in the civilized world." Her eyes darted up and out as she corrected herself. "Well, maybe not *any* street corner. They're harder to find near my work. I went to Ganheim Academy for school. We used to have one in every building. Now I have to walk over a kilometer any time I wanted to change my eye color."

"Wait, wait. What the hell are you talking about?" I said.

The unfrozen girl stared at me, the light of the low, oily flames dancing in the blue lakes of her eyes. "What? I don't understand," Zaea said.

I washed my face through my hands, exhaling a frustrated sigh. "Never mind. I don't think we're going to find any of that here. AutoLeks, flyders, or whatever. You're the first living person I've seen since I've been here. Well, that's not entirely true. I heard one woman yell something while that Louse... thing was carrying me – it's a long story. She was human, but you're the only other one."

"Louse thing?" Zaea laughed. "Now who's not making any sense?"

I frowned. "Yeah, you're right. That probably sounds pretty insane. You just woke up here. You haven't even been outside yet."

Zaea shook her head. "You're a bit strange, you know that, Daniel from California? I must say, I don't know who you are or how we met, but I've woken up next to far worse after a wild night." She extended her hand. "And I apologize for my terrible bedside manner. I'm pleased to meet you."

Jesus. She really thinks we slept together, that this is all just the aftermath of some drunken hookup she doesn't remember. Won't be long before she sheds that delusion...

I shook Zaea's outstretched hand. It felt cold and small, but familiar, too, like a touch I'd been missing all my life but didn't know I had been missing until now. "The pleasure's all mine, Frost Princess. And, I'm glad you're feeling better. To be honest, I didn't think you were going to make it for a minute there."

"Are you not always honest, Daniel from California?" Zaea said with a smirk.

"Um, it's just Dan. And, I'm not sure. I try to be honest. But I'd be lying right now if I told you I knew where we are or what the fuck is going on."

Zaea shook her head *no*. "No one is completely honest all the time. The difference between a liar and an honest person is, the liar doesn't know it. That's what my father says. Our people consider him a good king. And he is so funny. He tells the dirtiest jokes... things that should not be appropriate to say in front of your daughter." She laughed at the memory. "You'll see when you meet him. He will like you." Zaea pursed her lips suddenly, catching the comment on the tip of her tongue. She blushed and smiled. "Oops. I'm sorry. I probably sound crazy, talking about you meeting my family after one night."

"It's okay. He sounds like a great man," I said.

"He has his flaws. But, don't we all. Anyways, come on. Let's get up and get that wound treated. I'm feeling much better, and I need to stretch my legs." Zaea rose, shivered, and stretched. The fire was dying, and I didn't see any reason why we shouldn't, though I dreaded to see her sweet naivety shattered when she saw what awaited us outside the tombs. Just in case we wouldn't return, I grabbed the remaining half of the flame bud and the broken axe head. I let Zaea keep the Snowman's fur coat.

The lights died as soon as we passed Grandma. A loud *thunk* echoed through the endless hallways, and the unbroken beam of the single lamp flowed back out of its mirrored infinity, leaving us in pitch-black darkness. Zaea gasped behind me. "Dan?"

"I'm here," I said. I couldn't even see my own hand in front of my face. "The light should be motion activated, but it's not coming on. Looks like the power went out. We'll be okay. Here. Give me your hand." I reached and groped for her hand in the darkness, my fingers brushing something soft and warm.

"Hey! That is not my hand!"

"Sorry," I said. Her fingers found mine. "Hold onto me, okay?"

"I am waiting. Lead the way," Zaea said.

I reached out with my free hand until I felt the cold, mirrored glass of the left wall, and started walking. It took much longer to navigate the spider web of halls in total darkness, but eventually, we made it back to the entrance to the crypts, and the promising light of that shining, gilded archway.

"See?" I said, letting go of Zaea's hand to wag a finger at her. "I have an impeccable sense of direction."

Zaea blew a raspberry through her lips.

We ascended back into the station's high, domed hall, the smells of ancient death and cold dust seizing in my nostrils. The lights here were still on.

Zaea scrunched her face and covered her nose. Her eyes became discs as she saw the piles of corpses covering the floor and benches. A two-tone whimper escaped her lips.

"Oh, no."

I gave her hand a gentle squeeze to let her know I was still there. "Yeah. That was my reaction too," I said.

I suspected Zaea had been brought here by the same strange, unknowable happenstance that had brought me. I didn't think these were her people. But if I was wrong, I didn't want to say something that would add to the trauma.

Zaea walked among them, fingers slatted over trembling lips, breathing short, pale clouds of breath. Tears brimmed at the edges of her eyes.

When she'd taken a full survey of the room, she turned to me, blinked back her tears, fixed her stricken posture, and demanded, "We didn't get drunk and sleep together, did we. We've never even met before now, have we." Neither were questions.

I shook my head slowly. "No."

"Daniel, what's going on?"

"I don't know," I said honestly.

"What happened to them?"

I shrugged. "Your guess is as good as mine. Maybe they froze. But that doesn't make sense. The heat is still on down in the crypts, twenty feet from here. Or it was, until a few minutes ago. If they were freezing, why didn't they just... you know?"

"They didn't freeze," Zaea said. "We used to operate on cadavers that were preserved this way in medical school. These people were poisoned."

"Poisoned?" I took a second look at the corpses lying or sitting side-by-side in close circles, some leaning on each other, some fallen. I'd assumed that they'd done that to keep warm, but Zaea was right. There wasn't any indication the cold had been what killed them. There were, however, plenty of tiny, pill-sized glass cylinders littering the floor that looked like the bottles my anxiety medication used to come in back in the first months after the accident when I still took it – those were plastic, but the basic design was similar.

Of course. This would be the perfect location for an end-of-the-world suicide ring to get together and kick the bucket. Where better to find lethally poisonous preservatives than in a royal crypt?

"They killed themselves," I said.

Zaea shook her head. "Not all of them." She pointed to the few who had fallen outside the main groups, huddled in corners or curled up behind trash bins. "The others killed themselves. These ones didn't want to. But they weren't given a choice."

I suddenly wanted very badly to leave that sepulcher of sallow, sunken faces, parched leathery skin, and unblinking eyes. I saw a vision of despair in my mind's eye so empty and terrifying it shook me more deeply than I'd been shaken walking through the fields of frozen corpses on the surface.

"I need to get out of here," I said. "Come on. The exit's right there," I said, and began walking toward the stairs leading back down the platform.

Zaea put a hand on my non-injured shoulder to stop me. "No. That's the train station. Look. The sign says *Metro*. Can't you read Ithic?" she said, pointing to the strange, swirling script scrawled above the gate.

I shook my head *no*. Confusion washed over Zaea's face, then fear. "Dan... where exactly is California?"

"California is in the United States. On Planet Earth."

"And in which sector of the Paradigm is this Planet Earth?"

That was all that needed saying for both of us to truly see each other, and our surroundings for the first time.

"Zaea, where the fuck are we?" I said.

Zaea looked back at the sign above the subway gate, then at me, then the sign again, her lips parting like she was staring at a pattern her eyes couldn't follow. "I don't know, Dan. I don't know. I was wrong. That language isn't Ithic. It looks similar, but the accents are wrong. And some of the characters are different. It's like we walked into some kind of..."

"Parallel universe," I finished for her. "Or a wormhole. Magic wardrobe. A door to another dimension. Or... something."

"How long ago did you wake up?" Zaea said.

I shrugged, sucking air through my teeth to show my uncertainty. "I'm not exactly sure. It feels like days, but it can't have been more than a few hours ago. I wasn't as lucky as you. I woke up outside, in the snow. Still can't believe I didn't die."

Zaea's brow furrowed in consternation. "What snow?"

"I think we should go outside. It's easier if I show you. If that's not the main exit, where is it?"

Zaea gestured toward a sealed, ornate double door on the far side of the hall, opposite the stairs. "There."

We struggled for at least half an hour to get those doors open. The snowpack was thick on the other side, and the gaps between and underneath the doors had frozen solid. It took both of us slamming into it with our shoulders on a count of three just to get one side ajar, letting a slip of muddy, gray light fall in through the cracks. It was morning outside.

Two more well-timed shoulder thrusts and the door opened wide enough for Zaea to squeeze through. I waited in silence for a moment before calling out, "Zaea?"

"Sorry," her voice came muffled from the other side.

"Can you help me open this a little more? It's not big enough for me to get through."

"We're on the Surface?" she muttered to herself, then louder, said, "All right. There's a lot of snow. I've never seen this much snow before."

"You pull. I'll push. Ready?" I said, and we did, until I was finally able to shimmy through.

The pallid gray of the outside blinded me at first. I shielded my eyes with my hand and waited for my vision to adjust.

We stood on the remains of a stone promenade covered by a long overhang lined with statues. It was dawn. The promenade was a narrow bottleneck opening about a hundred feet long, where the shattered remains of revolving glass doors framed a serrated portrait of the ruined world beyond, a broken city rising piecemeal from the tundra as far as the eye could see.

Zaea shrugged the Snowman's furs off her shoulders and offered them to me. I shook my head. "No. You hang onto it. You can give it back to me later, when I'm the one almost dying. Deal?"

"Deal," Zaea said.

We started walking toward the shattered revolving doors. I paused to look at the graffiti someone had scrawled on the grimy, crumbling walls. I was seized by the strangest sensation. The longer I stared, the clearer the symbols became. Suddenly, that mutant, alien form of Cyrillic transformed into words with meaning and value, and in that instant I could read the characters as clearly as I could read English.

"A mouse alone is prey, but a family of mice overruns," the graffiti said. Beneath it, the artist had signed the name, *Vermin*.

That's what the woman yelled who rescued me from the Louse. This must be the Vermin's territory.

Zaea put a hand on my shoulder. "Dan? Can you read what that says?"

A frigid gust of wind blasted in. I wrapped myself in my own arms and said, "I can. The strangest thing just happened. I didn't understand jack shit when we were inside the building. But when I saw these words in daylight just now, I could." I chuckled nervously. "Maybe it's written in magic paint."

Zaea folded her arms too, shivering and glaring at me skeptically the way Carly used to when she thought I was lying. "And what does it say?"

"It says: *A mouse alone is prey, but a family of them overruns. Vermin.*"

Zaea nodded. "I feel very disoriented, Dan. We need to get out of here, and find someone who can help us figure out exactly where we are."

"You know what? That's a great idea."

I was first to climb through the shattered glass of the revolving doors, helping Zaea with one eye while I kept the other on our surroundings.

The crypts were located at the end of some kind of plaza lined with other grand buildings, all facing a huge, rectangular mirror pond. The ground was buried under six feet of clean, white snow. I couldn't see any footprints, but I thought the Lice might have been waiting to ambush us once we were out in the open.

It wasn't the Lice we had to worry about. As soon as Zaea had both feet in the snow, someone hissed, and six pale shapes rose from the snow, surrounding us with weapons drawn. They carried short, cruelly bladed spears, short swords, knives, and axes, and wore white fur jackets with hoods drawn. But they moved differently than the Snowmen had, intelligently, with swift grace and silent purpose. All of them were masked, wearing the faces of owls, mice, rabbits, mongooses, foxes...

The Vermin, I realized.

Their leader stepped forward, carelessly slinging her spear behind her neck and resting both hands on it. She was tall and slender as bones. The face she revealed when she slipped off her mask and blew a long, disappointed sigh at me was a chiseled oblong with cappuccino skin bedecked with scars, a crooked nose, and unfriendly eyes of frozen fire.

I recognized her voice when she spoke. She was the woman who had led the attack on the riverbank. "Good evening. You're not supposed to be here, are you? This is a sacred place. And it's ours. Trespassing is a crime punishable by death in the Burrow... at least, for your kind. But, before we get this done, I'm curious. Somehow, you freaks still look smart enough to talk. Where the hell are you from, anyway?"

"Neen," Zaea said.

I added quickly, "I-I-I'm from California."

The woman burst out laughing.

A woman in a bunny mask said, "See? They *can* talk! Y'ever hear of a Frosty talking before?" The other Vermin shook their heads. "Cheese Eater, you ever hear of a Frosty talking?"

The rest of the Vermin removed their masks.

A short, wiry youth with a pathetic stubble beard creeping over the edge of his bandanna and a rusty short sword in each of his hands, shrugged and kicked snow. "Hell no I ain't," the one called Cheese Eater said.

The girl behind the bunny mask was a skinny ginger with apish arms and a galaxy of freckles covering the bridge of her nose. "They look a lot different than in the picture books," she said, slipping out of her mask.

"Come on a few more of these little outings with me, and you won't be so surprised, Bunny Rabbit. Will she, Vermin?" the leader said.

"Hell no, sir," the other Vermin responded in unison. Bunny Rabbit retreated obediently.

The tall woman raised her arms. "Anything can happen out on the ice, can it not?"

"Anything and everything, sir!" the Vermin said.

"Very good." The leader turned her attention back to Zaea and me. "Now, I don't know what the hell the Oppressor – excuse me, our Beloved Sovereign - did to you to make you two all smart and shit, but that doesn't change what you are. And Frosties who cross into the Burrow get their heads and hands put on the Fence, to discourage more of your kind from tryin' to come here. Maybe that's fair and maybe it isn't, but that's the way it is."

"Who are you?" I said.

I felt the Vermin leader's spear in my gut before I saw it. I only had time to let out a painful hiccup before I fell to the snow. I thought she'd stabbed me, but she'd only hit me with the butt. It hurt like hell. Cheese Eater kept me down by pointing one of his swords in my face. We'd learned a few disarms in kendo, but his wrist was just barely too far away for me to grab, and he looked like the kind of guy who wouldn't let me take his sword easily.

Zaea sobbed. "Please, don't kill us! We were only…"

"Shut your goddamned mouth." The tall woman's words boomed across the mall. "Now. You can call me Barn Owl. What I say goes around here. So here's what's gonna happen. I ain't gonna kill you yet. You'll have the chance to explain yourself. My boss is gonna wanna see you, anyway. But don't get your hopes up. You crossed the Fence, and that means someone is gonna question the shit out of you, torture you, then hang you as an example to your fellow scum-sucking, flesh-eating brethren. And that someone is probably gonna be me."

"We didn't cross any fence," I said.

The woman called Barn Owl cast me a raised eyebrow. "Prepare for the opportunity of a lifetime, pusbags. You two are on your way to meet Our Lady of the Revolution, Queen Rat."

THE CITY

I SHIVERED and pulled the blankets closer under my chin. My brain hurt and my mouth was sour with the taste of alcohol. A warm, steadily breathing shape was curled up naked against me. Pounding pressure nagged at my bladder, too painful to ignore, despite that I wanted nothing more than to close my eyes and go back to sleep.

Clumsily, achingly, I rose from my bed, a Cartesian mind separated from my body by a trillion miles of space and time. I made my way to the bathroom where I pissed for a minute straight on the floor, the toilet seat, all. I had to brace myself against the wall so I wouldn't fall down. A shooting pain spiraled down my shoulder, through my arm, to the tips of my fingers.

Must've fallen asleep on it, I thought. *Fell asleep drunk on my own arm. Damage may be permanent. Great. Goddamn Kashka. Goddamn stupid hard mattress.*

I crashed into my kitchen table on the way back to bed. I was too drunk to feel the angled wooden corner of the table leg gash open the skin on my shin, too drunk to feel much of anything.

Kashka stirred as I slid back under the blankets. I lay on my back, watching the ceiling spin. She tried to cuddle with me, but every time she tried to roll over my arm to put her head on my chest, I pushed her away.

THE NIGHT COUNTRY

MY EYES rolled and there was a thousand-ton iron weight in my head, turning my nerves into gouts of fire. I didn't know who, or where I was. There were voices whispering around me, filtered through milk. A foggy haze of ground moved under me. When I tried to speak, my tongue was in the way. The simple act of opening and closing my mouth took superhuman concentration.

"Dan," someone whispered into my ear, so loud it could have been a bullhorn. I knew that voice. It was Zaea's. "Dan. Are you all right?"

Painfully, I nodded. The vague, pale shadows in the murk of my vision began to form distinct shapes. There was Zaea, walking next to me amidst the Vermin. Barn Owl was taking point. We were back in the ruined city, walking down a street that looked familiar. But as my vision cleared, I realized most of the ruins looked pretty much identical, and there was no way of knowing if I'd been here before. I also wasn't walking. Someone was carrying me.

As soon as that thought occurred to me, Cheese Eater shrugged me off his shoulders and I fell gasping into the snow. He had me in a fireman's carry, and I couldn't put my hands or feet down to break my fall. I was lucky he threw me down into a snowbank; otherwise, I would've broken something.

Ow SHIT

Cheese Eater loomed over me, grinning. "Like the taste of that, do ya? Don't fuck with me, mate, or I'll smash you again. And this time, it won't be with the blunt end of my blade. That's a promise."

I wriggled and tried to stand up, but it was no use. My hands and feet were tied. "Why... why?" I asked no one in particular.

Barn Owl's disembodied voice drifted back to me from up the street. "You looked like you were going to try something stupid, so we took precautions. By the book, Cannibal Man. Get back on your feet and keep moving."

"Cannibal Man," someone else said, chuckling.

Another responded, "He's no man."

The girl called Bunny Rabbit said, "He might sound like us, but Boss is right. He's one o' them! They both are. Look at that axe head he's got. And her coat! They'll try to eat us, first chance they get! We ought to roast their guts!"

"You don't roast guts, Bunny," the first Vermin said, taking on a tutorial tone. "You throw the guts out, and roast everything else."

Bunny scratched her head. "You do? I always thought they kept the intestines as a sort o' storage unit to dry meat in. How else would you make sausage?"

"She's got you there, Squirrel," another Vermin said.

Squirrel sounded horrified. "Sausage is made o' intestines? Oh, sweet Wanderer's wisdom. Vole, tell me she's havin' a laugh at me. I'm like to get sick if that's true."

Vole cleared his throat. "Actually, she's right. What did you think sausage was made of? You grind up the leftover meat after you separate the scraps from the good cuts, and then stuff 'em inside an intestine and smoke the whole thing. Goat. Pig. Sometimes cat or snake. Any intestine will do. But naturally, different animals are going to produce sausage of different sizes and flavors. My personal favorite is frost elk. But, those are hard to get. That's why we only eat it once a year, on Saintsfall."

"I'm going vegetarian," Squirrel muttered.

Zaea's clouded shape knelt down beside me. Cold fingers brushed the hair from my forehead. When Zaea's hand retracted, her fingertips were sticky with blood. "Dan, you have to get up," Zaea whispered. "Hurry. They'll kill us."

"It's not us you have to worry about, Dearest. At least, not out here," Barn Owl said, somewhere along the snowy road. Her voice carried like she was standing directly beside us.

Zaea helped me to my feet. It took me a moment to realize that her hands were free. "Wait. You tied me up, but not her? That's not very fair," I said.

Barn Owl chuckled. "She's smart enough not to fight us."

Zaea held onto my arm as we marched. I got weak a few times, and Zaea helped steady me so I wouldn't fall. I was so tired it was hard to keep my eyes open. Every time I closed them, the nagging, horrible pain in my skull, and a soft squeeze from Zaea made me open them again. Someone had wrapped me in a fur jacket while I was unconscious, which I guessed was a spare they kept for prisoners. It didn't do much to keep the cold away.

It wasn't until we'd been walking for at least an hour that I noticed the day wasn't getting any brighter. The sky was still the gloomy, charcoal gray of early dawn. There was barely enough light to navigate by as we threaded ruined street after ruined street, the buildings hollow shadows standing ten stories tall to either side, windows like empty, backlit eyes, the walls black murals of devastation.

We mounted the ridge of a small hill topped with a crenelated line of one-walled ruins. Woven through them was a shoddy fence made of sharpened spear butts, salvaged wood planks, and broken swords thrust deep into the snow, each bearing the severed head or hand of a Snowman.

The Fence, as Barn Owl called it, was a fence in name only, nothing but a series of disconnected markers running for perhaps four or five city blocks from what I could see in that dim, pre-morning light. The markers stood about twenty feet apart, with nothing to connect them. The heads had all been skewered through the neck and eye, the hands through the wrist and thumb webbing. All of the remains were frozen and crusted with frost, some beyond the point of recognition.

I caught a glimpse of the inside of one of the Snowmen's eyes. The sharpened pole it was impaled on had broken the stitches holding the eye shut, and the heavy, scar-covered lid had frozen open, revealing a deep, black hole inside. The Snowmen didn't simply sew their eyes shut. They cut them out entirely.

Zaea gasped, squeezing my arm hard. I swallowed back a bubble of vomit.

Beyond the Fence, the ground rapidly fell away to the white, sloping walls of a familiar valley, pock-marked by the open wounds of exposed subway tunnels and piles of stone that had once been houses.

The same giant, black disc I'd seen the night before hung in the sky above us. Its sheer size was finally apparent in the wan light of daybreak. The disc consisted of three parts. The disc itself was a huge obsidian plate, hanging a mile or two above the ground. Above the plate was a riddle of amber spires that I hadn't been able to see before, a gleaming skyline of smooth, radiant towers all redder than gold that stood tall enough to threaten the heavens.

There's a city up there, miles above us. An amber city floating above the clouds.

For an instant, the clouds had parted to reveal that shining metropolis, and the sight was so incredible I gave an involuntary sigh. It was more beautiful than anything I could've imagined.

"Ooh, pretty," Zaea said.

And I, "Impossible."

The clouds agreed, billowing to conceal their secret paradise once more. The cloud cover left most of the plate itself visible, though. I finally got a good look at what was hanging under it, a colossal, broken cone of tangled stone and twisted metal, held airborne by the plate's gravity.

In the grim, gray light, the cone appeared like the corrupted mirror image of the city it supported. Gnarled towers hung from tangled, upside-down battlements. Inverted buildings grew from inverted streets, lampposts dangling like desecrated baubles. Its lowest point nearly scraped the valley floor. No lights glimmered within that nightmare wreckage, only shadows casting deeper shadows.

"That is the Echelon," Barn Owl said, pointing at the plate. She had manifested beside me at some point while I was enjoying the view. The tall woman lowered her scarf and took off her hood, scrunching and wrinkling her nose and lips as she freed them from the furs. Her head was bald and covered with scars.

"Five minutes," she told the other Vermin. The Vermin obeyed, taking off their hoods and scarves, too. A few bent over to stretch. The others found somewhere to sit and check their weapons.

I counted three men and three women, including Barn Owl. The other two women were Bunny Rabbit, the thin, freckled girl with ginger hair and jade green eyes, and a silent, stocky woman with cutting brown eyes whose scalp was stricken by pattern baldness. The others called her Mongoose. The men were Cheese Eater, Squirrel, and Vole. Squirrel and Vole were complete physical opposites. Vole was freakishly tall, lean and hard, his neck full of veins and muscle, with black skin shot through with old scars. Squirrel was short, squat and had babyish cheeks and a diminutive button nose. His skin was deep olive, like a person from the Mediterranean's would've been, although I suspected there was no such thing as the Mediterranean on this world.

All of them were bald or their hair shorn so short it made no difference.

I didn't look at Cheese Eater's face for very long. His eyes were different colors, and one of his front teeth was missing. Every time I glanced his direction, he was staring at me.

"It's so much clearer in daylight." I said, gesturing toward the Echelon. "I couldn't see that there was a city up there the first time I saw it." I didn't want to get the shit kicked out of me again for saying something stupid.

Barn Owl narrowed her eyes. "Daylight? You think this is daylight?"

"It's not?" I said.

I thought Barn Owl would hit me, but she didn't. She only cracked her knuckles and said, "It is a false day, a passing lie, nothing more. They happen every once in a while. Sometimes they last minutes, sometimes weeks. But they always end."

"You're telling me the sun isn't going to come up soon and become morning?" I said.

Barn Owl glared at me with one eye cocked. *No, she thinks I'm testing her.* "Don't take that incredulous tone with me, Cannibal Man. There is no way of knowing when, or for how long, the false day will last. The brightness can be a rough indicator once it has already arrived, but it isn't exact. This one is dim. It will be dark again in an hour."

"Look, I think you've got me mistaken for someone else," I started. "Zaea, too. I'm not a cannibal. Never had the desire to eat human meat, or even the chance. I'm not one of those things. I'm not from here. Neither is she. So I really don't know what the hell any of what you just said means."

"Did you fall and smack yourself on the head? Where do you think you are?" Barn Owl said.

"His head looks fine to me. Maybe the Frosties threw him out because he was too stupid," Cheese Eater rasped.

Barn Owl gave a dry laugh. "No, he's not stupid. He's terrified, because he's lost. You lied to me boy. California, huh? Where the fuck is California? Tell me where you're really from. Which tribe? Or maybe you're both spies for the Amber City, and I should cut you open right now and steam you on the ice before you get the chance to run back to your master. You have seen our faces, after all," Barn Owl said.

"They have indeed," Cheese Eater said.

"We already told you where we're from," Zaea said.

Barn Owl shot her a look. "Shut your mouth."

"Right, he's from California," Squirrel hooted.

"And she's from the Monksblood Moons," Vole howled.

They all shut up instantly when Mongoose said, low and clearly, "He's lying. She's telling the truth." It was the first time I'd heard her speak.

Barn Owl seemed satisfied by that. More to Zaea than to me, she swept her hand across the horizon and explained, "This is the Surface. This side of the river is the remains of our capital. Down below us, in the tunnels, we call the Burrow. That black shadow in the sky is the Echelon, and that utopian metropolis you saw oh-so-gloriously shining atop of it is the home of our enemies, the Amber City. I don't recommend trying to go there, or anywhere up here on the Surface unless you fancy being burned alive by a company of Shells, or eaten while you're still conscious by a pack of your fellow Snowmen, or captured by the Amber Guard and taken up there to be turned into a doll for our Beloved Sovereign."

The tall woman smiled at me. "When True Night returns, and it *will* return, you best pray we're already underground."

"What is True Night?" Zaea said.

Barn Owl spoke slowly and softly. "True Night is this. The world we live in. Or, I should say *usually* live in until the random passing of a false day. It is the curse of our time, the Darkness Eternal. The Age without Sun."

"Where did the sun go? Has it gone missing?" I said.

"It was stolen," Barn Owl said.

"By who?" Zaea and I both said at the same time.

Barn Owl gave the slightest nod in the direction of the Echelon. "By him."

"Someone up there?" I said.

"Aye," Barn Owl said, "He who sits high where the light still shines in his Palace of Dolls. You must not say his name aloud, or death shall be upon you. You must never refer to him by anything but his title, or his Lice will come running."

Zaea and I exchanged a look. I thought she would be the one to ask, but when she didn't, I said, "So who is he?

Three words fell from Barn Owl's lips, barely more than a whisper. "The Crippled King."

None of us spoke, each lost in our own thoughts and the gnawing sting of the wind, until Barn Owl shrugged, spat, and started hiking down the ridge. "All right, Vermin. Get your hands out of your pants and your feet moving. Let's take advantage of this false daylight while it lasts."

I expected the Vermin to say "yes, ma'am," or "aye aye" or something, but they only nodded silently and we started our long descent toward the valley floor. Barn Owl's speech must have made me bold, because I called down to her, "Where are you taking us?"

She didn't respond, vanishing behind a snow devil blown off the slope. Instead, Cheese Eater hissed, smacked me on the ass with the flat side of his blade, and said, "Shut that flytrap before I sew it. You want to bring the Shells down on us when we're most vulnerable? Maybe you really are a spy."

"Ow! No I'm not. We are who we told you we are. Is it really necessary to keep hitting me?"

"I said, get silent before I cut you."

"Get silent before I cut you," I muttered to Cheese Eater's back as he marched past. "Get silent before I cut you. Cut me. Jesus Christ, what is wrong with these people...?"

I didn't realize Zaea was close enough to hear me until her fingers looped through mine and she squeezed my hand, giving me a sympathetic smile. We helped each other the rest of the way down the broken, debris-littered trail. Holding her hand felt like trying to grasp an ice cube in my palm, but I was glad she was there.

THE BURROW

WE ENTERED THE BURROW two-thirds of the way down the crater, a flight of stairs that was completely hidden between a five-foot drift and the shattered remnant of a house. I didn't even realize the entrance was there until half of the Vermin had descended it and Bunny Rabbit waved at Zaea and me to hurry in, too.

The stairs led to what had once been the basement of a wealthy townhouse, a large, man-made cavern held up by ornate marble pillars, where the rusted shells of strange, wheel-less cars lined the grime-blackened walls. Most of it was caved in, and the Vermin had a carefully routed pathway through the part that wasn't, which also would have been invisible to anyone who didn't already know the way.

A steep, sloping brick tunnel led us deeper underground to a series of cylindrical tunnels that I guessed were sewers, long dry and littered with piles of rat bones and unidentifiable detritus. We followed the sewers for miles, none of us speaking, a hollow drip of echoes out beyond the Vermin's torches drawing us ever forward through the suffocating darkness. Cheese Eater bared the first two inches of his blade any time Zaea or I so much as scuffed our shoes on the smooth, old stones.

It got warmer the deeper we went, until eventually, I could no longer see my breath. Then it clicked, and I felt like the biggest dumbass in the world. *They call themselves Vermin because they live underground. The undercity is their domain; they live here because it's the one place the Lice can't go.*

We passed through evaporated cisterns, derelict grain cellars, abandoned subway tunnels, and ancient sewers, all connected by precariously hidden modular brick tunnels so small we had to squeeze through them single file. Despite the Vermin knowing exactly where to go, there were no directions or location markers painted anywhere I could see; that is, until I saw Barn Owl using a small, handheld mirror to look at the ceiling. There wasn't anything written on the arched brickwork that was visible to the naked eye, but her mirror showed clearly-painted arrows to guide our way through that darkened maze.

They use invisible paint as a security measure, probably to keep their enemies from finding their base, but just as likely, to keep prisoners from escaping... which for the moment includes us.

Zaea noticed it, too. I could see her trying to nonchalantly peer over Barn Owl's shoulder any time the leader produced the tiny, handheld mirror from her sleeve to check where we were. Barn Owl would stop, flick her wrist, and the torchlight would glitter in Zaea's large, eager eyes as she popped up on her tiptoes to get a glimpse. *Carly used to do that, too, when dad showed us techniques in class and all the other students rushed in and grabbed up the best places to sit.*

They looked so similar it hurt. For a second I thought Carly *was* Zaea, and the odd girl I'd saved from freezing to death only hours before was some otherworld version of the girl I loved who had been dead for two years. But it was only a trick of the light. The thought vanished from my mind when Zaea turned, caught me looking and said, "Why are you staring at me?"

"Sorry," I said. "You just... you look like someone."

"I am someone."

"No. I mean someone else. Who I knew from before."

"Oh. Dan, are you okay? You look so sad," Zaea said.

Blinking back tears, I said, "I'm fine."

Barn Owl snapped for us to be quiet. She halted next to a small, medieval-looking iron door a short distance ahead of us, rapping six times between the fat, sharpened spikes. A window in the door slid open a crack, and the sound of a swallow chirping echoed softly from inside. Barn Owl cupped her hands to her mouth and *who who*'d in response. The door groaned and swung open.

A group of men was waiting for us inside the narrow, two-storied cellar. They were so well camouflaged that I didn't see them at first. It wasn't until they moved, relaxing taut bowstrings and lowering blades that had been poised to slash open our jugulars, that I was able to pick their black shapes out from the stage of dancing shadows.

The men rushed to check our bindings and search Zaea and me for weapons. "How much of this shit before you trust me to do my job, Gator?" Barn Owl said, a little disgusted.

The biggest of the men in black, who I assumed was their commander, a huge, beefy man with a back made of clothed barrels, gave Barn Owl an unfriendly slap on the arm and said, "How much shit before you let me do mine, little cousin? Where are you taking them? To the Salt Mine?"

Barn Owl cringed. "No. These ones are headed for the Last Station. Got my orders directly from the boss. Any captives we find are to be taken to her once they pass quarantine. So, here we are."

Gator estimated Zaea and me with a rising smirk. "Let me guess. I'm not supposed to leave any marks?"

Barn Owl stepped toe to toe with the big man, driving a finger into his chest. "You touch them at all, and I'm gonna forget what our grandmother said about not whooping your ass anymore. In fact, I'm gonna forget it's against the Common for us Vermin to hurt each other at all, and I'm gonna cut those tiny mouse nuts off and feed them to you. We keen, 'cos?"

Gator's smirk widened. "Sweet cousin, I was only kidding. But, fine. I'll give the next batch you bring me something extra to make up for all the fun I won't be having with these two. You may proceed."

Barn Owl shook her head *no*. "Actually, we're leaving them with you. Got another mission tomorrow, and we're already late to briefing. Wash and shave them – gently – and have them to the boss no later than two candles from now. We're going to try this on faith, Gazzo. You mess this up, and I can guarantee you'll lose this nice, cozy post you've got protecting our valuable ale stores. You'll be the newest member of my Surface Party before the end of the week."

It was the first time I'd heard any of the Vermin referred to by their real name. The smile fell from Gator's face. He swallowed and said, "Well, we wouldn't want that, now, would we? Come along, valued guests. Right this way. A nice, lukewarm bath, complete with soap and moss for scrubbing, awaits you just beyond that door…"

Gator grabbed me by the shirt and shoved me through another, smaller iron door to the rear of the cellar, into a torchlit stone hallway alive with the echoes of dripping water. My hands were tied and I couldn't prevent my face from smashing into the wall as I stumbled in. Gator chuckled and got even rougher. He pushed me into a tiny prison cell.

They took Zaea somewhere else. Her eyes flashed at me as they led her away. She didn't scream, except to say my name.

A few big men including Gator followed me into the cell and locked the door behind them. They made me take off my clothes and splashed me with freezing water from a bucket. Then they made me scrub with a sponge so hard it took off pieces of my skin. Gator grunted when he saw the wound in my shoulder, and made me turn around while I was shivering so he could get a closer look. He stuck his thumb in the hole where the shrapnel had gone in. I admit that I screamed, but I didn't cry. Gator kicked me in the gut and told his men to shave me.

I had already figured out by then that the reason everyone in this world was bald, or close to it (except for Zaea), was to prevent outbreaks of lice, since the people here lived underground. I hadn't realized that meant they kept their body hair shaved, too.

When they were done, they held a mirror up to my face and let me examine their handiwork. Their rusty knives had cut my scalp in ten different places. My chest and armpits weren't so lucky. Thankfully, they'd been gentler with my groin.

I was too weak from pain and exhaustion to protest. My burn hurt worse than any injury in my life, and the reopened shrapnel wound sent bursts of paralyzing aches all the way down my arm whenever I flexed.

I noticed something strange about my reflection. My scalp and eyebrows were shorn bald, only it wasn't my scalp, and they weren't my eyebrows. The face looking back at me from the handheld mirror belonged to someone else.

They drugged me, I thought. But I didn't feel like I'd been drugged. I studied the stranger's face staring back at me through the mirror: the large, dark eyes; the angular, scar-slashed jaw and hawkish, broken nose; the huge mouth split by an ugly cleft that parted my upper lip all the way to my left nostril; the giant, lumpy flaps of cauliflower tissue where my ears should have been. I was older, bigger, meaner, and I was ugly as shit.

No, it isn't a trick. This is my face. This is me. This is what I look like, what I looked like in the crypts when Zaea examined my wound. But it isn't me, too, because I'm not Daniel Harper. I'm in someone else's body. I am seeing through his eyes, hearing through his ears, feeling through his skin.

CORRUPTION

The men around me suddenly seemed anxious. Maybe they sensed that I was on edge, but they spent a lot of time muttering amongst themselves. They snatched the mirror away and bandaged my wound in a rush, applying a thick, smelly paste of herbs to my burn. They gave me new clothes, a tunic and trousers made from itchy bag fabric, as well as fresh blankets for my bed. Then they locked the doors and I was alone.

I lay on the moldy mattress and thought of Zaea. I hoped she was okay. I closed my eyes and pictured her whiskey-colored hair, the way the torchlight had clung to it, the same as Carly's looked sitting in front of the fireplace at Christmas when we'd sip hot Mexican chocolate and open each other's gifts. I hadn't had much time to think about it until now, but meeting Zaea had forced me to confront those memories, feelings I had suppressed for far too long because they were too painful for me to bear. Now that the gates were open, they resurfaced in a deluge of old regret.

I knew the next time I saw Zaea her hair would be gone, and I got sad. But I was asleep before I could think about it for very long.

III

Through shadowed wood Arkadius went
A knight of glory, heaven-sent,
Afore ten thousand razored spears
All broken men too mad to fear.

The trees were twisted, black, and old,
They whispered in the gnawing cold,
Evil words that pierced skin and maille
Their magic brought a sudden hail.

The soldiers cowered 'neath their shields,
But that grim spell would not repeal,
Chunks of ice that tore through their clothes,
Three-sided wounds that would not close.

The column halted, the men broke form,
Sanity's dirge an eldritch horn,
Bodies crushed under hoof and boot
To turn the snow as red as root.

"We serve the one you would dethrone,"
The trees chanted in subsonic tone,
"We are the Viwa,[2] true as stone.
You shall never pass this road."

But great men are not wont to die
'Til giving fate an earnest reply.
The Good Knight stood, gave up a cry
And charged the trees with blade held high.

---

[2]*Mythological forest demons who could summon storms

THE CITY

KASHKA WAS still asleep when I woke up, the warm autumn sun already shining high through the gap in the curtains. My body begged me to roll over and try to get another four or five hours of sleep, but my mind was racing, full of thoughts about Zaea, Carly, the Night Country and its Vermin. *What a messed-up dream,* I thought. *I need to write it down before I forget it.*

I checked my phone. It was 11:15 in the morning. I rose and stretched, trying to shake out the nagging ache in my left shoulder. I wasn't too hung over, just a little bit delirious from not sleeping. *I slept for ten hours,* I thought, simultaneously thinking, *I didn't sleep at all... I've been up for days. The hole from the Louse's shrapnel is still in my shoulder.*

It wasn't, though, when I went to the bathroom and checked. My skin was whole, smooth and unburned. What had I expected? It was just a nightmare. I always had those after a night of binge drinking. Ink had said something about the Blot, and the snow, that planted those images in mind. Then, the combination of stress, alcohol, missing Carly, and the endorphin rush of finally breaking my two-year sexual dry spell had culminated in me having an extremely lucid dream about some really crazy shit... or, so I told myself.

I pissed, drank a glass of water, and climbed back into bed to snuggle next to Kashka. I kissed her cheek and she grunted, pulling the comforter tighter under her chin. She looked older in the morning light than she did at night, with makeup and softer lighting. Even asleep, the lines at the corners of her mouth and eyes were more pronounced. She had big, hairy moles on the back of her neck and behind her ears that had been hidden by her hair.

I kissed her again, she woke up, and we had sex. It was better than the night before, probably because we were both hurting too much from our hangovers to care about putting on a performance. We didn't fall asleep again after. I got up and made us breakfast, half hoping she'd leave, and half hoping she wouldn't.

We didn't speak much as we sat and ate our scrambled eggs and pan-toasted country bread, except for minor fluff about how I made the coffee too strong for her taste, or how I had a nice apartment, or that my building was new and thus might be a target for thieves, or how quickly the weather had changed. "Amazing. You wouldn't even know it snowed last night," I said, pulling the curtains aside to peer out at the sunlight shining through the dead branches.

Kashka shrugged. "And tomorrow it will rain again. It is a land of extremes. I read on Internet today will be the last good weather of the year."

"Then we should enjoy it while we can."

"Did you sleep? You look very tired," Kashka said.

"I just drank too much. Had some crazy dreams," I said.

I admit I wasn't highly invested in the conversation. I couldn't stop thinking about my dream of the Night Country. I remembered every face, every word and detail. Dreams fade the farther they slip from us, because they are lies. The truth, however, doesn't diminish over time. It becomes more convincing, not less.

The more I thought about the Night Country, the more it felt like an actual memory rather than something imagined.

"Dan? Is something wrong? Do you want me to leave?" Kashka said. She was staring at me over the rim of her coffee cup, eyes angled in a defensive slant. Her eggs were cold on her plate, barely touched. I realized neither of us had spoken in almost five minutes.

She thinks I'm trying to make up some excuse to get her out of here. I decided I didn't want her to leave. I didn't want to let that spark go just yet, to flutter off and die in the wind. There was a person under all those weird neuroses and fake sex screams that I thought I could love, maybe have a future with, if I could save her. I didn't want to treat her like Ink would, to fuck her and chuck her like she expected me to. And, I didn't want to be alone.

"No, sweetheart. Nothing's wrong. How are you feeling?" I said.

Kashka shrugged, eyeing me, and slowly set her coffee on the table. "I'm a bit hanged over. You say hanged over?"

"Close enough. I understand. Do you want some Tylenol?" I said.

"What?"

"Painkillers."

"No, I'll be fine. Tell me, what are you doing today?"

"I'm supposed to be at work, but I'd rather hang out with you. I'll tell them I'm sick. You look like you're suffering a little. Are you sure you don't want something else? You didn't finish your eggs," I said.

A childish smile bleached the suspicion from Kashka's face. "Maybe beer."

I chuckled. "Oh, Jesus. Fine. Beer it is. I'm just gonna jump in the shower first, then we'll go."

"Okay. So, I am waiting," Kashka said.

I emailed my boss telling him I wasn't feeling well. He responded almost instantly, telling me not to worry, and that he hoped I would feel better soon. An icicle of guilt grew in my stomach over skipping work. What if somebody saw me? But the weather was nice, and the last thing I wanted to do was try to focus on translating *Arkadius*.

I took a ten-minute shower, letting the scalding water massage the pain from my shoulder with minimal success. When I got out, Kashka was still naked, lying on my bed and studying the picture on my nightstand.

"What is it?" she said, handing me the photograph.

It was the picture of Carly and me with my parents, taken at the West Coast Invitational Kendo Championship in San Francisco two years earlier. Carly had her arm around me and we were both smiling. Evan was bombing the back corner of the photo, throwing up dual peace signs like a moron. My mom and dad stood proudly to either side of Carly and me, though it was clear from their body language and whose shoulders they were grabbing who they were actually there to support.

The bundled tip of #41's *shinai* slashed toward me in my mind's eye. The memory replayed in slow motion, like the memory of a car crash, highlighting all the things I'd done wrong. I was too close, too slow not to fall for my opponent's feint. The crowd roared as the final men's match of the tournament burst into action, the point of his *shinai* flashing forward to tap me on the wrist, then the nose of my mask. I barely saw it coming.

"This was taken at my last Kendo tournament," I said, leaving out, *I didn't win*.

"You look strange. Why did you wear these clothes?" Kashka said.

"That's what you wear in a Kendo match. The clothes are padded to protect your body. You wear a mask, too, but we'd already taken our masks off by the time this picture was taken," I said.

"Your father, he does this sport, too?"

"Yes. He owned the school I used to train at. He was a champion when he was my age," I said.

Kashka pointed to Carly, her voice frying a little as she tried to control her jealousy. "And who is she?"

"That's my ex-girlfriend."

"What is her name?"

"C-Carly." It had been a long time since I'd said it aloud. I quickly added, "Don't worry. She's not a part of my life anymore."

Folding her arms over her chest, Kashka said, "So, why keep a picture of her next to your bed, if she's no longer part of your life?"

"It's a long story," I said. I took the picture out of her hands and set it down.

"Do you still think about her?"

"Of course I do."

"Why?"

"Because she died."

"Oh. Dan, I'm sorry. I didn't know about it," Kashka said, with remarkably artificial sympathy.

"I'm fine. You're fine. Everything's... fine. Listen, how about we go for that beer?" I said.

We walked through the Jewish Quarter toward the river, stopping at Kashka's favorite beer garden on the way, a place called *Fabryka*. We sat at a table in a courtyard patio covered by trees, under a giant, ancient oak garbed in swathes of bronze and gold and ruddy autumn brown. Most of the other tables and chairs were folded up to be put away for winter, but the tables that were still open were packed.

I got us beers and a piece of crusty apple cheesecake from the little hut next to the gate. I always thought America had the best cheesecake on Earth, until I tried the cheesecake in Country. I ended up wolfing the whole thing down in two or three bites, and had to get up to get another piece so Kashka could have some.

She giggled and stroked my hand when I set it down in front of her. "You like Countryish cake?" she said.

"It's phenomenal. What do they make it with?" I said.

"You call it... white cheese? No. Cottage cheese. I used to make it with my mom," Kashka said.

I couldn't believe it. "This is made with cottage cheese?"

Kashka nodded vigorously. "Yes. This is the style in the Old World. I think in the States, you use cream cheese, but it's not popular here. We like the old-fashioned way. I will bake you one."

"I wouldn't say no," I said.

The light in her eyes fell to an inquisitorial glow, though the smile remained firm on her lips. "Dan, tell me about Carly. Were you with her for many years?"

I wiped my mouth on a corner of the tablecloth – they didn't give us napkins – and said, "We were together for about ten years before she passed away."

"How did she... you say pass away?" Kashka said.

"Yes, that's the nice way of putting it. She died in a car crash. The person driving the car was drunk, and swerved to avoid another car going the opposite direction." I left out, *I was the person driving.*

Kashka nodded. "Thank you for telling me about it, and I'm sorry for your loss."

Despite the gnashing pain inside me, I made a show of casually waving away her condolences. "It was a long time ago."

Kashka sipped her beer. "What was she like?"

"You really want to spend our time together talking about my ex? Isn't that a little... weird?" I said.

Kashka shrugged and then nodded. "Tak. It is."

"Suit yourself," I said, and took a swig of beer. "Carly was a very sweet girl. She had a big heart. She was beautiful, extremely intelligent, and an amazingly talented martial artist. She held black belts in Judo and Jujutsu, and was the women's champion in Kendo for all of California. She won that title the night of the crash." I left out, *I was jealous she won and I didn't, so I got wasted at the after party. We got in a screaming fight, and she was too devoted – or perhaps willfully naïve is a better way of putting it - to let me drive home alone. All I remember after that is flashing lights, the sound of crashing steel and crunching glass, and patches of blood-soaked, strawberry blonde hair on the dashboard...*

"I can see this topic is still upsetting you. Maybe we should talk about something else," Kashka said.

Her lack of compassion made me angry. "Don't ask questions you don't want the answers to," I said.

Silently, Kashka finished her beer and rose, hoisting her purse over one shoulder. "I'm going for a walk," she said.

"Sit down. We're not finished yet." It came out harsher than I meant it to, but once the words left my mouth I was happy I'd said them. I was hurt, and furious she'd been so cold. I wanted to make her hurt, too, if only to show her I wasn't a man whose wounds she could poke just to poke them. I wondered if Ink would've approved. I thought he would.

Kashka ignored me and started walking toward the gate. Louder, I said, "Kashka, sit down." She halted. "I'm not asking," I added, shoving the last bite of cake into my mouth.

Kashka spun slowly on her heels and marched back to our table, taking her seat again as an impish smile curled up the corners of her mouth. *A test. It was a goddamned test.* That only made me angrier. But it was hard to stay mad at her when she blew me a kiss and started giggling playfully, as if she'd won some game where the objective was to make the other person angry. While part of me was on the cusp of flying into a rage over the frivolity of her game playing, another part chose to accept it, because that's just who Kashka was.

Carly never would've done this, I thought. *What happened to you to make you this way, Kashka? Was it the men who came before me, men like Ink, who taught you to wound other people's hearts so that your own could feel full again? Was it your family? Your culture? What happens if I choose not to play? Do we stand a chance at all?*

My questions were long forgotten by the time we reached the river. The sun was out, and the day was warm. We strolled for miles along the grassy promenade of the riverside, all resplendent with the moving neon flowers of joggers and packs of tourists riding rented bicycles. The buildings lining the banks were modern, communist-era abominations of concrete and glass, the water an ugly shade of toilet brown with a thick film of pollution and debris gathered where the river met stone.

Not a place you'd want to swim, I thought, watching clouds of white swans drifting in their arrowhead islands. *It's lovely, though, in its own, decayed fashion. There is always some decay in beauty. But there is always some beauty in decay.*

Kashka squeezed my hand, pulling me to a bench, where I sat and she laid her head on my lap, squinting against the brightness of the sun. The harsh afternoon light smoldered on her pale skin, erasing the lines I had found so detestable that same morning when I'd awoken.

I cradled her head, brushed her crow-black hair behind her ears, and kissed her, tasting the beer and her hesitant openness. I kissed her until she finally submitted, slid her fingers through my hair to close around the back of my skull, and pulled me down, down, into her ample, eager lips. A memory resurfaced of rusty blades scraping against my scalp, of fire scorching my skin, and an unfrozen girl screaming my name in fear as her fingers tried desperately to grab the bars of my cell. I shivered and pulled away.

Cupping my cheek in the palm of her hand, Kashka said, "I love you."

I froze, dumbfounded. "What?" I said.

"I love you."

"You love me?" I said, straightening my posture. "You barely know me."

"And what?" Kashka said. "I don't need a reason to know it. In Country we say: *we love for nothing.*"

She doesn't mean it. She's a pretty girl from a poor country, her best years are behind her. She's spent the last decade hopping from one foreign penis to another, and now her biological clock is ticking. She doesn't love me - she sees me as a parachute.

No. Look in her eyes, Dan. She loves you as much as Carly did. It doesn't make sense, but it doesn't have to. It never made sense with Carly, either.

"I love you, too," I said.

We kissed again, for a long time, until a man said something to us in Countryish from the bike path and we both sat up to look. Two cops were standing next to our bench, staring daggers at us. I hadn't even heard them approach.

The cop who had spoken repeated himself, louder and angrier than before. Kashka anxiously dug her arms under mine and said something in Countryish. The cop argued with her for a minute before tucking his nightstick back in his belt and departing back down the path, his partner lagging a few paces behind with an eye roll and a sigh.

When they were gone, I said, "What was that about?"

Kashka broke into laughter, hiding her face in her hand. "They said we can't do that here. They said we were being very naughty."

"What?" I said.

"They said these benches are not for laying down and kissing," Kashka said.

"You're kidding, right?"

"No. I'm serious," Kashka said. "They are strict here. They said it's against the law, and if they see us again, they will fine us one hundred crowns."

"I guess that makes us criminals, then," I said.

Kashka pulled me down on top of her by the collar of my shirt, buried her tongue in my mouth, grinned, and said, "Tak. Take me to jail."

THE CITY

KASHKA HAD to go home to get ready for work around six PM. I went to bed as soon as she left, trying to shake the feeling of nausea that had been growing in my belly ever since we'd left the riverside. My brain was ragged with the telltale headache that precedes a fever, and my intestines wound like a snake eating its own tail.

By seven I was sure Kashka had given me something. I talked to my parents briefly on Skype while I was huddled under the covers.

"Danny, you look so beat down and tired. You're not doing the up all night thing again, are ya?" my mom said.

"I didn't sleep much last night, but no. I've been trying to get eight hours a night. I'm just not feeling so hot right now," I said.

"Must have been a good party, man," my dad said.

"No, dad. I think that girl got me sick."

My dad's brow furrowed. "Oh, yeah. Sada? Karen? Kiki? No... Kasha?"

"Kashka," I said.

My mom adjusted their iPad on its stand, sending a crackling boom through the speakers of my laptop. I cringed. "Do you have a fever?" she said.

I held the back of my hand to my face. "No, but my head hurts. Stuffy nose. Weak and tired. So I can feel one coming on. It's crazy, though. I only started feeling like this in the past two hours. I was fine all day."

"Might be one of those twenty-four hour bugs. If your fever goes over 104, you need to go to the doctor," my mom said.

"Jeannie. He knows," my dad said.

"I'm not nagging him, Tim. I don't want to have another emergency while he's in a foreign country."

"Guys. Can you stop for five minutes, please? I'll go tomorrow. Besides, they use Celsius here, mom," I said.

"Well... we miss you," my mom said.

"Miss you, too. I'll talk to you guys later."

"Later, man."

By nine I was shivering so bad I thought my teeth would shatter. I pulled the blankets up to my ears and convulsed while tidal bores of magma and liquid nitrogen poured through my body, born on thoughts of falling into frozen rivers and the scorching pain of blue-white flames. I didn't have a thermometer to check my temperature with, but I knew in the back of my brain the mild delirium I was experiencing meant it was at least a hundred and three. It felt a lot higher.

My fever broke around midnight, and I woke up from my scattered watches of shallow, restless sleep in a pool of old sweat. I stumbled to the bathroom to vomit, but nothing came up. I didn't have the strength to stand again. I leaned against the toilet bowl with my face in my forearms and prayed for the sickness to pass. I stayed that way for a good forty minutes before I was collected enough to climb to my feet and prop myself up against the wall to take a piss.

When I looked down to aim, there was a black mark on my penis.

A lump rose in my throat. It looked like a little blot of black ink. I tried to rub it off with my fingers, but the flat, circular spot wasn't something I'd spilled on myself by accident. It was part of me. It didn't hurt or itch when I touched it, but hadn't been there a few hours ago, when I'd started feeling sick.

"No, no, no."

My first thought was that it was genital warts. But genital warts weren't pitch-black, were they? Neither were herpes, as far as I knew. *Maybe it's skin cancer,* I thought. *Dammit. No. Kashka gave me an STD. The Blot. This is the Blot. That's why I had that crazy dream. Holy shit. Ink wasn't kidding. This thing actually exists, and I caught it, all because I didn't wrap it up, because I didn't stick to my guns and stay away.*

I was suddenly disgusted at myself for the bitterness and anger I felt toward Kashka. I'd chosen to sleep with her, hadn't I? Weren't the consequences of that decision my own fault?

Ink's words echoed in my mind's ear: *"You don't want to catch the Blot, Boy Scout. You don't want to catch the Blot..."*

My memory filled with cascading visions of Snowmen, giant Lice, frost princesses, and a city buried in ice. *The Night Country.* Hadn't I really been there? It couldn't just be a dream, could it? If it was, why was there still a nagging phantom pain in my shoulder?

I fell asleep on my arm. I couldn't even feel it when I woke up, remember? It's that shitty IKEA bed. The fever is making me delusional.

Don't catch the Blot, Dan. You don't want to catch the Blot.

"The Blot." I said it aloud, the words soiling my mouth like rotten food. "The Blot. The Blot. The. Blot. Goddammit. No. This is not happening. Why? Why."

I stared at the black lump on my penis. My knees began to shake. I tried to catch my balance, but with my pants down around my thighs, I couldn't, and tripped and fell backwards into the shower. I burped up something foul, burped again, got to my knees and crawled over to the toilet seat, where I vomited until the cold light of dawn broke through my window.

ADAM VINE

THE CITY

I SPENT the next three days at home, taking turns puking and shitting my brains out as my fever came and went. When I wasn't hugging the toilet, I was in bed, not doing much of anything but staring at the ceiling or reading poetry and trying not to think of the black, alien spot quietly festering on my junk.

I emailed my boss, who said I was probably still adjusting to my move, and my body wasn't used to Country's bacteria and viruses yet. I replied sure, that was probably it.

I texted Evan again, hoping he'd be able to pull himself away from his pregnant wife or his video games or whatever the hell else he was doing for five minutes to talk to me, and ask how I was doing, so I could tell him I was fine, and how much I loved it here. He didn't answer. When I saw how many messages were on my side of the thread without a single response from his, I decided not to message Evan again.

I emailed Kashka, too, but her response was cold. She demanded to know why I hadn't visited her at work that day by the river. I'd forgotten that I told her I would before she left my house.

You did not come visit me, her message said.

Sorry. I got sick, I replied.

Why did you not come to my work, Dan?

I already told you. I came down with a fever. You gave me something.

Dan, I think you are not honest person. I keep thinking about this picture by your bed. Why have a picture of your ex-girlfriend at all? Do you still think of her often? We have a saying here: let the past be the past. But you don't. I don't trust you.*

You never did, I thought, but the response I actually wrote was, Why not?

I don't think you really love me. Maybe you still love her. I don't know. But it is strange you have that picture next to your bed. I think you still have a girlfriend back home, and you are hiding it from me. You said she died, but maybe you were lying. Maybe she is still alive, Kashka replied.

No. You gave me an STD. There is a black spot on my penis because of you. Thanks for the mistrust, but fu-

My hand hovered, shaking violently as I argued with myself if I should hit send.

In the end, my conscience won. I couldn't say something so cruel, not to her, and especially not over email. I deleted the message and replied, *She's dead, Kashka. She died in a car crash, like I told you. Also, I think you gave me some sort of sexually transmitted infection. You're the only girl I've slept with for the past two years, so please do not give me any more accusations. When I feel better, we both need to go to the doctor.*

Kashka responded: *Maybe she is, maybe she isn't. But I don't know, and I don't trust you now.*

Another message from Kashka popped up in my inbox. She wrote: *And it's not my fault you got some disease. You probably got it from some other girl. You are a bad person. Please don't ever talk to me again.*

I sat up in my sweat-stained pillows and read that message six more times. Who the hell *was* this person? I'd fooled myself into believing we were anything more than desperate strangers.

I thought I was smarter than that, but I guess I'm not. I said it back, I reminded myself. *But why? All the signs were there she was full of it, and*

CORRUPTION

I still believed her. Why did I do this to myself, when there were so many red flags telling me I should've walked away?

Jesus Christ, what is wrong with me? That's what Ink would say. This isn't me. This isn't who I am. My life isn't over. What's that line I just translated from Arkadius that I liked so much? "Every sin has its price,/ Some are great, some are small, / But the debt is inescapable / And eventually comes to call."

That was written in the 1200s. Why am I only now figuring it out? I ignored my moral compass and was a selfish asshole. Now I have to take the hit for my mistake, like last time. And if she really is the toxic one in this relationship, why does my heart hurt this much?

By the third night, I was feeling well enough to get out of bed and go for a walk. I went to the Old Town, looked for Kashka on the Main Square, at the corner of St. John's Street, by the King's Gate, even under the high, gothic arches of the basilica, but I couldn't find her anywhere. I hadn't eaten anything but scrambled eggs for the past three days, so I got a kebab and wandered the empty, spider-woven streets, picking at the greasy meat and sauce-smothered veggies with my fork and staring into the faces of the strangers all passing like ghost ships in the mist.

Eventually, I accepted the fact that Kashka was gone. By the time I started walking home, it was snowing.

BENEATH THE MASK

THE CISTERN VILLAGE was smaller than Hyro expected, little more than a few clusters of earthen brick houses and tents surrounding an open common. Huge stone pillars gave the villagers *some* cover as they fought and begged and fled, but like all the other little vermin eking out such a freezing, starving existence here in the Burrow - Hyro could not call it *living* - the villagers here had forgotten the first rule of war. They did not know their enemy.

The Ratkeeper stalked the scurrying, dying rebels through a dream of rows of burning slum houses and screaming children, and they could not escape him, could not do anything but die. Dreams are the will of the Spiral in raw, crude form. There is never any question about where to go, only the oneiric magnetism of purpose. Hyro-called-Ratkeeper did not hunt them with his eyes. Hyro had no eyes to see, only the mask.

The Brave Ones before him now were brave indeed, but they were not warriors. Old men and boys too gray of beard and weak of branch, all gnashing teeth, guttural challenges, and shaking hands barely strong enough to keep a grip on their own rattling farm tools.

The dozen of them who were still standing were huddled behind a makeshift shield wall, blocking his path to the last cluster of houses that were not on fire. Was this the force the Vermin expected to keep the home fires burning? They weren't even properly armed. He made a quick survey of their weaponry. Here was an axe, there a scythe, at last a shoddy rake - no, a rusty heirloom sword was there too, bearing a dozen unrepaired notches. The shields were even poorer than their arms, some large pots and pans, a few reclaimed doors to houses now burning elsewhere in the cistern.

One old man with an impressive mustache hissed a curse and spat over the shield wall. Interesting that the worst possible condemnation for these people was a nickname his own sovereign called him in friendliness.

He threw his chain and took the old man out at the knees. A spray of blood spattered and froze at his feet. The line of old men and boys slithered back a few paces to keep the distance, scurrying to stay low as they closed their ranks tighter. One of them yelped, "Father!" but an older, wiser hand pulled him back behind the shield wall before he could break away.

The Ratkeeper advanced.

If such unhewn boys and rotten old bags as this really were all the Vermin could afford to man the smaller settlements, then why, Hyro wondered, was the Lord Master concerned with an invasion plan at all? Why perform such black-hearted missions, such as murdering women, children, and the dregs of the Burrow's men? Why not send him, Hyro the Black Ward, who once commanded legions of men ten thousand strong to incalculable victories in half a hundred countries back on Home, into the heart of the Burrow with a hundred of the Amber City's hardest elites and simply take the rebellion's headquarters by force?

Yes, Hyro already knew. Because the Little Lord Master didn't trust him.

The crying boy got bold again and opened his section of the shield wall to throw a thrust with his spear, not much more than a sharpened wooden pole with a Wyvernwood knife lashed to the end. The boy howled, "For the Vermin!" and then a name.

He froze the boy with a breath, then shattered him into a maelstrom of hail. The freezing was the most humane way to pacify little Vermin that Hyro had yet found. He did not want his victims to suffer.

But the Brave Ones grew agitated all the same. They desperately broke form and rushed him, blades and war cries filling the smoky air of the cistern, and the Ratkeeper pacified them each in turn.

He was doing them a mercy.

But it was they who'd chosen to go about it the hard way, was it not? Yes, it was. It was better when they gave into their fear and let him trap them, ran themselves into corners or down dead ends where they could no longer flee or hide. Then he would take the ones he wanted in the soft amber glow of his lamp, and gently, peacefully give those he didn't want back to the Spiral.

Peaceful equilibrium is always better for both parties. Or is it?

When all of them were pacified or contained by the lamp, the Ratkeeper advanced.

He sensed movement to his right. The chain swept down and shattered one of the houses that wasn't on fire into a cloud of orange-red debris. A scream inside was cut suddenly short; then, a death rattle. The Blot told him it was a mother and her two children hiding beneath the cellar stairs. The mother and one of the children died instantly. The other...

The little girl sprinted through the back door. She was fast, despite a heavy limp from a freshly wounded right leg. Hyro struggled with himself whether or not to kill the child. The girl was seven, maybe eight years old. With her wound, she would be hard to move across the frozen wasteland of the Surface, but Hyro was not in the habit of letting prisoners escape. Yet.

But something was different this time. There was the book - yes, the Glass Book and all its pretty little secrets. There was the Little Lord Master's lies, not so pretty, no. There was the Visitor and the other one with all her precious little reasons for running. Different, yes. The rings were growing, stretching, becoming...

The fragment faded.

The running girl was making for one of the tunnels nearby. But human legs could not hope to match the speed of a Blotling traveling in Slow Time. Before the child could take another step, the Ratkeeper blocked her path and held his lamp into her face. A golden glow swelled in the wideness of the child's eyes. Then she was still. If the girl *had* escaped, it could have meant dire consequences for the plans ahead. Whatever such temptation Hyro may have had vanished. If he had let a rebel prisoner escape, it would be...

No. He couldn't...

But he could, couldn't he?

No.

Yes.

But it would be...

There was that word again, like a splinter slowly working its way under the clay edges of his mask. The word he dare not consider, lest all he was be destroyed in the unraveling.

He would take the girl to the Amber City, yes. Not to cold, miserable Ganheim where she would likely die of starvation or disease before she could be Transformed. The Amber City would give her a good life. Children always made the best gifts for the Lord Master. If they were the right age and had no prevailing health issues, they could be successfully indoctrinated back into elevated society. Some became successful citizens. In rare cases, the Lord Master gave them special positions among the regime when they got older, making them his advisors, cupbearers, elite bodyguards, and - yes – even his lovers.

Positions of honor.

Honor that had once been Hyro's.

But there was still much work to do to cleanse the village. There would be time later to become lost in the dream. Now was the time to let the dream move *him*.

An object had fallen from the girl's fingertips when her body wilted under the lamp. Hyro stopped to pick it up. It was a doll.

The doll was in the shape of a rat. It was hand-woven from sheep's wool dyed charcoal gray, with buttons for eyes, white thread for its little, gnawing teeth, and was that...? Yes, gold thread to form a makeshift crown. A rat king doll, Hyro reflected with amusement. No. Not a rat king. A rat queen. An expensive toy, likely the only thing of value the girl – perhaps her whole family - had owned.

Hyro let the rat queen doll drop back in the mud and took his new prisoner to join the others already gathered in the village's central common. And there the doll remained, long after the flames had grown and consumed the cistern village and the chorus of agony had faded, forgotten in the shadows and then eventually, the silence.

THE CITY

"ARE YOU OKAY?"

I looked up from the coffee I was brewing, my third double espresso of the morning, to see a strange, gangly little man leaning on the counter next to the coffee maker. He had tiny, flinty eyes and greasy hair. His skin was deathly pale, and a half-mowed lawn of gray perma-stubble clung to his neck. He wore a Star Wars t-shirt, cutoff jean shorts, despite the freezing cold weather outside, and the ugliest pair of closed-toe leather sandals I'd ever seen rising out of a pair of knee-high white cotton socks.

"Uh... sorry, what?" I said.

The little man waved at me with the huge, steaming mug of tea in his right hand. "You were out sick for a long time. I asked if you are feeling better."

"Oh. Yeah. Thanks for noticing. I'm feeling much better now," I said.

"Do you remember my name?"

I'd seen him around the office before. *He introduced himself to me my first day here. It starts with a K... Karl? Krzysztof? No, there a million Krzysztofs here, but he isn't one of them. This is the asshole that's supposed to be illustrating* Arkadius. *Only, he hasn't turned anything in yet. I'm supposed to have a meeting with Filip later today to discuss some problems with the book... probably because we don't have much to show, other than my translations.*

The tiny man helped me out by saying, "Karol. Or Lolek for short."

"Thanks. Sorry. I'm terrible with names," I said. "I'm…"

"Dan. Everyone knows your name," Lolek said. He took a long sip of tea and made a face like he'd just chugged from a bottle of vodka.

"Really? No one ever talks to me at this company," I said.

"Yes, because they are shy. Most of them aren't very comfortable speaking English," Lolek said. "And, you know, it's publishing. Most people came here from a video game publisher. A big office closed near here recently, about…" his eyes shifted toward the ceiling, then back to me like two lead pellets rolling in a bowl, "Maybe three months ago?"

I nodded. "I see. So, Lolek… we're supposed to be working together on this book project, except, I haven't seen anything from you since I got here. Are you planning to show me any of your illustrations?"

Lolek's smile dwindled. "Everything's on the wiki. Mostly sketches. Do you not have access to our wiki site?"

"I have no idea what that is. I mean, I know what a wiki is, I just didn't know we have one," I said.

Lolek chuckled. "Man… you were right. No one tells you anything."

When he saw I wasn't laughing, he said, "But actually, this is why I came downstairs. I'm working on some concept art for the demon - you know, this one that sits on the king's shoulder and controls him?" Lolek hunched his back and made a demon face, gesticulating like a puppet master with his fingers. I chuckled despite myself.

Lolek straightened up. "Anyway, I could use some feedback. You're translating the poem, so I thought you would be the guy to ask."

I took my mug out from the coffee maker. "Lead the way."

We went upstairs to Lolek's workstation. His computer had two brand-new, top-of-the-line flat panel monitors, both leagues nicer than the one I had, and a $500 drawing tablet. He opened the file on his desktop called *koszmar.bmp* ("*koszmar*" was the Countryish word for "Nightmare," which was the demon's name). Brilliant shades of red, orange, and burnished gold filled the screen, broken by black and gray smoke drawn with eye-popping detail.

Christ, this guy is talented.

I thought the image would be of Nightmare hovering over King Mirek's shoulder as he sat the throne in the Black Tower, because the King's possession was one of the story's major arcs. But the image was a portrait.

In it, Nightmare stood alone on a field of smoke and flame. He wore hooded black robes that fell around his inhumanly tall, slender form like creeping shadows. The belt around his waist was made of braided human hair. On his feet were snip-toed boots like the kind ninjas wore to silence their footsteps, and on his face, a mask, the details of which Lolek hadn't filled in yet. One of the hands was also unfinished. The other carried a bundle of dead rats tied together by the tails.

Lolek's depiction of the demon was exactly how I had pictured the character while reading the poem. The description of Nightmare in the poem itself was pretty vague; it said he wore a mask, but nowhere was the mask actually described. The poem said the demon liked gold, but little else about his motivations. My take on the character was that the demon saw Country itself as a kind of treasure where he could play and plunder as he willed. There was a line in Part III that said Nightmare saw the people of the Country as little rats scampering in his trove, suggesting he viewed them as pests, who could either serve him or be eradicated.

If the history of Europe teaches us anything, it is that land is far more valuable than any amount of material wealth; not only the strategic advantages and resources, but the culture, its sons and daughters, and most importantly its future. Country's own history was plagued by invaders and conquerors as far back as there was a written record.

The demon in *Arkadius* both represented Country's oppressors and predicted them. Nobody in the thirteenth century AD could have known about Nazism, or concentration camps, or gas chambers, or Josef Stalin and secret police that made people disappear. But the poem's unknown author hadn't needed to, because as I learned the longer I spent in Country, bad blood is forever.

I couldn't help but think of the Night Country and its Vermin, eternally running and hiding underground from a tyrant who had stolen the sun.

"Looks cool," I told Lolek. "But, how are you thinking of designing the mask? And what is he going to hold in his left hand?"

Lolek swiveled in his seat, looked up at me, and shrugged. "Does this guy visit you a lot?"

"What?" I said.

"You seem like you haven't been sleeping, man. This is his *right* hand." Lolek pointed to the blurry patch on the screen.

Shit.

Lolek raised an eyebrow at me. "You said *left*. Anyway, don't worry. I also don't sleep very often. Too much tea." Lolek took a sip from his mug and went back to clicking his mouse, adding and subtracting mask variants he'd already drawn. None of them seemed right, though.

"About the mask, I was hoping you could tell me. You are the story guy. I haven't read it since I was in school," Lolek said.

I scratched under my beard, thinking. "The mask should represent duality, the temptation he offers King Mirek - happiness, riches, women, power - all of which are supposed to come once the kingdom is united. But of course, the way that ends up happening is through bloodshed. The mask should also show the eternal nature of the demon. Not an infinity sign. That would be lame."

"A spiral, maybe?" Lolek said, filling in the blank space with a single, ebony line coiling outward from the center of the mask.

"Yeah. A spiral..."

Weird, I thought. *Why didn't I think of that? Maybe I'm not the right person to be translating this poem. I hope that's not what Filip wants to talk about... oh, shit.*

I checked the time on my phone. I was supposed to be in Filip's office three minutes ago. "Hey, sorry pal, but I gotta run. Meeting with the boss-man. Looks great, though," I said, already rushing for the stairs.

"One more thing," Lolek called after me. "What should I put in his hand?"

I halted, drumming my fingers on the doorframe. "Hmmm. Give him some sort of weapon. In the scene where Arkadius fights Nightmare, Nightmare disarms him. Arkadius only wins because he draws the blessed dagger the water nymph gave him from his boot and stabs the demon in the face. So it needs to be something that can disarm a sword."

Lolek saluted me. "Roger. I'll think of something cool."

Roger. He probably thinks Americans actually talk like that.

THE CITY

I RAN upstairs to find Filip waiting for me in his office. We sat in the chairs by the window and Sabina brought us coffee. I'd had too much already, but I wasn't about to say no. My body felt like it had been run over by an eighteen-wheeler. My exhausted, disheveled appearance was the first thing Filip commented on.

"So, Dan... Are you feeling better? You look quite tired," my boss said.

"People keep saying that. I'm all right. But it was a bad week."

Filip crossed his legs, folding his fingers over his knee. "I don't have much time, but I wanted to talk to you about some problems I'm having with the translations." I must have given him a dirty look, because he immediately added, "You didn't do anything wrong. You're not in trouble. I believe there was probably just some miscommunication."

He spread a few printouts of my work on the coffee table. There were two columns on each page. In the left column was the original, Countryish text of the poem; in the right was my translation. Someone had gone through and underlined certain words in the original text, and the corresponding places in my version where there were errors. There were *a lot* of underlines.

Filip's eyes looked nervous, but his voice was firm. "We've found some places where your rewritten version loses the meaning. Also, some of the rhyming structure is wrong. I don't attribute this to laziness on your part, or anything else negative. You probably didn't understand there was supposed to be more than one implication to some of these words, and we didn't pay close enough attention to what you were doing. But I'm afraid most of these passages will need to be rewritten."

At least he broke the news gently, I thought. Rage warped the edges of my vision. I waited until I was sure my voice wouldn't shake, and then spoke as clearly and evenly as I could. "With all due respect, this stuff took me more than a month. I double-checked everything; triple-checked, in some places. If I have to do it over, I'll be working on Part I until Christmas."

Filip tilted his head to show his sympathy. "Unfortunately, I think so. I know how frustrating it is to start over, but this is one area we can't compromise on. I'm sorry, Dan. You look sad."

I tried to play it cool, taking slow, deep breaths to let the fire out of my belly. "No, I'm fine. I've had a lot of work rejected over the years, from magazines, from... well, mostly magazines... it's part of the deal, y'know? Comes with the territory. Whatever you need me to do, I'll do it. That's what I'm here for."

"Great," Filip said with a big, paternal smile.

We spent the next hour going over the edits. I made notes in my phone, but I was too angry to pay much attention. I couldn't get the thought out of my head that it had been a mistake to take this job. I *knew* some of my word choices had been the right ones, and that my boss being persnickety was actually going to rob some of the meaning from the poem, not add to it. Hell, some of the lines he wanted to cut were the best work I'd ever done.

Before I left Filip's office to go back to my desk, he stopped me by the door to shake my hand and said, "Oh, by the way. I know it's still a ways away, and I'm really sorry, but I wanted to tell you early so you could make other plans. I actually can't host you this Christmas. It's not that I don't want to. I do. And I'm sad I have to break our plans. But, my wife's father is sick, so we will have to spend Christmas at her home, in the east of Country."

"No problem, Filip. Is he all right?" I said.

Filip rolled his head uncertainly. "We're not sure. We are trying to err on the side of caution."

"We can take a rain check next year," I said.

"Hopefully sooner. When things are a little less busy, maybe we can go out for a beer," Filip said.

"I'd like that," I said.

I spent the rest of the day surfing the Internet, trying to psyche myself up for my first Friday night out now that I was single and relatively healthy again. I signed up for the guest lists at a few dance clubs that looked promising.

I suppose I'd been single all along, but it hadn't felt that way. I had actually thought Kashka and I had something. I'd even started thinking about our future together. *Not the first time I've been wrong about that.*

While I was surfing the web, I came across a website called howtomeetwomen.com, which looked like spam until I saw the headline of the latest blog post, titled *America is Sick*. I read the first sentence, then the first paragraph, then the whole thing, feeling a growing sense of déjà vu at each new criticism of American food, culture, feminism, and belt sizes. The website didn't appear to have much to do with picking up girls at all.

I wasn't surprised at all to see Ink's dour, bearded face staring back at me when I clicked through to the author's bio. He looked younger in his author picture than he did in real life, his black hair cropped shorter and his corpse-green eyes squinted. One, long, bony finger rested on his cheek in a classic philosopher's pose.

I spent far more time on that website than I should have, reading post after post about the fallen state of modern America. The further back I searched in Ink's blog archive, the more frequently I came across posts about picking up girls; which opening lines to use, when the right time was to approach, how often a man should shave or what kind of soap he should use to "maximize attraction."

Before he first moved to Country, Ink almost never wrote about American culture, except how hard it was to get American girls in bed. He didn't write cultural criticisms at all. His oldest posts had titles like *How to Obey Your Boner* and *Which Nationality of Girl is Right for You?* The website had over a million views in the past month.

Most of it made me cringe. Some of it even turned my stomach a little. But while Ink's style was crude, and he certainly wasn't going to make friends with feminists any time soon, the advice he gave seemed to make a primitive kind of sense. Any of it could've been something my dad had told me about the birds and the bees back when I was still a clueless teenager. In some ways I had reverted back to that state after losing Carly. It wasn't hard to imagine how, in the modern age of video games and porn, a lot of guys never grew out of it in the first place.

I understood why Ink's website was popular. Taken on their own, those individual grains of advice sounded somewhat reasonable. What I couldn't get over was the packaging. Ink's entire worldview struck me as bitter, sad, and extremely nihilistic. My dad had always told me not to trust people whose views came off as extreme one way or the other - that most of the world's problems were caused by people being unwilling to walk a mile in the other person's shoes.

But what did I have to lose just by trying it?

By the time I got to the old city around ten PM, I was too depressed and exhausted to talk to anyone. I saw a few groups of girls, but no matter how much my inner voice screamed at me to talk to them, my legs and mouth and heart didn't listen.

Tomorrow, I told myself. *I'll try again tomorrow. Hell, there's always next weekend, too.* I knew Ink would've slammed me for giving up and packing it in, but I was too cold, and too tired to care.

I went home and slept, the first good, deep sleep I'd had in almost a week.

THE BURROW

MY EYES OPENED to a ceiling of smooth, ancient stones where guttering torchlight played a grim, unending marathon of silent movies. I gasped a deep breath of stale air. The smell of mold and piss stung in my sinuses.

I sat up, sucking my teeth in pain. My shoulder felt like it had been run through with a lance. There were men outside my door. Their voices fell silent and they gave me quick, nervous glances when they saw I was awake.

Aching and nauseas, I rose to my feet, shivered, and brushed the patches of moldy straw from my rough wool clothes. It seemed like weeks since I'd gone to sleep in this subterranean prison, though I knew it had only been a few hours. I was in a body that wasn't my own, a world that wasn't my own. My memories of that other place were already slipping away, fast fading into vagueness and darkness like the false days that slid by on the surface above.

I walked to the door of my cell. "Good morning," I said.

A giant meat chimney of a man with a handlebar mustache, who carried a spear with a red blade that looked like it was made of amber and wore a three-lobed fur hat with a large, floppy button on the top, said, "The fuck you say?"

"Gator, right?" I said.

The man cleared his throat and spat on the floor of his own jail.

"Uh... hi. Listen. I'm really cold, and I have no idea why I'm locked up in here. Barn Owl said I was supposed to meet someone named Queen Rat, which I assume is going to be some kind of hearing, or trial, maybe... anyway. I was wondering, can you tell me when that's going to be? And could I get some food and fresh water while I wait? I'm feeling pretty dehydrated, and I think it's been a long time since I had something to eat. There's a bucket next to my bed, but it smells nasty, and I think it probably isn't safe for me to drink."

One of the other men outside my cell, a jowly son of a bitch with a skinny guy gut and a month's worth of stubble slapped Gator on the chest. "C'mon, then! The little prince is hungry. What were we thinking, leaving him in a cell with nothing to eat or drink? Surely we can't expect him to sip from his own soil bucket, can we? We'll order him a nice, greasy piece of mutton from the kitchens right away..."

The man yelped as Gator grabbed his hand and twisted it in the direction it wasn't supposed to turn. "Tell her the guests are awake," Gator grunted as he held the cowering man in submission, steering him a full 180 degrees, then sent the interlocutor scurrying away down the hall with a swift, dusty kick on the ass.

Gator must've had decades of training to pull a move like that off. I guessed the other guy had little, if any.

Gator gazed through the bars of my cell.

I gave him my easiest, toothiest smile. "So, how about that water?" I said.

"That bucket is not for drinking," Gator said.

Then Gator did something I didn't expect. He wrapped his pinky finger around one of the bars of my door and pulled it open. It hadn't even been locked. "You are no prisoner of mine. This was for your own protection," Gator said.

I hesitantly walked through the cell door. I thought it might be some sort of trap. But Gator only spat again and folded his arms.

When I was sure he wasn't going to beat me bloody, I stretched and said, "How long was I out?"

"You slept about six hours. One full torch," Gator said. He gestured to the other end of the prison block. "C'mon. There's hot soup and mulled ale waiting for you in the chow hall. If you need a hot bath, you're welcome to that, too. I suggest you take one before you visit the queen."

"Um... Gator? Can I ask you something?" I said, as he put a gentle hand on my shoulder and we started walking.

"Knock yourself out," Gator said.

"Are you only being nice to me now because of what Barn Owl said? Or is there some other reason? I only ask because you seemed a lot meaner last night, while you and your... uh... friends, were shaving me. You guys were pretty rough. I've got cuts all over my body," I said.

Gator spat. "Everyone gets cut. Also, I apologize for spitting so much. Medical condition." He spat again. "But get something through your skull, friend. It's always night here. We don't have such things as *evenings* and *mornings*. Those ended with the Last Day of Sun. Here, we measure time in torches. You slept for one torch. You'll be awake for three. I'm told four torches is the length of time we used to call a day, but how the fuck should I know? The True Night started a hundred years before I was born. Try to remember that it won't be endin' anytime soon, and things will go easier for you."

"What things?" I said.

Gator scratched the stubble under his chin. "And, I don't give two piles of bat shit what Barn Owl thinks. You got one apology. Don't expect any more. I was... mistaken about who you were. We couldn't recognize you with all that fucking hair."

"Who I was?" I said.

"Aye, who you were."

Does he mean this body, with the ugly, beat-up face that looks like a caveman? This person who isn't me?

Gator fixed me with a gorgon's gaze. As if reading my mind, he said, "We were friends when you were alive."

We both fell silent for a moment.

Gator's eyes and chin fell toward the floor, his brow growing heavy with sorrow. "Of course, you're different now. Changed. You don't know the man you used to be. That man is gone. But, it's always that way with your kind."

"My kind? What do you mean?" I said.

"I wasn't sure until I watched you sleeping," Gator said. "Thought I recognized you when the Surface Party first brought you in, but it wasn't until I crept next to you and pulled up your eyelid that I knew for certain."

Even though I knew Gator could throw me through a wall if he wanted to, I was getting impatient with his unnecessarily cryptic way of speaking.

"Knew *what*?" I said.

Gator shrugged, eyes darting abstractly as he weighed each possibility, and said, "That you are not the same man we lost scouting in the snow for food stores four weeks past... that you're not Len. That you're not one of us at all." His eyes locked on me and narrowed. "That you're just... *visiting*."

Gator cackled and slapped me hard on the back. I choked, coughing thick, black liquid into the palm of my hand. Gator looked at me with disgust, then laughed even harder.

His laughter faded and his tone became thoughtful. "This is why we are showing you such gracious hospitality! If you really were a Snowman, I would've tortured and beheaded you myself. You should've said something sooner.

"Of course, nobody would've believed you. The men all thought you were some kind of abomination – that you kidnapped and brainwashed that poor girl, so you could take her back to your den while the meat was still warm. They were ready to cut your internal organs out and make the dogs fight for them. But I had a premonition. A talking Snowman? I told them. Don't be absurd!" His laughter boomed through the shadow-ridden halls of the jail.

Gator cracked his neck, his jovial smile falling to a hard, downward curve. "When everyone saw it, they quickly changed their tune. So, don't worry. They're more frightened of you than they are of Him." He pointed to the ceiling, raising an eyebrow.

He means the Crippled King.

I had so many questions I couldn't keep them straight. *Start from the beginning, just like a poem. Prioritize the information that matters, and make sense of that first. Then go back and fill in the parts that don't make sense later,* I thought.

"Wait. What was it you saw?" I said.

Gator leaned in close, lowering his voice. "The Spiral," he said, gesturing to his own eye with a finger. "You have it. Right there. The girl has it, too. As do all Visitors who return in the corpses of the recently frozen."

I didn't have time to ask Gator anything else. We arrived at a heavy iron door reinforced with struts and rows of one-inch spikes. Gator casually kicked it, and it swung open from the other side.

Behind the door, an old man draped under a musty bearskin robe nodded to us curtly. His head and face were hidden inside the bear's jaws, except for a narrow slit left open for his nose and eyes.

"Bob of the Knob," Gator told me, denoting the bear-man with his thumb. "Be cordial to him if you want to go anywhere in this shoddy shithole of a barracks we call the Last Station. He holds the keys to all the doors you might actually want to enter. Be polite, say hello… just don't expect much in return. He lost his lips to frostbite. Then he lost his dick and tongue to a Snowwoman. Legend has it she bit one off, while the other froze from being inside her too long. I'll leave your imagination to decide which was which. Did I get that right, Bob, or did I forget something?"

Bob's eyes slanted behind the bear's yellowed canines.

I bowed to Bob o' the Knob and hurried through the door into a dim hall bedecked with rows of slender, white marble pillars. The ceiling was high and vaulted, covered in time-blanched mosaics of hallowed kings and warrior angels. Shadows hid in the crevices like clouds of black, formless bats, ebbing and waning in the light of a hundred guttering torches. Rust-eaten armor suits lined the walls, their eyeless faces reflecting floating ghosts in the polished, tiled marble of the floor.

Gator led me to a well-lit dais in the back of the hall where two women sat talking at a long dinner table. I didn't realize until we were close that the small woman with the shaved head and skinny, bruised arms was Zaea.

They cut off her hair. Her cascading, beautiful, whiskey-colored hair.

The women interrupted their own conversation and waited for Gator and I to climb the steps up to the dais. Zaea's spoon swam nervously through the chunky, brown soup in her bowl. The other woman studied me with eyes like amber arrowheads.

"A feast fit for royalty," Gator exclaimed, placing both hands on the table, palms down. There wasn't much – a few baskets of stale bread and a large pot of the same, unappetizing soup that was in Zaea's bowl, warming over a hillock of embers burning in an iron fixture.

Gator picked up one of the stale rolls, tapped it on the armored plate over his chest, creating an audible *plunk*, then tossed the roll to me. I caught it with both hands. "Enjoy yourself. I still want to have teeth tomorrow, so I try not to eat anything around here that isn't liquid, if you catch my meaning," Gator said.

"Thanks," I said.

The woman with the amber eyes dismissed Gator with a look. He shrugged, took another roll, and shoved it inside his coat. "On the other hand, I might not get to eat before then, unlike you fortunate people," Gator said. "Maybe teeth are a luxury I can't afford. To your health," he said, raising the roll like a glass. Then, biting down hard and wrangling a piece of it free with his jaws, Gator left.

"May I sit?" I asked the woman with the amber eyes. She had to be someone important; the queen's personal attendant, maybe, or one of her high court ladies; no doubt, she would be the one to present Zaea and me in front of the throne when we were done eating.

The woman gestured for me to sit down. She was older than me, but not much, thirty-five or so. She had an unattractive, square-jawed face, and short orange hair, ghostly pale skin, and a sunburst of ginger freckles like mine. She wore a simple wool tunic tied with a leather belt, frayed and stained as every other garment I'd seen in the Burrow. The only accouterments that denoted a higher station than someone like Gator was her gloves, red leather lined with soft, delicate sable fur. I'd seen gloves like that in the posh store windows on Saint Mary's Street back in City, bearing price tags that would make people back in the U.S. feel poor. Her shoulders were decorated with a white stole embroidered with twin suns in red lace, one rising, and one setting.

I chose the other chair closest to Zaea, the three of us forming a crowded triangle at the end of a table that could've held thirty, the kind of table meant for huge feasts like weddings or Christmas dinners.

Zaea clutched my arm.. "Dan, are you all right?" she whispered.

I placed my free hand on top of hers and said, "Yes, although, I didn't really want a haircut. But they still gave me one."

Zaea's eyes brimmed with tears. She lowered them and stuffed a spoonful of soup into her mouth.

They cut her scalp, too. She still looks a little bit like Carly, even though I never saw Carly bald.

"Did they hurt you?" I said. Zaea shook her head *no* and dried her eyes with the back of her sleeve.

"Don't worry," the amber-eyed woman interrupted us. Her voice was warm and motherly, but with a deep note of gravel that suggested she wasn't someone you wanted to mess with. "We didn't harm your friend. I personally saw to her grooming myself. Didn't I, dear one?"

Zaea nodded.

"She did seem a bit overly attached to that beautiful golden braid, though," the amber woman said. "Unfortunately, long hair is an extreme liability here in the Burrow. Not only does it go up like kindling whenever one walks too close to a torch, but we have a recurring problem with lice. Not just the big kind you met up on the Surface, but the little ones, those microscopic bastards who crawl everywhere and make you itch like they're trying to dig tunnels to Hell through your skin. We've found that the simplest way to avoid an outbreak is to keep everyone's hair short. The only exception is beards and mustaches. I've had to make concessions there; one, because the kinds of bugs who live in beards and mustaches aren't typically parasitic – lice prefer the scalp and pubic regions – but also, because the men would revolt if I took them away. The beards, not the bugs."

Zaea squeezed my hand while she ate. Not knowing what else to say, I said, "I see."

The amber-eyed woman clapped. "Forgive me. Where are my manners? You must be starving." She picked up a bowl off the table and served me from the pot with a scummy wooden ladle. "Dig in," she said, pushing the bowl toward me.

Any attempt at being polite and not stuffing my face flew out the window the second the steaming broth passed my lips. It tasted strange, like watery beef stew gone wrong. There were root vegetables like potatoes and carrots, and a soggy leaf cluster I thought might be cabbage. The meat was stringy, gamey, and lean. It tasted familiar, but I couldn't figure out what it was. I was almost to the bottom of the bowl when I realized it was mutton. The only time I'd ever had mutton was up on my grandma's farm in Chico when I was a little kid.

The amber-eyed woman studied me while I ate. When Zaea and I were both finished, she took our bowls away and gave us each a small, leather cup the size of a shot glass, filling it with a clear, pungent liquor she poured from a flask. Her cup was already full.

"Alas, we are not as blessed with fallow fields and wide, sunlit golden pastures where we can farm cash crops and raise endless tribes of slovenly cattle and birds of meaty breast as is no doubt the case wherever you two are from," the amber woman said. "But there is always vodka. To your health," she said, and slammed back her drink. Hesitantly, Zaea and I both did the same. I frowned through that old, familiar burn. Zaea hissed.

The amber woman wiped a few errant vodka droplets from her mouth. "On the subject of where you're from. Tell me where that is, exactly?"

"Neen, the City Arcanum," Zaea muttered into her empty soup bowl, rolling it on its side so the final drops gathered and she could slurp them out. The amber woman hummed.

"I'm from California," I said.

"Well, no surprises there. I'm happy Barn Owl didn't kill you when she found you out there in... where was it that she found you, again?" the amber woman said.

"It was outside the Royal Crypts," I said.

"Oh, right... the tombs of my great, great, great, great ancestors, where I too might've been buried, if things had gone differently. Alas! Bats in the night, as we say here in the Burrow. I'm happy I wasn't deprived of so many interesting future conversations about your home worlds, and about why you've come to this one, over a simple misunderstanding."

She poured us all another shot.

"We're both pretty confused about what's going on too, to be honest. Why exactly *are* we here?" I said. The amber woman refilled my cup. "Hey, Gator said there was hot beer. Think I could I get one of those? The vodka is burning my throat a little."

The amber woman gazed at me like a cat stalking an oblivious bird, then surprised me with a loud, brow-raising cackle. "What makes you think I'm confused?"

My face flushed. I didn't like the way she was looking at me. I shook my head. "Uh, never mind. I guess you probably know everything, and you're going to tell us what we're doing here. Right?"

"You guess correctly - half-correctly, anyway. Drink," she commanded us, and we all turned our cup bottoms to the ceiling.

I bit back a cough as the caustic moonshine stripped my throat raw. When I'd collected myself, the amber woman folded her hands on the table and said, "I'm not confused at all about why you're here. I know perfectly well. Which is why I'm so embarrassed about the way my people treated you. It should've been obvious to them at first glance you are not our enemies. You are nothing but two unfortunate children who got lost in the snow. And you have no idea how or why, just as you have no idea where, or when, you are."

"I'm twenty-six," I said.

The amber woman ignored me. "There are some answers I can give you. Others, I cannot, and certainly none before we trust each other. You have no reason to trust me, as I have no reason to trust you... yet. I've given you bread, and yes, young man, I shall provide you with hot beer, which we must drink here instead of water, because we have no way to adequately purify our wells, and neither ice nor snowmelt are safe to drink so close to the Night City. Our beer isn't strong. There's barely enough alcohol in it to kill the critters you might be drinking, much less get you drunk. That's what this is for."

She tipped her flask to my cup yet again, and poured me another shot of vodka. Zaea tried to turn her cup over to signal she was done, but the amber woman flipped it back up and poured her one anyway. Zaea threw me a pleading look.

"That is, unless you're fool enough to drink the wyvern piss Gator brews in his hovel. But if his sanity is any indication, I wouldn't suggest it. Half the men have their own little distilleries hidden in the nooks and crannies of this place – a military establishment where there are more carboys and empty bottles than swords. Can you imagine that?"

The amber woman cracked her neck to each side, yawning into the back of one sable glove. "Shall we?" We drank a third time.

"However," she said, rolling her knuckles on the table, "I wouldn't put it past the Crippled King to send me a few young, wide-eyed reindeer pups like you two, who he had brainwashed and implanted with false memories, to infiltrate us. You may truly believe you are who you say you are. You both bear the Spiral, and you, at least, young man, come clothed in the corpse of one of our dearest recently departed soldiers. I bet you wondered why you were able to survive so long in a blizzard. Or maybe you didn't.

"If so, there's your answer. The few Visitors we've had over the years, at least according to Bookmother, have all been well-adapted to the cold. My theory is that since the bodies your kind have reanimated all died by freezing, you're able to tolerate longer exposure to the cold, as the Snowmen can."

This body is dead. The image of the other man's face in the mirror replayed in my mind's eye like an apparition. *A dead, human, body. I'm a walking, breathing, thinking corpse.*

The amber woman must've noticed me shivering, because she said, with a note of scorn in her voice, "Oh, yes, Sleepwalker. You, whom the Great Spiral has chosen, have come to us bound in the earthly remains of my own recently departed godson Len, may the Wanderer rest his soul. The men didn't believe it until they saw you with their own eyes. Word travels fast here in the Burrow. They didn't recognize you at first, when they saw you with hair. But once you were shaved, it was a different story. Within minutes, everyone knew that Len had returned to us bearing a Spiral in his eye."

She poured herself another shot, neglecting Zaea and me this time. "This has given some of our people hope, but has caused panic in far more. You must realize, most people here are not old enough to remember the last time we had such a Visitor. It was more than twenty years ago. And, you come to us at a difficult time. We lost both Len and his father, a man called Vojciek, who was my brother by marriage as well as this outpost's Master of Mats, within the space of a single week. We also lost our most promising ranger, a girl of immense talent named Katherine, who went by the alias Meerkat."

The amber woman's eyes fell deep into her cup. She went to pour me another round, found the flask was empty, blew a raspberry with her lips and put it away. "I knew the moment I saw you. I remember the last time one of you came here - a man who called himself Helm. On his world, every boy was called Helm until he distinguished himself in battle and earned the right to choose a name. I was only a child, a girl of thirteen, but Helm befriended me. He told me where he went when he fell asleep and no one could wake him up, when the Spiral would glow impossibly beneath his sleeping right eyelid. He told me how he sleepwalked home, back somewhere across the Endless Night, and resumed the life he lived there as if he'd never left. Then, when he went to sleep there, he'd return here.

"Helm's story matched what was written in Bookmother's tomes, and in the Sol Firma, our most sacred text, about the Spiral sending spirits across great distances of space and time into the bodies of the dead to serve its unknowable plans. Though I pride myself on being a woman of reason, I never questioned that particular point."

Zaea and I exchanged a skeptical look, but I wasn't about to start a debate about theology. "Well at least I know I'm not the only one going crazy," I said.

The amber woman hummed. "I didn't know the man whose body the Spiral chose for Helm to inhabit when he visited us, nor did anyone else. It was probably that of some refugee, one among millions who froze to death on their long march to the capital during the Last Day of Sun. It was, of course, a figurative *Last Day*. In truth, it lasted for many years. But when it ended, the world grew dark, and there was no light or warmth to be found anywhere but here, in these tunnels... and upon the Echelon, where only the Crippled King's elect were invited to live."

"What about her?" I pointed to Zaea. "You said this... person I'm inhabiting, who isn't me, but whose body I'm borrowing, was someone you knew. And I believe you. I didn't recognize myself when I looked in the mirror. This face isn't mine. These eyes aren't mine. Nor are these hands."

I held them up and gazed at them for dramatic effect, then set them back down on the table. "I'm pretty creeped out by all this, but I'll buy it for the time being. The thing that really bothers me is Zaea. She hasn't mentioned being in a different body."

"Curious," the amber woman said. "I've never seen this girl before in my life. And indeed, she may not have needed a new pile of flesh the way you did to serve the Spiral's purpose. But that means little. The Spiral has chosen her, as it chose you. She has come here for a reason, as you have."

"What reason?" Zaea and I both said simultaneously.

The amber woman rose. "Everything in time, my dearies." She stretched, yawned, and sadly checked her flask again for any drops she might've missed. She tossed the empty flask on the table and beckoned for Zaea and me to stand. "Come. We'll get that beer now. I owe you as much for listening to me prattle on like a sour girl who's just been impregnated by her village boyfriend and left to die in the snow. Just kidding, we don't have villages anymore. The last one in the Burrow was just found empty. Oh, joy. Who doesn't relish a good pogrom? Our enemies in the Amber City certainly enjoy them. For them, it's a time-honored tradition. Joyful, goody, candied gumdrops, looks like we're next. And that's where you two come in."

The amber woman yawned. "But I'm getting ahead of myself. Before we begin negotiations, I feel the need to stretch my legs. You didn't think you'd be able to escape negotiating with me, did you? Please, grow up. Ninety-five percent of interactions between adults involve negotiation of some kind. The other five percent is sex. What do you say? Shall we have a walk and a talk? I bet no one's given you a tour of this place yet, the lazy slugabeds..."

"No, they haven't," I said. "What do you think, Zaea? Want to go explore? This nice lady wants to show us around."

Zaea pursed her lips, glaring as if her vision could penetrate the smokescreen of the amber woman's friendly, drunken disposition. At last Zaea nodded and we both stood. I noticed her discreetly hide her soup spoon inside the belt of her tunic.

As we followed the amber woman out of the hall, the hairs on the back of my neck stood. We were being followed. I glanced back over my shoulder to see four men sliding silently out from behind the shadows of the pillars, one from underneath the table where we'd just been sitting. I let out an involuntary gasp. The amber woman chuckled.

The men following us wore black, hooded garments with soot camouflaging their faces. They carried cruel, curved daggers that looked like giant fishhooks, as well as ropes, throwing knives, and thin garroting wires tucked into their black, leather belts. Their boots and gloves were sable, like the amber woman's; only theirs were worn and ragged from years of hard use. They'd been watching and listening to our conversation the entire time. The thought that I'd been so close to someone who could reach out and slash my throat without me even knowing terrified me.

The shadow-men moved with us toward the rear door of the hall, as silent as the darkness that had borne them. The amber woman called them off with a quick snap of her fingers.

"Thank you, gentlemen. That will be all. You've sufficiently impressed our new guests. They are certainly too busy shitting their scratchy underpants to try anything now. Mommy loves you. You can take your one hour break. Good Moles. Nice Moles. Have a bite of stew, find yourselves something to drink, and be merry. I'll be fine. Please don't follow us."

The Moles halted in the middle of the room and removed their hands from their weapons to stand straight at attention. They saluted the amber woman and said in deep, booming unison, *"Yes, Your Highness."*

THE BURROW

OUR FIRST STOP was the subway platform from which the Last Station had taken its name. It was a few tunnels over from the Mess Hall. The Queen explained that the underground structures had existed for centuries, if not millennia before the True Night, as grain cellars, vaults, crypts, catacombs, sewers, and subway lines. Her people had repurposed them when the surface was abandoned on the Last Day of Sun. They had built new tunnels to connect the old, creating a self-sufficient matrix that spread for miles beneath the ruins of the city.

The Last Station wasn't as grand as the subway stop at the Royal Crypts, but it was a million times better maintained. The high, heaving arches were washed clean of dust and ash. The illustrious mosaics on the ceilings and walls were still bright and resplendent, their winged knights, fallen angels, and gingerbread churches all detailed in eye-popping color.

The platform was made of clean, polished marble, and the subway tracks still held their spit-shined gleam. There was a junked subway car on the train tracks completely blocking the subway tunnel in one direction. The other remained clear.

"Where does it go?" I said. My words reverberated back to me through the curtain of shadows. I pulled my weight off my toes at the last second before I lost balance, avoiding an embarrassing spill off the edge of the platform.

"That is the way to Salt Town," Queen Rat said, pointing down the empty tunnel with her thumb. Gesturing back toward the blockade, she said, "That way goes back to the ruins. Unfortunately, this little checkpoint is rather weak. If the enemy ever truly learned where we are, it would be very easy to overrun us. That is also the reason why this entire station, which I hope you've realized is a strategic choke point, is wired with explosives at every juncture.

"We can collapse the whole place at a moment's notice. Doing so wouldn't protect our own necks, of course, but it might give the people of Salt Town a chance to escape. To where, I have no idea. It's a last resort. But we are living in a time of last resorts. If this place is ever attacked, my life, and the lives of my Vermin will be forfeit."

"I'm guessing Salt Town is somewhere pretty important," I said.

Queen Rat gave me a look like she wanted to push me off the platform. "It's the last major human settlement in the Burrow. All others have been emptied or destroyed by the Crippled King."

"Why?" Zaea said.

"We're at war," Queen Rat said. "We always have been. We always will be. Our scouts found a village only last week where the home fires were still warm, the kettles still whistling. The people vanished as if everyone up and decided to drop what they were doing and leave."

"Where did he take them?" I said.

"Our information is admittedly limited," Queen Rat said. "There are records of settlements and villages in decades past being wiped out by disease, or poison in their food or water supply. But for the last several years, the Amber City has been ramping up the raids and taking more prisoners alive. We don't know why."

"But Zaea and I are supposed to find out?" I said.

Queen Rat smiled so wide the fillings on her back molars bled orange in the torchlight. "I only intend to make you an offer.

Whether or not you take it is up to you. Now, let's not waste more time here. There's plenty more I wish to show you."

Our next stop was the station library, which had been repurposed as the infirmary. There was a small, white-haired woman sitting and reading a gigantic, leather-bound grimoire in an old wooden rocking chair by the door. She wore huge bifocal glasses and a knit rainbow shawl that she tugged at nervously as she read, muttering secret passages to herself through her thin, wrinkled lips and sipping from a mug of tea that rested on the doily-covered table beside her. She didn't seem to hear us come in.

"That's Bookmother," Queen Rat told us at full volume. "I'd introduce you, but she couldn't hear a Louse's siren if it was in her bedroom. Part of me thinks it's an act so she can read all she wants without being interrupted by the rest of us. Hello, auntie," Queen Rat said, kissing the old woman on one pale, warty eyelid. The old woman looked up, smiled, and went back to reading and pulling her shawl.

Countless blankets were laid out on the floor between the dusty stacks of ancient books. The blankets were sporadically filled by the emaciated bodies of the sick and wounded, mostly children, all of them pale and motionless. Their gaunt, gasping faces held a queer, uncanny valley look.

It took me a moment to realize that they were sleeping despite their eyes being open. Each child's eyes were mismatched, one pink and one pale blue. Their skin was similarly blighted, divided into thick, alternating stripes of eggshell white and cadaver gray.

Queen Rat knelt beside one of the sick children, gently stroking the single errant tuft of translucent white hair on the crown of his head. "Hello, Eamon," Queen Rat said. She took the boy's hand in her own and kissed it. The child's wormy lips struggled to yield a smile.

"He can't speak," Zaea said.

"Nor can he hear. None of them can. But this lad isn't fully awake. He's in the place between the real world and dreams, where I hope he remains," Queen Rat said.

"What's wrong with him?" I said.

"The children in this sick ward are victims of the Blight. It affects one in four children born in the Burrow, and is usually fatal, disproportionately so in boys. We suspect the Amber City has similar numbers, but the difference is those children are all abandoned and left to die. We save the ones we can and bring them here, when we find them. It is... *unusual* for us to find them alive."

Zaea fidgeted uncomfortably. The prospect gave me a chill, too.

"Sometimes they gain their speech and hearing back if they survive to adulthood. Those ones usually end up fighting for us, for obvious reasons. Barn Owl was that way, as was Mongoose," Queen Rat said.

"Is the cause of the disease known? Is it bacterial, viral, genetic...?" Zaea said.

"Are you a doctor?" Queen Rat said.

"Actually yes, I was," Zaea said.

"Of course you were, sweet thing." Queen Rat sighed. "We don't know what causes the Blight, except that it isn't bacteria or a virus. The prevailing theory among our ancestors before the True Night seems to have been that it was genetic, and the symptoms only became active after prolonged exposure to darkness and cold. But, we have no way of knowing if that's accurate."

"When did the primary outbreak begin?" Zaea said.

"Our records indicate the epidemic started sometime during the Last Day of Sun," Queen Rat said. "People grew desperate. Folks dying in the street, the hospitals overflowing, mass graves, religious fanaticism, riots, structure fires, that sort of thing. It's one of the reasons we believe the current regime was able to rise to power."

She stroked the boy's hair again, kissed him on the forehead, and turned back to Zaea and me. "Any further questions?"

We both shook our heads *no*.

"In that case, we'd best be on our way. Visitors tend to excite them, and the best thing for these sweet, suffering babes is to get as much undisturbed rest as humanly possible. Sleep eases the indescribable pain that is their day-to-day lives, at least a little of it, though I'm told they cannot dream. I simply wanted to show you just who we're up against. This is an enemy who does not give a thought to the destruction of human lives... even the lives of innocent children."

THE BURROW

ZAEA'S GAZE lingered on the child as we followed the queen out of the infirmary and back into the tangle of brick tunnels outside. It was around that time that I noticed the torches on the walls weren't real torches at all – they weren't made of wood, for one thing, but iron – when the smell hit me.

It was a rank, specious odor somewhere between a metric ton of wet feces and a pile of dead bodies spilling from one of the nearby passages like a foul mist. Queen Rat noticed Zaea and I both making faces at the stench, and stopped to explain.

"Ah, yes. Your noses have made first contact with our most prized possession here at the Last Station, our Gourmet Mushroom Farm. Gourmet is a joke. But it's true, we eat and produce myriad kinds of mushrooms here: big ones, little ones, round ones, smooth ones, white ones, brown ones, frilly ones with brown edges that are white in the center, red and green ones that are poisonous... obviously those aren't for eating."

"There were mushrooms in the soup," Zaea said through the top of her shirt.

"Oh, there are mushrooms in everything, my dear. Stick around long enough and you'll see what I mean," Queen Rat said. "There will be less when you visit Salt Town, though you should still expect to eat them twice a day. We grow them here so the Townies don't have to deal with the stench. In exchange, they give us grain and livestock, which we don't have room to raise here. Y'know, the usual things that crawl, eat, and shit: sheep, chickens, deer, rabbits, snakes, pigeons, dogs, a few cows, mostly for milking. We turn some of that grain into vodka and beer, and some of those animals into sausages – our specialty - that we sell back to Salt Town at a premium. I'm sure it's no different than where you're both from."

We don't eat snakes or dogs, I thought.

"We're vegetarians in Neen," Zaea said. "Animal protein can too easily upset your gut bacteria. Plus, it causes irreparable damage to the environment to raise enough livestock to feed a large population. All our protein is synthesized from plants or beans."

The queen's lips were the only part of her that smiled. "I imagine that must be a pleasant luxury." She gestured down the tunnel where the smell was coming from. "Incidentally, the stables and vegetable gardens lie that way, too. Would you like a tour?"

Zaea and I both shook our heads *no*.

The queen frowned. "Hmm. Just as well. I suppose they're not much to look at – just a few hovels and planter boxes tucked into the corner of a cave... though I've always found the light of the hydropons rather therapeutic. So rot me, I like machines. And, it is a *very* big cave."

"Excuse me, Queen," I said, once we'd walked a bit and it was safe to breathe again. "Not to interrupt, but I'm curious. How do you keep animals alive with no sun? Or plants? There's no way you're growing vegetables by torchlight."

The queen made a tiny, almost undetectable swiping gesture with her fingers, and the torch on the wall nearest to us instantly brightened. She swept her fingers again and it brightened more, until the light was blinding, and the tunnel was washed in white. She swept the other way, and the light dimmed back to its normal luminosity. I'd already figured out that whatever the torches used for fuel wasn't oil, but rather something renewable, that could be grown. I wasn't expecting them to be motion-controlled.

"Indeed, we don't," Queen Rat said. She explained as we walked: "These torches contain a trace amount of the glowmoss we use to power the hydropons in our gardens and farms. Glowmoss was engineered by our ancestors to read human gestures. It still grows in the mines near Salt Town, but you didn't hear that from me."

"Incredible," I said.

"We use it on my world, too," Zaea said.

Queen Rat raised an eyebrow at that, but chose to ignore it. "The Ancients mastered the art of engineering life. They grew things to serve their every whim and fancy. Unfortunately, that knowledge was lost on the Last Day of Sun. The patches of moss that still cling to the deepest reaches of our Salt Mines are all that remains of it, so we tend to use our glowmoss sparingly. Sad, because it is quite pleasant when turned up to full bloom. I remember I used to sneak into the gardens when I was a little girl and sit and read under the hydropons for hours, basking in their lovely, golden light. Alas, no more. A queen has no time for books."

We arrived at the end of the tunnel. Letting out a grunt, Queen Rat gave the ornate wooden door in front of us a push.

The door swung open to reveal a small, candlelit chapel no larger than my apartment, all hand-carved from the rock of the cave. The pews, the prayer shrines, the ceiling dome, the life-sized statue of the faceless man levitating above the altar, every inch of it was drawn from the smooth stone of the cave walls and awash in the glow of a thousand candles like stars floating in a silver sea.

There was only one other person in the church besides us, a hooded man kneeling in the rearmost pew whose head was lowered in prayer.

I ran my fingers along the wall. The stone was soft and spongy. The queen gestured for me to lick my fingers, and I hesitantly tried a taste.

Salt. The entire church is made of salt.

"Salt veins are common in this area," Queen Rat said. "The chapel in Salt Town is even grander. This one's rather small by comparison. I've prayed here since I was a little girl. The pews have been rather empty of late."

The queen shut the doors behind us and we moved to the altar, where the queen raised her hand, palm out, to mimic the gesture of the statue there. "Has anyone told you why we live down here rather than up there?" She said. Zaea and I both shook our heads. "Because we did not accept that the Crippled King was the Wanderer Returned."

"Who?" I said.

Queen Rat slowly began circumnavigating the etched shrines that ringed the chapel, stopping at each station as she spoke. "The Wanderer was a man whose light was so brilliant that he brought balance back to the Spiral after a period of great darkness. In case you couldn't guess, we are in such a period again, although ours is more literal than theirs was."

The images at the center of each shrine told a sequential story. The first picture was of a group of people happily basking in the sun, on a beach near a beautiful, prosperous city. Even in replica, the water looked clear and inviting. "We believe this is what our world looked like before the Last Day of Sun," Queen Rat said.

She moved on to the second picture, which showed that same seaside city, now hovering over the water instead of beside it. The city looked far more advanced than in the first picture, but the people looked sad and unhealthy.

"The People of the Sun had grown so rich and comfortable that they spent their lives pursuing hedonistic distractions rather than anything meaningful. They became decadent, arrogant, and spoiled. They neglected the sweet, sacred light of the sun. They even stopped having children, until eventually they no longer could. They began stealing their children from other, more vigorous worlds."

Queen Rat moved onto the third shrine. The image depicted a civil war, citizen soldiers fighting through head-high piles of bodies that stretched for miles. "They knew their civilization was in decline, but could only watch as it collapsed. They turned to war to supply them with purpose. In their desperation, our ancestors became genocidal. There came a war so bloody the darkness spread across the stars, threatening to annihilate the Spiral itself. Until..."

Queen Rat moved to the fourth shrine, an image of a group of survivors kneeling at the feet of a figure clothed in light who greeted them with one palm outraised. Like every other depiction of the Wanderer I'd seen, his face was blank.

"A Wanderer came to them from an unknown world who taught that in every person there is a fire and a shadow. The fire gives us peace; it is fed when we follow our purpose, and our light radiates happiness to others. The shadow feeds off of our hatred, sapping the light of everyone else around us.

"Fire and shadow are compliments. One cannot eradicate the other. But lights go out, and darkness spreads with time. Only by becoming the fire can we keep the Spiral in balance. It must start in the smallest among us, the weakest. That is how justice spreads, always outward, from the bottom up; never the other way around. Yet from a single flame can grow a blazing inferno that reforges the world. That is what the Wanderer taught.

"The suffering, the downcast, the strong, the broken, the victims, the survivors began to follow him, until his army was so great they numbered in the billions, countless peacemakers who gave their lives to end the decades of senseless bloodshed. At last, the war ended, and the people slowly began to rebuild."

The fifth and sixth shrines showed images of the war-torn city in various stages of renewal. In the fifth, the Wanderer floated above the clouds, overseeing the reconstruction. In the sixth, the clouds were empty.

"When his own purpose was at last fulfilled, the Wanderer left this world, and was neither seen nor heard from again," Queen Rat said.

The seventh shrine showed a group of people standing with their palms outraised toward the sky, which was full of birds and brilliant sunlight. "But the Spiral turns whether we like it or not. Before he went, the Wanderer foretold that a new age of darkness would come even greater than the first. On that day, the Wanderer promised he would return."

"And that's why the sun doesn't rise? Because we're in some kind of age of revelation?" I said.

The queen moved to the eighth and final shrine, the dark crescent of an eclipse halfway covering the sun. The sun in this motif wasn't a complete sphere, but a broken spiral.

Queen Rat ran her fingers over the tiny crests and troughs, giving Zaea and me a rueful smile. "Depends on who you ask. According to those living on the Echelon, that age is over. They, the elect were saved by the True Night and the Crippled King's ascension. They believe he is the Wanderer Returned, and that we, the little Vermin who chose not to follow him, must suffer our heresy down here in the cold darkness of oblivion. As you probably have gleaned, we here in the Burrow reject his claim of divinity. We believe he is a false prophet."

Zaea, who had remained flippantly disengaged so far, finally took a grim interest in the conversation. The subject seemed to be making her uncomfortable. "If the world of your ancestors was so peaceful, utopian, and, as I imagine, democratic, how was someone like the Crippled King able to rise to power?" she said.

"We don't know," Queen Rat said. "Most of our records were destroyed or lost on the Last Day of Sun. The Blight, perhaps. Fear about the future. We know he was a skilled rhetorician, a hero of the people, despite his disability."

"What's wrong with him?" I said.

"He was born with a lame arm," Queen Rat said. "Rumor is, he still has it. His right one, if that matters to you. I believe his frailty actually helped him win his throne. He was the underdog, a victim of circumstance who was able to rise above… what my dear friend Gator would call a game-changer.

"But enough about politics. You want to know how we got where we are," Queen Rat said. "We don't know what caused the world to grow dark. We know the government had some knowledge it would happen. The people were warned the sun would cease to rise as it always had. Few believed it, at first. But as the world grew colder, the crops failed, and snows started falling in mid-summer, more and more began to believe. Many chose to follow the Crippled King, who promised them salvation."

"So he took advantage of a crisis, and that's how he seized power?" I said.

"Took advantage… or caused it," Zaea said.

"Only he knows for certain," Queen Rat said. "We do know that the Echelon was built before the True Night fell. We know that only the uppermost crust of society was given a place in the Amber City: scientists, doctors, and celebrities, not to mention his own party members. The engines of the Echelon were fired, and their promised land ascended to the heavens.

"Millions of refugees clogged the highways and roads. The camps ran for miles. Those who rejected his doctrine, like my forebears, were labeled heretics and hunted down. They were forced to flee underground, into the bowels of the undercity where it was still warm. The Crippled King blamed us for the catastrophe, said that terrorists operating on our side had somehow engineered the planet to go dark. The surface became a bitter wasteland, uninhabitable by anything but snow bats, fang rabbits, and the gruesome abominations we call the Snowmen."

"They made the people of the Burrow scapegoats?" I said.

"The Amber City needed an enemy to keep its citizens preoccupied, so they wouldn't question the regime. Who better than us sinners left to die down on the Surface? It was the Crippled King who gave us that name, but it didn't take long for us to adopt it for ourselves. A slur can't hurt you if you own it," Queen Rat said.

"What about the Lice?" I said.

"The Lice have a deep-rooted fear of being underground. They won't come down here. They're the Crippled King's greatest weapon on the Surface, but beyond that, our information isn't good. All I can say for certain is that if you see one, you should run," Queen Rat said.

"With all due respect, your highness, what exactly do you want us to do about any of this?" I said.

"I like someone who gets straight to the point. Our weapons and numbers are no match for the Amber City. We wouldn't stand a chance if they ever found this base and staged a full-scale invasion," Queen Rat said. "Even in the best-case scenario, Salt Town would fall in less than a day. These tunnels, which span the entire width and breadth of the Night City and several miles beyond it, have been fortified enough to serve as our smokescreen, and our shield. The spies of the Amber City have yet to learn our exact location. But if they ever did..."

Zaea hung her head. Was she embarrassed? *She's a princess, after all,* I reminded myself. *Or, says she is. Maybe her father did similar things to the religious minorities on her own world.*

At last, Queen Rat said, "I want you to serve me, both of you. I believe that is the purpose the Spiral has sent you here to fulfill. I understand accepting this offer will mean risking your lives..."

A strange glaze suddenly clouded Zaea's eyes, pulling my attention away from what Queen Rat was saying. A grimace wrenched Zaea's lips apart, and a flash of silver leapt from her palm.

Queen Rat turned with a calm, fascinated smirk that froze as she saw Zaea's soup spoon flying toward her. My feet had already left the floor. I tackled the queen in the same instant the pewter projectile sailed over our heads, striking the man standing behind the queen with dagger upraised with a juicy *thud*.

Only then did I realize Zaea hadn't been aiming for the queen at all, but at her assassin. It was the man who had been praying in the back of the church when we came in. He'd snuck up on us while the queen was monologuing. The dagger he was brandishing was a cruel stiletto. In his other hand was my flint axehead, fixed with a brand new wooden handle.

As his face contorted with pain, I recognized the assassin as the gangly gaoler who'd stood guard outside my cell with Gator that morning. Because both of our backs had been turned, neither the queen nor I had noticed him approach. Only Zaea had, and her split-second decision to throw the spoon had saved the queen's life.

The man shrieked and dropped his axe, struggling to dislodge Zaea's spoon from the socket of his left eye. The spoon came free and a crimson spray riddled with thick, squishy white spurted from his face. He lunged for the queen, gripping his wound and desperately slashing with his knife.

The queen crouched and slid off the line of the attack. The knife came back around, slashing for her jugular, but cut only air. The assassin's third attack was a straight thrust toward her stomach. The queen sprawled back and grabbed the knife with both hands, drove her elbow into the gangly man's nose, then grabbed his wrist with an entangling figure-four grip so the assassin couldn't get his knife hand free. Then the queen bent his arm like a chicken wing, drove her hips forward and stabbed the assassin in the liver with his own blade.

The assassin shrieked and struggled, but he couldn't escape. They fought that way for a few minutes, the knife going in and out, in and out, their feet slipping on the slick and the red. At last the man trembled, gave a final hiss, and dropped lifeless to the floor.

Queen Rat's right cheek was slashed open. I could see her teeth through the elongated crimson dimple the knife had made. She shot me a look of panicked relief, and quickly set about tearing strips from her tunic to pack the cut.

In that short instant I looked away, the assassin somehow made it back to his knees and made a grab for Zaea, who gave a surprised yelp before tripping and falling backward over a pew. The bastard still wasn't dead. Without thinking, I grabbed an iron candelabra sitting on the ledge of the nearest shrine and smashed it over his head. Before I fully comprehended what I'd done, the assassin stopped moving.

Wild breath scorched my lungs. A furious rhythm pounded inside my skull. I stared at the murky pool of blood spreading out from what was now my second kill with unblinking eyes. This time, I wasn't sorry.

"Thanks," Zaea said. She started to cry. The queen rushed to embrace her. Queen Rat clutched Zaea's head to her bloody breast, cooing, "Shh, shh, we're safe now, sweet girl, you're safe, you're all right, he didn't hurt you, he can't possibly hurt you now. Shh, shh. What else are friends for? Look at us, three brand-new siblings bound by an enemy's blood, bonding over the corpse of our first fallen foe. Excellent throw of that spoon, by the way."

Zaea's breathing slowed, and she laughed, wiping her face dry with the back of her sleeve.

The queen nudged the dead man with her boot. "Remind me to punish you for stealing good pewter from my chow hall, Zaea. Don't think you're getting away with that. But, later. We're going to get good and drunk now, and I don't mean on that pig's piss we had earlier. We'll break out the good bottle I was saving for the Feast of Saint Joanna. Where exactly did you learn to throw a piece of fine dinnerware like that, anyway?"

Zaea bit her lip. "My dad. He can throw anything. He used to show me things like that when I was a little girl. Said they'd be useful when I went to Ganheim. I was in military school before I became a doctor; I don't think I've mentioned that. I learned how to kill a human being with a spoon before I could do long division."

The queen must've thought that was the funniest thing she'd ever heard, because she laughed so hard I had to cover my ears. I couldn't take my eyes off the twitching mess of slashed cloth and pale, bloody flesh lying dead at my feet.

No. He tried to kill Zaea. He can rot in Hell.

"You must have some training yourself. That was quite the disarm," Zaea said.

The queen wobbled her hand in the air. "Enough to protect myself when my Moles aren't around. But I also had a fairly large advantage."

Zaea's eyes narrowed. We both said, "What?"

Queen Rat gave us a liar's shrug. "I knew the attack was coming. I haven't been entirely honest with you. I had a feeling this one was going to make a botched assassination attempt when we first entered the church. Not really the praying type, our friend Spider. Though I admit, I *was* surprised when he chose me as his first target instead of Dan, whom he was supposed to kill. You and I, Zaea, were only meant to be a nice bonus."

"I don't understand," Zaea said.

In an instant, the trust I'd felt for Queen Rat vanished, and my fear and post-fight jitters transformed into wrath. "You *knew* he was going to attack us? And you let him?" I said, more of a demand than a question.

The queen's smile faded, and she fixed me with a callous, analyzing gaze. "Of course I knew he would attack us, Daniel. I hired him."

THE BURROW

QUEEN RAT'S SOLAR was small and cramped, all dusty, empty bottles and untouched piles of ancient vellum scrolls. There was a wooden table and four chairs, which I guessed were luxury items in the Night Country, where trees no longer grew; also a gold candelabra with nine candles, a woven wool carpet, and a brick hearth, where the queen waved on a glowmoss log and Zaea and I sat and drank wine while Gator played music for us on his lute to mask our conversation from anyone who might try to eavesdrop from the hall.

The queen went to the bathroom to sew shut the wound in her face. When she returned, the severed flesh of her cheek was raw and swollen beneath the stitches, saliva murmuring through newfound passageways when she spoke.

"You have questions, and I've put off answering them for far too long. Of course, you understand why I couldn't. But now that I know you're both willing to kill for me, we've established a base level of trust, so at last, we can begin," Queen Rat said.

"Why don't you begin by telling us what the Hell is going on? No more bullshit," I said.

Queen Rat rolled her eyes. "Daniel, calm yourself, before you impregnate your trousers. You won't get to wash them any time soon. I promise."

I swirled my wine and stared at the fire, listening to Gator play. The bright notes sang in hypnotic succession. The melody reminded me of a church song I'd sang many times growing up, *You've Gotta Be Good to Meet God*. Of course, our little Evangelical congregation only had one singer, an electric guitar, and a keyboard – nothing as fancy or as masterfully played as the beautiful, hand-carved instrument in Gator's hands.

The Queen drained her wine and hissed as the alcohol scorched her wound. She patted it dry with a gauze pad. "I have long had suspicions of Spider's disloyalty, so I sent an envoy to him – an anonymous third party – with an offer to assassinate you, myself, and Zaea on behalf of the Crippled King. I had my catspaw tell Spider a rumor that you would claim to be the Wanderer Returned, and that the Crippled King would pay handsomely for your death. Not only that, but failure to kill you would result in nothing less than the fall of the Amber City. Naturally, they had been paying Spider for information about me for years... perhaps even since he was a child."

Queen Rat smirked into her wine. "Fool that he was, the pickle dick believed my ruse. The scene of the crime was supposed to appear as though you, Dan, had assassinated Zaea and I before succumbing to your wounds. That's why Spider was carrying your axe head, stolen from your possessions while you were incarcerated, as I'm sure you noticed.

"Whoever found us was supposed to think you were the Crippled King's spy, and in return, our creeping, crawling friend Spider was promised safe passage to the Amber City, where he was to receive a fully-furnished mansion, a pretty young wife, and all the food and drink he could consume until the end of his days. I think that last part is what sold him. Like so many of us here in the Burrow, Spider was a slave to distilled spirits."

"Care to explain yourself?" I said.

Queen Rat drained her wine. "I wanted to find where Spider's true loyalties lay, as well as yours. So I laid a trap for him, and he hustled on all eight of his spindly, spidery legs right into it. You must understand that I didn't know you, or Zaea, any more than a stone in my boot, and the only way for you to win my trust was by giving you the opportunity to kill me and have you not take it."

She sacrificed one of her own men, and knowingly risked her life, so she could see whose side Zaea and I were really on? What a callous, inconsiderate, unethical...

"Dan, you seem distraught. Is something I've said unclear?" Queen Rat said, refilling her glass.

I tried not to let my voice quiver. "Risking your own life is one thing. But how dare you risk Zaea's? She could have been killed! We didn't choose to come here."

The Queen eyed me scalp to toe. "Yes, I risked your lives. If you are who I believe you are, a little dismemberment and death is a small price to pay to confirm it."

"Who do you think we are?" I said, though part of me already knew.

"What does the widower say to his ceiling at night?"

"That doesn't answer my question, your highness."

"It's a roundabout way of saying your question was idiotic."

I got up and paced around the small confines of the room. Gator raised an eyebrow, but kept playing. "All due respect, Queen, but I think we're all a little too tired and frayed to start drunkenly philosophizing. Right, now we earned your trust. So what? Do you want us to sweep your floors? Search for frozen TV dinners on the Surface? What? If you're not going to tell us, I'm tired, and Zaea needs to get to bed, too..."

"I can speak for myself, Dan," Zaea said.

I sat down again, my face growing hot. Gator stopped playing to tune his lute.

The queen topped off our wine glasses. "You've won some of my trust, but not all. There is no depth the Crippled King will not sink to in an effort to stop our little revolution. We are a threat to his claim, both as king, and as the mouthpiece of god. I still cannot be 100% sure you are not spies. If you are not, you probably don't understand why I'm still suspicious of you. But the Crippled King possesses powers you are not yet aware of."

Zaea and I exchanged a nervous glance. "What?" we both said.

Queen Rat drew a spiral in the air with her finger. "The Crippled King can travel the Spiral, like you can. He has the ability to leave his body and inhabit another at will. Our spies in the Amber City have witnessed it. They report he is researching this power obsessively, though he is currently only capable of traveling short distances, and to do so puts great physical strain on his primary body. He is old, weak, and already quite vulnerable. However, he is making progress…"

I finished the queen's thought. "… You think it's only a matter of time before he's able to take control of someone here and open the gates. That he's going to use this power to sabotage you."

"Even in the best-case scenario, which one should never assume, it will be less than a year before the armies of the Amber City march victorious through these halls, and their banners fly over Salt Town," Queen Rat said. "I'm no pessimist, but we have no way of killing an enemy who walks among us unseen. This station is the last line of defense against such an invasion, and you've seen what a feeble bulwark it truly is. All of our other defenses have fallen to pogroms or disease."

"It is a time of ending," Zaea said, her eyes locked on the fire. "But an ending always means a new beginning, doesn't it?"

"That's funny. Our sources tell us that's exactly what the Crippled King told the freezing, starving refugees when he was inviting them by the millions to come to the capital to die. But there's no way you could've known that. Hear, hear." Queen Rat said, and clinked Zaea's glass.

She paused to collect her thoughts before going on. "As I said earlier, the Spiral sent you here to fulfill a purpose. You will return here, each night, until that purpose is fulfilled. I know, because it happened to Helm, too. Helm's purpose was to die for us, and he did. I do not believe you will share his fate, but it is possible."

"Here it is," I said.

The queen gave me a curt smile. "Serve the revolution until the Amber City falls, and then you can go home. For good."

"I don't understand," Zaea said.

"She means we'll be able to sleep again. Without the dreams. Without coming here," I said.

"You are as sharp as shattered glass, Daniel," Queen Rat said.

"Why us?" I said.

It was her turn to stand and begin pacing the room. "You are both Visitors. Thus, you both have an extreme tolerance to cold. My people can't remain on the Surface longer than a few hours unless there is a false day, but you can. We have recently learned of a secret facility run by the Amber City where our people are being held hostage. We have reason to believe they are being... experimented on."

"We're not soldiers. Well, she is." I motioned to Zaea. "And, uh... I guess I have some training, too... but neither of us are anywhere near that level," I said.

The queen swirled her wine. "Yes, it is possible you will both die. But I have faith in you. Besides, you'll have eight of my best Vermin to watch your backs."

"Fret not," I said.

"Once the prisoners are freed, leading them back here will be easy as pie. People of this country know how to defend themselves and travel in the cold. They won't get lost or accidentally walk off a cliff if you get too far ahead of them."

I wanted to see what Zaea thought before I said anything else, but her head was bowed low, her eyes full of firelight and masked intent.

"Again, why us?" I said.

"Daniel, are you truly going to deny where you are, and why you're here? You didn't fall into Len's body by accident. You were brought here for a reason. I think we both know what that reason could be. At least, we can hope."

She thinks I'm the Wanderer Returned. But why? I'm not a good person. I'm nobody's savior.

Not for the first time, Queen Rat read me like a book. She watched my mental wheels spinning with increasing amusement, before finally interrupting, "However, and this is a *big* however, we of the Burrow do not believe the Wanderer was divine. He never claimed divinity, or attempted to keep his power after his purpose was fulfilled. We don't even know his real name, or what he looked like. He forbade any image of his likeness. We believe *all* Visitors have the potential to fulfill this role. Whether or not they do is a matter of choice. And so we wait."

Zaea cleared her throat, and said, "Um, Queen? You were going to tell us how we can go home."

Queen Rat shook her head. "Oh, right. I tend to go on tangents when I'm a few cups deep. I also do it when I'm sober. Wine does make me love the sound of my own voice, though. The answer to your question is simple. To go home permanently, to rid yourself of this curse, you must kill the Crippled King. There is no other way.

Learn how he controls the Spiral. He will not share his secrets with you, otherwise. I promise."

"Oh, for heaven's sake," I said.

The queen tapped her fingers on her thigh. "You came to us in the hour of our greatest need, in the body of one of our greatest fallen warriors. We of the Burrow do not believe in literal prophecy. If we did, we would have no choice but to accept our oppressor, since he technically fits all of the qualifications. Instead, we believe that heroes and villains, saviors and tyrants create themselves. You need to want to help us, Daniel. As you must want to help yourself. And her." She gestured to Zaea.

"Seems rather convenient for you, doesn't it?" I said. "You're asking us to do the impossible. Otherwise, your own people would have already done it. So you tell us a bunch of pseudo-religious mumbo jumbo about how we were destined to come here, knowing perfectly well that we have no choice but to buy it. Sure, send us on a suicide mission. Who cares if they capture and torture us to death? You talk about choice as if we have one."

"Dan..." Zaea said, glaring at me the way Carly used to when I said something that embarrassed her.

"There is always a choice," Queen Rat said.

I closed my eyes and breathed, in, out, in, and out, my thoughts a tired web of drunkenness, pain, and worry. The blurred tip of Jaime Jimenez's *shinai* flashed toward me behind my weary eyes.

Maybe it is fate, I thought. *Or maybe it's just plain old stupidity. Maybe those things really aren't all that different.*

"I don't need to consider it," I said at last. "My answer is yes."

"And you, Zaea? What will you do?" the queen said.

Zaea took my hand and squeezed it. "Dan saved my life. Twice. I wouldn't be a very good friend if I let him go alone."

"Splendid," the Queen said with a clap. "Tomorrow. The expedition leaves at second torch. Your briefing begins an hour before that, in roughly seven hours. If I were you two, I'd get to sleep as soon as possible."

"We'll be there," I said.

"One last thing, Daniel. There was no shame in what you did. I thought I'd already finished the job for you, otherwise, I would have done it myself. And while it may have cost me my good looks – that's a joke – it was a necessary evil. Does anyone want more wine?"

I shook my head *no*, covering my glass with my hand as Queen Rat tried to pour me a refill from the nearly empty bottle. "I'll have a splash," Zaea said.

"Hey, wait just a damned minute," Gator said, slamming his fist on the wall. "She already had two glasses. What about me? Y'think I been sufferin' all this yik-yak for the pleasure of hearin' you people speak? Pay the musician."

THE BURROW

I DIDN'T IMMEDIATELY return to the tiny apartment Gator had set up for me next to the barracks. I wanted to see the man I'd killed.

I was glad Spider was dead. The image of his head splitting open, splattering his blood, brains, and skull fragments across the smooth stone of the church floor, gave me deep, intoxicating satisfaction. I wanted one more drink of it before I went to bed.

I found him in the morgue, next to the mushroom farm. I was careful to avoid being seen by the random shadows of guards and Vermin passing through the Station's halls. When the air got chillier, I knew I was close.

Spider's body was laid out on a table under a woolen blanket, entirely covered save for a jagged mountain range of toes poking out of the bottom. They had laid him next to a block of ice so huge it took up half the room. A few other cloth-draped corpses adorned that shadowy sepulcher, forever immune to the rotten stench permeating from next door.

I pulled back Spider's sheet and cringed. His wounds had been splashed with water and patted dry, but there was no way to truly clean them. His head was cloven into a blooming, pink flower of ragged flaps of flesh. Both of his eyes were closed, but the one Zaea had thrown her spoon into wore a monstrous, swollen bruise. One side of his wiry, milk-blue body bore a dozen puncture wounds from where the queen had stabbed the assassin with his own knife.

"Not so tough now, are you, asshole?" I said.

A hostile, alien thought entered my head that maybe the queen was wrong. What if Spider wasn't a spy, but another Visitor? *No*, I told myself. *No way. But what if...*

I'd dreamed of Ink drawing the Spiral in the dust on the outside of my window. If this curse could bring Zaea and me together, two strangers from opposite ends of the universe, if it could bring Helm to the Night Country, and who knows how many others, then was it really so crazy to think that Ink might be here, too?

I searched Spider's body for tattoos or any other kind of distinguishing marks, but found nothing other than his wounds. I must've been drunker than I thought, because I didn't hear Bob o' the Knob slip out of the shadows and walk up behind me. I didn't even know he was there until I felt his blade pressing into my side.

I spun around in time to see to see the old man in the bear suit relax his spear and give me a sour glare. He spat the nut he was chewing into a leather cup, lifted his free hand to his face, and pointed at his own eye.

Slowly, carefully, I nodded and bent over Spider's corpse to pinch his eyelids open, first the eye that was uninjured, then, with considerable more difficulty, the one that was swollen shut. Neither of Spider's eyes bore a golden spiral.

"Thanks," I said to Bob. Bob stuck a fresh, green nut in his mouth, chewed, and spat into Spider's face.

I went back to my room as fast as I could and climbed into bed. Despite the lightning speed of my pulse and the booming thunder of my own thoughts, I fell asleep quickly, drifting off to an uneasy blackness where I floated and dreamed of City.

IV

It is a lie to think men small
Ice-hearted leaders most of all
For they exist, though cruel and crass,
Only to turn this world to glass.

So into glass, the Good Knight gazed:
Spectacles seated upon a face.
The Good Knight's blade at last made free
The dead man stuffed inside the tree.

He ordered all the trees cut down,
Their black trunks growing sanguine frowns,
The peasants inside not hours dead,
Curs'd souls buried in cursed beds.

"King Mirek thinks us weak of heart,"
Arkadius told his silent lot,
"We bury them in Christian soil.
Then douse every tree in oil."

That beacon burned bright as a star
For days he watched it from afar
The ashes gave the light a scar
And the nights the blessed taste of tar.

For history is an open ring,
Coiling outward, not recurring,
A spir'ling, toiling, endless thing
That does not see the might-have-been.

THE CITY

"SORRY, DOCTOR. I don't mean to be rude. But, do you really not see what I'm talking about?"

Doctor Lekarski stared at me over the rim of his glasses, polishing the lenses with the corner of his starched white hospital coat. "I don't see anything. I think there is nothing wrong with your penis. Please, Daniel. Put your pants back on."

How does he not see it? It's right there. I gazed at the black spot, incredulous. It was twice the size it had been the week before. I pulled my pants back up. The doctor motioned for me to sit down with one hand, typing something into his computer with the other.

"Do you have any history of mental illness in your family?" the doctor said.

"No. Not that I'm aware of. But I guess I have been feeling somewhat... not like myself lately," I said.

"What do you mean?" the doctor said.

"I had a bad stomach virus last week."

Doctor Lekarski made a note. "And that was when you found the spot?" he said.

I nodded vigorously. "Yes."

"What were your other symptoms?"

"Vomiting. Diarrhea. Headaches. Nausea. Trouble sleeping. I went back to work a few days ago, but I still feel a little sick, and I'm always tired. I wake up exhausted after a full night's rest, then I lie awake for hours before I'm able to fall asleep at night." I didn't tell him about my dreams of the Night Country.

Doctor Lekarski sniffled and wiped his nose with the back of his sleeve. "Those are normal symptoms for a stomach virus. As for this spot you think you see on your penis, I don't see it. You are probably dehydrated. Severe dehydration can cause hallucinations and trouble sleeping."

"Are you sure it isn't herpes or something?" I said.

Doctor Lekarski smiled. "Did you ever have it before?"

"Definitely not," I said.

"Then I am 100% sure. I think it was dehydration."

"All right," I said, though I wasn't convinced.

"Your immune system might be low," the doctor continued. "I would like to do a blood test to make sure. The other possibility is that it was mononucleosis." He pulled out a pad of paper and a pen and wrote something. "I am making you a prescription for antiviral medication. You need to take the whole cycle, three tablets per day for ten days."

He handed me the note. There were three Countryish words, none of which were the names of any drugs I recognized, except the word for vitamin.

Vitamins? He's the only English-speaking doctor in City according to Google. And he prescribes me vitamins?

I mumbled the Countryish word for thank you, shoved the prescription in my pocket and returned to the reception desk, where I paid the equivalent of twenty American dollars for my visit. I still didn't have health insurance in Country, despite Filip's promises I would be getting a comprehensive government plan as soon as the paperwork cleared, but health care costs in Country were so cheap that it didn't matter.

My next stop was the pharmacy. Pharmacies in Eastern Europe aren't much different than they are in the U.S., though you never see them attached to supermarkets. Most pharmacies in the nations of the Former Soviet Union are still mom-and-pop's stores.

The nearest pharmacy was in the *galeria* next to the train station. I window shopped for a bit after picking up my prescriptions, which cost me a grand total of seven USD.

There was a jacket I liked, so I gave the one I was wearing to a homeless guy lying under a puke-crusted blanket inside the revolving front doors. It was a face-blistering two degrees Celsius outside, and I thought he would freeze to death if he didn't have something warmer. Plus, it gave me the excuse to buy a new one. I had always felt guilty about buying new clothes for myself, when so many people in the world can't afford them. That's partly why most of my wardrobe was ratty and old.

But I'd read on Ink's website that one of the first things a woman notices about a man is the way he's dressed, in particular his coat and shoes. Ink recommended that the cornerstone of any man's wardrobe should be a suit with a skinny tie and pocket square. Many of Ink's articles about going out to meet girls at the bars in Country started with him getting "suited up."

I ended up not just buying myself a jacket, but an entire three-piece gray suit, complete with silk tie and pocket square, as well as a new belt and a pair of wingtip leather shoes, from a boutique men's clothing store on the top floor of the mall, where the nicest shops were. All of it was hand-made in Country, and cost a quarter what the same suit would've cost back home. The clothes looked more stylish, too, fashioned with that Old World panache you saw in movies where playboys sat in parlors smoking cigars and drinking whiskey.

It was already dark by the time I started walking home. I was about halfway there when I saw her.

I usually watched the trams going by any time I walked on a main street in City. I'd look in the windows to see if there were any pretty girls I could hold eye contact with. It was a dumb game, but a harmless one. What I found was that people who ride trams spend a lot of time looking out of them, probably for the same reason. A few times a day, a pretty girl would catch me staring at her and smile; I'd smile back, and the game was won.

The tram trundling toward me in the direction of the main square was number 24. There was a pretty raven-haired girl with a pointed chin and big, sad eyes sitting in the window, her face framed by a forlorn finger and thumb. *Damn*, I thought. *That is one attractive Countryish... wait, is that? Oh, shit.*

Kashka's eyes met mine. Her face remained blank, her lips an emotionless, taught little heart, but the sadness in her eyes washed away and instantly became two smoldering coals, tracking me as the tram rattled past on its half-century old tracks, casting sparks off into the ruddy night.

If it sounds far-fetched that it took me that long to recognize a girl I'd dated for more than a month, it shouldn't. A lot of Countryish girls look alike, to the point where Ink had even written an article about it on his website.

The dirty look Kashka gave me from the tram turned to cinder as it lumbered by. She held my gaze until the tram passed and didn't look back. Then she was gone, and I was alone again on a street full of strangers all hurrying to escape the gnawing bite of the cold. I leaned into the wind and traipsed my way home over crunching patches of old snow, thinking of her, and how much I didn't want her, and how much I did.

I checked the time on my phone. Kashka was on her way to work. She'd probably already met a new guy at the square by now.

When I got home, I went straight for my laptop, logged into my email, and opened the compose message box. My fingers trembled over the keys.

Hey. Saw you on the bus. I miss you.

Not more than a minute later, my new message notification dinged. The email was from Kashka. *It was not a bus. It was a tram,* Kashka replied.

You know what I mean, I said.

Hi Dan, she wrote back. *Yes, I do. You did not smile at me.*

You gave me a dirty look, I wrote, then added a smiley face.

You deserved it.

I probably did. Are you at work?

Yes. I work whole night.

Do you want to meet me on your break? Or did you mean what you said about never seeing me again?

Obviously I didn't.

Then why did you say it?

Because you were bad to me.

I growled and waited a minute before replying, *You were bad to me, too.*

Yes, I can meet you, Kashka wrote, dismissing what I'd said without comment. *I will have thirty-minute break at midnight. Maybe we can go to Castle of Beer.*

THE CITY

"**WHAT IS** the worst thing you ever did?"

"Hmm. I don't know. This is difficult question."

"Think."

"I guess it would be sleeping with Maciek's friend after we broke up."

"Maciek was the guy you were with for seven years?"

"Tak."

"Damn. I thought you said *you* left *him*."

"I did. But I was still very hurt that he cheated on me. So, yes, I did it. I went to his friend's place one night, we got very drunk together, and I slept with him."

"Did he ever find out?"

"Maciek? Tak. He did."

"Ah-ha. Okay. So that's why he hates you. I get it now."

I reached out to smooth her hair, but she recoiled and reached down to grab one of the pillows off the floor.

"Hey, I'm not judging you," I said.

"Yes you are."

"I mean... that's pretty bad. But it's no worse than my past," I said.

Kashka propped herself up on one elbow, eyes narrowing. "What do you mean?"

I grabbed the pillow. "C'mon, will you put that down? You're being crazy."

"I know. Tell me what you mean."

She didn't let go. I pulled harder. "Kashka, seriously?"

Kashka harrumphed and finally let go. I threw the pillow back on the floor, and she crawled under my arm, resting the small weight of her head on my chest. I stared at the ceiling, playing with her hair and debating with myself about how much of the truth I was going to tell. The beer and post-sex endorphins got the better of me.

Finally it came out, a frozen memory belonging to another person who had once been me. "I killed my ex-girlfriend. Carly. The one in the picture you saw." I'd long since stashed that picture in the drawer of my nightstand.

Kashka's breathing paused, and resumed. "I know who she is. Tell me, how did she die?"

"I didn't murder her, if that's what you think," I said. "It was an accident, but I was the one who was responsible. I drove drunk, so it was my fault she died. Y'know, it's weird. I've never actually said that out loud."

"What happened?" Kashka said.

"You want the details?"

"Tak. And I think you need to tell them. Do you say, to get it on your chest?" Kashka said.

"Close enough. I was driving very fast and we were arguing. I swerved into oncoming traffic and almost hit another car. The car we were driving in flipped and rolled three times. The other driver and I were both fine, but Carly... she died."

"I'm sorry, Dan," Kashka said.

"Yeah. Me too."

Kashka slid from under my arm and propped herself up again. "I mean it. You loved her. Part of you still does."

I shook my head vigorously. "No way. It was a long time ago. That wound has long since healed."

"No it hasn't," Kashka said.

I mirrored her pose, reaching to stroke one of her bare, alabaster breasts. "Oh yeah? And how would you know?"

She batted my hand away. *Guess she's not in the mood.* "You still wear her necklace," she said.

My hand instinctively reached for the obsidian arrowhead around my neck. I had no defense. It hung like a pendulum in the empty air between us. I clutched its familiar weight and hard, defining edges. "Do you want me to take it off?"

"No," Kashka said, rolling over so her back was to me. "I don't."

"Then why even bring it up? Did you say that just to hurt me?"

"I said it because it looks strange. We have a saying here."

"Oh, Jesus Christ..."

She kept talking as I got up and put my clothes on. "We say that rain is worse than snow. Sometimes, when it is close to freezing temperature, and it starts to rain, you would much rather it start snowing, because rain is wet – it can get you sick. There are many worse problems from the rain, even though it is warmer."

"And what exactly does that have to do with us?" I said.

"It means I would rather you be bad to me than gray. At least then I would know your intentions," Kashka said.

The black spot on my penis caught my eye as I was pulling my boxers up, but Kashka had claimed she couldn't see it, just like the doctor had. Was I really the only one? Or was I losing my mind?

"I'll bet you would," I said, and got dressed. There was still about a quarter left in the bottle of plum-flavored vodka she'd brought over after getting off work, so I drank it, downing the sanguine liquid in one long, scorching-sweet pull. I checked my phone. It was five in the morning.

I sat back down on the bed and ran my hand along Kashka's shoulders. They were cold, so I pulled the blankets up over her, but she pulled them down just as quickly and got up so she could get dressed, too. Then she surprised me by saying, "I don't want to argue. I love you. You are still healing from losing her. I think you will be for many years, maybe your whole life. I will wait for you. I will wait forever if I have to."

"No you won't," I said under my breath.

Kashka picked up her purse and started for the door. "You are really cruel, Dan."

"Wait," I said. She halted with her hand on the doorknob, but didn't turn around. "Let's not leave things like this again. I don't want it to be like this, always breaking up and getting back together, not seeing you for weeks at a time. I'm sorry for what I said. Do you forgive me?"

She considered it over an obvious, dramatic pause. "Yes. I forgive you. But you are a vermin sometimes. No. You say pest? You are a pest."

Kashka kissed me. "Are we still going to the Concentration Camp Museum tomorrow? You said you wanted to go."

I rubbed my eyelids. They felt heavy. "I can't miss another day of work this year. Let's go to the museum next week. I also need to go to sleep early. I can't stay up this late again."

"All right. Goodbye, Dan."

"Kashka, are we okay?"

"Yes. We are okay now."

"Can I ask you something before you go?"

"Tak."

"Do you really want a future with me?"

"Tak. I do. Can you not see it?"

"I can see it. Sometimes."

ADAM VINE

"Then maybe you have something in your eye."

THE CITY

I DID EVERYTHING I could to avoid returning to the Night Country.

The first week I drank five cups of coffee a day. I didn't get to sleep until two or three A.M., and even then, I woke up every hour to go to the bathroom. I didn't drink alcohol because I thought it would help me sleep. I went for late night runs and ate big meals right before bed to ensure I wouldn't get a good night's rest. At night I would read about sleep cycles on the Internet. But instead of cutting back on things that prevent deep sleep, I increased them. Dragging myself out of bed in the morning felt like rising from the dead.

I didn't want to be anyone's savior. I'd spent my whole life fantasizing about being the hero. That redemption was my siren. I think most people have moments where they desire that. We all have our demons. That's what the Hero's Journey is about, isn't it? It isn't about saving the world, but saving us from ourselves, a compass meant to help us navigate through this blinding blizzard we call existence, and to find our way again when we stumble and lose our path.

But finding your way after you've lost it is a lot easier said than done. It's easy to be a good person if you've never done anything truly wrong. It's much harder to be one once you've hurt someone else, even if that harm was by accident. You carry that weight forever, if only in dreams.

Can a bad person become good? I don't know. I probably never will. But I like to think that it's possible. Ever since Carly died, I had staked my life on the proposition that it was. It was the only hope I had.

But now that someone had actually put their faith in me to really, truly be good, I didn't want it. How was I supposed to help anyone else? I didn't deserve to be the hero. To me, a hero is someone like Zaea, a person obviously carrying a great deal of pain and worry for the future, but who keeps it inside, who stands by and lifts up those who need her, those hopeless souls such as myself, even when she has no reason to.

Me? I wasn't the Wanderer Returned. I was nothing but a fraud, an imposter, and it was only a matter of time before the whole Burrow knew it.

I tried my hardest not to sleep, and it worked, for a little while. But sleep is a debt collector, not so different than one's sins. You can run from it all you want, but eventually it's going to catch up to you.

I wish there had been some cataclysmic event that broke my chain of sleepless nights, some epic fight with Kashka or a callous message from Evan, perhaps some harrowing betrayal at work that made me drink myself into a deep despair. But for once Kashka and I were relatively stable, Evan still hadn't written me back, and my work on *Arkadius*, while obnoxiously redundant, plodded steadily on.

It was an uneventful weeknight when I finally went back. I was simply too sleep deprived, and no amount of caffeine could keep me awake.

THE BURROW

"SNOWMEN HAVE two weaknesses. The first is that they're blind. Keeping your eyes is a privilege among the Eyeless. Only their alphas and children have them. The rest cut them out when they reach the age of the Ritual. What is the Ritual, you new people ask? It's the only one the Snowmen have. They sacrifice their own eyes to the Crippled King, who they worship as a god. Absolutely, skull-numbingly disgusting, right? Well, it gets worse.

"Their blindness may be compensated by extremely heightened senses of hearing and smell, but they still can't see shit. That's your first advantage. The second is that they're morons – almost as stupid as you, Bunny Rabbit. You gossip and giggle during my mission briefing, I guarantee I will march right down off this dais and stick my boot so far up your ass you'll be tasting leather. Am I understood?"

"Yes, ma'am. I mean, sir. Loud and clear, sir," Bunny Rabbit said.

Barn Owl, Zaea, me and the other Vermin stood gathered by the ice block in the Last Station morgue next to an empty table. When the Vermin's muffled laughter dissipated, Barn Owl cleared her throat and resumed.

"Some of you are going to die today. If you think that's a laughing matter, I implore you, for your own sake, to leave this morgue right now and stay home. You're wasting everyone's time, and the rest of us who take this shit seriously don't want you fucking up our program.

"The target location is heavily fortified. That means Snowmen, and not just a hunting party or two, but a few hundred, which means at least a dozen alphas. It means Shells, too... lots of Shells."

"Uh, Barn Owl, I mean sir, I have a question," I said, raising my hand.

"Go ahead," Barn Owl said.

"How many of these Lice... I mean Shells... are there going to be?"

Barn Owl shrugged. "How should I know? Could be two, could be two hundred. Our scouts haven't gotten close enough to the facility to get an accurate number. So, as usual, prepare for the worst-case scenario. Anything else?"

"Yeah, actually. What about weapons?"

Barn Owl cut me off. "While I won't say that's a good question, since it's not, I don't blame you for being green in the boots enough to ask. Every time I look at you, I keep seein' Len. It's goddamned weird thinkin' he's not the one in there askin' me this shit. Everyone, make a conscious note: this is Daniel speaking. Daniel, say hello."

"I'm pretty sure I've already met everyone," I started.

"Just do it," Barn Owl said.

"Uh... okay. Hi everyone. My name's Dan. I'm not from here."

"We know," the Vermin said in unison.

"To answer your question, outfitting comes *after* the briefing," Barn Owl said. "First, we need to do a little science project. You and Zaea are going to examine *him.*" Barn Owl looked around the room, like she was waiting for something, or someone. When nothing happened, she cleared her throat, and said louder, "*You and Zaea are going to examine* HIM."

"Shit, hang on, all right? This bastard is heavy," Cheese Eater's voice echoed from behind the ice block, to a loud scrape and a rustle of cloth.

Cheese Eater appeared dragging a huge, pale corpse under the arms toward where the rest of us were gathered around the empty table. Even though his back was to us, I knew from the smell and the crude, shoddily sewn fur mantle the corpse wore over its shoulders that it belonged to a Snowman.

Alternating between great, theatrical aplomb and short, struggling breaths, Cheese Eater brought the Snowman into the middle of the group, squatted, and hurled the corpse onto the table in front of us.

The Vermin all covered their noses. Zaea gagged and turned away, covering her mouth with her arm. The dead Snowman smelled worse than the most pungent garbage dump, a festering rankness of musk, armpit odor, urine and feces.

The Snowman's appearance was even more sickening than its scent. I hadn't gotten a good look at the one I had killed during the blizzard, only a cursory glimpse in the wan ghost light of the tundra.

Up close, the Snowman was a hundred times more hideous than any image my mind could have reconstructed from those frantic, scattered memories. It appeared to be male, though its genitals remained thankfully covered by its loincloth. Its belt was made from corded lengths of dark, greasy hair I could only assume was human. The Snowman's face was a Rorschach mask of scars and misplaced eyes, all sewn shut by fat, black threads. His mouth was a gaggle of rotten teeth the color of mud all filed to jagged tips. The fingers, hands, and arms bore hundreds of nasty, crescent moon scars from being repeatedly eaten.

I'd witnessed the Snowman on the tundra eating his own fingers in anticipation of the warm meat he thought he was going to get when he saw me, but it didn't make sense. No matter how hard calories were to come by up there on the frozen wasteland of the Surface, there couldn't possibly be any sort of net gain in energy from eating your own flesh – that small amount of meat wouldn't even cover the biting and chewing, not to mention the catastrophic deficit needed to heal the wounds. A theory formed in my mind that this behavior was a social mechanism meant to exhibit a high tolerance to pain. Infection probably wasn't as much of a concern at sub-zero temperatures, and the cold would act as a numbing agent. But if scars meant status in Snowman-land, this guy had to be pretty high on the totem pole.

"What's wrong with his eyes?" Zaea said, pulling me out of my philosophical tangent.

"I told you. They cut them out. Weren't you listening?" Barn Owl said.

"Yes."

Barn Owl cocked her head. "The Frosties are dumb as a sack of frozen breakfast links, but they're smart enough to know who's boss up there, and it ain't us."

"So what are we examining, exactly?" I said.

"Have you ever killed one of these things before, asshole?" Barn Owl said.

I folded my arms over my chest. "Actually, I have."

The tall woman's eyes narrowed. She turned to the others gathered around the examination table. "Y'know what? I just remembered. If these two are gonna be Vermin – as loathe as I am to let that happen, since I'd rather let their asses rot, but orders are orders – then, they need to have Vermin names. I say we call this one Leech." She gestured to me with her thumb. "'Cuz he sucks the fun outta everything."

"I do not," I said.

Zaea giggled.

Barn Owl quick-drew her dagger, almost faster than I could see, and poked the blade into the Snowman's torso. The pressure was hard enough to make an indentation, but not so hard it broke the skin. "Snowman's different than us, biologically. You kill a man-man, you slash his throat, bury your blade in his heart, or maybe in his liver, you stab his fucking eyeballs out. But a Snowman ain't got eyeballs, and his anatomy is tougher. You need to know where the soft parts are."

Barn Owl motioned for us to look where her knifepoint was pressing, at the top of the bowling ball-sized protrusion of the Snowman's belly. "The bladder is to Snowmen what our lungs are to us. You puncture or cut this open, right here, he won't die right away – he'll wet out slow - but the steam will scare him so bad he'll be outta the fight. You know that feelin' you get when you have to take a piss for hours and hours, but there ain't nowhere for you to go? That's the Snowman's whole life. His bladder is gargantuan, five or ten times larger than a man's. His urine is also very hot. He needs the extra water and the hotter temperature to thaw his meat. Not a whole lotta wood up on the surface to build campfires."

Nature didn't give them that adaption. Someone engineered that, I thought.

"I saw it once," I said.

Barn Owl raised her eyebrows in mock surprise. "Oh, really? You must be special, Leech."

Cheese Eater's voice piped up from the back of the small crowd. "No he's not. The kid just knows a thing or two about havin' cold meat."

The Vermin all laughed. Even Zaea.

I flipped Cheese Eater the bird.

"Watch what you do with that finger, boy. Wouldn't want it to end up on me necklace," Cheese Eater said. The little man stood on his tiptoes so he could see me through the crowd. He held up a corded band from around his neck that was strung with tiny bones.

"Hey, it's all good, buddy. No offense intended. It's just that where I'm from, it's considered rude to interrupt the teacher when she's talking, especially to make a low effort dick joke," I said.

Cheese Eater's brow furrowed. "Low effort...?"

Barn Owl hooted. "Hah! Don't make any plans to civilize this one, Leech. He's beyond redemption. But he has a point, Cheese. Save it for when we're back home drinking a celebration beer over the success of our mission. Then you can posture on each other all you want."

"Sorry, sir," Cheese Eater said.

"Moving on," Barn Owl said. She pointed her dagger at the dead Snowman's throat, lifting up his beard with the sheath to show us. "The throat is another good target, same as a human. But don't make it your primary one. Anyone want to explain why we don't attack their throats, for the new people?"

Mongoose raised her hand.

"Mongoose, go ahead."

Mongoose said something I couldn't hear.

"Louder, Auntie. We can't hear you," Barn Owl said.

"The beards," the stout woman spoke up. She drew an invisible beard in the air in front of her own fuzzy, rectangular chin.

"And why are their beards a problem?" Barn Owl said.

"They freeze."

"Thank you, Auntie. Frozen beards will be a problem if you try to slash a Snowman's throat in a fight. Snowmen have an uncanny ability to spill shit when they eat and drink, which is usually done on the Surface, where said shit freezes practically the instant it gets spilt. A frozen beard probably sounds silly to you greenboots – shouldn't it just shatter? Don't we have Wyvernwood blades forged by the People of the Sun sharp enough to penetrate a Louse's armor?

"Yes, and yes. A Frostie's beard won't stop a blade, but it can deflect your cut enough that you'll miss the killing blow. Anyone who's fought one of these things, 'specially the alphas, knows that's a bad idea. Even an error that small can end up costing you your life.

"Now, the Snowmen don't all have long beards, but most do, even the females. If you find one who doesn't, go ahead and give him – or her – a good old crimson grin. Otherwise, avoid attacking the throat unless it's your last resort."

Seeing no raised hands, Barn Owl moved the knife onto her next, and final point of demonstration. "Last one. The heart. Let's talk about the heart. A Snowman's heart is the source of his life, just like us. The problem with trying to hit a Snowman in his heart, or liver, or lungs, is what, Vermin?"

"He has a protective layer of fibrous tissue to prevent his vital organs from freezing," the Vermin said.

They either practiced that, or they've heard this same speech so many times they have it memorized, I thought. *But if that's true, greenboots in the Vermin must have an extremely low survival rate.*

Barn Owl offered Zaea and me her dagger. "Which one of you is doing the honors?"

"I'm good. I'll just watch." I said.

Zaea took the dagger, throwing me a dirty look, and stepped close to the Snowman's corpse. "Where should I make the incision?" she said.

"Make a four-inch cut over his heart. Deep as you can," Barn Owl said.

Zaea held the dagger up to the light, studying the edge. The light glanced off it like thrown fire. "Not Wyvernwood, just old fashioned iron, but it's sharp enough to shave with. I did this morning," Barn Owl said.

Zaea made a face and went to work, carefully placing the blade on the pale, soggy-looking flesh of the Snowman's left pectoral, then drew a line that bit the skin in two. The dagger cut easily through the fat and muscle, but was stopped short of the ribs by something that made an audible scrape, like the sound of fingers dragging on whiteboard.

Zaea gave Barn Owl a puzzled look. She lifted the knife and tried again, slightly to the left of her original cut. Again the barrier inside the Snowman's chest deflected her blade. Zaea seesawed the knife, and then tried outright hacking and stabbing at the Snowman's chest, but she couldn't penetrate its inner husk.

Finally, when Zaea was red-faced and huffing, Barn Owl took the dagger back from her, and with a powerful, single downward thrust, buried the blade in the Snowman's chest. The husk made a loud *pop*.

"Chest is a bad target," Barn Owl said. "Even spears and arrows don't always punch through. The gut is unprotected, though – 'specially the bladder."

"What about the skull?" I said, remembering the pink flower that had blossomed on the forehead of the Snowman I'd killed when I hit him with my makeshift wooden sword.

Barn Owl shrugged. "Or you could smash 'em in the head, if that's your style. Whatever lights your torch, Leech."

The tall woman clasped her hands behind her back and snapped her heels. In an instant the Vermin all stood quietly, their backs straight, heels together, and hands held up to their faces in a five-finger salute.

"All right, chuckleheads, it's time to go to the Armory and get these Greenies set up with some sharp things they'll no doubt end up hurting themselves with. If I see any of you walking, jogging, half-running, or going at any pace slower than a full sprint, you *will* be taking rear guard up on the ice. A little hint for you greenboots - that's not a job you want. Do you understand me, Vermin?"

"We understand you, sir!" the Vermin said.

"Then let's get moving."

THE BURROW

THE ARMORY was located in a low, vaulted chamber that at one time had been the catacombs of a church. There were dozens of crevices that ran well beyond the light of the two glowmoss lanterns by the door. The crevices were filled with piles upon piles of weapons: daggers, throwing knives, short swords, long swords, bastard swords, executioner's swords, small spears, big spears, halberds, staves, long axes, short axes, pick axes, ice axes, bows and arrows, crossbows and quarrels, whips, scythes, bear traps, and myriad other items for making war.

The weapons were well-organized, those of poorer quality occupying the lower alcoves, with the better ones up top. There were lots of low-quality weapons, but few good ones. The bottom alcoves, those nearest the floor, were practically overflowing with chipped, rusted, cracked, shoddy, and broken tools of every category, most made from wood and old, brown iron. The alcoves at waist height were much emptier, but the weapons there were made of steel and polished wood, some that looked quite decent, most in various states of disrepair.

The highest alcoves held weapons made of a metal I'd never seen before. It looked a little like Damascus steel, all clouded and layered with swirling whorls of color, but instead of varying shades of gray, these weapons were arterial blue, midnight purple, and bright, volcanic red.

"Wyvernwood," Barn Owl said when she saw me eyeing them. She took down a short thrusting sword similar to a Roman *gladius* and made a few practice cuts in the air. "It was engineered by our ancestors to be able to cut through the Lice's shells. So legend has it, anyway. My old martial arts master would say legends are always about what we want to be true, and never about what actually is.

"One thing's for sure, though. Wyvernwood is the most durable substance we know about. It can hold an edge for years, and it's the only thing we know of that can cut through solarite - that's the synthetic analog of the chemical compound of the Lice's shell, which the Amber City uses to armor its soldiers. Fools should've known that there's no such thing as invulnerable."

She spun her grip and offered me the handle. "Not that I'm about to let you touch my Wyvernwood on your first mission, but Len knew a thing or two about how to throw his cuts, and after talkin' to the queen, I've got a theory. Wanna give it a whirl?"

I reached to take the strange, crimson short sword, but paused when I saw Zaea standing alone by the armory door. The other Vermin were already shrugging out of their furs and rushing to grab up their weapons and armor, but not her. Zaea stared anxiously at the endless rows of weapons, wrapped tight in a bundle of her own arms. For the first time since coming to the Burrow I saw her shiver.

"Give me ten seconds, okay?" I told Barn Owl.

"Suit yourself. You've got five," Barn Owl said.

I rushed to Zaea's side. She shied away from me like I was going to sting her. Yet the look in her eyes was anything but angry. She looked sad. "Zaea... your, uh... your highness? Majesty? I still don't exactly know what to call you. What's wrong?"

"Call me my name. And, I'm fine. We'll talk about it later... if there is a later," Zaea said.

"Are you scared? Because if that's it, don't worry. I am, too. I've never been this terrified in my life. Well... once. But it wasn't the same kind of fear," I said.

Zaea pursed her lips. "I've got a bit of pre-fight jitters, but I've had worse. Competing in the women's royal grappling tournament for so many years made these things a little easier on my nerves. I won't deny I'm afraid, but Ganheim put us through extensive nerve-conditioning, which helps more than you'd think. So it's not simply that I'm afraid. I just can't stop thinking about my dad."

Her dad? I wondered. *Now?*

"Do you want to talk about it?" I said. Across the room, Barn Owl cleared her throat, a clear signal for me to move it along. "Look," I lowered my voice. "I can't count on anyone else here to have my back. For all I know, Cheese Eater would rather put a knife between my shoulders at the first opportunity he gets rather than let me complete this mission. They haven't even told us where we're going yet. We don't know these people, Zaea. We don't know that they won't just leave us to rot out there once the shit hits the fan. We need to look out for each other, all right? And to do that, I need you here with me. 100%."

Zaea nodded.

"Do they know about your... um... your lineage?" I said. It hadn't occurred to me that she might not have told them out of a desire to avoid unwanted attention or special treatment, until just then. But it seemed important. The look she gave me told me everything I needed to know. "Oh, crap," I said. "Why?"

Zaea's whisper was a lash of ice. "I don't know how it is wherever you're from, Daniel, but on most worlds, princesses don't fight. You might not trust these people, but that doesn't change the fact we need them. I plan to earn my daily bread. Not to mention, someone's been following me. I think there's a spy. I think it's someone in this room."

"What?" I said.

"Be quiet!" Zaea hissed. "Spider wasn't the only one after us. Someone else has been following me ever since we got here, and he's been following you, too. I saw him when you snuck into the morgue last night to look at Spider's corpse."

"Hey, wait a second..." I started, but Zaea cut me off.

"It doesn't matter. We'll face them when the time comes. He'll try to attack one of us, probably me, because he thinks I'm an easier target. So I agree with your plan. We stick together, no matter what."

"How do you know I'm not the spy?" I said. At last, Zaea smiled. "All right. That was a joke. But since we can't do anything about this now, let's solve the problem at hand. If you're sad, or homesick, or miss... someone... maybe I can help. We used to have a saying when I was training kendo: *if you bring baggage onto the mat, you'll carry it with you the whole fight.* It means..."

"I know what it means. We had similar idioms in the arts I trained," Zaea said. "You want to know what's bothering me? I was thinking about my dad because I'm worried about him. The situation with Spider got me thinking. My family has enemies, Daniel. My dad is a good man. He fights for our people. He's a peacetime leader. There has never been a war in our country on his watch. History will remember him as a benevolent king, a talented, charismatic diplomat... a great man.

"Yet people hate him. I'm worried that someone might... that something could... happen to him while I'm here, unable to help him. He's just so old. He never looked old before I went away to school. When I go back now, however..." Her voice trailed off.

I thought of my parents, too, and the way they looked older, grayer, more exhausted every time I saw them on Skype. I thought of Kashka and my inability to save her from whatever demons made her act the way she did. I thought about my own, bleak future, forever shadowed by the good man I could have become, but never would.

I nodded and said, "You're worried you won't live up to his legacy. That you'll die before you get the chance."

Zaea drew a deep breath, blowing it out as a whistle. "I've lived such a privileged life. And I've squandered it. I'm twenty-two years old, and I've done nothing to give back. I want to do something good, which will make my father proud, before he's..." she didn't say it, but I knew she meant *gone*. "He's my whole world, Daniel. The idea of never seeing him again makes me feel small." Zaea shivered and dried a tear with the back of her glove.

I put a hand on her shoulder. "It's funny, isn't it? That when facing death, all we can think of is the ones we love most." Carly's smile rose from the depths of my memory, a bright light shining through a thousand tons of ice. "Anyway, we'd better get suited up. These guys look like they're almost done, and we definitely don't want to be last. We all good now, Princess?"

Zaea stared at my hand until I let it drop. "Please don't use the P-word. I don't want them to hear. I'll be watching you out there, Daniel from California. Don't let anything bad happen to me, and I'll do the same for you."

"Deal," I said, thinking, *but it probably will, anyway*. "Maybe we should have a code word. I donno. A secret handshake or something."

"I don't think we'll have time for that in the middle of combat..."

"Just humor me," I said. I held out my hand and waited for her to take it. "First we do this," I said, giving it a solid shake. "Then we do this." I dragged my hand away and made a fist. "Give me a bump." Hesitantly, Zaea made a fist and tapped it against mine. I gesticulated an explosion with my fingers and made the necessary sound effect. Zaea rolled her eyes. "Wait. Get back over here. We're not finished. Give me a boot," I said.

"What?"

"Turn around and kick my heel with yours."

"This is stupid."

"That's how we do it where I'm from... *get stupid, get stupid*! You never heard that song?"

"No," Zaea said.

"Oh. It was pretty big when I was in high school. Well come on, don't leave me hanging," I said.

Zaea turned and touched her heel to mine.

"All right. Now we gotta do it all at once."

Barn Owl coughed at us again. "Wait. I have to teach her this," I said. "This is an important... spiritual... dance. My people cannot go into combat without it."

We ran through our secret handshake again, me counting the steps out loud and Zaea flowing through them like we'd been greeting each other this way since grade school. Nobody actually uses secret handshakes. It was a Hail Mary pass to try to get her to smile, to forge a bond with her that I knew both of us would need if we were going to survive out on the ice. And it worked.

Zaea threw me a smirk and a sigh. "Let's go get outfitted, shall we?"

The others were almost finished suiting up by the time we rejoined them. Barn Owl tossed us each a chainmail shirt. I put it on under my furs, and winked at her to signal that everything was good.

Side note: riveted chain mail is way lighter than you think. It is only slightly heavier than a windbreaker jacket. My first thought was, *They always show dudes drowning in their armor when they try to swim in the movies, but I could totally swim in this.* Then I remembered how cold it was on the Surface and thought, *but I seriously hope I won't need to.*

That was when Gator burst in, panting as if he'd just sprinted the whole length of the Last Station in one go. "Sorry I'm late. There was a crisis on the onion matrix."

"So nice of you to join us," Barn Owl said. "We're so happy you could grace us with your presence, cousin. Would you be so kind as to select your arms and armor, maybe do some light stretching to warm yourself, so we can please get the fuck on with the mission?"

The other Vermin hid their laughter behind clenched fists.

"Shit. I already apologized," Gator said. "What more do you want?" He plucked a half-eaten onion out of his coat and bit down hard, then motioned to the top shelf with the rind. "Can I take the Archangel this time?" Gator said through a mouthful of red-white mush.

Barn Owl's face became a circus of mock pity. "Oh, no. I'm so sorry, Gator, but you can't."

Gator popped the onion rind into his mouth and shrugged. "Why not?"

Barn Owl reached deep into the top alcove of the wall, fishing for something behind the carefully placed rows of Wyvernwood weapons resting on their oiled cloth beds. From that stygian darkness, she produced a slender, curved sword with a Wyvernwood blade slightly longer than a human arm, a red tongue shimmering like rippling blood in the dim light of the glowmoss. *A Wyvernwood katana.*

Barn Owl placed the crimson sword in my hand. "Metatron," she said its name, the negligible weight of it slipping from her grasp into mine. *Metatron was God's chief Archangel, the Avenger of Heaven in*

Milton's Paradise Lost... *or was he in the Bible, first?* I couldn't remember. It had been a long time since I'd studied Christian cosmology. *Why would they name a weapon that here?*

Coincidence?

Can't be.

I hadn't been to church or even prayed with any sincerity since the accident, but a few years without faith can't erase a lifetime of it. The sword called silently to me to remember that forgotten hope, that saccharine dream that I used to believe in, that the future could be better than the here and now, that we can be redeemed no matter how far we fall. The guilt of my unbelief was penetrating, but I clung to it, even as I relished the familiar lightness of the blade.

"You know how to swing that thing, kid?" Barn Owl whispered to me. "'Cuz if you don't, I just made one big-ass mistake."

Gator clapped sardonically. "Very funny. Great joke. Your skills as a comedienne are improving, 'cos. It was truly wonderful. Now hand over that weapon, son. Visitor or not, a sword that sharp will cut your tiny pecker off the second you disrespect it, and you don't have the prerequisite experience. Best leave it in the care of someone who does. C'mon. Give it over, before you hurt yourself."

I held the pommel with both hands in a high samurai grip, choking up all the way to the simple square cross-guard, raised the sword over my head and cut the air three times, once down, then horizontal, and then a huge, sweeping diagonal, finishing with the point down and then tucking the sword against my hip as if I were sheathing it. I tapped the cross-guard with the meat of my fist, the old samurai way of shaking blood off the blade, for flourish.

Barn Owl cackled. "Oh, he knows, all right. This boy knows. Find yourself another snow-picker-sticker, Gazzo. I think this Archangel has just been permanently checked out by another member of our fine organization. And here I was, thinkin' you were green as old mushrooms," she said to me, raising one eyebrow.

Gator growled and shot me a look full of death and hellfire before trundling off into the shadows.

Zaea meandered slowly past the untold piles of archaic weapons, wondering aloud to no one in particular, "Since we don't exactly know what kind of target we'll be attacking, can any of you suggest which kind of weapon I should take?"

"All of 'em," the tall, hawk-nosed man named Vole said, tucking a scalping knife into his belt. It was already heavily laden with throwing axes and the black coil of a whip tipped with a cruel iron barb. The spear on his back was almost as tall as he was, and bore a Wyvernwood blade as long as my forearm.

Squirrel chortled. "She'd be lucky to find one after you've been at it, you greedy shit farmer."

Vole raised a finger at the shorter man. "You wait one second, Squirrel. Just because I tend the mushrooms, doesn't mean you can make disparaging remarks about my profession, or the inherent scent that comes with it. You try working long hours down there, shoveling literal mountains of our own precious brown gold, and tell me you wouldn't catch a slight aroma. Someone has to do it. You're all eating my mushrooms, anyway. Have you thought about what might happen if I stayed home, and hung out in the bath pulling my little snake all day, like you do? Maybe you all should think about that. Maybe it's high time me and the other shit farmers, as you so indelicately put it, went on strike."

The Vermin all chuckled. Squirrel crouched and playfully cut at Vole's belly with the tip of his crimson-bladed short sword, blocking Vole's counterattacks with the buckler in his other hand.

Vole tapped the blade way with his knife and heaved a great, downtrodden sigh. "I wish you'd take me seriously, Squirrel."

"Start being serious, then," Squirrel said, blocking a slash to the head.

"You can't beat a well-made great sword," Gator's voice echoed from the darkness a few paces beyond the lamplight. "A full, two-handed, five foot-long and heavy as a boulder head-remover? You tell me who could say no to that. I couldn't. Hand-and-a-half? Peh! Who needs a hand-and-a-half sword, when you can wield a real one? Not me. Only weaklings need two hands to swing a sword meant for one. I never liked that piddly little piece o' scrap metal, anyway. If you think about it, any blade less than two meters is basically a knife."

Barn Owl rolled her eyes. "To answer your question, Zaea, choose whatever weapon you're most comfortable with. But if you want my opinion, a spear is always your best choice for a raid. You know I got mine. Whatever you choose, fast, light, and silent is the way to go for this mission. What Gator over here doesn't understand is that we're trying to get in and out of this place with our lives and the lives of the prisoners intact, without raising any alarms. Charging and barging is the tactic of fools. And I know *a lot* of dead fools."

The burly, middle-aged woman called Mongoose mumbled something I couldn't hear.

"Speak up, Auntie. We can't hear you," Bunny Rabbit said. She was bent over a longbow, which she was deftly stringing with a piece of hemp.

"I said we can always use more archers," Mongoose said.

"Why? You've already got the best one in the Burrow," Bunny Rabbit said, adding, "Me, if that wasn't clear to you new people."

Cheese Eater looked up from where he was sharpening his Wyvernwood sword on a whetstone and said, "Good thing those little arms of yours can't draw with enough force to puncture a suit of armor, Bunny, or we might have to worry."

"Good thing most Snowmen don't wear any," Bunny Rabbit said. "Only the alphas and some of their highest-ranking Eyeless. They wear shell pieces they pick off the dead Lice they find up on the Surface. Yuck."

Mongoose mumbled something.

Bunny finished stringing her bow, and tapped Mongoose's shoulder with one of her arrows. "Speak up, Auntie."

Mongoose cleared her throat. "Archers are force multipliers - the more, the better. Does Princess Stick-Up-Her-Ass know how to shoot?"

"Sorry, but I don't," Zaea said, playing it off like Mongoose was only having a go at her, and no great secret had been spilled. "I was always better at throwing knives. Archery was never my strong suite."

"Pity," Mongoose said.

"Don't be so hard on her, Aunt. Most likely, these are the last four torches either of them will spend alive. Why not let 'em enjoy it?" Cheese Eater said.

"Fast, light, and silent. Got it. May I have a moment to look around?" Zaea said.

"Sure, just be quick, and don't wander. These catacombs go on forever... real easy to get lost. We're leavin' as soon as everyone's geared up. This section is the only part we use, anyway. The weapons end over there," Barn Owl said, pointing to where Gator was emerging from the shadows with a huge, Wyvernwood great sword slung over his shoulder.

Barn Owl cupped her hands over her mouth and shouted, her voice rebounding off into the darkness of the tunnels. "All right Vermin, listen up. We're out of here in two minutes. This is the part where you pay attention. That means eye contact, Bunny Rabbit. Time to quiver those arrows.

"The target location lies within a sector of the Old City all of us are familiar with, but few have actually been to. Yes, you know which one. Back when this fine city was sundrenched and carefree, it was called Heroes' Park. We know it as the Icefall Maze: thirty square kilometers of treacherous glacier flowing off the foothills of Mount Gezel, where there are no ruins to use as landmarks, only sinkholes, crevasses, and freestanding pillars of ice big enough to crush a building, that can fall out from under you – or on top of you – at any minute.

"We'll enter the Maze through the tunnels to the northwest. Then we take the Plaszov Route south under the river. After that, we cross most of the way underground, but as most of you already know, these tunnels have opened up in places due to the movement of the ice, and those canyons are deep. We'll have to do some climbing. Anyone here not know how to climb?"

No one raised a hand.

"Good. I was hoping we wouldn't have a worst-case scenario. The facility itself is nestled up under the cliffs past the icefall, so once we make the Surface, we'll have to climb from there, as well. You all got ropes?"

A unanimous "No, sir," echoed through the tunnels.

"Just yanking your chains. I know you ain't got ropes," Barn Owl said. "Speed is the name of this game, and I don't want anyone getting exhausted from carrying a bunch of heavy-ass shit before we even get a chance to fight. That's why I sent our favorite Uncle Termite out ahead of us two torches ago to set the ropes and ladders. He's also laid a few stashes of ice axes and boot blades in case we need them.

"The facility is protected on two sides: to the north side by Lake Bagra, and to the south by the mountain itself. The east and west sides both have rail access, but we won't be going that way. We're going across the lake. Intel confirms the ice is thick enough. You all better pray that report was accurate.

"Once we get to the facility, we follow the usual protocol for a search and rescue. We hit the place hard and fast, entering and exiting through the back gate on the northwest side of the fence. We need to be out of there with the prisoners before anyone knows we're there. Kill anyone, human or otherwise, who might raise an alarm or compromise the mission – that is an order.

"Now, does anyone have any questions?"

Each of the Vermin looked around the room, making eye contact with the others. We all shook our heads *no*.

"I have one," Barn Owl said. "Where's Zaea?"

I hadn't noticed Zaea leave. The main door was still shut, and hadn't opened or closed while Barn Owl was speaking. There was only one place she could've gone.

A scream echoed from the catacombs' depths.

OSSUARY OF THE VOICES

I SPRINTED into that hungry darkness, diving through an arterial expanse of shadow and bone toward the sound of Zaea's cries. Somewhere else, Barn Owl shouted, "Goddammit, people! Move!"

The Vermin's footfalls fell in behind me. The light of someone's torch let me see far enough ahead to avoid crashing into the blankets of cobwebs and the sudden piles of ancient bones sprouting up from the ground like stalagmites.

"The Little Princess... (huff)... found the ghost... (puff)..." Gator said.

"Already? That was fast," Bunny Rabbit replied.

"Think she'll be dead by the time we get there?" Cheese Eater said.

"Donno... (puff)... Maybe. But maybe... not... (puff puff)... The waif is tougher... than she looks... (wheeze)..."

Another scream pierced the ruddy shadows, followed by a guttural groan of extreme agony. Light appeared at the end of the tunnel.

Zaea was standing with her back to the tunnel mouth, clutching her head like she was trying to self-exorcise a demon lodged deep in her brain. I dashed for her, entering a small Y-intersection where three tunnels conjoined. The domed chamber was lit by a smattering of torches. The walls were built from human bone.

Zaea was doubled over afore what appeared to be a waist-high marble birdbath fixed on a dais in the center of the room. The water in the pool was dirty and old, a verdant mirror bedecked with floating islands of sludge. Zaea must have heard me enter, because, without turning around, she held a soaking wet hand up to signal me not to come any closer.

I slid to a halt, almost eating a mouthful of dusty flagstone. Zaea didn't say anything. Her breathing was labored and excruciatingly slow. "Zaea?" I said.

A shriek exploded from Zaea's lips. She thrust the hand that had warned me away back into the scummy water.

I lunged for her, but Zaea growled, "Stay... back." I stopped dead in my tracks.

The Vermin flooded into the chamber and surrounded me. "I've almost... got it..." she said, grasping her own submerged wrist. Her voice was *wrong*.

Bunny Rabbit rushed to help her, but Barn Owl held her back. "Wait," Barn Owl said.

"Wait? Sir? It's going to kill her!" Bunny said.

"I said wait. Let's see how it reacts," Barn Owl said.

The Vermin and I watched in silence as Zaea rose and removed her trembling hand from the pool and closed a fist. Violent tremors jerked through her entire body, her left arm flailing like a thing possessed. She held it with her free hand until the demonic spasms subsided. When she turned to face us, her cheeks were drained and pale as frost, her eyes two bloodshot orbs.

She gasped and gave us all a bedraggled smile. "That hurt," Zaea said.

Barn Owl was the first to break the thick, electrified silence. She started clapping. "Who *is* this bitch?"

The other Vermin erupted in a chorus of applause.

"Woo-hoo! I cannot believe you did that!" Bunny Rabbit said.

"Bravo," Mongoose said.

Squirrel poked Vole in the side. "What a day this is, eh? Someone drew the bloody ghost! Bet you didn't think you'd live to see that again, did you, Vole?"

"Twice in one lifetime... makes me feel old," Vole said, sadly.

"Seems we might've been wrong about our new guest. This one, anyway," Cheese Eater said, pointing his thumb at Zaea.

"Speak for yourself, Cheese. I knew there was something special about her from the moment I laid eyes on her," Barn Owl said.

"Now wait just a damned minute, sir. Don't stand here and try to pretend that one minute ago, you didn't think she was going to fry, like the rest of us did. How old was Katherine when she drew it? Four, five years old? How many others have died in the attempt?"

"That'll be all, Cheese. Zaea, are you all right?" Barn Owl said.

Zaea gave a weak nod and steadied herself on the edge of the marble pool.

"Do you know what it is you just pulled out of that nasty-ass puddle?"

"I think so," Zaea said, massaging the meat of her left thumb. "But... these voices... (gasp) these... (ow!)... It's hard to think... hard to..."

"You were just chosen by one of the last weapons from the Twilight Age," Barn Owl said. "I say chosen by, because you can't decide to wield the ghost any more than I can decide to shoot fire out of my ass. The ghost picks *you*. Anyone who tries to draw it that the ghost doesn't like gets cooked alive from the inside out. We've lost more than a few new recruits that way. Yes, I admit I am surprised, and that when I realized you'd stumbled in here, I thought you were dead. It's safe to say we all did. But I am not above admitting when I'm wrong.

"And I was wrong about you, Zaea. If the ghost chose you, it means that it sees something great in you. It is an immaterial blade that functions by splitting the fabric of existence itself. The length and obedience of the weapon is determined by the will power of the one wielding it.

"Like Cheese said, the last person it chose was a child. That was more than a decade ago. She grew up to be one of our finest warriors." A note of sadness dimmed the excitement from Barn Owl's words. Tears gathered under the slate orbs of her eyes. "She died for us. Went missing in action during an incredibly important mission. Her name was Katherine, alias Meerkat. She was very brave."

"I'm... (ah!)... I'm s-sorry for your loss," Zaea said.

"We didn't just lose one of our best scouts. We also lost our only other ghost. Now that weapon has fallen into the hands of the Crippled King. The one in your hand is the last one that exists in the Burrow."

Zaea's lips tightened into a solemn line. "I will... (ow!)... do my best... (ssss) not to lose... this one."

Barn Owl approached the marble pool and took Zaea's hand in her own, gently rubbing her palm with three fingers. "The old man taught me how to do this. Katherine would get these pains, too. Grandfather Mouse used to tell Meerkat that it was the weapon's way of warning you of danger. Right now, I think it's just adapting to your body."

"Adapting?...(ssss... ow!)"

"Yes. You need time to get used to each other," Barn Owl said, letting Zaea's hand go. Whatever she'd done seemed to work, because Zaea shook her hand out and stared at it, raising her eyebrows in surprise. Barn Owl didn't let her get a word in. "Unfortunately, time is a luxury that we don't have. Nor is there anyone here who can train you how to use that thing. We'll have to go to Salt Town for that... *after* the mission."

"What? Are you... (ow!)... saying I'm not coming?"

"I'm sorry, Zaea. I can't risk it. That is the most powerful weapon we have. I can't risk one of our people being harmed by putting you in the field with it before you're ready. I also can't risk letting it fall into the enemy's hands. You're sitting this one out, okay?"

The princess's brow furrowed. She extended her hand, aiming toward the Vermin gathered by the door of the ossuary. They scattered with a cloud of yelps and frightened protests. The air around Zaea's hand shivered, and a slender, nearly imperceptible black line shot out of her palm. That hypnotic, penumbral blade split the world in two. There was a hiss of extinguishing glowmoss and a clatter of severed iron as Zaea cut the lantern off the wall like a wick. The Vermin glared at the perfectly bisected lamp lying piecemeal on the floor, glared at Zaea, then back at the smoldering ruins of the lamp.

Zaea sheathed the ghost and bowed to Barn Owl. "With all due respect, sir, I'd rather not sit this one out."

Someone clapped.

"Beginner's luck," Cheese Eater spat.

Barn Owl stepped toe-to-toe with Zaea, towering over the smaller, fairer-haired woman, and put a goliath finger on her chest. "I don't know who the hell you are, but if any of my Vermin get hurt up there because of somethin' you do, I promise you, it'll be your ass that gets snuffed out. We clear?"

"Yes sir," Zaea said.

Barn Owl turned to address the rest of the group. "Order rescinded. The princess is back on. All right, Vermin. We ain't got time for any more of this legendary bullshit. Who are we?"

"The Vermin, sir!"

"And what do Vermin do?"

"Survive and kill our enemies, sir!"

"And who are our enemies?"

"The Amber City, sir!"

"Why are they our enemies?"

"They murdered our kin! Put us in chains! Would hunt us to extermination, like they did all humankind!"

Barn Owl clicked her heels and threw us a hard salute. "Very good. Let's haul ass, folks. Break your boots. We've got shit to do."

We ran in a snaking column through the narrow, shadow-bitten tunnels, falling in two-by-two behind Barn Owl and Cheese Eater. I ran next to Zaea, in the second to last row. We chanted and hooted as we passed through the Last Station, mostly to psyche ourselves up, but also to let everyone else know that we were coming so they'd get the hell out of our way.

We passed the barrier of junked subway cars into the unpopulated part of the Burrow called the Undersprawl. The group spread out a little, adjusting to the slower, jogging pace set by our leaders. Safely out of their earshot, I said to Zaea, "So, how did you do all that? Did you already know how to use one of those things? I mean... how, or why did you even find the ghost in the first place?"

I couldn't see Zaea's matter-of-fact expression in the scarce light of the tunnels, but the tone of her voice was clear as day.

"Because it told me to," Zaea said.

THE BURROW

"ONE THING I couldn't help wondering back there, when I was seeing all those weapons, is why there weren't any firearms. The civilization that was here before was pretty advanced, right? It had to be if it built something like the Echelon. Not only that, but you say it has its own sun. The only thing I can think of that could act like the sun, but on a much smaller scale, is a stable fusion reaction, or a really big lamp – and I mean *really* big, like, the size of the city itself. That's all extremely advanced technology, more advanced than what we have on the world I'm from, and we have guns. So… why no guns?" I said.

We were taking a rest break near a five-point intersection of dank, dilapidated tunnels, one of which led to the Icefall Maze.

Barn Owl glanced up from where she was reading a set of hidden directions in her navigation mirror. "I don't know what the hell any of that means. But here's the thing, Leech. Wherever you're from, I'm sure it's probably a pretty nice place. Things work. Society functions. When society stops functioning, all of that precious knowledge you have in your universities and libraries burns. The only place it stays is in people's heads, and people's heads aren't exactly reliable media for storing information."

"So you're saying you used to have guns, but you lost them?" I said.

"At least an entire level of scientific understanding is lost completely during a cataclysm event simply due to media destruction and people dying," Barn Owl said. "Another will be lost as soon as the first generation of survivors passes. So we lost pretty much everything except the things necessary for us to survive: tunnel architecture, sustainable hydroponic farming, mining, medicine, methods to survive long-term exposure to the cold," Barn Owl said.

"I guess that explains why there aren't many advanced weapons lying around. But what about personal weapons? Family heirlooms, that sort of thing? Surely those didn't all just up and vanish," I said.

Barn Owl must've thought I was being pedantic. She gave me a dismissive wave. "Legend has it that the civilian population willingly disarmed and destroyed their guns long before the Crippled King took power and the world grew dark. Not that it would've mattered much if they hadn't. Regular weapons can't penetrate the Lice's armor, and by extension, the armor worn by the Amber Guard. Only Wyvernwood can... or a grenade housed in Wyvernwood that shoots Wyvernwood shrapnel. And before you say it, no, there ain't anywhere near enough Wyvernwood lying around for us to make bullets."

The tall woman snapped her mirror shut and pointed into the tunnel to her right. "It's that way. Tails up, folks."

We formed ranks and followed Barn Owl into the passage. I thought she was going to let the subject rest there, but she didn't.

"Look, Leech. I understand I don't know is never a highly satisfying answer. Believe me, we'd love to get our hands on whatever forms of weaponry the Amber City is using and reverse engineer it. The stories tell us that the kinds of weapons that once covered the world with hatred, violence, and mass death before the coming of the Wanderer were more advanced than you or I could possibly imagine. No doubt many of them fired some kind of high speed projectile. And you can bet your ass plenty of those are still being used to keep the peace up in the Amber City. We'd kill to get our hands on a cache of those, let our own weapons scientists have at 'em, but we can't exactly just knock on their doors and ask. You see what I mean?" Barn Owl said.

"Yes," I said.

A grim silence fell over the group at the end of the next tunnel as we exited into a large, man-made cavern held aloft by dozens of fat, round pillars each the size of a building. Burned mud and brick houses lined the cobwebbed avenues, an empty village sitting silent in the gloom, complete with market stalls crowding the central common, an open-air church where the Wanderer's image was carved into the otherwise smooth face of one of the pillars, pens and lean-tos for the animals now holding nothing but ash, a vegetable garden watched over by the charred gargoyles of dim glowmoss lamps where miniature black blizzards of flies swarmed.

An ancient waterline marked the pillars evenly at waist-height. This place had been a cistern once. The wind at my back told me that whoever had built the tunnels connecting this place to the rest of the Burrow had built them so that the air flowed continuously through, creating a natural ventilation system. I remembered watching a documentary on the Discovery Channel about how ant colonies were engineered the same way.

We all stopped and shared a moment of silence. The looks on the Vermin's faces told me everything I needed to know. The people who had lived here had been their friends and families. For all I knew, some of the men and women I was marching with could have even grown up here.

Barn Owl knelt and picked something up out of the mud. It was a child's doll fashioned in the shape of rat with a crown on its head. A tear formed in the corner of her eye, but she blinked it back, wiped the doll clean on the front of her furs, and shoved it into her satchel.

"Let's go," she said.

Nobody spoke again until we were a long way away, when Zaea cleared her throat and asked no one in particular, "Who were they?"

Barn Owl replied without taking her eyes from the tunnel ahead. "They were us."

That was the last anyone said on the subject of the burned village.

The walls of the tunnels started showing greater signs of stress and disrepair. Most sections of the Undersprawl were still pristine. Even the oldest passages were stable and well maintained. But here, piles of broken bricks lay in discarded heaps where they'd been spat from the withering walls, every few steps revealing newer and larger chunks of bare, frozen earth. Some wept and dusted us with cold soil as the world above trembled and shivered. At one point the tunnel had collapsed entirely, and we had to clear the bricks and hard, stony soil by hand.

At the second collapse, we took a detour that led us to a place where the ground had opened and broken the tunnel into a deep fissure. My heart sank when I looked down. The bottom was hidden by thick, impenetrable darkness. The crevasse may as well have been bottomless.

"How will we get across?" Zaea said.

"We're about to find out," Barn Owl said. "Do your squirrel thing, Squirrel."

The short, stocky Vermin saluted her. "Yes, sir, right away, sir, without a rope, sir, I'll happily engage in a risky climb with no anchor person to ascertain that tiny but important bit of information for you, sir."

"For us. And leave your lip up there, while you're at it," Barn Owl said.

"Pity I forgot to bring my detachable ones," Squirrel said, then gracefully shimmied out onto the furthest part of the ledge, where our path dropped off into fuliginous abyss. Squirrel grabbed a handhold and started to climb. I craned my neck to watch until his flashing baldpate disappeared above the jagged wound of the tunnel mouth.

A moment later, a disembodied echo called down to us, "There's a rope fixed between the cliffs. It's about four meters above where you're standing. I can't see the far anchor point, but the rope feels taught."

There was a loud twang and Squirrel hissed happily. "It's stable enough to hold my weight. There's a rope ladder bolted here, too - still coiled. I'm going to drop it down. Nobody stab it. Or, maybe stab it, if it attacks you."

The bottom rungs of a rope ladder appeared in front of the tunnel mouth. Barn Owl tugged the ladder. "We love you too, Uncle Termite. All right, Vermin. There's a zip-line up there with our names on it. We can't see it, because it's too dark, so consider this a test of faith in your fellow Vermin. When was the last time everyone rode a zip-line? Never mind; don't answer that.

"The procedure is simple. You climb up, put your sword, spear, bow, or dagger over the rope, take a grip with both hands on each side of your weapon, then kick off and ride it all the way to the other side. For you people using blades, make sure to hold them with *both hands* on the scabbard. Let me repeat, do not grab the handle of your blade while you are flying. Otherwise, it *will* unsheathe while you're in mid-flight and deposit you very quickly at the bottom of a probably long and definitely fatal fall into that there perilous ravine. We go one at a time. Squirrel, you ready?" Barn Owl said.

"Ready to fly," Squirrel said.

"Fly on," Barn Owl said.

A rush of air *whooshed* over our heads, and the shooting star of Squirrel's torch descended twenty or thirty feet in front of us. The scrape of boots scrambling on stone echoed from the far wall of the canyon. Squirrel's light dropped five or six feet, then stopped dead.

"Is it a clear drop?" Barn Owl said.

Squirrel's answer came a few seconds later. "Clear as vodka. Look at this." Squirrel flung his torch a few feet deeper into the opposite tunnel mouth, so we could see it from our side of the rift.

"Beautiful," Barn Owl said. "All right, Vermin. Volunteers. Who's first?"

Zaea went next. I went second to last. The scariest part was the actual descent. The darkness above and below me was so absolute, it was like falling into a black hole. I kept my eyes set on the distant flicker of Barn Owl's torch as I slid down.

Zaea stifled a laugh as she and Gator pulled me in. "Daniel, are you afraid of heights? You're white as ship rock."

I didn't answer. "Aye. Shakin' like a couple of snow elk mating, he is," Gator said, squeezing my shoulder with a big, greasy hand. "Don't worry, son. No one's brave their first time across this chasm. It's the next one that will really get your insides active."

THE NIGHT COUNTRY

WE MADE the Surface an hour later under an inverted black mountain of sky, ascending into perilous lunar fields of ash-colored snow and glacial fingers of ice all glowing with their nascent, ghoulish light. The weather was as clear as it got in the Night Country, which is only to say that there wasn't a storm, but a stinging wind howled across the plain like a cloud of knives, sending bitter snow devils to dance hellishly in our path.

Some of the Vermin used their weapons as walking poles. I was hesitant to use such a beautifully crafted blade as the Archangel at first, but after so many hours of walking, and so many of them on sketchy terrain that strained my ankles and made my lower back ache, I relented.

In daylight, we would've seen the Icefall from the moment we left the tunnels, rising over the world like a floating island. But the eternal, coal-gray gloom hid the Icefall under the shadow of Mount Gezel until we were almost upon it, when a sudden blue brilliance caught our torchlight. It was as tall as a skyscraper, its surface an uneven mirror of deep cerulean glass.

We ascended a span of switchbacks snaking up the shallow grade of the glacier's base. The snow giving our boots traction thinned down to bare, slippery ice, and the ground split beneath our feet into hidden crevasses. We descended into the shallower rifts, but had to cross the deeper ones using makeshift bridges made of wooden ladders lashed together. Thankfully, the man the other

Vermin had called Termite had already set those for us, and all we had to do was find them. Most of the chasms were only a few, breathless feet across, but all of them were deep enough that a fall would be fatal. I tried not to look down.

The higher we climbed, the steeper the grade became. Ragged forests of seracs like the up-thrust fingers of buried ice giants towered all around us, threatening to fall at any moment. Gator told Zaea and me that those freestanding pillars of ice were the biggest killer on the glacier. The seracs slept under camouflaging blankets of snow that made them indistinguishable from the rest of the icefall – you could be climbing one, thinking you were on stable footing, and you wouldn't know you were wrong until it was too late.

The second big fissure was twice as large as the first, and we didn't have the aid of a zip-line to cross it. Instead, there were three ladders lashed together and laid lengthwise across the gorge, with two long ropes fixed to poles driven deep into the ice on either side to use for handholds. The ladders looked like little toothpicks that would buckle and snap the second someone set foot on them.

Barn Owl wasted no time in crossing the makeshift bridge. She pulled an oilcloth bag from where it was secreted in a nearby crack in the ice, removed one of the sets of toe blades Termite had left for us, and started strapping into them. I didn't understand why until she stepped out onto the ladder. The climbing blades on her boots extended the length of Barn Owl's step, acting like little hooks that grabbed onto each rung where her boot alone would've fallen through.

Slowly, but steadily, Barn Owl overcame the gaping maw in the ice, while the rest of us hurried to get our blades on.

Once she was safely on the other side, Barn Owl held the ropes to make it easier for the next person to cross. My blades were already on, and I was still salty about Zaea and Gator insinuating I was a coward, so I volunteered. From my first step onto that rickety bridge of ladders, I wanted nothing more than to turn around.

The conventional advice given to people who are afraid of heights is to never look down. That's impossible when you're crossing an ice crevasse on a bridge made of ladders. If you don't look down, you can't set your boots properly between the rungs, and you fall and die. But being able to see how deep the abyss is that you're trying to cross – or not seeing it, which is worse – fills your mind with images of slipping and falling, which doesn't exactly help you stay calm.

I did some technical climbing back when I was in Boy Scouts, and while all of that knowledge and experience didn't immediately come flooding back to me, I had retained enough of it to matter. I clung to those ropes like a true believer, taking one step and then another until I was across.

Before I knew it, my feet were back on solid ice, and Barn Owl was giving me a high five. I was so jittery from the adrenaline that the full weight of the accomplishment didn't really sink in until later, but damn, did it feel good... so good that I raised my arm up over the chasm and flipped Gator and Zaea the bird.

Mongoose crossed next, then Zaea, Gator, and Vole. Squirrel took the rear guard, and only went once all of us were to safety.

When all the Vermin had crossed and our short rest was over, we started back up the blue spine of the icefall, ropes and ice axes quickly replacing cut backs and walking poles. I was the worst climber among us second to Zaea, but I kept up, and only managed to endanger the lives of my friends on one occasion. I lost my footing, fell on my ass, and slid about twenty feet down the slope. I rolled onto my stomach and slammed my ice axe into the snow to break my slide like they taught us to do in the Scouts, and came to a skittering halt just before I would've crashed into Vole, who was next in line behind me.

No one except Zaea was overly impressed by my save. "Do they have many mountains in California?" she said to me, as she struggled over the ledge of a low gully the group was currently working to cross.

I helped Zaea over the ledge. "Yes, we do. There's the Sierra Nevada Mountain Range, which has Mount Whitney, the tallest mountain in the continental United States. There's also Mount Shasta to the north. That's closer to where I grew up."

"Five minute break," Barn Owl called down to us. "Rest up, get your gear tight, take a piss, do whatever it is you need to do. This will be your last chance until after the objective."

"Have you climbed it?" Zaea asked me, brushing clumped snow off her furs.

"Which one? Mount Whitney? Or Shasta?" I said.

Zaea *hmmed*. "The taller one."

I couldn't help but smile as those distant memories resurfaced: the emptiness of my lungs and the camaraderie of my fellow scouts, all huffing and puffing like tired dogs, sharing Cliff bars and going to the bathroom in plastic Ziploc bags as we toiled our way up wastelands of gray granite and naked sky. "I have, actually. I was part of a group called the Boy Scouts from the time I was a little kid until my eighteenth birthday. I earned the rank of Eagle Scout," I said.

"Is that high?" Zaea said.

"It's the highest rank we had. My troop went on several mountaineering trips every year. It was my favorite thing to do, other than take my twenty-two shooting at the rifle range." Zaea nodded like she knew what a twenty-two was. "We climbed Mount Whitney in a single day," I added.

"And how old were you?" Zaea said.

"I was sixteen."

"Sounds like quite the accomplishment."

"It's a difficult hike, but most people can do it with the right training, as long as they don't get altitude sickness. It's a hell of a lot safer than this," I said, looking down. "The view at the top, though... you can see for miles and miles, just mountains, nothing else, running all the way to the horizon."

Zaea heaved a sigh of accepted discomfort. "That sounds lovely."

"How about you, Zaea? Where'd you learn how to climb? You've obviously had some practice."

Zaea kneeled to tighten the blade straps on one of her boots. "We didn't have organizations like yours at my school. I learned to climb in our Combat Fitness and Readiness program. It was mandatory."

"I'll bet. Didn't you say it was a military academy?"

"Good memory. Yes, it was. It was called New Ganheim. I can't say I ever enjoyed climbing indoors, but now that I'm finally putting it to use in the field, I'd like to do this again someday, preferably in daylight. Really feel the nature, y'know? Maybe catch a view like the one you're describing. That is, if we survive, of course," Zaea said.

"If we survive," I said. "How about this, then. I'll make you deal..."

"Dan," she cut me off, her voice growing fraught with exhaustion. "As much as I'd love for us to make a pact to find each other when this is all over, and climb some far-flung mountain together, we both know that won't happen. I don't mean to shoot your idea down. It really is something I'd want to do in a different life, and when I say I'd want to, I mean *really* want to. But now isn't the time for wishful thinking."

"You're probably right. It was a dumb idea," I said.

Zaea's voice became soft as vapor. "Look. Nothing would make me happier than climbing with you under different circumstances. But something about this place is messing with my head. I don't only mean in the obvious ways."

"I don't understand," I said.

Zaea lowered her scarf, exposing her nose and mouth to the cold to wash her face through her hands. She returned the scarf over her face. "Ever since the briefing, I've had this unshakeable feeling that I've been here before. I had it when we first came to the Burrow, as well. Something about these streets, this architecture, even the way people speak here – specifically, the idioms they use – gives me the feeling that this is not the first time I've visited this land. Only, I can't remember when I was here."

"Jesus Christ," I said.

"What?"

"Uh, nothing. Are you sure? Do you think that maybe…"

A shout cut me off, echoing from the cliffs above. "All right, Vermin. This is the big one, the final push up the frozen ass crack of Hell. So what do you say, Vermin? You all still hard enough for the task?" Barn Owl said.

The Vermin answered, "Sir, yes sir!"

"You don't look hard to me. And you sure as crotch rot ain't gonna look hard after climbing that." Barn Owl waved her thumb at the wall of ice behind her, a sheer, hundred-foot face of midnight blue where a single, black strand of rope hung from the scattered abutments.

"The name of the game is watch where you put your goddamn feet. You climb no faster, or safer, than the Vermin above and below you," Barn Owl said. "I'm going to pass a rope around. Tie it once around your waist, and then hand it to the person next to you. This is your lifeline. It's going to keep you, me, and all of us alive. So be nice to it."

"We'll talk more later," I whispered to Zaea. She nodded.

Once the other Vermin had all finished tying themselves in, Gator tossed the rope down to Zaea. The order was her, then me, and then finally Mongoose at the bottom of the line. A sharp tug traveled down to us as the other Vermin started climbing, and the rope slowly floated upwards until it grew taught.

The climb was easier than I'd imagined, at least until the halfway point. The blades on my boots and the dual-line system we used to ascend helped negate the slipperiness of the ice. There was also the comfort of knowing that all of us were in it together, undertaking such a dangerous task as a group. Despite the wind lashing at my face and the constant fear I was going to fall and die, I didn't feel that cold or tired.

Len must have been a damned good climber, I thought.

Around the halfway point, I realized the tiny, dark shadow standing directly above us at the very top of the cliff wasn't some kind of metal anchor, but a strong, wiry little man who was holding our rope steady so that it wouldn't blow asunder in the wind.

Termite-

A hand grabbed my ankle and yanked it off the ice. "Traitor!" Mongoose shouted above the howling of the wind.

I slid, nearly losing my grip on the rope, but I caught it and held on. "What are you doing?" I yelled, as Mongoose began overtaking my section of the rope.

She grabbed the base line above my feet, then hooked my legs with her own in a scissor. She let go of the rope and took hold of the knot anchoring my waist to the line. A weight like a ton of bricks suddenly pulled me down. It took every ounce of strength I had just to hang on.

Trying to cut me off the line, I realized. *She's trying to kill me. Mongoose is the spy.*

But there was nothing I could do. I tried to kick away from the cliff and throw Mongoose off me, but she had control of my legs. I tried to pull myself higher on the line, but couldn't. I couldn't draw the Archangel, because I needed both hands to hold onto the line. Like her namesake viciously taking down some poisonous snake, Mongoose had taken me by surprise when I was most vulnerable and wouldn't let go until I was dead.

None of the Vermin looked down or even noticed our struggle. My cries for help went lost in the aural siege of the wind. I was on my own.

In one quick motion, Mongoose took her hand off my rope and pushed us away from the wall. We slid about ten feet, taking all the slack out of the line above us. A small, curved knife appeared in Mongoose's fist. She slid the knife under the rope around my waist, and I gasped as the iron bit deep into me. She shouted into my ear, "Best regards from the Amber City!" and slashed.

An arrow sprouted from Mongoose's eye.

A guttural hiss escaped my assassin's throat, as the knife, and the hand holding it, fell limply away. Mongoose's legs released their hold and the dead woman fell back to her old position at the bottom of the line.

I instinctively braced myself for the hit, holding on for dear life as her weight yanked the line taut again. I thought the force would tear me in half, but somehow, miraculously, the last remaining threads of my rope belt held.

Thanks, Uncle. I glanced up in time to see the old man at the top of the cliff lower his bow and throw me a casual salute.

Mongoose's corpse dangled ten or twenty feet below me, an impossible weight that neither I, nor the remaining cord about my waist could bear much longer.

Somewhere above me, Zaea shouted my name. A powerful gust of wind pushed me sideways, causing me to scramble laterally along the slippery ice. That sudden wall of black noise drowned out the rest of what Zaea said, but I could read her lips:

"Dan! Cut! The! Rope!"

I drew the dagger I'd taken from the armory as a sidearm, reached down, and slashed off Mongoose's dead weight. The line instantly went light. My hands were shaking so violently that I couldn't get the dagger back in its sheath, so I let it drop.

I don't know how I finished the climb, but I did. By the time I reached the top, my hands and arms were numb. My lungs burned like I'd inhaled toxic fumes and sweat steamed through the gap between my scarf and the hood of my furs, forming a pale halo that surrounded my vision. A lean old man with bottlebrush eyebrows helped me up over the ledge.

I took a few steps and collapsed into the snowbank next to Termite's bow, where the other Vermin were already sitting, stretching out aching joints and massaging the numbness from their limbs. It took me a long time to recover my breath.

Eventually Barn Owl walked up behind me and started massaging my shoulders. "There a reason you look scared, Leech?" she said.

Everyone laughed. Everyone but Cheese Eater, that is, who only sat unlashing the blades from his boots and giving me an eerie, dichromatic stare.

"She.. (gasp)... tried to... (huff)... cut my line... (wheeze)...." I said.

"We know, kid. Everyone saw it. Mongoose was an old friend, but I can't say I'm surprised that raggedy bitch decided to turn tail on us. Her whole family was taken by the Blight. She didn't have much to live for. Always thought that meant she'd live for the cause, but I guess I was wrong."

I laid in the snow with my eyes closed. "She... (huff)... said... (puff)... the Crippled King... sent her (wheeze)."

Barn Owl titled one eye at me. "Maybe he did, maybe he didn't. But you should forget it. For now, anyway. We won't know who-did-the-what-now until we get back to the Burrow, and we have a mission to finish. You owe Termite a drink."

"No, he doesn't," the old man said, already crouching to re-attach the ropes for the climb down. His voice was soft, but gruff, deeply accented with a slow, meditative drawl.

Barn Owl chuckled. "Mmm-hmm. Keeping a special eye on him, were you? I suppose you would."

Termite finished what he was doing and rose, walking over to us to stand in our glimmering circle of torchlight. He was bald, with a long, skinny face covered in scars that reminded me of the ancient dolomite front of the oldest churches in City, and a braided, forked beard speckled with streaks of black and gray poking out from inside his hood. "Yes, I was. Had to see it for myself. But he's Vojciek's boy, true as the Wanderer's wisdom."

"I can't believe Auntie would just turn tail like that," Bunny said.

"You can ask her to regale you with her grievances on the way down," Barn Owl said. She cracked her back and yawned into her fist. "C'mon, Vermin. We've still got a whole shit load of ice to cross, and it ain't getting any warmer. Leech, you going to thank this kind gentleman for saving your ass?"

Termite helped me to my feet. It was a little easier to talk now that the cold air had chased the fire from my lungs, but not much. "Sorry, sir. Didn't mean to be rude. Just having a little trouble breathing. Thank you. That was one hell of a shot," I said.

The old man examined me, the white bristles of his eyebrows becoming a single, downturned line. "I bore no great love for my twin brother, but blood is blood, even in this abominable form you've taken. I'll accept no thanks, and no damned apologies. Pay it on, and help your own brothers and sisters when the time comes. Our father taught us that sacrifice is a virtue, though I didn't know what that meant until I was already gray."

Termite clapped me on the shoulder. His grip belied a monstrous strength far greater than his diminutive frame suggested. "If there's any part of you in there that's still my nephew, I'll speak to him, now. Your father loved you, and he watches over you still, no matter what the faithless old fool believed about our savior and the path we all must take up the Spiral, or didn't. You were a troubled boy, Len, but I hope that wherever you've gone, you've found peace. That's all I wish to say."

Barn Owl cleared her throat. "How's the lake looking, Unc?"

Termite's hand fell from my shoulder with a final squeeze. "Frozen solid. Checked your path thrice for soft spots hidden by the snow. You should be good to cross," the old man said.

"And the facility?"

Termite stroked the twin prongs of his beard, blowing a thoughtful sigh. "I kept my distance. Didn't get closer than the Graveyard of Trains. It's heavily guarded. The scouts underestimated."

"You going to be all right getting back?" Barn Owl said.

The old man spat off the cliff edge.

"I'll take that as a yes," Barn Owl said. "Okay. You heard the man, Vermin. Time to get where we're going. There's enough Frosties for everyone. Blades out. And if any one of you makes a single, goddamned peep, I will make you rue the day you joined."

THE NIGHT COUNTRY

A half-hour march through waist-high snow and bitter wind led us to the frozen shore of Lake Bagra. The giant, black mirror of the lake stretched in an even plane nearly to the foot of the mountain, broken only by scattered islands of bare granite rising through the ice like the scalps of giant, stone heads. The lights of our destination glittered far out beneath that veiling darkness.

Barn Owl warned us not to follow the lights, as theirs was a false path that might lead us onto ice too thin to hold our weight. Instead, she used her pathfinding mirror to plot the trail of invisible dust the scouts had left for us.

The way across the lake was winding and treacherous. Barn Owl and Gator both killed their torches, leaving only the scarce traces of the facility's distant floodlights for us to see by. We each kept one hand on the shoulder of the Vermin in front of us. Even with that small security, my heart slammed into the inside of my chest the entire way.

We're completely exposed. The worst danger here isn't the ice. It's having nowhere to run. No wonder the Vermin wanted to wait for a good omen before attacking this place.

Yet despite my apprehension at being so out in the open, that fear didn't come to fruition. The worst thing that happened was Bunny Rabbit losing her feet, causing a ripple of hushed laughter to erupt through the line.

"I thought archers were supposed to be nimble," Squirrel whispered.

"Really? I always thought that was a myth. You seen this one try to string a bow? It's about as graceful as watching a glowspider fuck a mushroom," Vole said.

"Both of you can grow mold," Bunny said, struggling to get her feet back. She slid again, but this time Cheese Eater caught her and helped her up. Another giggle spread through the group. Bunny went for her dagger.

"Save it," Cheese Eater told her, placing a gentle hand over the scabbard. "We get over that ridge, and you can cut up all the icky bastards you want."

Bunny spat in Squirrel and Vole's direction. "Is that supposed to be a joke? These cave-divers aren't worth any more of my time. I'll probably kill twenty Frosties before they even get one, between the two of them."

Barn Owl's voice hissed back at us across the ice. "Shut the hell up back there. Not another word."

No one spoke until we reached the opposite shore, where a long, black beach sloped steadily up to a wall of abandoned train cars lying half-buried in the ice. The trains formed a kind of labyrinth. Some were connected, while others weren't, making it difficult to tell if we were progressing forward or just moving in circles. We would've easily gotten lost if not for Barn Owl and her magic mirror.

Once we reached the perimeter, we crouched inside one of the ancient, ruined cars for a final huddle. There was a clear view of the facility from the car's rusted-out side windows. Barn Owl gestured for us to be silent, and we waited about ten minutes while she surveyed the objective.

The facility itself was small, only a few clusters of buildings all orbiting around a much larger main one, but the outer yard was gigantic, surrounded by a nasty razor wire fence full of squat watchtowers all pouring their floodlights down onto an icy common that ran for miles. The satellite buildings, which I guessed were prisoner barracks, looked brand-new, their brick walls and tiny jailhouse windows all crisp and shuttered. One building appeared to still be under construction.

The main hall was a single, behemoth four-story tower with two adjoining wings, both several centuries newer than the core. The tower itself wasn't constructed of bricks, but of huge blocks of ancient, blue stone. There was ornate statuary decorating its crenellated abutments. It had large, panoramic windows, and the first floor was built straight into the cliff face. I suspected that its bowels ran deep under the mountain.

It looks like some billionaire's Hollywood mansion, I thought. *No, more like a rich private hospital. Or a school.*

Barn Owl's voice stirred the silence of the rusted train car. "Well, folks. We ain't getting over or under it. The only way in is to go through. I don't like it any more than you do. Intel says the back gate should be right over there." I looked to where she was pointing at a pair of twin watchtowers guarded by a group of Snowmen shivering in the light of a single lamp.

"How many in the towers?" Cheese Eater said.

"Who knows? I'm not worried as long as we stay clear of those floodlights. The real problem is going to be the Lice. But all I see on that yard is Frosties, which tells me the Lice are sleeping, and won't come out to play unless there's an alarm. Intel couldn't spot them directly, either. Only their tracks."

"Maybe your intel was wrong," Gator said.

"My intel is never wrong, asshole."

"They must have good archers in those towers," Bunny Rabbit said.

"Then you'll just have to be better, won't you?" Barn Owl said.

Bunny chewed her lip and nodded.

"What you see is what you get, people. The guard is heavy enough for no one to get out, and to keep anyone brash or imprecise from getting in. But we ain't brash or imprecise, are we, Vermin?"

"Sir, no sir," the Vermin said.

"Damn right. We're the goddamned razor blades of God."

"You think there's any possibility it's a trap?" I said.

"Sure I do," Barn Owl said. "Everything we do is walking into traps, Leech. Or did you forget who we are?"

"Oh. I see. No, sir, I didn't," I said.

"Good. How's that arm, Princess?"

Zaea was kneeling under the red ruin of the car window, vigorously massaging some hidden pain in her forearm. "It hurts a little. I think it's reacting to my anxiety about passing next to those towers. I'll get it under control."

"You better turn *I'll get* into *I've got,* five seconds ago. Can I still trust you to use that weapon without dismantling any members of this team?" Barn Owl said.

"I can handle it."

"You can handle it, *sir.*"

"I can, sir."

"Awfully humble for a princess, ain't she, Vermin? Where the hell did you say you're from, again?" Barn Owl said.

"I'm not a princess here, sir," Zaea said.

"Good. Any thinking you are, and that your life is more valuable than any of ours, is going to get us, or you killed. So we ain't gonna encourage that type of thinking in this unit. From now on, you're Little Mouse. And you're gonna be silent as a little mouse out there, aren't you, Zaea?"

"Yes, sir," Zaea said.

How come she gets a good nickname, and I got stuck with Leech?

Barn Owl made a final survey of the compound, tracing an invisible path through the back gate and across the yard to the nearest cluster of prisoner barracks with an outstretched finger. "We make our approach there. That way Bunny has plenty of time to take out those four Frosties at the gate. How close do you need to be?"

"Twenty meters," Bunny Rabbit said.

"Can you kill two at thirty?"

"Yep. Yep," Bunny said.

"Then I'll get one with my spear, and Vole will take the other one. Little Mouse could use the ghost, but I don't think that's a good idea. We don't want to destroy anything big enough to wake up the Lice before we know exactly where they are. So keep it sheathed until my signal, Mouse. That's an order."

"Yes, sir," Zaea said.

"Once we're in, we'll split into two groups. I'll take Gator and the newbies underground. Bunny, Cheese, Squirrel, and Vole, you guys work on clearing those barracks. I count twelve buildings, but intel says less than half of them are occupied. Maybe none are. That report was a week old. They might've moved everyone into the main facility for all we know. When you find our people, move directly to extraction. Get as many of them as far away from this place as you can. If you make it all the way home, wonderful. If not, we'll rendezvous at the foot of the icefall. If those buildings are empty, you come find us in the main hall immediately. All of that clear?" Barn Owl said.

"Yes, sir," the Vermin answered.

"Good. Run fast, and stay low. The yard has been salted, so there's no snow, but there could still be patches of black ice, and nothing will fuck up this mission faster than if one of you slips and pulls a Bunny Rabbit."

The Vermin chuckled. Even Bunny was forced to smile.

"One more thing before we go. Even if you don't believe, I want to see everyone take the hands of the Vermin next to you and say a prayer. I'd better see those goddamned heads bowed, people, and you'd better bow them low."

We did.

Barn Owl prayed: "Lord, Son of the Spiral and Sower of Seeds, give us strength so that we might do your good work. We ascend the Spiral by your grace alone. Move us now, so that we may be your flame, for you are the ember, the light, and the sun that will return. All together now, everyone. We are the fire."

"We are the fire," the Vermin reprised.

V

Far below in the valley green
An army camped by rushing stream
Standards limp in the early mist
The soldiers sav'ring sleep's last kiss.

Hidden in thick pines high above
The Good Knight flicked a battered glove,
His hussars[3] poured down 'pon the glen
Their winged song a fell siren.

For weeks he'd watched the birds of prey
That haunted the highest, crook'd ways,
Observed their predatory make
God's own terror in avian shape.

The whore, Ola designed the wings
Of countless faggots, feathers, strings,
She'd worn a costume once onstage
When the late Queen Ania she had played.

The king's men died still in their tents
With covered ears and bowels spent.
By sunrise, lo, how they had lent!
Their armor cleaned, their standards rent.

A new force rose in that red haze
Ten thousand ghostly royal shades,
Dead men marched, false banners raised,
To meet the king in three short days.

[3]*Winged knights who fought on horseback. Their wings were constructed of wood frames holding the feathers of hawks or ospreys, and would create a terrifying, high-pitched shriek.*

THE FACILITY

WE RAN at a low crouch across the no man's land that hemmed the outer darkness of the compound, eight scampering Vermin clothed in shadow and snow. The four guards standing watch astride the gate didn't hear us until Bunny had already let her arrows fly. The shafts sprouted between the leather stitches of their eye sockets, their cries of agony caught sputtering in their throats.

Vole took another Snowman down with a throwing axe at twenty paces. It whistled through the air and sunk into the creature's belly with a raw, meaty smack. The Snowman doubled over, his groan cut short by a second axe growing from the bridge of his nose. Barn Owl took care of the fourth, chucking her Wyvernwood spear through his stomach and pinning the creature to the permafrost, where it thrashed, croaked, and died.

We halted under the north gate tower, kneeling in the snow to keep out of view of the sentries prowling the walls of the compound. Even from this distance, I could see the Snowmen up on the battlements still had their eyes. They were alphas, and the bone arrows they carried by the dozens in leather quivers on their hips were likely as accurate as Bunny's.

Cheese Eater tested the monstrous, iron slab of the gate for a weak point, but was interrupted by an arrow thumping into the snow between his feet. Before the sniper could shoot again or raise the alarm, Bunny soundlessly shot him out of the gate tower. She pulled the arrow from between Cheese Eater's feet, examined it, and stuck it in her own quiver with a shrug. Cheese Eater went back to checking the gate.

The gate was solid iron through and through. We weren't going to chop it down or open it from the outside. Squirrel took Vole's leather whip and tied a four-pronged metal hook to the end, creating a makeshift grappling hook. He wrapped the hook part in cloth to dampen the noise of impact before tossing it up into the gate tower and scrambling up to disappear into the dark, slatted window above. The clash of steel and the muffled sounds of a fight drifted down. A few seconds later, a Snowman - who I guessed had been sleeping at his watch - flew out of the window, fell two stories, and impaled himself on Vole's awaiting spear.

A lock clicked open on the other side of the gate, and the giant, iron slab swung inward.

The crack Squirrel opened was barely large enough for each of us to squeeze through. I saw why once I'd made it to the other side. The gate had to be opened by hand, either pushed or pulled to the side you wanted it to open, and was heavy enough to require the strength of several men to move. I should've noticed how strong Squirrel was down in the tunnels, when he'd pulled his own bodyweight up a naked cliff face with no equipment and a parkourist's ease. The guy was a head shorter than I was, but pound for pound, he was practically superhuman.

We knelt in the shadows of the gate and waited for Barn Owl's signal. It was a clear shot to the prisoner's barracks, but we'd have to time it correctly if we were going to avoid the floodlights. Their paths sliced wandering half-moons from the dark stretches of rock and ice. Snowmen carrying glowmoss torches patrolled the perimeter walls with slow, clockwork gaits. I still couldn't see any Lice, but I knew how fast those things could move across open ground.

Barn Owl gave a wave and we broke cover. The cluster of buildings was farther than it looked, but before I knew it, I was diving behind the stairs of the nearest barracks. A guard came around the corner walking with that careful, suspicious prowl that is the trademark of a clueless henchman who's about to get dropped. Cheese Eater did the honors, smacking the creature's head off with his sword and sending a rain of hissing blood to freeze on the cracked, flinty soil.

We waited under the stairs until Barn Owl was sure no other patrols were coming, then split into two groups. Cheese Eater, Bunny, Squirrel, and Vole set about trying to find a way into the barracks. Barn Owl, Gator, Zaea, and I headed straight for the main hall, nestled in its midnight nook at the base of Mount Gezel.

The main doors of the tower were unguarded. A large glowmoss lamp in an archaic glass casket brightened automatically as we approached. Barn Owl waved it off, but not before I saw the inscription carved into the ornate stone archway above the door.

The building's name was written in the same, pseudo-Cyrillic script I'd seen in the Royal Crypts and everywhere else in the Night City, which I knew now was called Old Ithic, the ancient common tongue of this world.

The name above the door read *Ganheim Military Academy*. Beneath it, in smaller script, there was an oxidized bronze plaque bearing the warning: *Access restricted. The punishment for trespassing is death. Imperial Army of Yesaeda.*

A queasy sensation drifted up from my stomach, to my neck, ears, and fingertips. *Ganheim... where have I heard that name before? Wasn't that the name of Zaea's school?* I turned to face her, and the hollow look in her eyes told me everything I needed to know.

Her legs wilted and I lunged to catch her, but she held out a hand and shook her head.

"I'm fine," Zaea said.

"The hell's the matter?" Barn Owl hissed. "Get your cover, you two. Now!"

Zaea pulled her eyes away from the inscription and we both slid into the protective shadows under the monstrous archway of the door. The stone was black and pitted like petrified wood, all covered with thousands of tiny facets that caught the light like a miniature manifold sky.

Barn Owl tested the door with her fist. "Locked," she said, unsurprised.

The door was perfectly smooth, not made of wood or stone, but carved from a single, giant slab of some translucent, blood-red metal. *Not metal*, I realized. *Amber.* I didn't see a latch.

"I can open it," Zaea said. She gave a pained little gasp and clutched her forearm until the agony passed.

Barn Owl scratched under her cowl. "Do your magic."

Zaea left the shadows of the archway, trailing her fingers along the smooth surface of the door. She placed her palm on the center and closed her eyes. There was a sound like distant glass breaking, so soft I second-guessed if I'd heard it at all, but the accompanying shiver of the air and the door swinging suddenly inward confirmed that it hadn't been my imagination. The ghost's slim, fuliginous blade slithered back into Zaea's palm.

Without a word, she stepped inside.

"Wait!" Barn Owl said, but Zaea was already gone. "Shit. Who the hell she think she is, walking in like she owns the place? Don't you dare follow her in there, Leech, or I will court-martial your ass. Goddamn. I knew bringing that uppity bitch was a bad idea..."

"I say she's confident about what she wants. Walks with purpose, like she knows where she's going," Gator said.

"Yeah, you could learn a thing or two from her," Barn Owl said. "Goddammit. This is horseshit. Gator, you get our perimeter on lock. Make sure that stupid idiot didn't set off any silent alarms. Leech, I changed my mind. Go find her. Mouse is now your personal responsibility. You'd better get this under control fast, or we are all dead. You understand?"

"Yes, sir," I said.

"Then get your ass in there."

BENEATH THE MASK

THE WOMAN on the operating table moaned, drawing his eyes from the pages of the Glass Book. It was normal for those undergoing Transformation – or those aiding the process of new research so that others could be Transformed, like this Brave One - to get fussy and cry out in their dreams, but this was different. It wasn't the fear in her moan that alarmed him, but something else.

He set the book down on the chair and rose to her, checking her vital signs and the placement of the pins keeping her open. She was still semi-conscious, held in that otherworld between dreams and fully-formed thoughts that Hyro knew so well. From the readouts, it looked as though the woman had had a nightmare. Not uncommon for his patients, no. There was a characteristic sheen of cool sweat on her forehead. Her lips trembled, opening and shutting in unheard, indecipherable prayer.

What worried Hyro wasn't the fact his patient had an upsetting dream, but why. Under this particular cocktail of anesthetics, she should have been all but immune to stimuli from the outside world. But stimuli from the Spiral...

Someone could contact her that way, yes. Or if she was sensitive enough, and slipped into the proper dream-state, as the drugs no doubt were capable of creating, she could sense their presence.

But why not him? He was a Blotling. One of the first. One of the oldest sentient beings to ascend and travel the Great Spiral at will. His strength in the Blot had grown over the centuries to such proportions that he and the Little Lord Master's small, tribal people back on Home would have called him a god. They had low standards for that word, yes, as he once did himself. That was plain to see from the other side of it. But he should have felt the unbalancing long before it touched the woman's dreams.

One of the first talents Hyro-called-Ratkeeper had learned was being able to sense others like him. Another Blotling, one who had mastered this art and path; or perhaps a Visitor, one with raw ability but no idea of how to control it; even just one of the more dangerous tools leftover from the Twilight Age that flirted with harnessing this immense power; Hyro should have felt it.

But he hadn't?

Was his grasp on the Blot weakening, as the mask's grip was weakening on him?

How could that be possible? Hyro was the strongest he'd ever been. His skill was almost parallel with the Little Lord Master's. Maybe even surpassed it.

No. Such thoughts were...

The woman moaned again, louder this time, and twitched in the throes of another nightmare. He felt it too, this time.

The Visitor was here, inside Ganheim. He had a ghost with him. No. One of his party did. The girl, yes, the Special Brave One who had run.

Someone had been shielding them from him, but Hyro couldn't tell if that concealment had been done from within their party, or from a distance. It made no difference now. They were too close for such amateur's tricks to work. And he had little time to waste.

He had to put the book away, yes. That was the most important thing. There was time for fighting, time for killing and dying, a thousand little deaths if he must, but without the book all of it was pointless, just another meaningless spinning.

Whether the rebels or the Lord Master found it in the end, Hyro's only hope of waking up from the dream was to finish the Glass Book. Perhaps he wouldn't remember all of it, or any of it, but the secrets it contained might finally provide the impetus for him to...

For him to...

A sound, somewhere else in the facility. A door opening, then closing, too soft for human ears to detect. But Hyro felt the wrongness of it, could almost see the trespassers through the dream-weaving sight of the mask. They were close. Too close. He had to act.

The machines would keep his patient alive long enough for him to spare a few minutes away.

He couldn't bring the book with him in Slow Time, no. It was too delicate. He had to walk like a true analog, the way his old self had in the dreams of dreams of his memories that came to him through the Blot. Walking was a cumbersome thing, but at least this old fortress had many secret ways, nooks and crannies and artfully hidden passages that led anywhere one needed to go without being seen.

He made for the Archives.

A memory bubbled up to him through the Blot while he was en route. One of the earliest, from when he'd been a child back on Home.

In the memory, he was reading a book by candlelight, a book much like the one his present self was carrying, only thicker and bound in deer leather rather than stained glass.

Even as a boy of ten or maybe eleven years old, he knew this book was sacred... and that it was forbidden. It had no title, only the simple image of a Spiral on its cover.

The Mainland People, who wanted the True People of the island where Hyro and the Little Lord Master had seeded from to change their religion - a movement which was quite unpopular with the True People, and which Hyro's own adoptive parents violently protested - they called this book *The Patrios*. But that was an awfully big word for Hyro, even at ten, so he simply called it the Spiral Book.

It spoke of a Great Spiral, upon which the world, and all other worlds which had ever been or would ever be spun in tandem, a Spiral made of a multitude of stories. For what was matter but the crucible of life, and what was life but the crucible of stories? It spoke of great men and fathers and grandfathers, of strength and bravery and courage and war, all subjects which the Mothers of Home found to be intolerable, the filth of the Mainland not meant to infect their precious, pure island of True People.

But Hyro loved the stories. Even as a child, they gave him something much deeper than the kind of joy or comfort or permissible sorrow other stories, even religious ones, seemed limited to.

The stories of the Spiral Book gave him meaning. Purpose. What the Spiral Book called "the gravity of the soul." He only read it by candlelight, in the darkest corners of the night, when he could build a blanket fort next to his bed and hide himself from the world.

He kept the book stashed on the highest eaves of his room, where his mother couldn't see, let alone reach. If his mother found it, she'd beat him. If his father found it, Hyro would be dead, a sacrifice to the Old Mothers, who recoiled from the spilling of blood, but somehow still demanded it for certain transgressions.

Hyro was abnormally tall even as a boy, already over two meters by his tenth birthday, with long, dangly limbs and huge feet and a veritable carpet of coarse black body hair that looked strange on his midnight-colored skin. His appearance made him self-conscious, but without it, he never would have learned how to fight and defend himself from the crueler, smoother, and lighter-skinned children of Home.

Those fights had lasted years. Some had never truly ended.

In the memory, his mother's footsteps echoed down the hall. She'd heard him moving about. Quick as he could, Hyro hid the Spiral Book once more on its high eave and raced back to his bed, where he pretended to be sleeping. A crack of light slipped in through the open door, stayed for a moment, then went.

The memory faded.

Deep in the bowels of the facility at Ganheim, the Ratkeeper set to hiding a much different, rarer, and perhaps even more powerful book. It felt remarkably like the first time.

GANHEIM

METATRON'S HANDLE rattled in my grip as I followed Zaea through the amber door into the bowels of the tower. The place looked as dead as anywhere else in the Night City, the branching hallways leading to the east and west wings all empty mouths of shadow yawning wide as I passed by. There was dust everywhere, covering the furniture, the lights, and the checkered flagstone tiles of the floor in a thick cloak of pale ash.

I found Zaea less than a hundred paces from the front door, standing in a large ballroom at the foot of a grand, teardrop-shaped staircase that wound upward to the second floor. Her clenched fists shook violently with the sudden remembrance of memories long forgotten.

Did she used to call this place home? I wondered. *It can't just be a coincidence. I can't imagine what she's feeling right now. What if this was my home city, and I was just now seeing it for the first time? What if it was me, walking through the long-dead ruins of San Francisco... or... or Arcata?*

Zaea's eyes never left the giant teardrop of the stairs as she said to me over her shoulder: "Don't worry, Daniel. We're safe, for now. They're all on floors B3 to B6. They can't hear us up here, but we should be careful. This entire place is monitored, and the systems are still running."

"Zaea, was this your school?" I said.

Zaea rubbed at her temples. She shook her head. "No. I went to school at New Ganheim, in Neen. This is the old Ganheim. It hasn't been used as an academy for over a hundred years. But I've been here before."

"When?"

"I don't know. I don't know anything. I'm so confused. I'm so... oh god, this hurts."

"What hurts? Is it your arm?"

"Everywhere. Everywhere hurts," Zaea said.

"Because of the ghost?" I said.

Tears slid down the frost-flushed balls of her cheeks. Zaea squeezed her eyes shut and hastily wiped them dry. "I don't know. I don't..."

Barn Owl put her arm around my shoulder. "Hi." I jumped, drawing snickers from Gator and even a reluctant one from Zaea. I hadn't heard the two of them approach.

Barn Owl looked at me like I was the most hopeless greenboots she had ever brought into the field. "Battle senses, Leech. Work on 'em."

"Really, sir? Because I don't see much of a battle going on," I said, trying to recover some of the face I'd lost.

Barn Owl crouched to examine the staircase. "That's what I'm worried about." She ran her fingers through the fragile skin of dust that covered the stairs, banisters, and everything, then paused and retracted her hand when reason got the better of her.

"Anyway, the perimeter's clear. I'm guessing neither of you found anything, either. No guards. No alarms. Not even a pair of goddamned footprints. This is supposed to be a top-secret prison camp. Seems to me like intel was wrong, and they ain't even using this place to store their dirty laundry anymore.

"Trouble is, we know they brought our people here, at least three hundred over the last year, if not more. The fence is still guarded enough that some uncritical asshole might look at it and think whoever's in charge of this place simply let his guard down. But that ain't us. I'm inclined to think you were right about what you said earlier, Leech."

"My intel's never wrong," Gator said under his breath. Barn Owl ignored him.

"You think this is a trap," I said.

Barn Owl's eyes narrowed. "Honey, I know this is a trap. The question is when it's gonna spring, and who's gonna spring it. As long as I can rely on you and Miss Mouse here when it does, I'm not worried."

"What is the name of this planet?" Zaea said, her eyes finally parting from where they'd been fixed for the last five minutes, at the top of the stairs.

Barn Owl cleared her throat. "Why you ask? We got all sorts of names for it. You already know the Night Country. There's also the Iceberg, the Ice Cube, the Ice, the Big Freeze, sometimes just the Tundra, or the Cold-As-Fuck. The name our ancestors called it was *Yesaeda*. It means..."

"I know what it means. *Yesaeda* means *Paradise* in old Ithic, which this world was before the True Night," Zaea said.

Barn Owl unslung her spear, rolling it cautiously through her hands. I didn't think she would attack Zaea, but the look in the tall woman's eyes made me nervous. "Where did you say you were from, again?" Barn Owl said.

Zaea's voice was almost too quiet to hear. "I've been here before. Inside this building. I know it like the back of my hand." Her voice wavered. "How did this happen? I don't remember any of it. That floating city. These monsters you call the Snowmen. Why?"

"This same building, huh?" Barn Owl said. Her gloved fingers closed tighter around the shaft of her spear.

She thinks Zaea is a spy, I realized. A bead of cold perspiration slid down my forehead.

Zaea gazed at Barn Owl's spear, then at the taller woman's eyes, then at Gator and me. "Yes. I lived here, in the west wing. Did a medical survey on level B4. It must've been a long time ago. It looked... different."

We all fell into an uncomfortable silence as we tried to puzzle out the paradox of Zaea's words. I knew she wasn't lying. The only conclusion I could draw was that whatever had brought her here not only acted across vast distances of space, but of time, too.

Maybe the Night Country isn't a different world for her at all, I thought. *It is her world, only in the future. Or rather, in her future.*

The sound of a door opening echoed from somewhere in the building. In an instant, Barn Owl's spear was poised over her shoulder, ready to throw. Gator and I both drew our swords, too.

Zaea's features were gripped by an eerie calm. "It's automated," she said. "That blast door you heard opening leads to the stairs that go to the basement. We always took the lift, because we usually had specimens to move, but the lift seems to be out of commission."

Zaea pointed toward the back of the ballroom, behind the teardrop staircase. Barn Owl clicked her tongue at me to go look. I raised my sword next to my right ear so I could easily thrust it through anything that jumped out at me, and went. I found the elevator where Zaea indicated I would, in the deeper shadows behind the stairs. The doors were gone, and the elevator shaft had been filled in with several tons of rubble.

"She's right," I reported back. "Elevator's filled. We can't go down that way."

Barn Owl gave me an affirmative nod, then said to Zaea, "How did you do that?" She made no attempt to mask her suspicion this time.

Zaea shrugged. "I used the facility's Link. Every resident is given a private access node in their biosphere the day they're admitted to the program. Or, they used to be given one... obviously, not anymore. I simply logged in with my student ID number. As I said before, the old systems are still running."

Barn Owl gesticulated a slow, silent clap, then held out her hand and said, "Lead the way."

We moved through the belly of the tower with Zaea taking point, our weapons drawn, but relaxed. There was no one in the building, at least the part that was above ground. The place was much larger than it appeared from the outside, full of cavernous, twisting hallways that anyone unfamiliar with the floor plan would've easily gotten lost in, but Zaea knew the way, and soon the four of us stood gathered around the black, empty vessel of the basement stairs awaiting Barn Owl's command.

"Mouse is the only one of us who knows what's down there. I'll take point. Mouse, you follow me, and then Leech. Gator you take rear guard."

Gator's unintelligible complaints resounded softly behind me for the whole descent. Zaea stopped us at the landing of the first basement level to peer through the barred porthole in the stairwell door. She shook her head for us to keep moving. "This used to be the armory. Looks like they're using it for cold storage."

"Storage of what?" Barn Owl said. Then she sniffed the air and said, hanging her head in solemn rage, "Oh. Goddammit."

The sweet, biting smell of rot hit me, too, and I understood. *This is where they keep the corpses. The ground is too hard to bury them. They probably burn them, which means they either have a set day of the month (or... the week?), when they burn them all at once.*

Gator made the sign of the Wanderer. "Glory be to the heroes..."

"May their bravery carry them up the Spiral," Barn Owl said softly. "C'mon. Let's go."

Zaea stopped again at the landing of the third basement level, where harsh, flickering light fell in striped shadows through a barred iron door. Zaea stood on her tiptoes to get a glimpse, careful to lean into the light so she wouldn't be seen. "Have a look," she said, popping down.

Barn Owl went first, pressing a stealthy eye to the bars. Her scowl deepened. "They're there." She counted quickly in her head. "Thirty-two prisoners. Our people. I only see four cells. Snowmen got 'em packed into cages like animals."

Gator scratched his beard with the edge of his great sword, flinching when he accidentally cut himself. "How many Frosties?"

"One," Barn Owl said. "Leech, you wanna look?"

I took my turn at the window. A single Snowman strolled lazily up and down the hall, tapping the cell doors with his bone club. There were two doors on each side of the hall. Ragged, human arms spilled through the bars, retracting when the Snowman's club swatted at them, then extending again once he'd passed.

They're waiting for food? No. They're hanging their arms out because they have nowhere else to put them.

The kidnapped Burrowers were being held eight to a cell, and the cells weren't much bigger than a small bedroom. Their faces were grimy and sunken, their eyes full of pleading and madness. The smell of unwashed bodies, human waste, and general despair cloyed in the air, as pungent as the rankness of death had been on the floor above.

I stepped away from the window so Gator could take his turn. He scowled. Barn Owl waved for us to continue down the stairs.

"We're not going to free them?" I whispered once we were out of earshot of the guards.

Barn Owl shook her head *no*. "We'll work our way from the bottom up. Easier that way. We're just getting the lay of the ice, kid."

But there was only one other floor to clear. The levels below B4 were flooded, the stairwell filled with dark, stagnant water.

"Must have seeped in from Lake Bagra once regular maintenance stopped being done on the lowest floors," Zaea said. "Levels B5 and B6 used to be the library and fitness center."

We huddled next to the stinking, fetid pool and prepared our weapons while Barn Owl surveyed the hallway beyond the barred door of the landing. When she was done, we each looked. I counted two Snowmen, both alphas; towering, muscle-bound abominations with faces full of black, wide-open eyes, each leaning against the wall opposite the other and cleaning the filth from his teeth with a bone dagger.

This floor didn't appear to be a prison, but some kind of infirmary, with brighter lighting and solid metal doors with thick glass windows rather than bars. The windows were too small and far away to see inside, but a sick feeling gnawed at my gut. I suddenly didn't want to find out what lay beyond those doors.

Barn Owl gave her signal and Zaea cut the lock off the stairwell door. We raised our weapons and charged.

We hit the Snowmen hard. We'd already covered half the ground before they knew we were there. The nearest rushed Gator with his axe. Gator broke the bone weapon with a horizontal slash of his huge Wyvernwood blade, a single stroke that split the creature and its weapon in two. Barn Owl took the other one out with a feint and a thrust, plunging her spear through its bladder. She pinned the dying creature to the floor with her boot as she pried it free, pressure-washing the tiles in a steaming deluge of red.

Four more Snowmen heard the racket and came running, rounding the corner of the hall in time to see their comrades fall.

Barn Owl and Gator barely had time to take defensive stances to deflect the oncoming rain of blows, axes and spear points filling the space between the walls with cacophonous bladesong.

A harsh screech rose above the din. The ghost's black beam split free of Zaea's palm, slamming through the open mouth of the Snowman attacking Barn Owl. The Snowman's snarling face stilled in an instant. Gnashing jaws fell slack, and a sputtering croak rattled in the creature's throat. Its death throes were short and violent. The ghost returned to her palm, and Zaea cried out in painful triumph.

I watched these events unfold in a matter of seconds, my knuckles wound white around Metatron's hilt. Yet even in that short, infinitesimal period, another Snowman had closed the distance toward me and lunged in attack. The razored edge of his axe head flew at my carotid artery, and my instincts fired. I cast Metatron into a high block, then down with the full force of a killing head cut. The Snowman's axe slid off the red tongue of my blade with a shower of sparks, a crimson canyon opening in his skullcap as Wyvernwood met pale, mottled flesh. The dead Snowman crashed into my legs, his feet still moving with the momentum of his charge.

Several thoughts occurred to me in the uncanny valley of that moment. The first was that I hadn't fought as Len. I had used the power of Len's muscles and the tree limb reach of his arm, but the instincts I employed to make that block and cut had been mine. Whatever share of skills and knowledge that remained in Len's body or brain, which I was now able to draw from, I must also have imprinted equally on him, though he would never live again to use them.

As I would learn many times over the millennia to come, you cannot be touched by someone else - in your world or any other - without you also touching them.

The second thought I had was about the laboratory. Whatever sort of "research" was going on here, the Snowmen were only meant to serve as watchdogs, a crude sort of alarm system to warn against intruders. Whoever was running the place and performing the actual experiments, the doctors or scientists or whoever, had to be fully human.

Anyone still on this level would have heard the fracas and had time to escape. The possibility of an endless stream of Snowmen flowing down the stairs within mere minutes, cutting off our only exit out of this place, instantly removed the fog of combat from my mind.

"Get a taste for that smell, kid. There's going to be a lot more of it," Barn Owl said.

Gator wiped the blood from his great sword off on one of the dead Snowmen's fur tunics. "Aye. That was a decent cut, though, cousin. Shouldn't we be impressed? The boy's got a flashy counterstrike. Would've made old Vojciek proud. Red's a good color on him."

"Not now." Barn Owl crept along the wall and peeked into the adjoining corridor. Seeing nothing of interest, her posture eased and she patted Gator on the shoulder. "Here's hoping we didn't just bring the roof down on our heads. We ready to see who's hiding in there? You know we didn't just clear this entire floor."

She motioned to the door with the sign reading *Surgery*. The other door was labeled *Recovery*, but a newer plaque next to the door read *Prion Immunity Research*.

What the hell…? I thought.

"Guess that means I'm taking point," Gator said, heaving the crimson pylon of his greatsword up into a high guard and slamming his heel into the door.

ADAM VINE

THE INFIRMARY

WE RAN into a nimbus of hard white light, ready to cut apart anyone or anything waiting for us. But the ambush never came. My eyes adjusted and a large, brightly-lit basement with ceilings of vaulted, mirror-smooth stone took shape. An array of freestanding stage lights cast looming half-moon shadows in the high arches. Rows upon rows of stone operating tables stood beneath them, riddled with nebulas of old blood the color of dead autumn leaves.

This was the overflow room, which would only have been used once the main infirmary was full. It was now being used for medical storage.

Glass jars holding body parts suspended in some clear fluid I could only guess was brine crowded the shelves lining the walls: hearts, bladders, stomachs, diaphragms, vocal chords, eyes, and brains. Except, they looked *wrong*.

I had never studied anatomy, but I remembered enough high school biology that I could tell these weren't human organs. The eyes were too small; beady, pale little marbles, like the eyes of a wolf. The hearts and bladders were grossly oversized, like those of a cow. The diaphragms and vocal chords were fluted, the stomachs triple-chambered. The brains had about ten to twenty percent less volume than the brain of an adult human, like the brain of a child. The largest vats held specimens of dense, rubbery membrane, all in various stages of growth or decay. I realized with a bubble of rising vomit in my throat that this last, strangely familiar organ was the inner husk of a Snowman.

All of them were. These jars contained the Snowmen's vital organs, or at least the ones that differed significantly from those of human beings. I had known the Snowmen weren't fully human, but witnessing the actual, biological differences infected me with indescribable unease.

There were other objects on the shelves, too; preserved fetuses in various stages of gestation, rabbits, wolves, and a strange, white-haired ape that looked similar to a chimpanzee. There were vials, drums, and kegs of sedatives, cleansers, and preservatives, trays of unused scalpels, speculums, bone saws, and clamps; and spools upon endless spools of surgical thread and medical tape.

"Adaptation," I said to no one in particular.

Zaea raised an eyebrow at me. "What are you talking about?" she said.

"These all show adaptations meant to help an organism survive in an extremely cold climate. The big heart is to pump more blood to the extremities. The three stomachs are to better digest cold, raw meat. The fluted vocal chords are to produce high-pitched sounds for optimal communication during a blizzard. That oversized bag of a bladder is to hold large volumes of superheated urine…"

I shuddered, remembering the Snowman I'd watched cannibalize the frozen body of a child outside the Night City.

Barn Owl had been listening to our conversation from the other side of the room. She came over to join us.

"The Snowmen… they're not some other, alternate species, are they?" I said. "They're not some product of divergent evolution, not some distant, biological cousin of us? They *are* us. Except someone engineered them to be different, so they could survive up on the Surface. Someone *made* them."

"Pretty keen, Leech," Barn Owl said. She didn't sound impressed at all, only distant, and a little sad.

Zaea folded her arms and shivered.

An anguished moan echoed from behind the door to the infirmary proper. It was human.

Barn Owl, Gator, Zaea and I exchanged a round of nervous glances, then Barn Owl turned and marched toward the source of the noise. The rest of us followed her through the swinging double doors of the infirmary proper.

I can't say I was excited to see what we all knew awaited us beyond those doors, but the reality was a thousand times worse than what I had imagined.

Gator whined.

Barn Owl stuttered, "No, no, no, no…"

Zaea hid her mouth inside the crook of her arm.

I fought back my vomit, so I wouldn't disrespect the still-living, fully vivisected woman lying on the operating table in the center of the infirmary.

THE INFIRMARY

THE SAVAGE GLOW of the spotlights spared the poor woman no secrets, on the outside or in. Her arms and legs were held in place by thick leather straps; the clean, bloodless flaps of skin where her torso had been opened from clavicle to groin carefully secured by long steel pins.

She didn't struggle - not that she could have, if she had wanted to – the woman on the table only lolled her head toward us so she could see who had come in. Her eyes fluttered weakly. The quiet, muttering sounds that came from her lips weren't actual words, but there was a spark of recognition in her gaze. Though heavily sedated, she was aware enough to know we were there.

I admit that I looked away. But in the madness of that moment, as the potential for absolute cruelty that we human beings are truly capable of dawned on me for the first time, I thought that this woman deserved more than my weakness. I faced my fear and opened my eyes.

Some of her parts had been replaced. The new Snowman parts appeared similar to the organs I'd seen in the specimen room, but some were better, more streamlined. They'd been grafted in. The machines that kept her alive gave constant measurements of how the grafts were taking. Some scrolled seemingly infinite strings of symbols that I thought could be some kind of real-time genome mapping.

Testing to see how the new models work, I thought. *They made her into a prototype.*

Barn Owl was the first of us to speak. "Help me get the straps," she told Gator and I. "Gently."

Gator, Barn Owl, and I carefully undid the leather restraints from the woman's wrists and ankles. Once they were off, Barn Owl knelt by the operating table and cleared the greasy, sweaty tendrils of hair from the woman's forehead. Then, she started to pray.

"Dan," Zaea whispered. Her voice was a tiny, high-pitched whine. "I'm scared."

"I don't think we should stay here," I said. "Whoever did this left in a hurry. They're going to come back."

Barn Owl must've heard me, because she rose and said, "I for one ain't going to leave her like this. This is something I gotta do, and I don't give a damn what you people think about it." Barn Owl drew her dagger and slowly placed it on the woman's throat.

"Wait," Zaea said.

Barn Owl paused.

"I... I... It has to be me. Please," Zaea said. Her face was slick with sweat. I had never seen her so worked up before.

Barn Owl nodded and stepped away. Zaea took her place, gently setting her palm on the dying woman's forehead.

There was a hiss and a soft *drip, drip, drip,* beneath the operating table. The woman's gaze slowed, then stilled. Her heart stopped beating in the open cavity of her chest. The machines pumping her blood and lungs began blinking silent alarms as she flat-lined. The woman herself was gone, her suffering ended by the ghost's eternal kiss.

Zaea leaned on the edge of the table and hung her head. Her breath steamed in the stark, sterile light. She grabbed her temples and screamed.

"*GYAAAAAAAAAAAAhhhhhhhhhhhhhhhhhhhhhhh!*"

"Hey, hey! Shut the hell up!" Barn Owl moved to grab Zaea.

Zaea hissed and thrashed, trying to break free of the taller woman's grasp. The ghost fired, its blade carving a dusty line from the ceiling and wall, finally coming to rest in Barn Owl's collarbone. Barn Owl gasped and doubled over.

Zaea's eyes went wide. The ghost evaporated back into her trembling hand. "I'm sorry... oh, god... I'm sorry..." Zaea said.

Barn Owl fell to one knee and clutched her ruined shoulder, breathing the pain out slow. Blood bubbled through her fingers. Gator hastily cut a strip from his tunic and stuffed it over the wound. "Knew... that bitch... was crazy..." Barn Owl said through hard-clenched teeth.

"It's just a scratch. Try not to talk," Gator said.

"Why shouldn't I talk, dumbass? She didn't hit my neck," Barn Owl said. Gator cut more strips from his shirt, and Barn Owl let out a stifled shriek as he tied off the slapdash bandage. "Ow. Wanderer's fucking wisdom. Who taught you how to do first aid?"

"You did, sir," Gator said.

Barn Owl rose. "We need to get outta here. Now. You. Wait." She pointed to Zaea. "Accidents happen. I take full responsibility for letting you in the field without proper training. You'll face some punishment when we get back to the Burrow, most likely corporeal. I'll do what I can to make sure it isn't harsh. But this will be your last mission with the Vermin. You understand?"

Zaea nodded.

Barn Owl stumbled, found her feet, and the four of us left that starched white cloister of death, returning to the tall shadows of the specimen room, where Zaea burst into tears.

"Dan, I don't know why I did that. I can control it... you know I can. I just... I didn't mean to hurt her. It's these memories. Why do I have them? They're not mine. They're not..."

Zaea's plea was cut short by a sound in the hall outside.

The four of us froze. There was someone out there who wasn't a Snowman, who moved slow, whose footsteps were silent, but who did nothing to hide the telltale *clink, clink, clink* of a heavy chain dragging on the floor. They'd heard Zaea's screams. We were done.

THE INFIRMARY

CLINK, CLINK, CLINK.

The sound of the chain came closer, stopped, and a shadow fell through the one-inch gap under the door.

I unsheathed Metatron as slowly and quietly as I could and stepped back into a fighting stance. Gator and Zaea did the same. But Barn Owl shook her head *no*, and signaled for us to hide instead.

I crouched behind one of the stone operating tables and waited. Zaea hid beside me, Barn Owl and Gator on the other side of the room.

I had barely sunk down behind my cold slab of stone when the creak of the door opening penetrated the silence. The light fixtures above the operating tables flickered off and on, overtaken by a much brighter, yellow glow slowly advancing across the floor. The person who had entered the specimen room was carrying some kind of lamp.

Clink, clink, clink.

The newcomer's lamplight threaded between the operating tables, drawing closer and closer with each strike of his chain on the old, gray tiles.

Only Zaea was in my line of sight. Gator and Barn Owl were hiding on the other side of the room, behind tables of their own. Despite the throbbing protestations reverberating like thunder in my heart and stomach, I leaned over a few inches to try to catch a glimpse of our pursuer.

I could only see the vagueness of his shadow silhouetted behind the golden flare of his lamp, but it was enough. He was seven feet tall, and carried a twisted lantern in one hand and a long, spiked chain in the other. His cloak swirled like the ocean on a moonless night, the cloth a color deeper than black. His eyes were invisible behind the pale, broken moon of his mask, carved in the fashion of a spiral. Three slender, bladed hooks like tiny jaws were fixed on the end of his chain that snapped and bit eagerly as they bounced along the floor.

Clink, clink, clink.

Zaea saw him, too. She covered her mouth with both hands, but couldn't stifle the sound of her whimper.

The masked man stopped and gazed in Zaea's direction. Zaea tried to break cover and run. The masked man casually threw his chain, like my dad would've thrown a baseball when we played catch when I was a little kid. Zaea's table disintegrated, solid stone exploding into a rain of dust and shale, and Zaea went down. When the debris settled, she lay prostrate on the floor, a red stain quickly blooming from the side of her skull.

Oh god Jesus that's blood oh please no

I didn't know if it had been rock shrapnel or the chain itself that had struck her, but I didn't have time to find out.

The masked man moved to finish Zaea off. Across the room, Barn Owl yelled, "Hey asshole."

His lamp flickered as he turned and was impaled by Barn Owl's spear. There was a blink and the spear passed through him like air, striking uselessly against the far wall.

Barn Owl didn't miss a beat. "So you really are the Ratkeeper. They say your lamp steals souls. That you turn people into dolls for your master. Well, you ain't getting me, honey. My soul belongs to the Vermin."

Two cruel, red, crescent moons grew from Barn Owl's fists, slashing at the masked man's neck as she leapt. Barn Owl dodged his chain once, twice, three times, but one of its gnashing, bladed mouths caught her on the backswing and she went down.

Gator and I both broke cover and charged. The masked man struck the table Barn Owl had fallen under with a roll of his chain, turning it over on top of her. Her scream was cut short by a mountain of rubble.

He's trying to distract us. Focus. Focus. Oh, crap. Goddamn son of a... Focus. Breathe.

I didn't know if Barn Owl was alive or dead. I raised my sword and advanced toward the masked man. I held Metatron firm, pointing the tip of the blade at my opponent. I stared into the pits of oblivion where his eyes should have been, and slowly bowed. It felt like walking through an earthquake.

The masked man accepted my challenge. He twirled his chain but did not strike. All I could see in the eddying vortex of his robes and the pale glaze of his mask was the tip of #41's *shinai* angled at me as I stepped onto the center of the mat.

I had already lost this fight once, and it cost me everything in the world I had ever loved. I wasn't going to lose it again.

The masked man tapped the tip of my blade with his chain. I checked his thrust and hit him with my own downward cut. But my blade cut air. He reappeared one pace to my left, but I'd seen what he'd done to Barn Owl and pivoted, bringing my sword up in a rising block. His chain rolled off Metatron's edge. I cut diagonal, the last of those three, little moves I had practiced for over a decade, the combination that had only failed me once before, when I was too slow.

But again, I missed. The masked man flickered like a shadow cast by a strobe, reappearing inches outside the path of my blade. I thought I saw him flinch as Metatron's tip sailed past him and down into one of the operating tables, carrying me with it. My blade bit stone and ricocheted, sending a bolt of pain spiraling up my arm.

Before I could raise my sword again, the masked man struck. Time seemed to slow as those razor-sharp jaws floated toward me. There was nothing I could do.

In an instant the chain skewed, missing my face by fractions of an inch. The giant crimson leaf of a Wyvernwood great sword plunged through the masked man's torso. A familiar mustachioed grin appeared over the masked man's shoulder.

"Told ya I'd get the drop on him," Gator said.

Gator moved to withdraw his blade, but couldn't. Inhuman vocal chords hummed deep within the eternal twilight of the masked man's cloak. A nauseous plummeting sensation spilled through my body. The masked man wasn't dead. Wasn't injured. His cloak floated open. Gator's sword hadn't hurt him at all.

Inside his cloak was a void.

In a single, rippling motion, the masked man turned and breathed into Gator's face. Gator froze. *Actually* froze. It happened so fast that if I hadn't been watching, I might've thought someone had replaced the real Gator's body with an identical statue made of frost, all shimmering and blue-white.

Gator's final expression was some incalculable mix of surprise and sadness. But it didn't last. The masked man swung his chain and shattered Gator into dust.

I don't remember much of the next few minutes. I remember the cold flurry that had been my friend only seconds before covering the masked man and I both with a rain of hail. I remember screaming at the top of my lungs and running the masked man through, aiming my sword deep into the center of the spiral in his mask. I remember him raising his lamp into my face and the light flaring just as my blade was about to thrust home, a golden spiral burning beacon-bright in the center of its tarnished, ancient glass.

These memories are vague. When I recall them it is like recalling memories from early childhood. They aren't full images, but the pieces of pieces, the edges all torn and frayed, the centers made murky by time and self-doubt, some elements real and some imagined.

I don't know if I dropped my sword willingly or if I was forced to. I don't know if my legs and arms moved of their own volition or someone else's as I went and scooped up Zaea off the floor. I don't know if I bent my knee on purpose and offered her to him, or if I could simply no longer walk and fell helpless at his feet. I don't know if I called to Barn Owl for help, or cried out Gator's name, or Zaea's, as he took her and hoisted her over his shoulder.

What I do remember vividly was the thought, *He knows. He knows I'm a Visitor. He knows Zaea is, too. And he isn't going to kill us. He came to pick us up so he can take us home.*

In that haze I found a deep happiness. The longer I stared into the light of his lamp, the more it washed away all of my fears, anxieties, and sorrows, until every last drop of darkness within me evaporated and only an unshakeable contentment remained.

A gentle, long-needed splash of California sunshine enveloped me, and a voice called to me from somewhere inside that infinite paradise. I followed her voice into the light, and for the first time in years, I was whole. It was a voice I knew, that my heart had begged a god I no longer believed in to hear every waking second since it had vanished from my life, that sated my tired soul.

"Hey my love," Carly said.

???

"HEY MY LOVE, can we talk about something? I mean something kind of important."

"Sure. What's up?" I said, under-hooking her arms and pulling her in close. I kissed her and then pulled away to brush a curly, whiskey-colored lock of hair behind one ear.

We stood half-dressed in our hotel room in San Francisco amidst a bed riddled with post-sex sheets and a floor covered with clothes exploded from our suitcases. We had to be on the mats in less than an hour. The gym where the tournament was being held was at a local private high school across the street from our hotel, but if we were even a minute late my dad would be furious, and he wasn't a guy you wanted to piss off when he had his *sensei* hat on. The dude had been world champion for a reason.

No. This is wrong. We were in a rush, weren't we? It wasn't like this.

Yes it was. It had to be. We didn't rush. Everything was perfect.

"Babe?" I said.

Carly took a deep breath, cupped the side of my face, and said, "Dan, relax, okay? Nothing's wrong. I just want you to know how much I love you, and that even though you're nervous, you're going to kill it today."

No. This is all wrong. She didn't...

She did. You know she did. She encouraged you.

Carly smiled at me and shrugged into her *gi* top, the patch of our dojo flashing purple on her left lapel. The patch showed the image of a mountain framed by the red ball of a rising sun in a violet sky, the words *North Coast Martial Arts Center* embroidered in white along the fringe. Carly stepped into the ample, black fabric of her *hakama* and pulled them up around her waist, tying the strings at the top to secure the skirt pants in place.

She was so beautiful.

Was? She's standing right in front of you.

"Thanks, babe. I don't know why, but I just feel kind of… off today," I said, putting my own *hakama* on.

Carly finished tying her belt and leaned over to kiss me on the cheek. "Just jitters, love. Everyone gets 'em. Myself included."

"I know, but everyone's gonna be there. You. My parents. Evan. You know he's never been to one of my tournaments before?" I said.

"Dan, don't start this, okay?" Carly said.

"That guy's always got something going on. The fact he came all this way, planned this whole after party thing for me… at a bar! He actually called a bar. I donno. I just feel like I'm gonna choke."

Carly rolled her eyes. "Now you're just being Mr. Negative. Do what my dad says. Empty your mind. Let it go. Picture yourself winning. Victory is ninety-nine percent mental."

What is this? What's going on? Where am I?

You're in your hotel getting ready for the West Coast Invitational Kendo tournament. Get it together, man. If you mess this up, you'll lose your title.

I gave Carly a playful shove. "Ninety-nine percent, huh? That's interesting, Carl. Normal people need things like technique and speed, too. I guess we can't all be superhuman."

"Stop. Oh! I almost forgot." Carly knelt to dig through the smaller pockets of her suitcase.

"I thought we had to be there half an hour early," I said.

"Half an hour early is when we're *supposed* to be there, Daniel."

"Don't worry. We'll get there with plenty of time for you to sit on the bleachers posting on Instagram."

"They won't have bleachers. They put them up. More mat space."

"You checked?" I said.

"Your dad said they hurt his back."

Of course she knows that. That thoughtfulness is why I love her.

No, this isn't happening. Why do I feel like I've already been here, said these things, stood contemplating that same godawful geometrically patterned carpet and felt like I'd become unstuck in time?

It's just a bit of déjà vu. Everyone gets it. Chalk it up to nerves, like Carly said.

"Has anyone ever told you you're an overachiever?" I said, pulling Carly in close to kiss her on the lips.

She turned away and scrunched her lips like my kiss was full of plague. "You are *literally* the worst. Here." She handed me a small, plain white cardboard jewelry box.

"You used literally, even though we both know how much you hate it when people use that word improperly. So, I guess this must be serious," I said.

Carly folded her arms impatiently. "Open it."

Inside the box was a tiny arrowhead carved from volcanic glass with a silver chain attached to the non-business end so it could be worn around the neck. "Holy shit, Car. Is this obsidian?" I said, gently taking the necklace out of the box.

"Yup," Carly said. "My dad found it in our yard while he was digging the foundations for the shed, back when I was like, eight years old. He even asked that nice lady who works at the library about it…"

"Dorothy. She gave me that nice illustrated edition of *The Divine Comedy* for high school graduation. I thought that was such a lame gift until I actually read it. Ended up being my favorite poem of all time."

Carly nodded. "Right. Dorothy. Anyway, Dorothy used to be a docent at the Native American Museum, and she said the Native Americans used arrowheads made from obsidian because it has a conchoidal fracture. That means it makes razor sharp edges when it breaks. So it's great when put to good use, but dangerous if left lying around. Sort of like you." She grinned.

"Such a comedian. Are you here all week?" I said.

"Since it's been sitting on our living room bookshelf for, like, ever, I... I mean, *we*... wanted to give it to you."

"So you're saying your dad made this from some obsidian he bought online and hid it in the backyard so you'd think it was a magical Indian arrowhead?" I said.

Carly growled. "Ugh, you are so..."

I pushed her onto the bed and kissed her. "So what?"

No I didn't. I wanted to, but we didn't have time. Right...?

We rolled and kissed and groped each other for a blissfully long moment before she pulled away. "Later, okay? We gotta go. But I promise, we are going to have the best victory sex of your life when we get back," Carly said.

"And what if I lose?" I said.

She tapped a finger on my chest. "Then that big, bruised ego of yours is going to need me to take care of you. Either way, it's a win-win. Now, c'mon. Get the gear. We need to go."

"Yes, ma'am."

The audience at the convention center was a sparse scattering of familiar faces, *senseis* and senior students from schools all over California, most of whom were my dad's friends and many I had trained or competed against before. Kendo is a small community, so the turnout at these things was always relatively low. A hundred people would have been considered a good crowd.

Carly and I found my parents and Evan sitting with the other people from my school on the metal folding chairs lining the mats, stretched, and put on our gear, and then hugged everyone for good luck. I thought we'd have some time to drill before my first match, but I was one of the first names called when the buzzer sounded.

I won my first match with a straight head cut, and then my second with a head cut-block-wrist cut combo. When the final elimination round was revealed, I was paired up against #41, Jaime Jimenez, the dude who had won all kinds of kendo and western fencing tournaments on the East Coast, and who'd been the subject of a feature article on Bullshido.com only last week.

What the hell is a New Yorker doing in our tournament? Did he fly out here just to sandbag?

You know why. He's here to steal your title.

I'd hoped someone else would've eliminated Jaime before the final round, but I should've known that was foolish. Jaime was one of the best kendo players in the country. If I didn't fight him, and win, it would mean losing a title I'd held for the past six years.

Our names were called, and we both bowed and stepped onto the mat, mirrored shadows clad in nightmarish robes and masks of empty, featureless mesh, the bundled tips of our *shinai* angled and ready, drawing closer and closer together as we circled each other, two lost planets falling into each other's gravity.

The buzzer sounded and the match began. The ten or so seconds we spent sizing each other up with tiny, noncommittal jabs at the ends of each other's swords seemed to last hours. Then everything exploded. #41 lunged, flying forward off his toes and throwing a tiny, lightning-fast cut for the top of my wrists.

Two paths unfolded before me in my mind's eye. In the first, I reacted like I had so many times in training, checked his blow and counter-struck with my own thrust to his mask, winning the match and keeping my title. At the trailhead of that other, much darker road, I choked and checked him a fraction of a second too late. He cut me on the wrist and head, and it was his *shinai* that hit home, costing me the match, my title, Carly, my entire world.

I checked his blow and slammed the tip of my *shinai* into his forehead. We collided, both carried by the momentum of our strikes. The ref called the match. I won.

The cheers of my friends, family, and dozens of strangers rising from their seats to give me standing, howling applause rose to a deafening din. They were all screaming my name: Carly, Evan, my parents and fellow students. Their hoots and cheers went on for a long time, even after #41 and I bowed to each other and exited the mat. I watched Jaime as he returned to his corner. He didn't throw down his sword and mask like I did when I lost, didn't do anything but fall into the condoling arms of his fellow students and loved ones.

But I didn't lose. I won. Beat that asshole to the jump, just like she said I would.

No you didn't. That isn't how it went down.

I returned to my own corner and took off my mask to a flurry of handshakes, embraces, and head rubs. Carly jumped on me and covered me with triumphant kisses. Evan wrapped me under one arm and said, "I'm proud of you, man." My mom hugged and kissed me ecstatically. My dad shook my hand and told me he was proud of me, before leading me to the podium, where I was crowned Kendo Champion of the State of California, Adult 18-26 division, for the seventh year in a row.

CORRUPTION

No. This is wrong. I lost. Got hit with a wrist and head cut. He beat me with my own goddamned combination. I. Lost.

An hour later Carly won her first two matches, then lost in the finals. After, we went to celebrate at a dive bar in the Haight called *Teddy's*, courtesy of Evan, who'd booked the place for the competitors and their families until 10PM. Carly even convinced my parents to take shots with us. We lined up next to the bar and drank the caustic, cheap vodka out of a ski with shot glasses glued to it. Nobody could stop talking about how I'd beaten one of the best kendo players in the country by a fraction of a second.

Carly spent maybe ten minutes sitting by herself staring glumly at the bar, but she was always better at thinking herself out of holes than I was. The next time I looked over to where she was sitting, her chin was up and she was splitting a pitcher of margaritas with my mom. The next time after that, they were both laughing so hard Carly slipped and fell off her stool.

It was the best night of my life.

No it wasn't. I tried to have fun, but couldn't, and the more everyone basked in Carly's glow, the drunker and angrier I got. She wasn't the one sulking by herself at the bar. I was. Until Evan told me to cheer up, and then...

We took a taxi back to our hotel, had loud, drunken sex, and fell asleep in each other's arms. We did it twice the next morning after we woke up, too, then showered, packed and ate breakfast with everyone before saying our goodbyes. I wanted to get an early start, because I had something special planned for the drive home, something I'd been thinking about doing for a while, but whether or not I actually would was predicated on us both leaving the tournament victorious.

We stopped at Salmon Creek State Beach on the drive home, just outside of Bodega Bay. It was my favorite place in California. I'd planned on proposing to Carly there ever since we started dating back in high school. I pulled off Highway 1 into the unmarked back alley that led to the parking area, making up some excuse about how I needed to get out and stretch my legs. I didn't have a ring, because Carly had always told me she wanted to wear her great-grandmother's when – never *if* – we got married. I'd also nearly gone broke paying for our hotel room for the tournament, and had less than ten dollars to my name until my next paycheck. But I knew she wouldn't mind. Carly was one of the good ones.

It was a hot summer day, a dichotomy of white clouds and the dark saw-blade of the windblown Pacific rising beyond the amber, ice plant-crested dunes. The smells of salt water and spilled beer from unseen beer bottles left wantonly behind by high school bonfires stung my nostrils, intermingling with the dumb howls of the gulls.

We walked down the beach and found a good place to sit far away from the crowds. My heart was racing faster than when I'd stepped onto the mat with Jaime Jimenez. Bolstered by the confidence of that win, I did what I should've done long before she died.

Kneeling, I said, "I'm going to dip my legs." I took off my shoes, then took Carly's hand. With the other, I touched my pointer finger and thumb together to offer her a ring. "Carl, will you marry me?"

Carly covered her mouth and gasped.

No she didn't. I never proposed to her, because she's dead.

Carly's mouth was hidden behind a steeple of fingers, but the wideness of her eyes gave me her answer. She fell to the sand next to me and tangled me in her arms and lips. She finally pulled away enough to whisper in my ear, "You know I will."

No. She's dead.

CORRUPTION

The car flipped and rolled, headlights flashing in soundless oblivion. The impact buried me in shattered glass. Minutes or years passed before I was able to breathe again. We had landed right side up, but something was wrong. Carly wasn't screaming anymore. Why wasn't she screaming?

My head felt like someone had gone to work on it with a pickaxe. My lungs burned with every breath, and there was a hideous mixture of bile and blood settling in my mouth. I smelled smoke, and thought that meant that I should run, because if the car was on fire it could explode, or suffocate us. *Us. Why isn't she screaming?*

She isn't screaming because she's dead.

Attempting even a simple movement like turning my head to look at the passenger's seat brought on sharp, sudden pains through my entire body. I grunted and gasped. In my haze of confusion I didn't realize how much worse the impact had been on the other side of the car. I'd swerved across the opposite lane to avoid the Ford F-150, then we had rolled...

Carly...

Oh, fuck.

Her body had been turned into a fusion of woman, metal, and glass. What was left of her was slumped over her seatbelt, her head dangling almost to the dashboard, where a sanguine marsh of blood and whiskey-colored hair pooled beneath the shattered spiral her forehead had imprinted on the windshield.

She's dead.

My eyes opened and I saw the masked man rising with Zaea slung over his shoulder in a fireman's carry. His chain was sheathed, but the light of his lamp still held me in its imprisoning trance.

He's going to take her away.

I wanted to reach out and wipe the bloody, fleshy chunks from the whiskey-colored bristles of her hair, but I couldn't move, couldn't speak. Even my thoughts were not my own. I was a slave to the will of that warm, golden light.

I pushed through the agony of raising my arm, unlooped it from the tangled prison of my seat belt and reached over to cup Carly's face. She was warm, but still. No breath rose in the ruined altar of her body. Her lips flagged open in silent, final confession. She didn't respond when I screamed her name. Tears clouded my vision, and the world became opaque and wet. I tried to tuck her soaked, sticky hair behind her ear, but her ears were gone.

I begged God to bring her back, then he didn't, and I threatened to hate him, said that I wished I'd never known him, and that now I never would.

Somewhere in the distance, a siren whined.

"It took you this long to ask?" Carly said, helping me back to my feet. She clutched my face in both hands and kissed me, then gazed into my eyes and smiled. *Thank you God for this moment,* I thought. *Thank you for everything. Thank you for her.*

I brushed the sand from the knees of my pants, took Carly under my arm, and we watched the furious ocean and its guardianship of stalwart clouds for what might've been days. For the first time in my life I knew I didn't have to say, or do, or want anything, because I was happy.

What a perfect day.

Eventually, Carly took my hand and said, "As much as I wish we could stay here forever, I think it's time to go, so we can start the rest of our lives together. We are going to have a ton of planning to do if you still want to have our wedding in a castle in Scotland. Don't you think so, baby? Our first road trip as fiancées... pretty soon, it'll be as Mr. and Mrs. Harper."

I opened my eyes again and strained to keep them open. If I could just move my hand, only an inch, I could reach Zaea's boot. The light flared again, draining my will. Yet the blood on Zaea's hair forced me to keep going. My eyelids felt like they weighed ten thousand pounds.

"Baby?" Carly said, tugging at my hand. She had already started walking back toward the car, but paused when she saw I wasn't coming. "Dan. Is something wrong?"

She's offering me a way out, a way to un-see that bloody hair, to undo the downward spiral of the last two years. She's offering me a new life.

The sirens blared, then cut short, a blue strobe flickering through the mangled, missing windows of the car, turning her blood the color darker than black.

Carly's eyes widened, filling with the ocean's missing shade of blue. "Babe? Come on. I'm worried about you. Talk to me, my love. Please?"

I let her hand fall and walked down to the water, swimming my fingers through the warm, lapping waves. *But the water is never warm at Salmon Creek. It's always freezing, even in summer.*

And then I realized where I was. I was inside the lamp, seeing some kind of hallucination about the life I could've had. Or maybe it was real, and I really was getting a second chance, on the dunes of some other Salmon Creek on some other possible world, where the water was warm, where I'd beaten Jaime Jimenez, where I'd never driven drunk, and where Carly was still alive.

But if that was true, then it meant that there was also a world in which Carly had really died, and that if I got back in that car and drove away to live happily ever after with her, somewhere else, in the world where I was still gazing into the masked man's lamp, I would be condemning Zaea to death, or something much, much worse.

The thought kept me rooted in place. *I'm never going to marry Carly. I lost that road a long time ago. I watched them bury her, didn't I? I stood at the bottom of that hill and watched them put her in the ground, because her family wouldn't let me join them at her grave.*

The girl I loved is gone. But Zaea is still alive.

When I opened my eyes for the third time and gazed upon Zaea's bloodied scalp, the runnels of red dripping down the cheeks that looked so much like Carly's had, I was able to flex the tip of my index finger. The lamp brightened, but its hold on me was weaker. I pushed and pushed, and found I could close a fist.

I raised my hand and reached slowly for Zaea's boot. I thought of the car crash and the way the blood that had wiped off on my fingertips had stained my soul, the years of my life annihilated by a single, thoughtless instant. The masked man looked at me, flaring his lamp to cow me into submission, but I was already there. I grabbed the knife out of Zaea's boot, the same one she'd tried to stab me with when I found her thawing in the Royal Crypts, and thrust the blade through the glazed, pale clay of his mask.

It was a wild, desperate, stab, but Zaea's knife bit home, smashing through that thin disc of fired clay as easily as it would paper. An otherworldly howl split my skull and shattered pottery fell away. Finally I was free. I could move of my own volition.

The no-longer masked man dropped Zaea to the floor, clutching his face in agony. His scream was the sound of worlds splitting, of earthquakes rending continents and black holes swallowing planets into unseen nothings, a wrong chord played in the symphony of existence. I caught a glimpse of his face in that tiny fraction of a second when his hands fell away before he turned and ran. It was nothing but a shadow floating in an endless abyss, a dark, shapeless blot feeding some far deeper darkness.

CORRUPTION

Then he was gone, leaving only a horrified echo of screams quickly fading into the bowels of the facility.

In that moment I realized that the Ratkeeper hadn't always been a monster. He was a slave, too. He'd probably enslaved dozens, if not hundreds of innocent people using the hypnotic power of his lamp, but it wasn't by any choice of his own. Someone else had done it to him first, and the one who made him, too, a vicious cycle carried down through the ages. The mask had been his shackle. Without it he was free to resist the compulsion. He was free to say no.

The shrill notes of utter terror and revulsion in his wailing told me that the one called Ratkeeper wouldn't be returning to serve the Crippled King any time soon. Perhaps, I hoped, he would never go back to his master, but abuse has a funny way of convincing us we can't function without it.

Regardless of where he went or what would become of him, I doubted I would ever see the Ratkeeper again.

WITHOUT THE MASK

AWAKE. Free. The agony of unshackling. The darkness, bittersweet. The memories. Horrible stabbing knives.

He could remember. The line between dream and real at last solidified. Firm. Unbreakable.

Free.

He was his own again. Responsible. The string was severed. He was responsible. Centuries of death and pain. His. His own. But free.

Guilty. Yes, guilty. No denying. The knives. The relentless stabbing knives.

To be free means, means what?

Your guilt is your own.

Your failures are your own.

Your triumphs are your own.

You are your own.

Free. Guilty. Guilty, yes. But no longer condemned.

The path unfurled.

His. His own. His own path to walk, to fly, to blot.

The Spiral lay naked, a little tiny thing.

Free.

Free to remember.

Free to forget.

Free.

Utterly, terribly,

        free.

THE INFIRMARY

I RUSHED to Zaea's side to see if she was all right. She was still breathing and her pulse was normal. The gash on her head looked worse than it was. It wasn't deep, but there was a lot of blood. She must have been hit by a piece of rock shrapnel, not the chain itself, I decided, or the wound would have been much worse. Her face was paler than usual. The blood she'd lost crept in dark splotches across her skin and clothes.

I picked Metatron up off the floor and bedded it back in its scabbard. I was scooping Zaea's legs to hoist her over my shoulder when the pile of rubble Barn Owl was buried under shifted, and Barn Owl moaned.

Barn Owl's gloveless, debris-dusted arms poked free of the rubble.

"Hey! Easy! Easy!"

I helped Barn Owl dig herself out. The pieces of the smashed table trapping her were mostly small, but a few big ones had fallen over her legs, thankfully landing in such a way that they'd only pinned her down.

I pulled Barn Owl free and examined her wounds. Miraculously, they were mostly superficial, and she was more aware and together than should have been humanly possible. Two of the fingers on her right hand had been crushed by a large rock. Both of the end joints leaked red pulp, barely held together by the shredded flaps of skin. They'd need to be sewn back together or amputated as soon as we got back to the Burrow. I realized with a tightening in my stomach that I would probably be the one to treat her wounds, as well as Zaea's, unless Bunny, Squirrel, or Vole were better at first aid. I also strongly suspected that she'd suffered a concussion, but there was nothing to be done about it now.

When I was sure she could stand, I helped her to her feet. "Can you walk?" I said.

"Yeah. I think so."

"Take a few steps. I need to see if you can balance."

Carefully, Barn Owl obliged. She stumbled at first, then walked slowly to the other side of the room, where she collected her spear, and limped back to where I was standing. "Head feels funny," she said. "And my hand fuckin' hurts. Shhhh… ah!" she gasped, grabbing her fingers to throttle the pain as if feeling it for the first time. "I think I blacked out for a minute. What the hell happened?" she said.

I pointed to the broken pieces of the Ratkeeper's mask where they still lay smoldering on the floor.

"Did you do that?" Barn Owl said.

I nodded.

"I'll be damned… Little Leech, the Ratkeeper-Killer. Never thought I'd live to see this day. You'd better take that or no one's gonna believe you did it," Barn Owl said.

I scooped up the broken clay pieces and shoved them into my coat.

Barn Owl cringed as she checked the damage to her fingers. "I'll be fine. I don't need all of my fingers, anyway. We need to get Princess Mouse somewhere safe, and fast. Looked pretty bad when she went down. And I'm guessing we'll have company soon. Where's Gazzo? I mean, uh… shit. Where's Gator?" Barn Owl said.

I shook my head.

Barn Owl hung her head in her hands, squeezing her eyes shut to stem the sudden flow of tears. "Oh, no. No, no, no." The tears came anyway, carving glistening canyons in the dust of her cheeks. When she spoke again, her voice was a hard, thin whisper. "Was it the lamp?" Barn Owl said.

I shook my head again. Barn Owl followed my gaze to the blanket of frost and tiny ice chips covering the floor where Gator had died and let out a long, heavy sigh. "That stupid son of a bitch." She choked back a sob, holding onto me as she lurched forward and nearly lost her feet. "You won't be forgotten, Cousin. But I'll save my mourning until after our asses are out of the fire. Now, Leech. You're gonna have to carry her. Think you can do that?" Barn Owl motioned to Zaea.

"Yes, sir."

Barn Owl wiped a wayward dribble of blood from her forehead. "Damn. You hear that? They're already coming. Or is that just the ringing in my old, busted-ass head?"

"No, I hear them, too," I said.

Somewhere outside, a Snowman howled.

GANHEIM

THEY CAUGHT US on the stairs. Their bloodthirsty howls carried down to us from the top of the stairwell. I hauled ass as fast as I could, but no one can run at full speed carrying a human body over their shoulders. We had only made it to the B3 landing before the Snowmen's meaningless, guttural voices flooded down the stairwell to meet us.

"Where?" I mouthed to Barn Owl.

"We need to get what we came here for." Barn Owl said.

A harsh cry boomed down from the uppermost landing three stories above us. A bone-tipped arrow sailed past my face, missing Zaea by inches.

So much for sneaking out.

I ducked and ran as arrows rained down on us from the floors above. I heard one bite flesh, thought for a terrified instant that it was Zaea. Barn Owl yelped in pain. She'd taken one in the knee diving for cover.

I kneeled to jiggle the door handle. "Locked."

Barn Owl winced, snapped the shaft of the arrow stuck in her leg, and tried the door herself. "Wake her up," she said. "I know you can hear me, Mouse. You ain't dead yet, but you about to be if you don't open your eyes and do something with that ghost hand. This is not a drill."

"I'm... awake," Zaea said, her voice a whisper somewhere between sickness and sleep-talk. She reached out her hand and the ghost's black line bloomed into the iron bar blocking the door to the landing. She shot the two guards watching the cells as they came running, cutting one off at the knees and the other, the neck.

Eager faces peered out through the barred iron doors. A sudden clamor of awareness rippled through the cells, the prisoners scrambling and posturing to see what was going on. A thrilled, collective gasp rose when they saw us, then a cheer.

"Shut the hell up," Barn Owl said.

Zaea tapped me on the shoulder. "Put me down!" I slammed the door shut as the Snowmen clambered onto the B3 landing. "Step back!" Zaea said. I did.

Zaea made five or six quick cuts at the ceiling, blocking the door with a landslide of fallen stone. Wails of bloodlust and anger filtered through the gaps in the makeshift barricade, followed shortly by the hiss of poorly aimed arrows that ricocheted harmlessly off the walls.

Barn Owl cringed, favoring the leg that didn't have half an arrow sticking out of it. "Zaea, get those cells open."

I held Zaea steady as she sliced the locks. Once all four of the cells were empty, the prisoners began arming themselves, filling their thin, quivering hands with bone spears, flint knives, or loose arrow shafts reclaimed from the floor. Their grimy, half-rotten faces were twisted and afraid, thirty pairs of red, tired eyes locked singularly on the rubble pile where the stairs had been.

"Where's everyone else?" Barn Owl said. She was met with a bevy of sad looks and downcast glances. "This is it, huh? Shit. Wanderer damn him. Is there another way out of here?"

"Aye, there is," a lean, gray-bearded man said. He'd donned one of the fallen Snowmen's fur mantles as his own, and was brandishing a pilfered bone axe casually in one hand, like he'd done it a thousand times before. The graybeard saluted and identified himself. "Name's Vampire, from Catacomb Town."

"I know who you are, sir. Report," Barn Owl said.

"This floor weren't made a prison until a few months ago, when they moved us from up top. There were too many of us, and they're planning for a whole lot more. This used to be the archives. The caves connect a ways back, becoming a matrix of honeycombed tunnels. The Frosties only use 'em for storage. Grub here thinks they go all the way back under the mountain, but we never got the chance to explore that far. The few times we were able to slip out of our cells, the place was too heavily guarded."

"Confirming that report, sir. They barely keep 'em sealed off," a bald, friendly-looking man twenty years the graybeard's junior said.

The two men both held their salutes while Barn Owl considered what to do. "Thank you, gentlemen. At ease. I hope you're all ready for a fight, because there's about to be a bad one. They knew we were coming. Big Nasty sent the Ratkeeper to get us, but Leech here wasn't gonna let us get got. Cut off the bastard's mask and sent him running scared. Y'all hear that screaming a few minutes ago, sounded like somebody throwing a cat into a bottomless crevasse?"

The prisoners nodded, exchanging looks of excitement and disbelief. Barn Owl put her uninjured hand on my shoulder. "Oh, that was him, all right. And you can thank Leech here as soon as we get back to Salt Town *alive*... keyword, people. You all know the backup plan is waiting for us as soon as we walk outside. This facility was wide open when we got here. It sure as hell ain't gonna be wide open when we leave."

An arrow struck the wall a few feet from where Barn Owl was taking cover. She shot an irritated look at the barricade. There was already a considerable gap. "Is there anyone who can't fight?" Barn Owl said.

None of the Burrowers raised a hand.

"All right, people. I know you're all craving that sweet revenge you've been fantasizing about ever since they threw you in here, but we stop only if we absolutely must, and that includes for fighting. We can safely assume they already know where we are, and where we're trying to go. So now, we gotta run. Column up. Two lines," Barn Owl said.

"Wait," Zaea said. She had to repeat herself twice to be heard over the din of the moving crowd. Finally, Barn Owl heard her and silenced them with a whistle.

"We can't leave through the tunnels. Grub is right... they do delve under the mountain, some all the way to the other side. But they're a maze, and impossible to navigate without a map. The area was originally a training ground for students to practice subterranean warfare and survival skills. Some of the bloodiest battles the Yesaedans ever fought were on worlds covered with mines or ancient cities with vast undersides, including this one, where there was a civil war that lasted over a hundred years. The point is we won't make it. Students at the old academy studied for years before they took the Cave Trials. Most needed days - some, weeks - to successfully navigate the tunnels. Some came back. Many didn't."

"Old academy? What the rot is she goin' on about? She some kind of deserter?" Vampire said.

Barn Owl waved him off, leaned on her spear and scowled. "Well, Miss Mouse, if we can't go that way, I hope you've got a better idea. You're the expert. Tell us. Where should we go? And can you tell us on the move?"

"It's over there, at the end of that hall," Zaea said, pointing. "I'll show you. Dan, help me."

The prisoners followed us to the adjoining hall, ducking, weaving, and covering their heads to avoid being hit by the Snowmen's wayward arrows.

"That big door leads to the vault," Zaea said. It was a squat rectangle of solid metal sealed by three gargantuan combination locks. "The brass used to store important artifacts in there, things even the doctors didn't have the clearance to access.

"More importantly, behind that door is this facility's emergency safe room. I remember it. The students were supposed to stand their ground and fight, but the top brass, VIP staff, and president of the student body were supposed to lock themselves inside that safe room until the worst of the danger passed, then evacuate to the Surface through a hidden escape tunnel."

The column stopped in front of the vault door and parted to let Zaea and me through. She made a quick slash with the ghost that severed the ancient metal. But even with three strong men pushing it, the door seemed impossible to move. I heaved and lurched, Len's tremendous, inexhaustible muscles screaming, but it was like trying to move a mountain.

Just when I thought Zaea would have to cut the door off the wall, the hinges moaned and the door creaked inward. The gap was barely wide enough for us to squeeze through single file, but the prisoners moved fast.

When everyone was inside the vault, four of us pushed the door shut while Zaea and Barn Owl led the others into the safe room. I didn't think the vault door would hold longer than a few seconds once the Snowmen caught up to us, and we couldn't lock it again.

The vault itself was a series of connected, low-ceilinged caves each wide enough for two or three people to stand in side-by-side, and long enough for about five. There were six caves that I could see, and another vault door on the back wall, which Zaea immediately began trying to cut open.

The place would be a deathtrap if the Snowmen got inside before Zaea could get everyone into the safe room. I searched for anything I could use to block the door. There was nothing except some modular, opaque cabinets lining the cave walls.

Actually, those might work, I thought. They were stacked floor to ceiling, and made from some kind of thick, durable glass. There were tiny red lights on the fronts of the drawers to indicate they were locked. The drawers bore no labels, only numbers.

I tried to move them. Some of the prisoners milling about in the caves saw me struggling to block the door and rushed over to help. The cabinets were heavy, but they weren't bolted to the floor, as I'd feared. We needed at least ten of the stacks to create an adequate blockade, maybe twenty, but we'd only moved two when the first loud bang reverberated through the vault. A cacophony of guttural, Snowmanly howls echoed from the other side.

A sudden silence gripped the Burrowers, then chaos. I was too tunneled into my task to realize that Zaea and Barn Owl had already started leading them into the escape tunnel.

"A few more should do it. We only need enough time to get the last ones out," Vampire said.

The door moved. The volume of the Snowmen's cries rose exponentially. It moved again, toppling the peak from the small mountain of cabinets accumulated there. The barrier held, but it wouldn't for very long.

"Brace it!" Vampire yelled. "You, lad! Leech, was it? Three more – just three more! Then, we run!"

Vampire, Grub, and the other prisoners who had stayed behind put their shoulders to the blockade while I added the last of the moveable stacks to the pile. Yet the more resistance we added from our side, the more force the Snowmen added from theirs. They were hitting the door in a concerted effort now, pushing into it like a battering ram, each SLAM, pause, *one two three SLAM,* shortening the distance between us and them a little more, until I could see their beady eyes and gnashing, rotten teeth, could smell their cloud of piss and foul rotten meat breath.

"Retreat!" someone shouted. I looked back over my shoulder. All of the prisoners were inside the safe room. The men holding the door scattered. For an instant, I was alone. The next strike felt like trying to hold back a tsunami. My feet lost purchase and slid. A deluge of cabinets crashed all around me, and the door opened wide enough to let their arms and weapons in. One more and they'd be inside.

My legs moved of their own volition. I turned and ran, navigating that minefield of fallen cabinets for the low overhang of the safe room door. Adrenaline dumped into my veins, making time seem to flow simultaneously far slower and faster than normal.

I noticed the light on one of the fallen cabinets was green. Falling from the pile must have unlocked it and spilled its contents. The number on the cabinet was forty-one. Inside was a small glass-bound book, now cast halfway out onto the rough-hewn stone of the floor.

I can't say what it was about that slender volume, all wrought in stained glass so old I thought it would turn to sand when I touched it that caused me to stop and pick it up. Those precious seconds nearly cost me my life. Yet something about the book beckoned to me: the jagged brown-yellow of its pages, the smooth vertebrae of amber wire coiling up its spine, the twin crescent moons setting over a triangular plane emblazoned on the cover.

An unnatural urge came over me to sit down and read it, right there amidst the raucous storm of my enemies' war cries that would soon transform into blades if I didn't move. But seeing that book, feeling its surprising weight in my hands, filled me with a deep, inner calm, until a spear bounced off the cave wall next to my head, breaking my trance.

The Snowman who threw it had squeezed halfway through the door and was wriggling fanatically to get his other leg in. I picked up his spear and gave it back to him through the soft spot under his jaw. He stopped wriggling.

I tucked the Glass Book under my arm, drew Metatron, and ran.

GANHEIM

VAMPIRE AND GRUB were waiting for me inside the safe room. The others had already exited through the escape tunnel and were on their way back up to the Surface.

The room itself was bare bones, nothing but a few bunk beds cut crypt-wise from the rock of the cave, a small kitchenette with dining table, an empty bookshelf, and a rusted, time-devoured machine that I guessed had been some kind of wireless communication device. The bathroom was a tiny, closet-sized chamber adjoining the main room, with no door and a hole in the floorboards that opened over a natural crevasse.

Brings the saying "don't fall in" to a whole new level.

I was oddly calm, my thoughts swimming in a cloud of cool detachment. My adrenaline stores had been thoroughly depleted by the events of the last half-hour. I was resigned to the fact that the three of us were unlikely to leave this place alive. And that was fine. My life, and the lives of Vampire and Grub were a small price to pay so that Zaea and the prisoners could live.

"Help us get this shut," Vampire yelled at me. I rushed to help them reseal the door.

We were too late. The Snowmen were already upon us. We braced the door with our shoulders, and they shoved it open with theirs. Vampire cut down the first two who came through. The third stabbed the old graybeard through the eye with a three-sided bone knife.

It seems shitty, leaving one of your friends to die – even if I'd only known him for a grand total of fifteen minutes – but practice beats planning in a fight, and I was used to running from my problems, even if that meant leaving others behind. In fact, it was the only thing I had ever really been good at. I was already ascending the nearly vertical corkscrew stairs of the escape tunnel when Vampire's blood hit the floor.

Grub fell a few hundred stairs later, less than a dozen steps from the exit, to a Snowman's bone axe that took him in the hamstring. I heard the bone blade bite into flesh, tried to spin and grab him before he tumbled, but only got his collar. Before I could pull him up, the Snowmen had him by the legs.

Grub's eyes widened. He let out a sharp yelp of pain as the Snowmen below did something to his legs. If I let him go, the stairwell would be clogged long enough for me to reach the Surface.

"Go!" Grub screamed, his voice two-toned with resolution and terror. I let go of his collar and sprinted up toward the snow-shrouded mouth of the tunnel.

As soon as I stepped outside into the jaws of freezing wind and sideways-blowing snow the Vermin surrounded me to ask where Grub and Vampire were. When they heard the Snowmen coming up the stairs, their questions ended. A group of them pushed a huge, strategically placed boulder in front of the tunnel mouth. It had been put there so it could be used to seal the tunnel in case of just such an emergency, but also to camouflage it as part of the landscape of the prison yard.

When the tunnel was sealed, I caught my breath and took stock of my surroundings. We were standing a dozen paces from the east wing of the main hall, behind a small, granite outcrop atop a hill overlooking the prison yard. Barn Owl, Zaea, and the Burrowers were all crouched among that scattered forest of cracked, icy stone, hidden, or so I hoped, from the guards patrolling the perimeter fence. My eyes scanned across the snowy reaches of the yard, all strobe-spotted with the bright, raking fingers of searchlights, finally coming to rest on the back gate.

Still unguarded, I thought. *But why? They know we're here. Something's wrong. Those patrols aren't guarding shit. We're only meant to think they are. Someone put them up there so that we'd think this place was lightly guarded, but no one is this incompetent. They knew the bait was strong enough that we'd overlook the fact this is an obvious trap, either out of haste, or willingly. There's a bigger fish waiting for us somewhere, and I'm guessing it's close.*

I ducked over to the rocky outcropping where Barn Owl was hiding, but before I could say anything about the guards she pushed a finger to her lips and pointed down toward the prisoners' barracks.

Four silhouettes emerged from behind one of the buildings, half limping and half running in a drooping H configuration. Cheese Eater took point, with Vole, Bunny Rabbit, and Squirrel behind him. Vole and Bunny were carrying Squirrel under the arms. He'd been wounded. No one else was with them.

Barn Owl signaled to the prisoners to get ready to run. Thirty pairs of gaunt, shivering hands tightened around stolen bone axes, arrows, and knives. Barn Owl clicked her head to the side, indicating I should help Zaea.

I made an under hook beneath Zaea's armpit with my free arm and hoisted her to her feet. Len was strong enough to swing Metatron one-handed, but I prayed I wouldn't need to. My cuts wouldn't be accurate, and more importantly, there would be no way for me to dodge or use the proper footwork if we were attacked. Still, the warmth of her small shape next to me was comforting.

We broke cover, descending the hillside in a silent mass of white-eyed shadows. Despite one searchlight coming a little too close, we made it safely to the shadows of the barracks without incident.

Bunny and Vole met us by the same stairwell where we'd split up. Squirrel had taken an axe through his arm. Even in the wan, ambient glow of the yard I could tell he'd lost a critical amount of blood. Vole had dressed the wound with pieces of his shirt, which made me wonder briefly why none of these people carried first aid kits.

Squirrel's labored breaths and pained, unconscious groans haunted the short debriefing that followed.

"We didn't find anyone," Bunny Rabbit said.

"Place is emptier'n my guts after a bad night of drinking," Cheese Eater said.

"No shit," Barn Owl said.

"Seems like they was still getting the place ready for the next batch of customers. Seems like the next batch of customers they was intendin' to have here, was us... those from Salt Town and the Last Station. Seems like that was the whole reason this facility was built," Cheese said.

"Most of these buildings is empty," Vole added. "They ain't even put the floors in yet. Part of me was thinkin' they wasn't real, and was built as some sort of distraction."

Barn Owl sighed. "We got played. This place is a goddamned morgue. Still, thirty lives is better than zero." She checked the bloodied field dressing under her shirt with two fingers and gasped.

"We did what we could," Bunny Rabbit said.

"It ain't over yet, youngblood. We're gonna have big problems when we try to walk out that gate," Barn Owl said.

"Cheese and I were just sayin' the same thing. So, what's the plan? Charge in screamin' for blood and justice? Or try to do it sneaky-like?" Vole said.

"Dan… can you… hear it?" Zaea said.

"What's that?" I said.

"Can you… hear it?"

"Hear what?"

Her voice was a threadbare whisper. "They're… singing. Their song… their song is… the axle. That's… all… I'm trying to say."

I panicked. The blow to her skull had been worse than it looked. I was losing her.

Barn Owl licked the blood off her fingertips, poking the ground with her spear so she could lean on it. "I'll tell you the plan. We're going out the same way we came in, and we're gonna kill anyone who tries to stop us. Leech already got the Ratkeeper. Cut his mask off like it was paper. You shoulda seen that motherfucker run."

"You did that, Leech?" Bunny said, eyes widening.

"Wanderer's wisdom," Vole said.

Cheese Eater slapped me on the shoulder. "And here I was, thinkin' you wouldn't survive more'n five minutes."

A wave of impressed musings rippled through the crowd, then hushed as Barn Owl raised one hand. "Does everybody have a weapon?" The prisoners murmured in the affirmative. "All right. On the count of three, we're heading for that back gate. Do anything you have to to get outside. We can lose them in the train graveyard, but if we get stuck behind that fence, we're all dead. On my count."

"Dan. It's the final stage. They took everyone… because I left… now it's empty, like a grave…" Zaea said.

"One," Barn Owl said. A chilling wind rose off the prison yard.

"Dan…"

I held Zaea's head close, cradling it under my arm. "Stay with me. We're going to get through this. You and I can get through anything, together. I need you to hang on for me, okay?"

"Two!" Barn Owl said. The wind howled, lashing my face with frozen knives and rending snow devils from the dormant drifts of the yard to spiral up through the scattered, probing beams of the searchlights.

"Dan."

She was slipping away. It wouldn't be long, now. The breath caught in my chest, choking, suffocating me. "Hang on. Please. Don't do this again, Car. I can't lose you again."

"Dan, I know who I am," Zaea said.

"Three!"

The group charged, splintering off from the shadows of the barracks into a free-for-all of vague shapes of men and women sprinting wildly in the pale dark. I did what I could to help Zaea along, keeping my eyes locked on the distant beacon of the gate shining through the moving, periodic walls of white, but we fell behind.

Barn Owl hung back to help, but it didn't do any good. We could only move as fast as Zaea allowed us to, barely more than a slow limp.

A chorus of heartless screams tore above the wind far behind us on the hill. I glanced over my shoulder to see an army of Snowmen pouring into the yard from God knows where. It looked like they were coming from the mountain above the academy's main hall.

Caves? I wondered, but I didn't have time to contemplate the living conditions of the Snowmen. They'd catch us before we were even halfway to the gate. There was nothing we could do to escape them that didn't involve leaving Zaea to die.

"Dan, I know who I am," Zaea said again, louder and clearer than before.

"Zaea, we really don't have time…"

"No. Listen to me."

"Wanderer damn this," Barn Owl said.

"Listen! It's important! I remember who I am. Why I know this place. Getting hit like that, it woke me up, shook me out of this foggy haze I've been wandering through ever since I woke up with you in the Crypts. I know why I was there, why this place is so familiar. And I know what the ghost is saying."

"Leech, if you don't shut this bitch up and haul ass *right now...*" Barn Owl started.

"Zaea, what the hell are you talking about?" I said.

"It's for brain surgery," Zaea said. "The ghost is a precision instrument invented by Yesaedan neurosurgeons for fine operations inside the human mind. That's what it's for. It opens a new axle on the Spiral that divides matter, but it can also heal. It wasn't meant to be a weapon."

She's lost it. That blow to the head didn't kill her... it just made her batshit insane.

"Did the ghost tell you that? Are you hearing voices? Because now is not the time to be listening to them," I said.

Zaea's voice was calm. "No. It reminded me."

"Can you stop being such a cryptic asshole? If you've got something important to say, say it."

"I didn't kill that woman, Daniel. The ghost reunified her consciousness with the Spiral. The ghost is the Spiral's axle. It wasn't meant to be a weapon. We used them for surgery. To make..." Zaea said.

"What? I can't hear you. Speak up!"

"To make..."

A deafening crash split the air, drowning out the last of Zaea's words. Zaea, Barn Owl, and I all watched in silent horror as one, then both of the gate towers shook, shuddered, and blew apart in a rain of mangled wood and barbed wire, and the two Lice that had been sleeping inside them stretched and rose.

The Lice let out a blood-curdling shriek. Their lures bloomed, brightening the ground all around us. The prisoners froze under those twin cones of scorching, brilliant white, clutching each other and weeping in the shivering cold.

And now the trap is sprung. We almost made it, too, I thought.

All around the perimeter of the yard, the guard towers quaked and shattered, a chain reaction of rending wood and iron shrapnel giving birth to a dozen other colossal, insectoid monstrosities. A roll call of shrill sirens sounded from each flattened tower where a Louse now stood. Hundreds of filament legs danced into motion. Flame buds primed, spitting blue-white spears of fire into the frozen night. Their translucent carapaces gleamed like clouds of ghostly mist moving on an invisible wind.

In an instant we were surrounded.

I'm going to die. This truly is the end. I'll never be able to overcome my failures. Carly, Kashka, Evan, mom and dad. Not only am I going to die, but Zaea is, too; and Barn Owl, Bunny, Cheese Eater; everyone I've grown to call my friends here on this lost, desolate world.

But maybe I deserve this. Not just this place, but this end. How would Arkadius meet his death? How would Ink?

"Dan. You're not listening," Zaea said again. I hadn't realized she was still talking. "I wasn't here a century, or a year ago. It wasn't even one week. The ghost chose me because I've been *trained* to use it. I've been using this instrument for years. Well, not this exact one, but there are many here at this facility. I used it to make the Snowmen, and to pilot those tundra drones, that you call Lice."

"Wait. What?" I said.

"That's what I keep trying to tell you. I can control it. I can control *them*," Zaea said.

I didn't believe a word of it. But there was no other choice. "So do it," I said.

Zaea extended her hand, and a dozen slim, ebony beams grew from her palm, curving, swirling, giving birth to dozens, then hundreds of smaller ones, until the yard was covered with a gargantuan black web of interwoven spirals.

The ghosts found their endpoints and the Lice stopped cold, each bowing and falling to trembling, triple-jointed knees as slender filigrees of shadow entered their brains. I knew from the blank way they swayed and stared at her that they weren't dead.

They're awaiting orders. Holy Jesus. She was telling the truth. Thank God. Thank the Wanderer. Zaea was telling the truth. She can control the Lice.

The sirens ceased. The bloodthirsty cries of the Snowmen ceased. The despair on the prisoners' faces transformed into overwhelming joy.

Cheese Eater walked over to the nearest Louse and hacked its shin open with his sword. The Louse didn't move. He shrugged and hacked it again until Barn Owl took away his weapon.

Zaea summoned one over to us. It skipped silently above the snow and kneeled at her feet. Zaea stepped carefully into the bent stirrup of the Louse's lowest knee, grabbed a handful of its flame bud, and pulled herself up onto its back. She placed one hand gently over the Louse's brain and spurred it into a canter, circling left, then right, then finally, back to where I was standing.

"How?" I said, crisp and biting over the stunned silence of the crowd.

Zaea raised her head, triumphant. "Because I was the doctor here."

THE NIGHT COUNTRY

THE BATTLE was short, hardly enough to be called a battle at all, save for the streaming gouts of blue fire that lit the night like fireworks. The Snowmen scattered. They ran back into the bowels of the mountain, the facility, or through holes in the perimeter fence left by the destruction of the watchtowers, to anywhere they could to escape Zaea's Lice. The Lice scoured the prison yard with the cold efficiency of a unit of pack predators in the bloodlust of a hunt, all led by Zaea on her tall, crystal-armored mount.

I was too distracted to join in the prisoners' revelry. The familiar squawking of a bird drew me to a distant corner of the yard, where I found a large, white hawk circling over the battlements. The errant floodlights caught its brilliant, moon-white feathers every time it wheeled close, like an indecisive shooting star.

The hawk had been watching the fight with rapt attention.

I've seen that bird before, I thought, but as soon as it noticed me watching it, it took to the sky and quickly vanished from sight.

The prisoners spent some time scouring furs and weapons from the dead Snowmen. Many were already showing mild signs of hypothermia. Zaea led the desperate, shivering crowd out of the compound some time later, through the melted ruin of the same gate we had come in, the battle-weary Vermin trailing close behind. We crossed again through the Graveyard of Trains and the frozen mirror of Lake Bagra. Barn Owl stayed close by me the entire time, silent and deep in thought, giving Zaea the occasional signal.

It made me nervous walking so close to the Lice. There were twelve of them, and less than forty of us including the Vermin, not to mention they had us completely boxed-in. If Zaea lost control of them somehow, it would be a massacre.

When I tried to mention this to Barn Owl, she ignored me. Maybe she didn't believe any of this was happening, or still thought Zaea was a spy and was waiting to get us out on the thin ice before finishing us off. Zaea's words echoed in my mind's ear: *I was the doctor here.*

I thought that the descent down the glacier would take at least as long, if not longer than the way up with so many more bodies to move and so many of us exhausted from the fight. But in fact, it was much faster.

Zaea commanded several of the Lice to descend the icefall ahead of us. They were remarkably well suited for climbing due to their anatomy and weight distribution, appearing as nimble as spiders as they picked and leapt their way down the slick, sheer cliffs. She made the rest of the Lice stand directly above them on the cliff's edge, and then ran ropes down to those acting as anchors at the bottom.

This crude elevator could lower five people at a time. I was one of the last to tie in, choosing to remain topside with Cheese Eater and Barn Owl in case the Snowmen decided to ambush us when we were most vulnerable. I fought the urge to put my feet on the ice and rappel during the short, jerky descent. Zaea said the friction might confuse the Louse, and cause it to stop feeding the rope. All that stood between me and a deadly plunge to an icy death was the rope slipping out of my anchor's grimy chitin claws.

My eyes stayed fixed on the white hawk circling high above the cliffs the entire way down.

CORRUPTION

The hawk followed us all the way back to the entrance to the Burrow. I should have been happy just to be alive, and proud of the glory and praise that would be showered on me for defeating the Ratkeeper. But touching the shattered pieces of his mask inside the pocket of my jacket did not elicit the visceral satisfaction I expected. For that whole, cold and lonely climb home, I felt nothing but the same familiar emptiness I had felt every day since I arrived in Country.

THE BURROW

FOR THREE DAYS I didn't sleep or leave my room at all. Queen Rat announced there would be a party thrown in Zaea's honor on the twelfth torch after we returned to the Burrow. But I didn't care. I was so enraged and overcome with the sadness of Zaea's betrayal that I lay awake, thinking the same thoughts over and over:

She's the Crippled King's daughter. The Crippled. King's. Daughter.

Sometime before the feast I began to feel the strangest sensation, a tingling that ignited in my chest and grew until it became a scorching inferno consuming me head to toe.

The physical part of that revelation is almost impossible to describe, as all such experiences are. May as well ask somebody what it feels like to be touched by God. The description I've given here is an appallingly threadbare approximation. But spiritually, mentally, even rationally, I knew in that moment what Len's body was trying to tell me.

It was telling me that I was in control of the Blot, and not the other way around. That I was the one in control of where and when I went and always had been, but up until that moment only my subconscious mind had known it.

I stopped tossing and turning on my moldy straw mattress and concentrated. The more I focused my thoughts on becoming the string rather than the marionette, the more the sensation condensed into a single point that seemed to be floating inches in front of me, directly between my eyes, a magnetic pulse pulling me upward out of my body. I let go and surrendered to that pale vertigo, plummeting up toward the new gravity spiraling away from the here and now toward the infinite unknown.

I was no longer in a body. Len was lying dead on the straw mattress several feet beneath me, just a corpse, a riddle of matter that had been preserved by the revitalizing force I'd breathed into it, that would now be seized by rot and time once more.

But I wasn't in my own body, either. I wasn't back on Earth. I was still in my room in the Burrow, clinging to my tiny, single thread of the vast unwinding that had brought me here. And I was *so cold*.

There was a knock at my door, someone bringing me food, or - had it been twelve torches yet? - maybe even to summon me to the party.

I swung on that string and the unwinding thing carried me outside into the hall. I was warm again, had hands, feet, a mouth, a gut gnawing itself with hunger at the smoky smells of meat roasting somewhere else in the Last Station. I looked down my long, crooked nose to legs that seemed miles longer than I was used to. I wasn't as strong as Len, but I was taller. I had the nagging urge to wash my clothes, or other people might think I smelled at the feast - like a rancid combination of fertilizer and moldy mushrooms - even though I couldn't smell it myself.

I pulled the dagger out of my belt, pricked Vole's thumb, gasped as the blood welled, and woke up in my own bed a few feet away, on the other side of the apartment wall.

THE BURROW

THE AIR WAS FILLED with laughter, song, and the smell of spilled beer and roasting meat. The queen's dining room had been transformed from an empty cellar into a roaring carnival.

Every living soul in the Burrow seemed to be there. Long tables packed every inch of the chamber. Fires blazed in open braziers, pigs, chickens, rats, and snakes sizzling over the embers on slow-turning spits. Horns of ale and open bottles of young potato vodka made orbital rotations around every table. A five-piece band composed of strings, wind instruments, and an accordion played lively polkas at the foot of the dais, where I sat at Queen Rat's table with Zaea, Barn Owl, and the rest of the Vermin.

I barely said two words the entire feast. I picked absently at my food - there was probably more on those tables than the people of the Burrow produced in a year - and avoided smalltalk with the Vermin sitting next to me. It wasn't hard. There were constant interruptions from the Burrowers who approached the dais to see the shards of the Ratkeeper's mask and to give praise to Zaea. A steady procession formed that seemed without end, all of them repeating the same tired platitudes:

"It's a good thing, what you did," a random old man with a face full of scraggly stubble told me.

Another one said, "Tough guy, you are. I wonder how you'd do against my own boy. He's sixteen, but he's the best fencer in the Burrow since Katherine left us."

"I can't believe it. That whoreson killed my aunt. Thank you for avenging her. Leech, was it? I'll say a prayer to the Wanderer for your soul," a plain-looking woman with twin baby girls clutching her bosom said.

Bob o' the Knob took a long look at the clay shards, grunting as he ran his fingertips along their jagged edges, but said nothing.

"Took my own brother is what they tell me, the bastard. Your - 'scuse me, I mean Len's – father, Vojciek. May he rot," a very drunk Uncle Termite said, then raised his glass, spilling half of the vodka inside it down his beard, and shouted, "Glory be to the heroes!"

"Glory be to the heroes!" the Vermin all chanted, slamming their glasses down on the table. A moment of silence gripped the Vermin as they remembered the ones they'd lost. Everyone took a deep, hearty drink. The music resumed.

They want to see the mask, but they're not here for me, I thought, swishing a mouthful of mulled wine. Hot spice, orange and cloves danced over my tongue, spilling down my throat to warm my insides, but the wine brought me little enjoyment.

They're here for her. The one they think is the Wanderer Returned. The spy of the Amber City who walks among us. The Crippled King's own fucking blood.

I drained the rest of my wine and held my glass up over my head. A scrubby boy carrying a huge, earthenware pitcher rushed to our table to refill it.

"I remember hearing stories about the Ratkeeper when I was a girl," Bunny Rabbit said at last.

"When you were a girl? Did you become a woman when we weren't looking?" Cheese Eater said. The Vermin broke into rolling snickers.

"Grow mold," Bunny said, but even she was forced to smile. "I was about to say that in the stories I heard when I was a little kid, the Ratkeeper was always portrayed as some mindless automaton."

"A mindless what?" Cheese Eater said, biting into a hunk of crusty, fresh-baked bread.

"It means a drone or golem, an empty vessel without a brain of its own. You should know all about that," Bunny said. Cheese Eater chuckled, chewing with his mouth open. "Anyway, from the way Leech described it, old Ratty wasn't exactly an automaton. He was enslaved by that mask, the way Leech is enslaved by the Spiral in his eye. The Ratkeeper was just following orders."

"Are you suggesting we should feel sorry for him, the son of a rutting bitch who killed Grandfather Mouse, Meerkat, and no less than half a hundred of our other friends and allies? Because if you are, that's the stupidest thing I've ever heard," Cheese Eater said.

Bunny folded her hands on the table. "No. I'm not suggesting that. I'm making a rational assessment based on the evidence. Maybe you should try it sometime, you mean, squinty little man." Cheese Eater cringed at the word *little*.

Bunny gave a frustrated sigh, finished her mug of beer, and let out a loud belch before finishing, "The point, and I did have a point, is that former slaves are always resentful of their masters, especially if they were mistreated, which we can assume old Ratty was, if he needed to wear a magic mask to be compelled to do things. If we could somehow find him and take him alive, he might be willing to tell us the Crippled King's secrets. An informant like him would be worth a hundred spies inside the Amber City."

"She's got you there, Cheese," Barn Owl said. "Bunny, you just earned yourself a new pay grade."

"Thanks," Bunny said. Barn Owl clinked Bunny's empty glass and drank.

"Wanderer damn you both," Cheese Eater said, and then to me, "And you, you braggadocious bastard. What the hell are you looking at?"

I shrugged and sipped my wine. I was happy to have something other than the mission to think about. The grim cloud over the table had evaporated. It allowed me to take my mind off of Zaea's falsity, the frozen sorrow of Gator's face shattering into a million particulate pieces, and the vision of Carly I'd seen inside the lamp.

"I've got my own theory. Not about the Ratkeeper, though," Barn Owl said. She leaned over the table, lowering her voice to a whisper. "This one's about Miss Mouse. Our very own little princess lost. Don't you dare say her name, Cheese. I see it jumping on the tip of your tongue. She's had enough on her plate today. We don't need to add to it. Besides, if the wrong people overhear our conversation, the kind of people who ain't smart enough to have figured it out for themselves already, we could unwittingly put her in danger."

"I thought it wasn't polite to discuss religion at the dinner table," Cheese Eater said.

Barn Owl laughed. "Well, it's a good thing we ain't known for being polite."

"You think she's the Wanderer Returned," Bunny Rabbit said. It wasn't a question.

"Are you saying you don't?" Barn Owl said.

"How should I know? I never paid attention in church. I always thought it was boring," Bunny said.

"Who gives a shit?" Cheese Eater said, submerging a bite of bread in his bowl of cabbage and bacon soup.

"The Spiral turns through light and dark. Sometimes it brightens. Sometimes it dims. But it always finds balance in the end. The last Wanderer was a man. Why wouldn't she be a woman this time?" Barn Owl said.

Cheese Eater shrugged, popping a soup-soaked hunk of bread in his mouth. "Never said she wasn't. I tend to more metaphorical interpretations of the whole Saga of the Wanderer, myself, and believe that it's all just a pretty way of saying humanity is rotten by default, and that we need good people with bright ideas to make us better.

"But the cycle of murder and squalor always finds a way to continue, doesn't it? Look at this world. It was paradise. Peaceful. Perfect. Now it's even darker physically, not to mention morally, than it was before. You really think some girl with a princess complex, who could be one of the Crippled King's spies for all we know, is the Wanderer Returned just because she did some fancy tricks with a weapon from the Twilight Age that none of us have any idea how to actually use?"

"I said it's possible. And I'm not the only one who thinks so," Barn Owl said, nodding to the other side of the table, where the woman with the twin girls was handing Zaea a woven glowmoss bracelet.

No sooner had we set foot in the Burrow than the story began circulating about how Zaea had freed the prisoners by taming the Lice. Now, three days later, many in the Burrow believed her to be the Wanderer Returned.

Zaea blushed and thanked the young mother and slipped the bracelet over her wrist. The glowmoss bloomed to full brightness as Zaea waved to the small crowd of Burrowers gathered at the foot of the dais, casting a white halo of light from her hand. The hall fell silent, then the entire room erupted into raucous applause.

Zaea seemed embarrassed by the attention. She held her hand upraised, modeling her brilliant jewelry for everyone to see. The applause increased to a full-on din, ripped through by whistles and hoots of adoration. One of the tables started a chant that spread through the hall until everyone was stomping their feet and pounding their fists, shouting, *"Zae-a! Zae-a! Zae-a! Zae-a!"*

I chose not to join that miserable incantation, instead pouring myself another glass of hot wine and draining it in a single, burning gulp. I didn't care if I destroyed the inside of Len's mouth or upper digestive tract with the scalding liquid. I deserved the Burrowers' adoration, not Zaea – dishonest, traitorous, falsely caring Zaea.

No, Dan. That's yourself you're thinking of, Carly said in my mind's ear. *Zaea is brave. She does the right thing, even when it is the hardest thing to do. She acts despite what she is, not because of it. Can you say the same for yourself?*

Queen Rat urged Zaea to her feet as the chant reached its apex and devolved into formless noise. Zaea's cheeks turned beet soup red. She waved and smiled like she was some kind of religious icon.

You didn't want this… remember? You didn't want to be anyone's savior, thought you didn't have it in you, or more likely, that you didn't deserve it. You only came back to the Night Country because you had to.

Above the clamor, someone shouted, "Fuck the Crippled King!"

Projectile droplets of spilled beer showered my face as another voice added, "Praise the heroes!"

And a third, "She is the fire!"

The applause continued until Zaea dimmed the bracelet, gave a final bow, and sat down again. Yet the Burrowers' looks of hope and longing for salvation lingered, all fixed upon that single face, that girl who looked so much like Carly; the girl with the whiskey-colored hair who I'd unfrozen in the bowels of the Royal Crypts and nourished back to life; the girl whose life I'd saved, and who'd saved mine; the girl who was the offspring of my enemy.

I could tell them. Turn her in. Blow her cover. Then those would be my praises they're singing. I was supposed to be the hero, wasn't I? It's not too late.

It took me another three hours, two more plates of roast chicken, fried cabbage and dumplings, and another six glasses of wine – not to mention all the shots of vodka I took with my fellow Vermin – to confront her.

I followed Zaea outside and waited for her to go to the bathroom. There was no one else in the tunnels except Bob o' the Knob, who was standing watch by the main door to the feasting hall. I waved him off and he quickly vacated the area.

When Zaea re-emerged from the privy caves, I blocked her way and said with a friendly smile, "So, Zaea. I've been thinking about what you said during the mission, about you being the doctor at the facility..."

"Oh, here it comes," Zaea said, her eyes falling to the floor.

I made no effort to hide my scorn. "You're from the Amber City?"

Zaea looked up and gave me a long, red-eyed stare. "Yes. I was."

We were both piss drunk, verging on obliteration, which made it all the easier for my wrath to boil. I tried to be firm, but not threatening. Zaea was the closest thing I had to a friend, on this world or any other, but I was disgusted that she could deceive me after I'd saved her life, that she could deceive *them*.

"You say your dad's a king. Well, there's only one king in the Amber City. You're the Crippled King's daughter, aren't you?"

"Yes. Why do you think I'm still here?" Zaea said.

"You tell me."

The word took a long time to pass her lips. "Guilt."

"And yet you still think about going back to him. Just waiting for the right opportunity to split and run. You need to choose. Pick a side."

"I already have," Zaea said.

I leaned in close, breathing hard into her face. Zaea didn't flinch, only returned her gaze to the floor. "When are you going to tell them, Zaea? How long are you going to continue this charade?"

Zaea's brow furrowed. "I'm not going to tell them. It wasn't an easy decision, but I believe it is the right one, not only for my own safety, but yours, and theirs, as well."

No. She's not like Carly at all. Carly was honest.

"So instead of letting them know you're a traitor and that you're the one they should blame for their own people being abducted and murdered, you're going to sit up there and let them praise you like you're their messiah? Man, I've seen and done some twisted shit in my time, but that really takes the cake," I said.

"I don't work for him anymore, Daniel, and I never will again. Not only for my own sake, but for the sake of the people of the Amber City. They don't even know about this place, or that the Surface is covered in darkness and cold, that the real sun has gone missing. They have a false one. And the King's - my father's - Pax Eterna keeps them blind. He shows them deceitful visions of how the world ought to be on their screens of dancing glass, lies they willingly accept.

"I need to show them what he's done, not just to the people of the Burrow, but to themselves. He's made them into monsters complicit in the murder and degradation of millions, perhaps billions of human lives. If I can somehow wake them up... show them what it's really like outside their perfect little bubble, maybe there's some tiny fraction of a chance we won't have to wage this war alone. Some of them may join us. Or at least give us a way in."

I said nothing.

Zaea's eyebrows rose and fell. "Do you still believe I'm a traitor? Do you even believe me at all? What must I do to convince you? I don't want to lose you as a friend, Daniel. You're the only one I have."

A conciliatory smile cracked the edge of her lips, but I wanted none of it. When I didn't respond a second time, she said in a more serious tone, "If you are still my friend, you won't tell them, either. You'll let them continue to believe that the reason we're both here is to fulfill some ancient prophecy, even though we both know the truth. That is your *only* choice if you want any of us to survive."

"And what truth is that, exactly?" I said.

Zaea's mouth became a hard, thin line. "That we are both here because of the man you call the Crippled King. Neither of us knows how, or why, but that, too, is by his design. You cannot begin to comprehend how powerful he is.

"Neither of us wants to be a pawn in his game, nor will we be any longer, if we can help it. But if these people discover the truth about me, they'll execute us both just to be certain I won't turn tail on them and go running back to daddy... and in doing so, they'll lose the only people they have who possess any real chance of ending this war.

"You'd not only be condemning me, but yourself, along with every man, woman, and child in the Burrow. His endgame is nothing less than the total extinction of every human being not living in the Amber City, because everyone who knows the truth - everyone who he can't control - is a threat to his rule. There won't be a peace treaty. My father can be a ruthless man, and there is nothing a ruthless man hates more than being proven wrong."

I still didn't believe a word of it. "So why the sudden change of heart?" I said.

"I remembered why I was in the Royal Crypts, back when we were in the prison camp, why I couldn't remember how I got there or anything else. It came back. Daniel... I tried to kill myself. I would've been successful if you hadn't stopped me," Zaea said.

"Stopped you...?" my voice trailed off.

There was a long pause before Zaea spoke again. "The Ganheim Research Station was my first job after university. My father specifically requested my transfer there from the lab I did my internship in. I worked in Prion Immunity Research, which is a fancy way of saying, *finding ways to let people eat human flesh as a long-term survival measure.*

"That's what the Zoanthrope Project originally aimed to do - Zoanthropes are what they call Snowmen up in the Amber City - it was about keeping humanity alive outside the Amber City through the duration of our Fall Through the Darkness, in case the Amber City should ever fail.

"Of course, I didn't know about any of this until after my transfer. Only the top, top military brass was privy to those secrets. When I found out, I couldn't live with what I'd done. Or maybe I should say, *what I contributed to.* All those innocent lives... I can still see their faces..."

There was another long pause. Zaea continued. "So I made a plan. I stole a jar of the preservative we use on our test subjects. It cools the body into a state of torpor so we can operate without killing them, but in a high enough dose, the compound becomes lethal. I ran away, found a place where I knew I would die alone, and drank the whole thing down. You turning the heat back on and waking me up is the only reason I'm still alive. Sure, I couldn't remember where I was, or..."

"There's one major hole in your story, Princess. The heat was already on when I got there," I said.

Zaea shook her head. "No, it wasn't. You walking down the subway tracks from outside is what turned it back on. The system thought you were a train. Maybe I didn't take an exactly lethal dose of the poison. I'm not sure, since I'm the only person I've ever tried to kill with it, and I don't recall you giving me anything but Panacea Bars when I woke up. But I *am* certain that I would have frozen to death if you hadn't come," she said.

"Fine. What were you going to say before I interrupted?" I said.

"I think maybe part of me wanted someone to come, that what I really wanted was forgiveness, not to actually die. But I didn't think anyone would."

"You want me to forgive you?" I said, unable to hide my incredulity.

"No. I want you to listen. Memory loss is a side effect of the FR-BD9 preservative, but it usually isn't permanent. Now that I remember everything, I don't want to die anymore, but there's no way I'd ever go back to my father's house or the Amber City unless it was at the head of a conquering army. Their whole system is flawed and corrupted by design. There is no salvaging it. It must be destroyed and completely rebuilt. I believe I am the person to do this, and you, if you're willing to help me."

I don't think she expected an answer, because she didn't stop for me to give one. "Does this explanation for my horrible treachery suit you? Or shall I keep going?" Zaea said.

She tried to kill herself? Goddamnit. How could I not have seen it? But even if she's telling the truth, how can I forgive her?

"I... I'm sorry, Zaea. I didn't know. I believe you, all right?"

"You're not going to kill me?" Zaea said.

I released the handle of Zaea's boot knife that I'd been gripping under my cloak and stepped aside to let her past. Zaea muttered a small, "Thank you," kissed my cheek, and vanished back in the direction of the feast hall.

I was alone again, or so I thought, until a familiar voice startled me from the shadows just beyond the reach of the torchlight. "Bravo, Leech. It's never easy forgiving a friend after they've broken our trust. For a second there, I thought you were going to turn her into carpaccio," Queen Rat said.

She stepped out of the darkness holding the Glass Book in her hands. My first thought was, *She heard everything,* then *Hey, that's my book. I hid that thing under a mountain of blankets. She had her people turn over my apartment. So she didn't trust me.*

Bob o' the Knob stepped out of the shadows next to the queen, his hand resting on the pommel of his Wyvernwood sword. I relaxed my posture to show them both I wasn't going to try anything. "You couldn't just ask?" I said.

Queen Rat gave me a pitying smile. "No, Leech. I couldn't. Wonderful moniker, by the way... Agatha was right. You really do suck the fun out of everything. This lovely game of find-the-egg, for example. You hid this very special golden egg in your bed, so I wouldn't find it. I looked everywhere, and found it I did. Now, who couldn't see the fun in that?"

Queen Rat handed me the book. I took it. I assumed Agatha was Barn Owl; I'd never heard her called by her real name before.

"How do you know it wasn't going to be a gift? That I wasn't planning to share it with you as soon as the feast was over? There hasn't exactly been a good opportunity," I said.

"A gift," Queen Rat mused. "Indeed, it was. Let's say I buy this little play of yours. I don't, but let's pretend for a moment that I do. Let's say you wanted to read me that book, since you're the only one in the Burrow who can, and not in fact keep what might possibly be the most invaluable source of intel on our enemies we have yet discovered hidden from me. Or do you know someone else who can read Old Ithic?"

Zaea can, I thought, but shook my head *no.*

"Have you read it yet?" Queen Rat said, the eagerness catching fire in her eyes.

Visions of lost planets falling through black, dark space, of promised second suns that would never come, of native species enslaved by an oath, replayed in my mind's eye.

Slowly, I nodded. "I read it this afternoon."

"All of it?" Queen Rat said.

"Every word."

The queen clapped. "Splendid. In that case, here's what we're going to do. My dear friend Bob here is going to escort you to my chambers, where you're going to read me that book. Not the whole thing, mind you. It's a bit too late, and I'm a bit too drunk, to sit through that right now. Later on, perhaps..."

She stepped close to me, her hand trailing up the front of my leg. I tried not to flinch as it brushed past my groin, stopped, and squeezed. "Tonight, I only want to hear the really *juicy* parts. Highlight the plot points, give away the twists, and reveal to me what you've learned during your wild ride through the mind of the Crippled King. I want to hear everything."

"What happens if I say no?" I said.

Queen Rat shrugged and let go of Len's crotch. I expected her demeanor to become cold, but her smile widened. "You want me to threaten you? You actually want to cause a conflict between us, so you can justify acting on those thoughts of betrayal rooting around in your brain like a hungry hog? Please, Leech. You're smarter than that.

"Besides, that's all rather boring, isn't it? I realize you're sad that the little princess is actually the daughter of our worst enemy, and still somehow managed to steal all your precious glory. However, if the reason you're acting like a rebuffed teenager is because you feel you're not getting your proper slice of the praise, then I promise this proposition will interest you."

"What proposition is that?" I said.

Queen Rat placed both hands on the glass-bound object in my arms, pushing it lightly into my chest. "I want you to do something for the cause that she never could. We both know what this is."

"And what will happen to Zaea?" I said.

"Unlike you, I believe our little princess when she says she's one of us. But that doesn't change what must happen. She'll be arrested, interrogated, and likely tortured before four torches burn. If that effort proves fruitless, she'll be allowed to stay and fight," Queen Rat said.

"You're going to torture her?" I said.

Queen Rat laughed. "This coming from the boy who was about to slash her to ribbons? Don't worry, it won't be anything too medieval, just enough to show that she's really who she says, and that her moral 180 is real. I'm much more interested in the contents of that book than some stupid, ancient prophecy. For what else is a prophecy but the hopes and dreams of a people? I don't want to give my people hopes and dreams, Leech. I want to give them a future. Now, are you going to read it to me, or not?"

THE BURROW

I STOPPED BY the Infirmary to see Squirrel on my way to Queen Rat's chambers. I asked Bob o' the Knob if a quick visit would be all right. He gave me a curt grunt, clicking the nub of his tongue as he pointed at the Infirmary door, which I took as a yes.

I found Vole waiting by Squirrel's bedside, sucking his thumb amidst a silent sea of sleeping children. Vole quickly straightened up and wiped his thumb on his trousers when he saw me enter. The next bed over, where I'd seen the blight-sick boy on my first day in the Last Station, was now empty.

"How's he doing?" I said, keeping my voice low.

Vole glanced up, exhaustion sagging his usually wide, vigilant eyes. "His best days are behind him, I'm afraid. The doctor said he might not live to see the torches change. It's only a matter of time. Lost too much blood, and the trauma wasn't the worst part. Now, there's an infection. The blade that cut him was poisoned."

Squirrel's arm had been amputated, and the bandages hadn't done much to stem the bleeding. His brow was glazed with a glistening sheen of sweat. His eyes darted beneath shut eyelids, deep in the throes of a fever dream.

I didn't know what to say, other than, "I'm sorry."

I offered him my hand. Vole clenched it, cringing back tears. He let go of me and brushed his angled, hawkish nose as if he'd been fighting an itch. "You of all people got nothin' to apologize for, Leech. Without you and Zaea, we would've been dead little Vermin.

How was the feast, by the way? Wish I could've been there. Would've liked to honor her, and you. I would've liked that very much. But I can't leave him."

A sob escaped Vole, and a few of the bodies sleeping nearby stirred and moaned. Vole didn't try to hold back his tears. They came in a steaming deluge that carved canyons from the grime of his cheeks.

"He's my best friend, Leech. My only true friend. The only person who ever cared about me. I don't know what to do. He's always been there for me, even when others left. He loved me like I was his brother, and never asked me for nothing. I don't want him to go."

I knew that nothing I could say or do would ease Vole's pain, so I did the next best thing and cradled his head in my arms until he'd cried himself dry. I said a brief, quiet thank you to Squirrel, and left them alone in the silence.

THE BURROW

"SOME WINE, before we begin?"

Queen Rat filled my goblet up to the brim. *Shame I'm not going to finish it. It's probably the best she has. Gotta be hard to grow grapes down here. Still, only one of us is getting blacked out drunk this torch, and it isn't going to be me.*

The queen lounged in front of the fire, stretching out and yawning as she topped off her own clay goblet. The book sat on the table between us, its stained glass eye staring at me like a splinter out of time.

"Let's start from the beginning. Why don't you confirm for me exactly what this book is, and who wrote it," Queen Rat said.

"This book is the private journal of the Crippled King, written before his rise to power, when he was studying as an acolyte of the faith, at a church called St. Aram's," I said.

"The Lost Cathedral. Yes, every child in the Burrow's heard that story. St. Aram's was the cathedral that was hidden on the Last Day of Sun, whose greatest treasure is supposed to be the Crippled King's secrets," Queen Rat said.

I already knew from reading the diary that the Crippled King had feared the contents of the Glass Book could undermine his rule, so he buried it deep beneath the Night City. He created a magic barrier that would keep the structure immune from outside elements until the end of time.

The book contained plans, mathematics, diagrams, and astrophysical concepts that together created a framework for moving an entire planet to a new star system in the case that a civilization grew so old that it outlived its parent star, as this world had.

After reading the Crippled King's diary, I now believed that this was the watershed moment that the people of the Burrow referred to as the Last Day of Sun. Only, for some reason the Crippled King's plan to give his people a new star failed, and their planet had fallen into unending darkness, which the people of the Burrow called the True Night.

"Tell me where you found it, again?" Queen Rat said.

"It was in an unlocked cabinet in the prison camp archives. At first, I thought the drawer was unlocked because I'd knocked it over. But thinking back on it, those drawers were pretty much indestructible. We used them to blockade the door against more than a dozen Snowmen. It was unlocked because the Ratkeeper had been reading it."

"And why would he, a loyal servant of the Crippled King, have hidden a book in an archives where he could read it in secret, rather than return it to its rightful owner?" Queen Rat said.

"Because he wasn't a loyal servant. No one knew the Crippled King's crimes better than the Ratkeeper. My theory is that the Ratkeeper's loyalty died a long time ago. He was looking for a way out. The Ratkeeper wanted to be free, maybe so he could finally search for a new beginning, or maybe because he could no longer live with himself after all he'd done, and was looking for a way to finally make it end, like Zaea. But because he was enslaved to the will of his master through that infamous spiral mask, the Ratkeeper didn't have a choice. He couldn't free himself. I had to do it for him."

"Are you saying that he let you win?" Queen Rat said.

"I'm saying that it's possible. When I was drawn into the vision caused by gazing into his lamp, there were certain inconsistencies that make me believe he *allowed* me to slip out of the hallucination and wake up so I could destroy his bonds before he would be forced to kill me," I said.

One of the cover's stained glass corners bore a spider web of hairline cracks, like it had been dropped inside a bag that protected it from shattering entirely, and there were fine blood splatters along the outer rim of the pages. Someone else had found the book before I did, some other Vermin who hadn't survived to tell the tale.

Queen Rat sipped her wine, rolling her fingertips over the uneven, blood-spattered paper. "Which leaves me to ask how what is perhaps the most precious artifact relating to this rebellion ever discovered moved from Point A to B, if it ever was in St. Aram's to begin with. I believe it was, and that the Lost Cathedral isn't merely a myth. But if you've got any theories about this particular hole in your story, Leech, now would be the time to indulge me."

I took a sip from my own cup. "Simple. Meerkat and Grandfather Mouse found St. Aram's. That's the *mission of great importance* you sent them on, isn't it? Only they never made it back to the Last Station. The Ratkeeper killed them and took the book for himself. I think he had to know what it said before he could fully turn on his master, before he could truly let one of us win."

Queen Rat gazed into her wine. "If your theory is correct, then St. Aram's was most likely destroyed."

"I agree that it's probable," I said. "But, who knows?"

Queen Rat tipped her cup to me. "I must say, Leech. I'm impressed you put all of this together on your own. I told you of Katherine's, excuse me, Meerkat's, and Grandfather Mouse's deaths. I did not tell you that their final mission was to find the Lost

Cathedral. Perhaps I should consider promoting you to revolutionary intelligence."

"I admit that it was a guess, and you only now just confirmed my suspicion. One thing I've learned here is that if you want to get information out of someone, the best way to do it is to confidently pretend you already know it. I learned that from you, actually," I said.

"You're learning to play the game. Pity. It's always a shame to see a good person corrupted by politics. But I suppose it's unavoidable. All bright things fade over time," Queen Rat said.

"Thanks for your vote of confidence," I said, clinking her glass. I decided that finishing one more glass wouldn't hurt my chances of pulling off what I had planned.

Queen Rat's gaze drifted toward the ceiling. "Of course, the book could be a counterfeit meant to deliver us false information, to draw us out and misplay our final hand. And make no mistake, we are in the days of final hands being played."

"It could be, but I doubt it," I said. "You didn't hear the Ratkeeper scream."

"Though I sorely wish I had, you're right. I suppose I'll just have to trust your judgement on this one," Queen Rat said.

"Also, and perhaps more to the point, if I can say anything about the Crippled King after reading his entire life story, it's that even as an adolescent, he was a perfectionist. Every idea he had, experiment he conducted, and number he crunched is reported here in painstaking detail, including the science behind how he hid and sealed the Church of St. Aram. I don't think that kind of detail could be faked," I said.

"Explain," Queen Rat said.

"I don't completely understand the science myself, but the way he explains it in the book is that he used something called an atemporal lever, which didn't physically move the cathedral at all, but instead paused its momentum through spacetime, causing its position in our four-dimensional universe to change. The end result is basically what you and I would call teleportation, but it's still just technology; an extremely advanced form of technology, but technology, nonetheless. And technology is only magical if you don't know how it works."

Queen Rat drummed her fingers. "I can't say I understood much, or any of what you just said. Fortunately, I know many talented astromancers in Salt Town who will. You're right that a belief is never more damaging than when it is misplaced. If I put my faith in this book and you're wrong, then many people will lose their lives. So you'd better hope you're not wrong. Shall we begin?" Queen Rat said.

I took the book in my lap and opened it to the first page. "I'll start from the beginning."

THE GLASS BOOK

I HAVE WALKED with the Prophet. I have shared his rice and salted fish, and have spoken his name. He has made me his disciple, and I truly believe that he will be the one to lead my people out of perdition.

My old centering scrolls were lost during our escape from the flood back on Home. I had neither paper nor charcoal to write on the ship that carried us across the Sea of the Gods to this world of light and endless water, for our quarters there were cramped and inhumane, like the quarters of servants. Our food consisted of a substance similar to liquefied rice, which we drank twice a day, once upon waking, and then before lights-out. We slept three to a bed, and there was always a long line to use the privy. Sometimes you'd have to wait for hours. Sometimes the privies broke and people continued using them anyway, or made their own privies in the darkest stretches of the ship.

We were forced to lie on the floor for many days at a time, both at the start and end of our journey, and the result left my legs weak and unsteady. My good hand has since taken a steady tremble, and I have difficulty drawing or aiming a bow. I will say nothing more of our journey here, for I do not wish to remember it.

("Well, that's our first piece of evidence, isn't it? The Crippled King would be, of all things, a cripple..." Queen Rat said. I continued reading.)

They call this place Paradise. When we first arrived, it was difficult to see why. We spent months in starched white tents, as crowded and brutal as our accommodations aboard Gadov's ship. But the people here are friendly, and above all, kind, despite the vast differences between our two tribes. They went to great lengths to understand and respect our customs, morals, and linguistic oddities. Many of our tribe from Home thought them demons, and plotted to kill them.

It was not until the Prophet confronted the conspirators in front of the whole tent city and put a stop to their murderous nonsense that it was ended. The conspirators were given over to the Yesaedan authorities as a symbol of good faith. I do not believe any were beheaded, exsanguinated, or even executed. Such punishments seem too crass for this world, where the men do not gaze at each other as animals, but as fellows in brotherhood. Even the women here are different. They do not seem to me all that much different from the men.

("Leech," Queen Rat said, "while this is all very interesting, it hardly constitutes evidence. Mind skipping ahead to the point?"

"I do mind, actually. You'll see why in a minute," I said. Queen Rat rolled her eyes. I read on.)

This Yesaeda is a world of ancient, indescribable magic, of islands full of flashing lights and towers as tall as the sky. We glimpsed the blue curve of the planet briefly from above, as Gadov's ship was making its descent. It is a water world. By day, the sea is a shade of blue so deep it could never be imagined. There are uncountable archipelagos of city-islands. Some cities even float above the water like the garden towers of Ito, but a thousand times larger. Some swim deep beneath the surface like gargantuan whales made of luminous glass. By night, this world is a mirror of the Spiral, a scattered, star-studded multitude of lights.

("Pretty," Queen Rat mused. "All right. I'm listening.")

CORRUPTION

When we were finally released from the refugee camp (kindly named Welcome City), I visited the shore and bathed my toes in the sea. The burning, black sand was as fine as powdered obsidian. I expected the ocean to be freezing, like the fast-flowing waters of the river Ist back on Home, but it was as warm as taking a bath. It didn't take long for me to change my opinion that this truly was paradise.

The people here are kinder, too. I hate to say it of my own tribe, but the fact of our closed-mindedness and hostility to other tribes has become so apparent this past year, it is impossible to ignore. We are only of one color. Back home, any person of a different shade was known not to be trusted, until the Prophet, and even he required many miraculous deeds to convince our people to follow him.

The Yesaedans are of many colors, as many shades as the birds of the jungle, and yet it doesn't affect their relations. They are also a polyglot people fluent in many languages, including our own river country dialect of the Yubiq, which they call "Low Ithic," and which everyone here speaks. Where a canyon of tongues would prove an impassable barrier back Home if no translator could be found to bridge it, here, it is not a problem. The Yesaedans either already know the language in question, or carry a magic device in their pockets that does.

Never was the abstraction of human ideas made clearer than when I arrived here and witnessed people not solving their quarrels or addressing insults with the blade, but with words. When our own quarrels erupted into violence in the camp, the offenders were quarantined and reprimanded, but they were never treated as brutally as prisoners were back on Home.

An amazing thing seems to happen when people stop being told they are bad and instead are assumed to be good. They start to believe it.

Standing there with my toes in the warm Yesaedan sea was the first time in my life that I truly wondered if the traditions I had been raised with might be wrong. The Yesaedans had every reason to hate us:

...We had come to their world uninvited, demanding they take us in, even as we threatened to detonate the ship that had transported us here, an explosion which would have killed billions of their people. Yet they did not kill us or even treat us as enemies. They built refugee camps for us to stay in and offered us free schooling while they figured out how to best integrate us into their society.

...When we violated their laws, they gave us fair trials, and treated us no worse than they would their own citizens. And when we were finally released and allowed to join their civilization, they treated us as brothers and sisters, rather than an invading horde, which is the way we would've treated them had the sandals been switched.

...Even the Prophet was given a position of power. His Holiness was given the keys to Neen, the City Arcanum, and named our Sovereign-In-Exile until such time that we are able to go back Home, or we find a new one. The Twelve Houses unanimously supported him. The Prophet's teachings have spread far and wide, penetrating every facet of Yesaedan society. The Yesaedans now consider him one of their own great thinkers, an acceptable guru of the ten thousand-year Yesaedan canon.

If only they knew the Prophet was a son of their own world, and was himself a refugee when he fled to Home...

("Leech," Queen Rat interrupted me again. She'd polished off another two glasses of wine while I was reading. The bottle was empty. She got up to get a fresh one. "Though long have I yearned to know my enemy in such intimate detail, how does any of this prove..."

CORRUPTION

"Just wait. I'm about to get to the good part," I said. *I continued reading.)*

War is the one area where I have found the Yesaedans to be like us. One would think that on such a peaceful, prosperous world, war would have been eradicated long ago. And this is true, except in the case of the Shadashim...

("Leech..." Queen Rat slurred, one eyelid already drooping. My plan was working.

"Your Highness, you're going to want to hear this," I said.)

The Shadashim are the creatures indigenous to this world. They are a sentient species resembling colossal armored insects with translucent shells, who live both on land and underwater, though they seem to prefer tropical beachfronts. Their diet consists of fish, roots, and large fruit, and they cook their prey the way humans do, using targeted spears of flame. Mother Sea has given them the ability to shoot fire from their mandibles. Underwater, these flames turn into boiling spears that can cook entire schools of fish from a dozen yards away. The Shadashim are truly miracles of nature.

The Yesaedans, like our tribe from Home, did not seed from this soil. They came here many aeons ago on ships that carried them across the Sea of the Gods. The Shadashim, on the other hand, were here millennia before the arrival of humans, though they keep no written records. It is said their memory is genetic, and thus, eternal. The Yesaedans call them 'crabs' for short, but I think this is meant to slander them as unintelligent. Nothing could be farther from the truth. The Shadashim are peaceful and do not use technology as we know it, but they are beings of enormous intelligence. I hope someday the Yesaedans realize this, even if it is at their own peril.

("The Lice...? What else does it say about them?" Queen Rat said.)

The Yesaedans conquered the Shadashim ages ago, in a long and brutal war that was mostly one-sided. Today, most Shadashim work for the Yesaedans as servants, manual laborers, or as city peacekeepers, doing the types of dangerous, mundane jobs the Yesaedans don't want to do. The Yesaedans rarely do any kind of work that doesn't involve sitting in front of screens. Yesaedans have weak, strangely proportioned physical bodies, and the ones who don't only exercise at special places called wellness centers.

"Wellness center." I've never heard anything that sounded more dystopian.

But the Shadashim don't seem to mind doing the actual work that keeps Yesaedan society running, because this arrangement yields them twelve hot meals a day, and comfortable beachfront slums to live in.

Back on Home, we would have called such an arrangement "slavery." The Yesaedans have a different word for it. They call it "The Diversity in Labor Initiative," though to me, that too sounds abhorrently dishonest.

Most of the Shadashim willingly accept their bonds, but there are still some who resist. I understand there has always been an underground faction of them who did not accept Yesaedan rule, though it is small. No less than three nativist rebellions have been violently put down since I arrived on this world. Of course, these short, brutal massacres – one could hardly call them battles - are far away and scarcely reported on. When the Yesaedan news media does mention them, it is similar to when our own urban poets used to cry the royal affairs back on the busy street corners of Ito. They scrub their words to the point of bleaching, but a discerning person can always read between the lines.

Though Yesaeda may be paradise for Yesaedans, and perhaps someday it may be for us who crossed the stars from Home, too, the motto here seems to be, "Paradise is a place for some, but not all."

("He was a fish out of water who admired bigger fish out of water," Queen Rat chuckled into her wine glass. I ignored the comment, but before I could go back to reading, she added, "All cheap shots aside, I am curious to see how someone so invested in the ideal of social justice, who was so against inequality and political falsity, could go on to build a place like the Amber City."

I paused, holding my place on the page with my finger. "It says here that he found religion, though not in the way you would imagine," I said.

Queen Rat slouched back in her chair. "I'm all ears.")

My own placement proved to be disappointing. They have asked me to join the Order of the Brothers and Sisters of Cultural Anthropo-Moral Preservation, on account of my disability.

("His arm," Queen Rat said.

"Yes."

"Sorry. Continue.")

Apparently, on this world, I am unfit for any kind of physical work – not because I am actually unfit, but because of their labor laws – despite the fact that they have the ability to replace my lame arm with a new one made of silver and glass. I am told something called the Integration Affairs Committee fears it would cause a public backlash for me to receive such an extremely expensive surgery while tens of thousands of Yesaedans are still on the waiting list.

So they want me to be a church librarian. Me, last scion of the Sturgeon House and heir to Stag Horn Castle, a *librarian* - even though I have never professed belief in their god, and remain loyal to the Five Mothers of Home, at least in the privacy of my heart. Indeed, the coup in Ito at the hands of our own monotheistic clergy, and the five-year civil war it started, were the events directly leading to the cataclysmic flood that caused us to flee Home on Gadov's ship.

One might say that my opinion of organized religion is somewhat dim.

Yet some Yesaedans, however few, still attend regular services, despite being mostly godless in their day-to-day-lives. My duties will be more akin to that of a museum curator than a monk, my sole purpose to safeguard some otherwise forgotten aspect of their culture. Ringing bells, sweeping floors, creating interesting displays in the main hall, kicking horny teenagers out of the catacombs, that sort of thing.

What would the Prophet say, if it was he being forced to work for the office of a false and dying faith? I haven't seen him in months. He's too busy traveling and preaching, trying to grow his movement. But I think he would say that there is a lesson I can glean from all this.

Back on Home, I was heir to Stag Horn Castle and all of its attendant lands, but I never would've truly ruled there. If I had stayed and taken my father's seat, my advisors would've made the important decisions for me, and I would've spent my days hawking and hunting in the Spider Web Forest, drinking with my fellow lords in their keeps along the Eagle's Nest Trail and growing older one day at a time, until I was a withering relic incapable of changing or impacting the world around me.

Here, I have no bow, no arrows or hawks. But I have power. It may only be over this one tiny corner of a dusty, ancient church, but it is power just the same.

I will do my duty. I will wear the lilac robes and give comfort to those few people who come to listen to the God-Word in this mausoleum of belief. I will clean and polish and make this time-wracked ruin as beautiful as the Old Quarter that surrounds it, will make its colorful entanglement of spires shine once more. They will call me brother, though the color of my skin, hair, and eyes, my strange accent and my disability will forever mark me as one not of their own, but of the tribe who came across the stars from Home. I will spend my afternoons and nights studying these confounded mountains of old books, until I have mastered all their strange systems of mathematics and science. I will lose all connection to Home, my former friends who came with me on Gadov's ship...

All except for the Prophet, whose body I carried through the torrential downpour up the thousand steps of the Animus Tower. Perhaps one day, together, we will change this broken, artificial world.

THE BURROW

THE FIRE gave a final lick and paled to ember. Sitting up, Queen Rat said with a drunken slur, "Almost makes you feel sorry for him, doesn't it? I never knew the wretched bastard was an immigrant. A spoiled rich kid immigrant, but still, it's a harder lot in life than I would've guessed. Sorry, I should say *political asylum seeker*. I know not making that distinction can cause certain people's undergarments to bunch up and cause discomfort to their genitalia."

"My undergarments don't bunch easily," I said.

"I'll bet they don't." The queen gazed at my crotch long enough to make me uncomfortable, burped, and rolled her glass through thumb and forefinger, fruitlessly trying to shake up any last drops lingering at the bottom. "So, our Dear Leader started his life as an invalid. He left his home, lost his friends and family, and came to this world under what sounds like rather uncomfortable conditions. His only friend was a religious fanatic, and his job was studying old books and sweeping dusty floors. That all sounds pretty awful to me. But, what the hell do I know? I never saw his personal battles, his triumphs, his unhappiness, or his loneliness. I only suffered the lasting effects of their reimbursement to society."

Queen Rat took the Glass Book from my hands. "May I?" she said. She smirked as her fingertips trailed down the page. "His name was Jun, Son of Sen, Heir of the Something House... what did you say his family name was? I know I heard it, I just can't remember, and I don't know what this word means. Some symbol that looks like a fish."

"It's *sturgeon*. I thought you couldn't read Old Ithic," I said.

"Jun, Son of Sen, Heir of the Sturgeon House," Queen Rat said, the name filtering through her teeth like a taste of something vile. She repeated the word several times with increasing distaste. "And, I can read a little, though certainly not as well as you can. I mean, as well as Len could."

The queen returned the book to me, still open to the page where she'd found the name of the Crippled King. "Why don't you skip ahead a bit, past all the mundane details of our Beloved Sovereign's boyhood? His moral formation – his *bildungsroman,* if you will - while interesting in terms of knowing one's enemy, so far has not disclosed any information that could give us a strategic advantage," Queen Rat said.

"You're in luck. Here, the account jumps ahead five years."

Queen Rat leaned forward with exaggerated interest, knocking her wine glass off the table. It broke on the flagstones with a crash. The queen dismissed the shattered vessel with a shrug and a sigh. "And what was the reason for this five-year gap?"

"The war," I said.

"And which war would that be?"

"The Great Passage. The war your legends say the Wanderer came here to end."

Queen Rat chewed a fingernail. "Of course the Crippled King says he lived through the Great Passage. That would only strengthen his claim that he is the Wanderer Returned."

"Why don't you have another drink before we go on? You might need it," I said.

"I'll have two," Queen Rat said.

"I think it's better if I paraphrase this part," I said.

"Paraphrase away." The queen poured herself another glass while I went on.

"Remember what you told me in the Salt Church, that the War of the Great Passage happened because the people grew too complacent, and could no longer reproduce? Well, according to this, it's more complicated than that."

"Go on," Queen Rat said.

"Yesaeda isn't a normal world. It's what's called a *rogue planet*. Do you know what I mean by that?"

Queen Rat shook her head *no*.

"Most worlds are tethered to their parent star by gravity, the same force that caused your glass of wine to fall toward the ground when you knocked it over just now."

"I know what gravity is, Leech."

"No doubt. Anyway, some worlds don't have a parent star. These are called *rogue planets*: worlds ripped free from the star that gave them birth, usually by some cataclysmic event. These planets are doomed to fall through the darkness of space, without sunlight or warmth, forever, or until another star catches them in its gravitational field. You still follow me?"

"Few people in the Burrow have ever actually seen the stars," Queen Rat said. "I never have, myself. I was tutored in rudimentary astronomy when I was in school, so I know what you mean by *stars* and *gravity*, though I admit this phenomenon of rogue planets is new to me. Still, I'm not a moron."

"My understanding of it isn't much better," I said. "But, according to Jun the Acolyte, your Crippled King, the people of Yesaeda left their parent star and became a rogue world *on purpose*."

Queen Rat glared skeptically over the rim of her cup. "What?"

I flipped the pages of the book to the chapter on the stellar gateways. "According to Jun's diary, the people who settled this world thousands of years ago - your ancestors - were the richest human civilization to ever exist. They wanted to create a world that was not merely a physical paradise, but a social and political one, as well, free of any corruptive outside influence."

Queen Rat *hummed*.

I flipped forward a few pages to find the reference I wanted. "Apparently, they wanted to escape something called the *Paradigm*, which I assume was some kind of large, galactic federal government."

"Fascinating," Queen Rat said. "In our language, the connotation for that word is highly negative. You would only use it for systems that are inherently tyrannical. We call the Amber City a paradigm, for example. It's also what edgy children say when they don't want to go to church," Queen Rat said.

"Moving on."

"Please."

"In order to build their perfect society, the Yesaedans came to this world, which back then was a land of beauty and plenty. They conquered the peaceful, sentient natives, and immediately began constructing the most expensive project in the history of the human race... a string of gates scattered all across the galaxy that would allow this planet to jump from star to star without needing to be anchored to a single one.

"Jun the Acolyte didn't write down exactly how long the gates took to be completed. They were built thousands of years before he arrived here as a refugee. What he does say, however, is that the Yesaedans used seed-worlds to build the gates – worlds they terraformed, and then implanted with people.

"The Yesaedans engineered the societies of their seed-worlds to be heavily feudalistic, never allowing them to move beyond their respective dark ages. They mostly did this through religion, but they also had elite military units who would lead purging parties to the surfaces of these worlds to assassinate rebels and thought leaders any time talk of revolution started to foment."

"Their perfect world was built with slave labor," Queen Rat said. "Of course it was."

"It gets worse," I said. "What Jun the Acolyte realized while he was writing this account was that the grimy, medieval world where he and the other refugees had come from, the world they called Home, was a Yesaedan seed-world. Not only that, but the planet-wide flood that had destroyed Home and caused Jun's tribe to flee was caused by the Yesaedans' own negligence at keeping the planetary systems running. As you can probably guess, Jun started to resent the Yesaedans for the suffering they'd caused him and his people. And the more he learned, the more that hatred festered."

"Oh, wonderful. I love a good tale of bloody revenge," Queen Rat said.

"Do you want another refill?" I said.

The queen shook her head *no*. "I'm good for now."

"When the gates were completed, the Yesaedans somehow found a way to detach from their parent star and fall out of its orbit. I don't know how they did it, and neither did Jun. He had some ideas, but my math is too low to understand the equations. The important thing is the reason.

"The Yesaedans cut this entire planet free from the gravity of its parent star so it could fall into the first gate. The first gate aligned with the second, and the second with the third, and so on, forming an infinite ring around the galactic center. Their daytime was the periods when Yesaeda was outside of a gate, falling next to the light of a star. Night was when the planet was passing through the gates.

"Once this chain of gate jumping started, it was supposed to be unbreakable. The Yesaedans were too blinded by their newfound power to realize there was a flaw. In making their planet invisible, they had become like gods. Instead of being influenced by the Paradigm, the Yesaedans suddenly controlled it. No single army or coalition of worlds could touch them. And for a while, they enjoyed their secret paradise as any of us would, happy and carefree.

"Of course, it didn't last. People started getting sick. An unknown, incurable disease started spreading through the Yesaedan population."

"The Blight..." Queen Rat said.

"Exactly." I nodded. "You already know that one in four children were born infected. Those numbers haven't changed to this day. The mildest case will leave a person sterile. The worst prevents the body from forming the right pigments in the skin, hair, and eyes, causes the brain to lose the ability to dream, so that you don't rest, even when you sleep fifteen or twenty hours a day. Eventually, your body just gives up, and you die of exhaustion. Boys are more likely to be affected than girls. Most don't survive past early childhood. Those who do are forever changed. In Jun's society, they became social pariahs or holy men, living secluded lives far away from the rest of society."

"The great judgment of our times. And theirs, apparently," Queen Rat said.

I nodded. "The doctors never learned where it came from. Some thought the cause was genetic, a mutation caused by some unknown side effect of the gate jumps. Others thought it was a virus engineered by the Shadashim, their revenge for the genocide and enslavement against them.

"Either way, Yesaeda unraveled over the course of a few, short generations. People got scared. They stopped having children and starting families. By the time Jun and the refugees from Home arrived, Yesaeda was hanging on by a thread. What Jun saw as utopia was actually a period of steep decline. By then, the Yesaedans had accepted, at the cultural if not the individual level, that they had no future as a people. What he saw as love and human fraternity was a threadbare act, a front people used to keep them from devolving into violence and chaos. But that, too, didn't last.

"A black market slave trade had arisen centering around children from the seed-worlds, who the rich Yesaedans needed to replace the children they weren't having and the Blight was taking. As things got worse, the Yesaedan military even started false flag wars on those planets, so it would be easier for the slavers to get in and do the kidnapping."

"My ancestors… (*hic*)… did this?" Queen Rat said.

"Yes. And it gets worse."

She finished her wine. The bottle was empty again. I got up to get her another one.

"People on my world have done equally bad things," I said. "But there were always good people who tried to fight back and stop those bad things from happening, just like there were good people here. Unfortunately, it didn't work out so well for Yesaeda. The cities were torn apart by civil war, not just over the lives of the millions of kidnapped children, but for the soul of Yesaeda itself."

"Dan (*hic*)…" Queen Rat said, covering her wine-stained teeth with the back of a hand. "I'm getting tired. I want to go to bed… (*hic*)… with you. All of this is… well, but what's the really big piece of cheese?"

Damn, she's drunker than I thought. So am I, but still. Mission almost accomplished.

The way the queen was staring made me uncomfortable, until I remembered what I was doing. If I faltered for one second, even for a meaningless, drunken screw with a powerful older woman, I would stray from my path and lose my only chance to get what I'd came here for.

Besides, she doesn't want to screw me. She wants Len. It's him she sees when she looks at me. She probably wanted him long before he died. Maybe they were screwing. I mean, the guy was ugly, but he's built like a fire truck, and from what people say about him, he was a good fighter, and highly intelligent.

She doesn't really want me, just like Kashka doesn't really love me, she loves the idea of me. Everywhere I go, I'm someone I'm not.

That made it easier to defuse the queen's proposition. Smiling, I said, "We'll go to bed soon, all right? But I need you to hear this next part. It changes everything."

Queen Rat rolled her eyes and waved me on. "On with it... (*hic*)."

Finding my place on the page again, I read.

THE GLASS BOOK

The churches are full. Every day, more people come to join our movement. But they come not for me, the nameless brother in my midnight purple robes. They come for the Prophet, to see him, to touch him, to hear his voice.

In these past five years of bloodshed and hatred, he has become a symbol of hope to them. The fighting and death yield no sign of ending. Yet the Prophet's followers, those who have given the Promise of Peace, number greater than ever – into the hundreds of thousands at least, even the millions according to some.

Many have taken to sleeping in the main hall of the church. I am glad the renovations to the cathedral were completed before things got bad. We wake to the shaking of seismic bombs raining dust all over us. The display of Gadov's old ship, which we moved here piece by piece from the Museum of Culture so it wouldn't be destroyed by the extremists, gives me some hope we won't be crushed to death in our sleep by falling stone and wood. The Old Powers of this world fear the Prophet. He has become the symbol of their decline.

It is not difficult to see why. His message has caught the hearts of the Yesaedan people like wildfire. It is strange to think that my friend and mentor, Aram Gezel, who I met on the highroad crossing the Izo Pass getting drunk on rice wine and smoking his fish while I was on the run from my father's retainers, has come to mean so much to so many.

CORRUPTION

("Stop... (*hic*) there. Did you say Aram Gezel?" Queen Rat said.

"Yes, why?" I said.

"Aram Gezel is one of the names attributed to the Wanderer... (*hic*)," the queen said.

"You think Jun's Prophet was the actual, historical Wanderer?" I said.

Queen Rat's lips slid back and forth over her teeth as she thought. "Perhaps. Whether it's an historical document, or a... (*hic*) or a fabrication - my gut tells me this book is somewhere in between - it's impossible to ignore the thought. Besides, who better to emulate a religious fanatic than his own, favored disciple? (*hic*)"

"I think so, too," I said.

"Does it say how he died, this Prophet?" Queen Rat said.

"Unfortunately, it doesn't, only that he died sometime during the war. The closest thing to a description I could find was here." I turned to the page about the Prophet's funeral.)

I buried him in secret, in the dirt under the altar where he used to lead his people in prayer. It was his favorite place. I will erect a statue of him, and his body will be preserved in solarite until the end of time. I hope he will be given a proper burial someday, one with all the glory and honor he deserves. But I cannot risk his enemies finding him. They would profane his body, as they have already profaned this place a dozen times, simply for now bearing his name.

Aram Gezel, better known here on Yesaeda as the Prophet of the Thousand Faces, was the best man I ever knew, far greater than any legend could tell. He wasn't always a good man. When we first met he was a drunk, a thief, a liar, and a whoremonger. He was a man of violence, a killer. But he died with all the dark sickness of the universe on his shoulders; forsaking treatments that might've saved him. He liberated a thousand worlds, saved the lives of a thousand times as many children, because he believed he was a bad man who owed his life to the world.

That was his final lesson to me: that virtue isn't something good people do to continue being good. Virtue is what bad people do when they decide to change. A bad man *can* become good. That was the lesson that Aram taught me.

(Queen Rat scoffed).

THE BURROW

"WHAT A LOAD of... pedantic... philosophical... pig shit... (*hic*)," Queen Rat said. She slumped deeper in her chair, head lolling over and bare feet kicked up on the table, her toes dancing to an unheard tune.

She was almost where I wanted her. Almost, but not one hundred percent. "Reading between the lines, the implication here is that the Prophet contracted the Blight, but chose to continue his activism to end the child slave trade rather than receive treatment, a choice which ended up killing him. Of course, that wouldn't make any sense if the disease was genetic," I said.

"Could've activated... late..." Queen Rat said. "Or perhaps he lived with it all his life... and found some way... to suppress it... (*hic*)."

"It gets even more interesting," I said, eliciting the yawn from the queen's mouth I'd been hoping for. "Almost as soon as the Prophet was dead and buried, the war ended, the peace treaties were signed, and the diurnal cycles on Yesaeda started to change. The days and nights became chaotic and unpredictable.

"The official opinion of the Yesaedan scientists was that the gates had been tampered with during the war. Remember that at the peak of the fighting, the bloodshed hadn't just consumed Yesaeda, but over a thousand of its seed-worlds. Jun the Acolyte, however, thought that the breakdown of the gate ring wasn't due to sabotage, but disrepair. He did the math, and according to him, the gates were simply getting old. But by then, society was in such disarray that fixing them would've been impossible."

Queen Rat's eyes narrowed. "And so we arrived at our metaphorical Last Day of Sun."

"Right," I said. "Jun's theory, laid out in literally dozens of pages of equations throughout the latter part of this book, was that the only way to save Yesaeda was to give it a new sun. He calculated the best way to eject the planet from the gate ring cycle so that it would immediately fall into the orbit of a new, viable star. But without the original engineering plans the scientists had used to build the gates thousands of years before, it couldn't be done, not even by a mathematical genius like Jun."

"A new sun," Queen Rat echoed, sighing forlornly at the ceiling. "Sweet, fabled sunlight falling on our faces once more. Wouldn't that be just grand? But, pardon me if I... (*hic*) if I have a hard time believing *that* was the Crippled King's end game. Sorry, Leech. But I'm no longer convinced. You've unconvinced me."

Dammit, that is not how this was supposed to go.

I shoved the book in her face, causing her to shy away and bat at me with a goblet-filled fist until I relented. "Read it for yourself. It's all here," I insisted. "And it wasn't just *his* goal. He became so obsessed with the idea that he built an entire cult around it, mostly made up of the Prophet's old followers, who had become radicalized after the death of their leader. And guess what it was called?

"Jun's followers called themselves the Cult of the Wanderer. Jun the Acolyte became Jun the Disciple. He even convinced the Shadashim to swear allegiance to him, promising to support them in their own fight for liberation once the war for Yesaeda's soul was over.

"Together, Jun's cult and the Shadashim staged a coup against the shattered remnants of the Yesaedan government, overthrowing the powers-that-were in a single night. Jun the Disciple became Jun the Messiah. The people flocked to him, and his rule was solidified. For a while, at least, the political situation on Yesaeda stabilized.

"Jun's new government set into motion a vast, worldwide resettlement plan to help prepare the people for the coming cold and darkness as the planet traveled from the last gate to its new parent star, a period that was meant to only last two years in the best case, but even that relatively short time had the potential to cause mass death and chaos.

"King Jun built his Amber City as a life capsule for Yesaeda's elites in case the worst came to pass, and his plan failed. Refugees flooded into the cities, where they were promised food and warmth. The days grew dark, and the people waited, but Yesaeda never reached its new sun. Something, somewhere along the way went very, very wrong, and I think we both know the rest of the story," I finished.

"Is this your great secret, that the Crippled King stole the sun so that he could one day give it back to us? Well… (*hic*), let me let *you* in on a secret, Leech. He didn't. So, fuck… him. (*hic*)"

"Agreed," I said, raising my glass. I was worried that if I argued with Queen Rat in any capacity, it would wake her up, and my plan would be toast.

The queen slumped back in her chair, letting her anger out with a slow hiss. Even calm, she was so drunk I had trouble understanding her. "This is clearly the portrait of the man that you *want* me to see… (*hic*). So. Go on. Close the book. Make your conclusion. We have other… (*hic*) business… to attend tonight."

I feigned a humble bow. "I have no ulterior motives, your highness. To me, it makes perfect sense. The most genocidal, evil dictators in the history of my own world have all believed they were doing what was right for their people, even when their ideas resulted in millions of deaths. They all had savior complexes that led them to believe that the evil they did wasn't evil at all, only a necessary cost to achieve their plans for the greater good. Maybe Jun truly believed his plan would succeed and give Yesaeda a new star. For some reason, it didn't, and a hundred years later, here we are."

"Oh, go rot with your lousy… (*hic*)… moralizing," Queen Rat said.

"That's not only my opinion, queen. It was his, too. He says so right here…"

The soft, rhythmic wheeze of Queen Rat's snore drew my eyes up from the page. Her wine glass rolled out of limp fingers. I caught it before it fell off the table. Her eyelids fluttered, but she didn't wake. I would never get this chance again.

I picked up the book and slid it under the fold of my jacket.

THE BURROW

MY SKIN was hot and sticky with sweat as the Glass Book slid under it. I hadn't taken my jacket off while I was sitting in front of the queen's fire. She'd been too drunk to notice. I shuffled my feet toward the door to quiet my footsteps, opening it with the knob already turned, so it wouldn't click.

I stepped outside to see Bob o' the Knob standing there with his hand on the pommel of his sword, accompanied by four dangerous-looking men in black, who wore black furs and had black camouflage on their faces. Light gleamed on the naked, twisted steel in their hands.

The Moles. They know.

I smiled and faked a careening, drunken lurch toward the silent doorman with my arms outstretched. "Bobbbbby! Hey, buddy! My Moles! What's goin' on?"

Bob ducked my hug, put his palm on my chest and pushed me away. He surveyed my clothes, probably searching them for blood, then gave me a disgusted grimace.

I pretended not to understand. "What's the matter? Queen's passed out. You guys wanna go grab a drink? I'm wasted, man."

Bob o' the Knob clicked his tongue and drew an invisible line with his thumb in the air, signaling the Moles would cut me gullet to groin if I tried to run.

"You're not going anywhere, yet. You're going to wait right here until we can make sure the queen is asleep, safe and sound in her bed. Then, you're coming with us," the leader of the Moles said.

"Knew it was a bad call to leave her alone with this demon," another muttered.

The first Mole straightened up, tucking his dagger back into his belt. "The queen does what the queen does. He's not going to try anything. Look how hard he's shaking. You three, tie him up. Mr. Knob, mind letting me in there? Her Majesty's door locks automatically. I need the key to open it from the outside."

But I wasn't shaking because I was scared. I was drunker than I'd planned, and my nerves were shot, making it hard to concentrate on the sensation of falling upward toward the pull of the spiral growing inches in front of my forehead.

One of the Moles hissed, "Watch out!"

Another, "His eye!"

"Shit!" Another said, drawing his knife. But it was too late. I blotted into him like I had taken Vole several hours earlier. In an instant I was the one holding the knife. I stopped the blade mid-thrust. The tip slashed open Len's chest, leaving a deep cut in his left pectoral, but it missed his heart. Len fell backward, eyes still open, but lifeless. The only light behind them was the fading, burned-in trace of a golden spiral.

I drove the knife hard into my own belly and blotted again.

The harsh clamor of confusion descended on the other three Moles and Bob. I watched the Mole I'd killed double over and die twitching, then slashed my own throat and blotted a third and a fourth time. I made the next two Moles stab each other in the neck, falling dominos of black and spurting red.

I was back in control of Len before he even hit the floor.

Without a word, Bob o' the Knob kneeled, closed his eyes, and lowered his head. His hand dropped from the pommel of his sword. He hadn't drawn it. The blade was still bedded in the scabbard on his belt. Bob wanted me to kill him. He knew he couldn't beat me in a fight now that my ability to control the Blot had awakened, and wanted me to give him a good death.

But I had other plans. I bashed the old man's skull against the brick archway of Queen Rat's door. The blow was hard enough to knock him unconscious, but not enough to kill him. The thick fur of his bear pelt hood likely spared him from any permanent damage.

I hadn't wanted to kill the Moles. I'd only done so because it was their lives or a prison cell and a quick, likely inevitable execution. It's easy to say in hindsight that there could have been another way, but in that moment, I did what I believed was necessary to survive and finish my plans.

I hid the bodies the best I could, in a natural alcove in the cave walls down the hall from the queen's chamber.

Then I ran.

I stumbled and lurched through the endless, dim passages of the Last Station, clutching the Glass Book under my jacket with one hand and the biting wound in my chest with the other. The cut was deep, and my clothes were already soaked with dripping eyes of blood. Thankfully, the place was mostly still empty. Those who weren't already passed out were still partying hard in the feast hall on the other side of the station. My blood would leave a trail that I didn't have time to cover, but I hoped I'd be gone long before anyone found it.

A thousand questions burned in my mind. Were the Blight and the Blot related? If catching the Blot from Kashka had been what brought me to this world, then was she here, too? Was Ink? Would I find them where I was going?

I knew the reason why the Crippled King's plan hadn't succeeded, and why Yesaeda never reached its second sun. I never said it to Queen Rat, but the answer was as clear as day. At some point the Crippled King had made a choice. He chose the darkness, the cold, and the absolute power those things gave him. And I had no doubt about when he'd had this change of heart. It was when he learned to control the Blot.

That realization led me to another: why *I* was able to control it now, as well. Something had changed inside me when I'd defeated the Ratkeeper. Some of his power had transferred into me when I'd cut off his mask, or awoken a dormant ability that was already there. My control of the Blot was messy, unrefined, like a white belt in kendo sparring for the first time against a live opponent after only passively drilling technique. But with enough time and training, I knew I could master it.

One thought still lingered like a thorn in my mind. *But what will happen to Zaea?*

My hand instinctively moved to clutch the arrowhead necklace under my shirt. The necklace was somewhere else, in another world and time, but suddenly that place no longer seemed so far away. I could be there and back in the blink of an eye. All I had to do was fall.

THE CITY

I WOKE UP to Kashka banging on my apartment door. We'd made plans to visit the Concentration Camp Museum outside City at ten, but I'd slept through my alarm, and I could tell she was pissed off as soon as I opened the door and saw her standing there.

"Why did you not answer my messages?" she said, storming over to the bedside table where I kept my phone.

"I didn't hear it go off. I just woke up," I said.

Kashka was silent as she scrolled through the unread message notifications. She put the phone down and glared at me. "Are we still going today, or not?"

"Yeah, of course we are."

"I don't know. It might be too late. The museum closes at three PM. You should not have slept so late. Where were you last night?" Kashka said.

Images of prison camps buried in snow, of Snowmen dying as Zaea tamed the Lice with her countless tendrils of shadow, of reading Queen Rat to sleep next to a withering fire, and of stealing the Glass Book all flashed through my mind like fragments of a fading dream, though I knew it wasn't.

I wiped the sleep from my eyes, pulled on a pair of jeans, and approached Kashka slowly, cradling her face in my hands. I tried to kiss her, but she moved her face away. I kissed her on the eyelids instead. "Three o'clock, babe? That's five hours from now. We've got plenty of time. I just need to brush my teeth, then we can get going."

Kashka shook her head, fuming, as I hurried to the bathroom. "No. It is too late. We will already miss this bus. The next one doesn't leave until eleven."

"Eleven's fine. Stop being crazy," I said through a mouthful of toothbrush.

"I'm not."

"You are, and you know it."

"I do." She leaned on the bathroom doorframe, a slight smile curling the corners of her lips. She frowned and said, "Babe, is it really the truth? Did you not go out last night at all? Not even for one beer?"

I spat out the toothpaste and rinsed my mouth under the faucet. "Kashka, why do you ask me things like that? No, I didn't. Why would I lie to you?"

"Maybe you were with other girl."

Christ. This again?

"You know that I wasn't. I was home."

"No, I don't," Kashka said.

"You have issues."

"No. You do."

"You're not wrong about that. Come on, let's get going," I said.

There was already a long line for the bus by the time we reached City's central station. We barely made it on. Kashka argued with the driver for about five minutes before he took our money and printed our receipts for the hour-long ride to the museum, which cost a grand total of four dollars and fifty cents. The bus was one of those crappy little minivan busses that can only hold twenty people at maximum capacity. We sat on the floor next to the driver, uncomfortably bumping and lurching as he barreled down the twisting country back roads. There were only two highways in

Country, and neither of them went anywhere near the Concentration Camp Museum.

I said a silent prayer that we wouldn't crash, then spent most of the ride thinking about what would happen when I returned to the Night Country, but those plans no longer seemed urgent. I could go back whenever I wanted, and there was something I had to do here first.

It was noon by the time we bought our tickets and entered the museum. The sign above the archway of the camp's infamous main gate read *Arbeit Macht Frei,* a German phrase endemic among the concentration camps of the Holocaust, which meant "work for freedom." The perimeter was closed in a riddle of barbed wire fences punctuated by wooden watchtowers, the grounds a silent sepulcher of autumn trees all weeping their leaves. Tour groups full of Japanese, Chinese, Russians, Israelis, and Americans meandered through the gray gloom of early afternoon, reading the signs and taking dishonorable selfies in front of the camp's most morbid sights.

We didn't say much over the next three hours as we explored the matrix of brick buildings where Jewish, Russian, and Countryish prisoners had once slept and starved body-to-body under thin, threadbare blankets. The rooms were long since converted into museum displays depicting the timeline of the camp's role in the Holocaust, from the Nazi occupation of Country in 1939, to the liquidation of the Jewish ghetto in City, to the forced migration of those who were to be murdered into the concentration camps and their eventual deaths at the hands of Hitler's genocidal regime.

We'd watched *Schindler's List* in high school, studied the pictures of the mountains of pots, shoes, and disembodied braids of hair, even the dead themselves, emaciated and skeletal from months of starvation. But there was something about actually being in that place where those horrors had actually happened, feeling the chill and tasting the dusty concrete flavor of the air that transformed those images from abstract ideas into the harrowingly real.

Kashka clung to my side, but even her comforting warmth couldn't shake me out of the dark, hallucinatory visions conjured by the evil of that place.

We saw the hair, hills upon hills of seventy year-old braids shorn from the heads of five hundred thousand murdered women, and all I could think of was that it could've been hers.

We saw the shoes, endless piles of shoes that could have just as easily been on Kashka's feet, or Carly's, or Zaea's. The styles weren't much different from the styles women wore today; high heels, flats, strappy little sandals.

We saw the pots, a towering stack of them filling a room larger than my whole apartment, and all I could think was that any one of those countless pieces of enameled metal could have been the one Kashka and her family cooked their meals in back on her farm.

We approached a ruined courtyard where thousands had been marched toward a wall now covered in flowers and shot.

We walked through a low brick bunker with concrete floors and square ventilation holes in the ceilings. I didn't realize until we entered the incinerator room that we were standing in a gas chamber.

We saw the prison cells where gypsies, pregnant women, and the mentally ill had been held without water or food, then taken away to be subjected to the most brutal experiments in human history.

Kashka was mostly quiet for those few, eternal hours we spent wandering the camp, seldom offering to break the silence with a whispered "I love you," or some tidbit about the last time she'd visited during a school field trip in the fourth grade. She mentioned that the museum had been funded by the Russian Government to preserve the memory of the tens of thousands of Russian soldiers who had been murdered there, then quickly added that in her opinion, Russian people were dishonest and always tried to make everything about themselves, so therefore the displays about Russian losses couldn't be trusted.

I was too lost in my own head to care about most of what Kashka said. One thing did stick out to me, however, that echoed in my mind long after we'd climbed back on the bus for the hour-long ride back to City, as I watched a red sun set over fleeting quilts of fallow fields and old, dense forests.

Kashka said, "For us, this is not something shocking that happened many years ago, that we see in movies or that we learn about in school. It was really here. My grandparents told me stories about it. One in five people died when the Nazis came. Our cities and villages were turned to rubble. Even the people who did not lose their lives lost everything. My grandfather had to start over from zero.

"Countryish people have suffered many times throughout our history. The Second War was probably the worst instance, but it wasn't the only one - not even the most recent. Suffering is part of our lives. It's who we are."

Hearing her say that put an arrow in my gut. It brewed and grew and tangled me up inside, until I finally admitted to myself what I'd known all along, that I was being incredibly unfair in wasting Kashka's time. I wasn't going to marry this girl. In the U.S., maybe that wouldn't be so bad, but here, it was.

I could no longer lie to myself about the fact that each day I led Kashka on further limited her options for having a happy future. In Country, she didn't have a choice to stay single into her thirties, to be carefree and independent like people did back home. She'd be poor and seen as a failure by her family and peers. Unfair? Absolutely.

But Kashka couldn't opt out of doing as the Romans do simply because something was unfair. Kashka was in Rome whether she liked it or not.

Ink would've told me not to worry about it, that Kashka's problems weren't my problems, that I should sleep with her until I got sick of her and then find someone younger and prettier. Ink would've told me not to attempt to see things from Kashka's side at all. But my indecision wasn't just leading Kashka and I to an inevitable bad breakup. I actually had the power to destroy the life of someone I cared about, and I'd sworn to myself two years ago I was never going to make that mistake again.

When we got off the bus in the old quarter of City, a harsh autumn storm had rolled in, sending freezing, sideways gales of rain to howl down the ancient, crooked streets.

"I need a drink," I said.

"You want to go to Castle of Beer?" Kashka said.

"Sure."

We rushed to find shelter from the storm. I stopped us outside the door to Castle of Beer, under the overhang where I'd kissed her the night we first met, I took her by the arms, and pressed her gently against the slick, dimpled stones. She closed her eyes and lifted her chin for me to kiss her, waited, and opened her eyes.

"You don't want to kiss me?" she said, already knowing the answer.

Do the hard thing, I told myself. *Do the right thing. Be a good man, or at least, try.*

"I don't think we should do this anymore," I said.

"What?"

"This. Fight all the time, then break up and get back together. It just isn't working for me. And it's not just the fighting. It's your past. I never know where you are or what you're doing. We've been dating for two months and I haven't even been to your flat. Why? How can you accuse me of hiding parts of myself from you, when you're not open with me at all?"

"My flat is very old and ugly. I don't even have a shower, just a tub with a gas heater. I don't have enough money to move. I didn't want you to think I was poor," Kashka said quietly.

"I'm wasting your time, and it isn't right. I don't want to do that to you," I said.

Tears glistened in the corners of her eyes. Her lips quivered downward into an involuntary frown. "Dan. Please. I love you. I want to marry you. I want children with you. Do you not want it anymore? Truly? You really don't love me anymore? Because I don't believe you."

"Sometimes love isn't enough. We're not good for each other, Kashka."

She stared at me like I was her last glimpse of sunlight before the golden afternoon of her life vanished into dusk. She fought back her tears. I tried to hold her but she pushed me away.

Kashka's eyebrows slanted. "I loved you with my whole heart. That's the truth. I'm not a bad person, and I think you will not see it until it's too late. But all right. It's okay. My heart will heal. It's been broken before. I thought you were the one who wouldn't break it, but I was wrong. I will not argue with your decision. We say here that everything happens for a reason. I think you were sent here to punish me for my sins."

"You're just saying that to be cruel," I said.

Kashka shook her head furiously. "I'm not. I believe it. And now you will never change my mind. When I told you I loved you for nothing, I meant it, because you made me happy. I will be happy again, someday. Someday, I will be happy. Goodbye, Dan. I hope you have a good life. I wish you the best luck in the world."

"Goodbye, Kashka. You, too."

It took me hours to get home. I wandered aimlessly through the cold and the rain. I walked as far as the river, where I found myself standing alone under the slender, curving abutments of the Lover's Bridge, one palm gripping the metal hand railing littered with its rusted padlocks all bearing a thousand forgotten names, the other snaking inside my shirt to grasp the familiar shape of Carly's arrowhead necklace.

I thought of Carly, of Kashka, of the life I'd left back home and the one I'd found in City, of Ink, of Zaea, the Night Country, and the Blot, of the man I had been, and the one I would never be. Instead of feeling happy, or at least satisfied with my decision to let Kashka go, I was emptier than when I'd left my parents at the airport in San Francisco.

Maybe I would see her again. Or maybe I never would, and Kashka, like Carly, would become nothing more than a memory. Who are we to say what is possible and not? The universe is much larger than a simple yes and no, black and white, can and cannot. The universe is maybe, and maybe is deep and wide.

I tore off Carly's arrowhead necklace, pricked the tip of my finger with the obsidian point one last time just to feel something, cocked my arm back, and threw it into the river.

THE CITY

THE NEXT FEW DAYS were a vodka-induced blur. I got drunker than I had since my first week in Country, staying at the bars until closing, throwing back shot after shot of scorching, questionably-sourced liquor until I was too hammered to see straight.

I scoured the empty streets for pretty women to approach, but City's nightlife was dead due to the Feast of Saint Nicholas. The holiday didn't exist in America, but it was one of the four or five times per year in Country when everything except bars and restaurants shut down for three whole days, even the grocery stores, and the students all went home to their villages to spend time with their families.

I wasn't even thinking about sex. I just wanted someone to talk to. The truth was, I didn't think I could have sex if the opportunity presented itself. The black spot on my genitals was growing. It had started as a single bump, but had begun spiraling outward, giving birth to a coiling tendril of black, that I had the horrifying premonition wouldn't *stop* growing until it covered my entire body.

The worst night of my post-Kashka streak was the night I went to Drinks Bar, and the cute bartender fed me multiple shots of a 140-proof vodka with a name I couldn't pronounce. It was distilled from plums. The bartender was the same girl who'd poured me my drinks on my first night out in City, the one with the dyed-red hair and facial piercings. She was wearing a black tank-top that revealed a full-sleeve tattoo on her right arm. The tattoo depicted hardened Slavic knights in shining armor battling a hideous demon in the ruins of a medieval palace.

I'd spent enough time obsessively re-reading *Arkadius* that there was no mistaking that scene. The artwork was nowhere near as good as Lolek's subtle, nightmarish illustrations. The bartender's tattoo was drawn in a cliché, Ed Hardy style, and didn't look at all like what I'd imagined when reading the poem, but I leapt at the chance to ask her about it, hoping my expertise would impress her.

"Act IV," I said, drunkenly pointing at her tattoo. "The scene where the Good Knight slays the demon. Climax of the poem. Fugging... epic."

The bartender raised an eyebrow at me. "What?"

"When Arkadius stabs the demon in the face and frees the Kingdom," I said, almost falling off my stool as I leaned in closer.

The bartender recoiled, squinting at me. "Oh, yes. You mean my tattoo. *Arkadius* is my favorite story. I've reread it every year since I was a girl."

"Why?" I said.

"Pride in my homeland, maybe. It is our tradition. Plus, I like swords, and this guy has a cool one. Look." The bartender flexed her bicep, and the Good Knight's tiny, gleaming blade plunged back and forth into the black depths of the demon's hood.

Cool optical illusion, I thought. *But that isn't what happens in the poem.*

"Wow. You're a nerd," I said.

The bartender smirked. "You're the one who commented on it."

"I had to read it for my job," I said.

"Oh. What do you do?"

"I'm a book translator."

"A what?"

"A book. Translator."

"Oh. Okay. You don't need to yell."

The bartender smiled pityingly and put the bottle of plum vodka back on the shelf. I thanked her and promptly stumbled home, but I was so drunk I couldn't find the keys to the front door of my building. I passed out on the front lawn next to the gutter.

I woke up to the gray light of dawn in a pool of my own vomit. I was shivering, and my head hurt like I'd been brained by a Snowman's axe. Thankfully the temperature had stayed above freezing. If it had been any colder, I would be dead. Some nice person had draped my coat over me like a blanket at some point during the night. They even left my wallet, though there wasn't much cash left after my three-day bender.

My keys were in my coat pocket.

In the painful cave of my apartment, where my hangover bloomed and then deepened, I thought back on the chain of events that had led me to this place of suffering and regret so far from my home. I thought of the people who were no longer in my life, who my failures or choices had driven away (some of them, for good); my dad, my mom, my sister Delia, her husband Nick, their little girl, Evan, Carly, and God.

As if summoned, my phone buzzed on the bedside table. It was a text from Evan.

Hey man, sorry for the delay. Life tough with the baby. Always busy. Glad to hear you're doing well. Talk soon, buddy.

Rage spilled down my fingers into the touch screen of my phone as I drafted my response:

Seriously? It took you two fucking months to send me a goddamned text saying hello? What kind of guy leaves his best friend hanging that long, when I'm in a foreign country? I'm not okay, Evan. I'm not okay at all.

But I didn't send it. I'd fantasized about burning Evan for his disappearing act since I'd moved to Country, but now that I finally had a chance, it seemed stupid and childish. Ink would've scoffed at me for acting like such a little baby.

I deleted the message. I never wanted to talk to Evan again.

THE CITY

LOOKING UP at the inside of Saint Mary's Basilica was like standing under a starlit ocean. Vaulted ceilings rose into waves of blue marble speckled with gold and amber studs, huge marble pillars as thick as kelp forests holding that false sky aloft between a robber's sanctuary of chapels. The nave was riddled with arcane stairways and vining pulpits branching off from the main church's ground floor. The altar was a hollow mountain of stained glass and black, ancient wood depicting the story of Christ from his birth to the Resurrection.

The place was large enough to hold thousands. Schools of tourists swam errantly through the timeless stones, quieting only for the garden of grandmothers praying in the rearmost pews. And yet wherever I sat, I was still completely alone.

One of the first things I learned after moving to Country was that beautiful old churches aren't merely conduits to the divine. They are funnels that force-feed you with awe. You think to yourself, *how could anyone build something so beautiful? How did they dedicate their whole lives to such a selfless act? Will anyone remember what I do when I'm gone?*

I sat in the back rows of the church, as far from the tourists as I could, bowed my head and prayed. It had been two years since I'd spoken to God. I asked him to forgive me for everything wrong that I'd done. I asked him to help me become a good man. I asked him to help me forgive myself for Carly's death.

If God couldn't help me do those things, I didn't think anyone could. If he didn't answer me here and now, in the last fleeting moment before I slipped and fell into my own shadow, then I would carry this pain forever. There would never be peace in my heart.

I prayed, I listened, and I waited. I knelt, I begged, and I cried. I asked God for forgiveness, but God wasn't there.

THE CITY

"WERE YOU SICK AGAIN?"

I turned around to see Lolek ascending the stairs of my apartment building with his girlfriend Marzena, both of their arms heavily laden with plastic grocery bags from the convenience shop downstairs. Marzena was the receptionist who worked the front desk at our office. She was tall, thin, and had a village-pretty face and almond brown hair that fell almost to her waist. Like most guys in Country, Lolek was batting far above his league.

"Hey Lolek. Hey Marzena. Yeah, I was sick. Do you guys live here?" I said.

Lolek shifted a grocery bag across his hip. "Yes, of course. Didn't they tell you?"

"We found you, um... we found your flat for you," Marzena said. Her English wasn't as good as Lolek's, and she spoke with that lilting, wooden false-British accent that my co-workers called "school English."

"Nope. Nobody tells me anything," I said.

They both laughed. "Those bastards," Lolek said.

"Anyway. Been out for the last few days. Some kind of stomach virus. Again," I said.

"Well, don't worry. They don't tell me anything, either. I just found out today we have to redo the whole second part of *Arkadius* again. This will be the third time. They did a survey, and the focus group didn't like the artwork. They said it wasn't what they imagined when they read the poem in school," Lolek said.

I rolled my eyes, throwing my hands up in the air, and said, "Well, we're in the same boat with that one. I have to redo all of my shit, too. You guys doing a little grocery shopping?"

"Weekly supply," Lolek said, holding up one of the bags. I counted eight rectangular boxes of Earl Grey inside the overstuffed, translucent plastic.

"Jesus Christ. You're addicted," I said.

Marzena smiled politely. I don't think she understood my joke.

"Anyway, yes, we live on this floor, right over there, at the end of the hall. Flat number forty-three," Lolek said. He quickly added, "I can't believe you haven't seen us here before. Marcin didn't mention that we live here?"

Wait. Dammit. This means he must have heard all those screaming, humiliating fights. Months and months of fights. And not just Lolek, but his girlfriend, too. I'll bet everyone at work knows how much Kashka and I fight... or rather, fought.

No. They seem like good people, like Evan was, before everything changed. They wouldn't do that to me, would they?

"No," I said. "I had no idea we were neighbors. We'll have to get together sometime."

Lolek's grin dissolved into a flat, inquisitive line. He raised an eyebrow at me and said, "Actually, I wanted to talk to you about Christmas. I was going to come over later, but then we saw you leaving and thought it was better to just ask now."

"Christmas?" I said.

"It's not important. Will you have time to talk about it later?" Lolek said.

"No, sorry. I've got plans tonight," I said.

"Oh. What plans?"

"I'm going to a magic show," I said.

"A magic show?"

"It's at the Old Theater on St. John's Street. I know the guy who's putting it on. He's another American. A bit eccentric, but the guy is crazy talented. Plus, I need to get out of the house for a while. But I have a minute now. What did you want to ask?" I said.

Lolek and Marzena exchanged a look. "I heard that Filip had to break his plans with you to visit with his family. We wanted to invite you to have Christmas at my parents' place. We don't want you to spend Christmas alone."

"Is it far from here?" I said.

"No. My village is maybe an hour east of here. And technically, it would be two Christmases - one with each family. So, six Christmas dinners, because in Country, Christmas lasts for three days."

My stomach rumbled. I hadn't eaten anything since yesterday but scrambled eggs.

"I'll be there," I said.

Marzena patted Lolek on the back. "Also, this one is, um... special holiday, for us. We want you to, um... be a part of it."

"What makes this one so special?" I said.

"It is our last Christmas as, um... boyfriend and girlfriend," Marzena said.

"We're getting married in the spring," Lolek explained.

"Wow. Congratulations. I'm so happy for you guys."

"Then it's a date," Lolek said.

"You can't, um... say that it's a date," Marzena scolded him.

"Why not?" Lolek said.

"Because he's a man."

I chuckled. "I'll mark it on my calendar. So, do you guys want help with those groceries?"

THE OLD THEATER

RED CURTAINS drew over an empty stage. The ancient velvet snapped and slithered across the brightly polished wood, revealing a maze of disjointed floorboards, crowded amplifiers, and microphone chords. It was an old, grand theater on the smallest scale, with less than a hundred seats. The rows of folding, disintegrating cloth chairs were packed so tight together the audience had to sit knee-knee with their neighbors. The balcony was a contradiction of plaster angels and claustrophobia. A full house awaited Ink's entrance, a mix of stoned college students and middle-aged, mildly interested eccentrics all chatting loudly and checking their smartphones. The air smelled of must, stress, and borrowed time.

The stage lights flashed, and a ripple of silence spread outward from the front row, where I sat with my feet touching the foot of the stage. The lights dimmed to total darkness, and a single white beam appeared at the corner of the stage. Ink manifested from that velvet sea, wearing a top hat, a pince-nez, and a black, three-piece suit.

The crowd gave a hesitant round of applause. Ink confidently walked to center stage, bowed, and three white doves sprung out from under the rear of his tailcoat. The crowd gasped and roared with applause as the squawking birds frantically tried to find an exit among the theater's high rafters. Ink gave a dramatic snap, inhumanly loud above the din, and the doves stilled and fell, fluttering strangely on the air as if made of paper.

A wave of startled *oohs* and *aahs* spread through the audience. The doves *were* paper, nothing more than origami.

One of the paper birds sailed down into my lap. I picked it up and unfolded it. It wasn't made of normal paper. It was a folded ten-crown note. The old grandmother sitting next to me snatched it away and gave me a dirty look, like she was going to fight me for it if I tried taking it back.

Sounds of pleasant surprise punctuated the air all around me as the crowd snatched up the money birds where they fell.

Ink silenced the audience with a gesture and said in a booming voice that filled the musty corners of the theater with his deep gravel, "My name is Ink. I come from America. I arrived in Country four years ago with nothing but the coat on my back and some pennies in my pocket."

A tiny flame appeared within the white-gloved gyre of Ink's hands. Ink spun the flame like a loom. The flame-wheel flickered and grew.

"Yet tonight, I am here to entertain. You will witness the wonders learned by a wandering soul. I've traveled to places strange beyond all imagining, outside the limits of space and time. I have trained with masters of the macabre and the arcane, men who could bend the laws of this universe, and others, to their will. Tonight, you will see a thousand centuries of the dark arts distilled to the head of a pin. Tonight, I will show you the meaning of awe."

The wheel of flame between Ink's hands shivered and stretched into a slender oblong, and then elongated into a rectangle the size of a large picture frame. Flaming stars and stripes populated the inner space, a blazing simulacrum of the American flag.

Ink wove the burning flag into fiery replications of famous American landmarks: Mount Rushmore, Yosemite, the New York skyline. "Why did I come here, you ask? Because my country is no longer free. There, men can no longer be what we were born to be. America, once the land of the free and the home of the brave, is now the land of the fat and the enslaved, a place where you pay more to get less, where having fun is wrong, and telling the truth will put you in jail."

Ink turned the flames into the bars of a jailhouse door, then erased them with a slash of his finger. The fire curled into a ring once more. Inside it, Ink drew a Vitruvian Man.

"Men are, above all things, playful beings. We are not merely born for games... fighting, war, love, sex..." the crowd gave a nervous giggle, "...in fact, we need them to live and thrive."

Ink hacked the center of the circle six times, extinguishing each of the fire man's limbs one-by-one.

"Without games, men cannot be. And without men, civilization cannot be. Where America leads, the rest of the world follows. So here we all are, in the great spiral, tail-spinning down toward a beautiful oblivion."

The Vitruvian Man vanished, and Ink shrunk the ring of flame back to a ball no larger than his glove.

"There it is, my friends, my dear fellow surfers on this slow, crumbling wave of decline. That is why I left. I quit being responsible. I quit being honest. I quit being good and started practicing the fine art of living for myself rather than those who only wanted me in my place, who wanted to hold me down. And I would encourage each and every one of you to do the same."

Ink drew a figure eight, summoning a tiny nude woman dancing in the palm of his hand. "Yes, you have stability. You have traditions. You have Catholicism. Family values. Closed borders. You have strong men and pretty, feminine women. You have loving grandmothers, perfect weddings in beautiful churches, three Christmas dinners a year. You have culture, language, and morality... for now. I promise that someday, much sooner than you'd like, all of that will be gone, evaporated like snow in the sunlight."

Ink closed his fist, snuffing the dancing woman out.

"I have seen it a thousand times before and will see it a thousand times again. The fall is inevitable, the shadow ever falling over the horizon. You can't escape it, nor should you try. We struggle to thrive, and then we grow rich and comfortable, until comfort turns to contempt, and we tear down the towers that made us tall in the first place. The corruption of all good things is written in their design."

Ink whispered into his fist, like he was blowing the audience a kiss. A hot spear of fire shot out over my head, turning the dimness of the theater as bright as day. Fearful gasps echoed all around. The gout of fire stabilized above the crowd and began rotating, circling outward until the theater was filled with countless, spiraling rings of flame.

A few audience members yelped in panic. I buried my face in my sleeve, wiping away the thick streams of sweat suddenly drawing from my skin.

"So my friends - my, good, honest people of Country – do not fight corruption. Corruption is our duty. It is in our nature to fall," Ink said.

He retracted his hand, and just like that, the flaming spiral was gone, leaving only the smell of gunpowder and a few, hesitant claps that turned into rolling, thunderous applause.

No way. That was impossible.

The show picked up, and from there moved at breakneck speed. Before I could collect my thoughts, Ink had already moved onto his next trick: making his albino hawk, Mr. Snow appear and disappear on his arm in time with the stage lights shutting off and then back on again.

Once Ink had adequately teleported the hawk onto various parts of his own body, he made Mr. Snow appear at various points throughout the theater, too; once up in the rafters, once at the rear doors, once on the balcony (where a group of drunken hipsters shouted and tried to shoo the big bird away with a beer bottle), then finally on the back of an old woman's seat.

After the bird trick, Ink performed the card routine I'd seen him do on the street, in which the magician shuffled and juggled a deck of playing cards, and then threw knives through the cards he was juggling while they were in mid-air. Only this time, instead of tumbling back down to the stage when they were hit, the cards exploded like miniature fireworks, filling the theater with tiny panoplies of color and sound.

When Ink went to fetch the fallen throwing knives from the stage, they turned into wriggling, poisonous snakes. Ink offered a snake to the front row, and then stuffed it under his top hat. When all the snakes were put away, Ink removed his top hat to show us the snakes were gone.

The grand finale of the show was Ink's own twisted variation of the infamous magician's sword trick. Big Ben came out dressed up like a medieval executioner, black cloth mask and all, leading a pretty brunette Countryish girl by the arm. The girl was so dolled up it took me a moment to recognize it was Iza, the high school girl Ink had taken home from Drinks Bar the night Kashka gave me the Blot.

Big Ben looked like an overweight American dad dressed up to take his kids out for Halloween, all questionably obtained muscle barely hidden under a cheap-looking costume. Iza was the opposite, dressed to the nines in a tight black dress, fresh curls in her winter branch brown hair, a thick slathering of stage makeup, and a floppy, pointed black witch's hat.

"Everyone, please allow me introduce my two lovely assistants. This giant, fleshy homunculus is called Baldanders. I know that's a mouthful. Blame him. He chose the name himself. It comes from a great work of science fiction literature. You'd be surprised that such a massive, meaty fellow could read at all, but old Baldy here consumes at least two books a day. Literally. He eats them." The audience gave a polite laugh.

Ink flourished his hat and took a deep, theatrical bow in Iza's direction. "And this perplexingly beautiful damsel in distress is named Margarita. She just arrived from Moscow on her broomstick. Unfortunately, she couldn't bring her black cat. Baldanders ate him, too." More nervous snickers murmured from the crowd.

Big Ben and Iza approached center stage, where the Executioner handed the Witch off to the Magician and returned backstage. "Double unfortunate is the fact that here in Europe, and especially in Country, people don't have a high tolerance for witchcraft. So sorry, Marge, but your days of joyriding with the devil are over," Ink said.

Iza pretended to be terrified while Ink held up his tailcoat like a curtain, leaving only the girl's head visible to the audience. Big Ben returned carrying not one, but two *katanas* bedded in black, lacquered scabbards. I wasn't 100% sure, but they didn't look like stage swords. They looked like real, razor-sharp steel *nihonto*.

No way are those actual Japanese blades. No one's that stupid. Not even Ink.

Big Ben drew the first, then the second sword, and placed them on opposite sides of Iza's neck, forming a bladed X with her head in the middle. From where I was sitting, I could see one of the swords edge-on, and the stage lights were bright enough that there should have been at least some light reflected off the edge if the blade had been blunted. It wasn't.

No. He wouldn't. Would he?

Iza, too, seemed to sense the danger she was in. In an instant, her pretend terror became real. Sweat beaded on her petite, porcelain forehead, gathering under the brim of her hat in visible droplets. Her eyes widened, fixated on the two razor-sharp edges caging in her neck. Her lips quivered, and her whole body began to shake.

Did that prick really not tell her what he was planning to do? I wondered.

Dismayed whispers rose to a full-on clamor as Ink raised his coat-curtain up to cover Iza's head, too, hiding her entirely from the audience. Ink gave a subtle nod to Big Ben.

The Executioner drew a quick double breath and slashed with both hands.

Three things happened simultaneously: Iza let out a blood-curdling scream; the sound of metal slicing meat rang as the swords scissored closed; Ink flourished his tailcoat, and then dropped it, revealing...

The crowd gasped. Iza's head wasn't merely separated from her body. Iza's head was gone, and so were her clothes.

Iza's naked, decapitated body stood with her hands on her hips, still swaying from the impact of the makeshift guillotine. Ink placed a hand on her lower back to steady her and gave the audience a huge, self-confident smile.

No. No, Ink did not just murder that girl. That son of a... where is her head? Where are her clothes?

Ink presented the girl's nude, headless body to us with a white-gloved *ta-da* as silent horror enveloped the audience. Hands clasped over mouths. Stifled cries rippled through the seats behind me. There wasn't any blood, neither on Iza's neck, nor on the blades of Big Ben's swords, which he was swiftly putting away behind the far curtain of the stage.

Ink put his tailcoat back on and held up a hand to quiet us. "My good people of Country. Before you storm the stage with your pitchforks and tear me to pieces for taking the life of this poor girl, I would point out that Margarita here isn't dead."

I couldn't believe my eyes, but Iza's body was still moving. Her hands scoured the flat line at the top of her neck where the cut had been made just above her trachea, searching for the head that wasn't there. Their motion was smooth and controlled, not erratic like one would've expected from a freshly decapitated corpse. I'd read somewhere that the heads of decapitated people stay alive for a few seconds after being separated from the body. But did that also apply to bodies deprived of their heads?

I didn't think it did.

"What's that, Margarita? Do you want to tell us something?" Ink asked the headless girl.

Iza said something too quiet to hear.

Ink hushed the audience with a wave. "One more time, dear?"

"You didn't tell me you were using real swords," Iza's nude, headless body said. Her voice sounded wheezing and muffled through the open piping of her neck, but it was unmistakably hers.

"Sorry. Anything else? Maybe you could tell us how you feel, now that you've lost a bit of weight? Oops. I mean, not that you needed to, or anything. Forgive me that faux pas, my love. Doesn't she look thin, everyone? Oh, dammit. She's not likely to forget *that one* anytime soon," Ink said.

"You're an asshole," Iza's headless body said.

The tension gripping the theater eased, and a few anxious laughs punctured the silence.

"See, folks? This scrumptious, unholy tart is still in perfectly good health. Sure, she's a few kilograms lighter, but bikini season *is* right around the corner. By the way, Margarita, baby... have you considered shaving?"

"Give me back my head," Iza's body said.

The audience roared.

"Don't worry. I will," Ink said."

"Well, where the hell did you put it?" Iza said.

"It's somewhere safe. Do you want to say any final words before Baldy calls the curtain and gives it back to you?" Ink said.

Ink placed both hands on the stump of Iza's neck, twisting it back and forth, like Iza was shaking her head *no*. "A little hard to do without all the equipment," Ink said.

"Stop that," Iza said.

Ink let go and gave us a Cheshire Cat's grin. "Oops. My apologies. Since moving to Country, I've developed the horrible habit of not listening to anything a woman says. That's why I love you guys. You can take a joke. Unlike some people..."

Ink pointed to Iza, who had begun searching the stage frantically for her head. She stumbled over a bundle of speaker wires and fell over. The audience lost it.

"Seriously. *Kocham Kraj.* You guys are the best. Thank you so much!" Ink said.

The curtains fell to uproarious applause, a single, claustrophobic wave that boomed through the darkness of the theater. When the curtain rose again, Ink, Big Ben, and Iza – Iza, who was whole again, her head and clothes reattached – raised their hands to the ceiling and gave three deep bows.

The crowd cheered and showered the stage with bread.

THE CITY

I FOUND INK in the alley behind the theater, one hand leaning on the grimy bricks, the other wiping tears from Iza's eyes with ritualistic detachment. I hung back, not wishing to interrupt them, but Ink noticed me standing there and waved Iza away. She stared at him incredulously. He waved her off again, pointing at the street and then clicking with his tongue to get the point across.

I hadn't heard what they'd been arguing about, but it must've been bad, because she gave Ink one of the dirtiest looks I've ever seen in my life before storming off.

"Spierdalaj," Iza said over her shoulder as she disappeared back into the golden glow of the City night, a broken bird fleeing back to the infinite nest from which she'd fallen. I knew enough Countryish to know that Iza had just told Ink to go fuck himself. From the way she'd been crying, and the callous aloofness Ink had demonstrated, I didn't think he would be seeing her again.

"They'll surprise you," Ink said to me.

"Uh... what?" I said.

He beckoned me to come closer. "It was a fight. A broad doing what broads do. It's not gonna stain your clothes, buddy. C'mere."

"Okay." I edged closer to where he was leaning on the back of the theater. "Uh... you need a cigarette?"

"The fuck? No, I don't need a cigarette. I don't smoke. Neither do you, Boy Scout," Ink said.

I pulled the pack of Marlboro Reds out of my coat pocket. "Actually, I do. Started yesterday."

"You're a little old to be entering your 4Chan phase, don't you think?" Ink said.

"I broke up with my girlfriend. I guess that makes two of us. You don't mind?" I said. Ink threw me a quizzical glare. I lit my cigarette. "You did tell me it was a good way to meet women, remember?"

"Daniel, sometimes I think you must be a fucking idiot to believe half the shit I tell you. Don't smoke. You want to die when you're forty-five? No. You want to live forever. Give me that." Ink snatched the cigarette from my mouth and extinguished it under the heel of his shoe. I withheld my protest. "I'm sorry to hear about your girlfriend. I didn't know you and that girl were serious. What was her name again?"

"Kashka," I said. "And we weren't. She wanted to be, but I decided it was better not to waste her time."

"Give her a few months. She'll be back. So will that one." He nodded toward the direction Iza had gone. "You called it off. You know what that means? It means she'll be checking her phone every five seconds for the next forever until she hears from you again. Then it'll be easier than it was the first time."

"I'm not sure I want…" I started to say, but Ink cut me off.

"You enjoy the show?" he said.

"Uh. Yeah. It was great. That's why I came back here to find you. I wanted to tell you…"

"Hey, thanks, man… really awesome that you came out tonight. Thank you for supporting me and my work, from the bottom of my heart."

Ink extended his hand for me to shake. I shook it. "Actually, I was wondering if maybe we could go somewhere to grab a drink and talk. It's kind of important," I said.

A slow, frozen breath blew from Ink's mouth. He rolled his top hat through his hands, squinted, and said, "That's not in the cards tonight, Boy Scout. But let's meet up another time when I come back to Country."

"You're leaving?" I said. "Why?"

"It's time for me to move on - past time, actually - Benny's already on his way to the airport."

"Where are you going?"

"Romania. Greener pastures. Thinner waists. Better asses. Well, maybe not better asses. Countryish girls have the booty game on lock. But my buddy told me it's going off down there. Catching a flight out tomorrow. Gotta go home and pack."

"I don't understand," I said. "I thought you said this place was paradise? I read that on your blog."

"Paradise has fallen. Paradise always does. I'm getting sick of the bitchy attitudes, the iPhones, Tinder, blue hair, and facial piercings. Female flakiness has risen 200% in the last two years. This country is becoming too westernized for my taste. You should've been here two years ago – that's when it was *really* good. Every other girl in the club gave you fuck me eyes like you were a movie star. Alas, not anymore. Now every Aga, Paulina, and Magda has her naked ass all over Instagram and has had her brains banged out by a dozen horny Spaniards and Italians when she was on holiday.

"No, I'm just rambling. I really did love it here. This city gave me four of the best years of my life, and too many decent lays to count. But places change, y'know? And I'm coming to realize that, as much happiness as this place has given me, happiness is transient, and my time would be better spent somewhere else. You understand," Ink said.

"It almost sounds like you need that drink more than I do," I said.

Ink chuckled. "Maybe, but I gotta pack. Plus, Mr. Snow gets cranky if he doesn't get his sausages within thirty minutes after a show."

An awkward moment of silence passed. I didn't know what to say. If Ink was leaving, who else could possibly help me?

"Well, shit," Ink said. "It's been good getting to know you, Boy Scout. You're a solid individual. I see great things ahead for you in this land of withering carnal opportunity. Just don't get any of these crazy fields you're plowing pregnant. Then you'll witness the true insanity of the Slavic female, and trust me, that isn't something you want to experience."

Just ask him, I thought, but the words caught behind my teeth. It was a struggle even to dance around what I wanted to say. "Actually, when I said I wanted to talk to you, I meant about something other than girls. It's… personal. I think you might be the only one who knows something about this."

"Is it serious?" Ink said.

"I really need your advice, man. Twenty minutes of your time. That's all I'm asking for."

"And what personal subject is that, Dan?"

Don't be afraid of him. He's made of flesh and blood, just like you. Just ask.

"It's about the Blot. That thing you mentioned the night you introduced Iza to me and Big Ben. The one they say rots your brain, turns you crazy," I said.

CORRUPTION

The alley became a grave of echoes until finally, just when I thought Ink would turn and walk away, he said, "We can meet at Drinks Bar, all right? One beer. Meet me there in thirty minutes."

THE CITY

"YOU THINK this girl gave you something, huh?" Ink said with a yawn.

"I'm not sure, but I think so. Nasty bitch," I said.

We were sitting in the back room at Drinks Bar, at the same corner table where I'd met Ink and Big Ben my first night out in Country. We sat huddled over a slowly amassing collection of empty beer glasses and cigarettes disintegrating to ember in the ashtray. We were the only two people in the joint other than the bartender, a big, bald Countryish guy who looked like a soccer hooligan. The cute one must've had the night off.

For weeks, I'd fruitlessly scoured Google for any information I could find about what Kashka had given me. I tried every search term I could think of: *Blot, the Blot, Blot* and *Country* together, *STD nightmares, viral hallucinations,* and more. Nothing came up regarding the Night Country, or sexually transmitted dreams. Ink became my only hope of figuring out what was happening to me.

"Girl game is a real thing. Sounds like you got played," Ink said. He gave me a sympathetic tip and sip of his beer. "Don't take it too much to heart. Every player hits a speed bump once in a blue moon. Hell, I've caught things before. We won't discuss the particulars of those thankfully infrequent episodes. But it happens even to the best of us. As long as it's nothing permanent, don't consider yourself out of the game just yet. Unless she gave you HIV, then I doubt you've been struck down in your prime, Daniel. Even herpes…"

"She didn't give me HIV or herpes. It's something else," I said.

"Hmmm. You mentioned earlier that you thought it might be this, what did you call it?" Ink said.

"The Blot. That's what *you* called it. Remember? That night we were here with Iza," I said.

Ink blew a raspberry into the dregs of his beer. "Yeah, I remember. But I was just kidding around, man. How do you know I wasn't just talking out of my ass, that I didn't make it up on the spot?"

"Because there's a black mark on my dick, steadily spiraling outward," I said. "Because I'm sick all the time. I'm having recurring lucid dreams about the same group of characters, in the same screwed-up world, and it isn't ours. Any time I fall into a deep sleep I go back there, without fail."

"Did you go to the doctor?" Ink said.

"Yes. The doctor couldn't see it. He told me I should take folic acid and vitamins."

"Vitamins. Classic," Ink chuckled.

In the most honest tone of voice I could muster, I said, "Listen, Ink. Normally, I'd never beg someone else for a favor. I have way too much pride for that. So, trust me when I say that it is taking everything I have to set that aside and ask this of you right now. But, from one man to another, I truly, deeply need your help. I don't know what to do. I have no one else to turn to. So if you have any idea about what's happening to me, please, just tell me."

Ink took a long time to respond. When he finally did, his voice had lost its typical, jovial aloofness, and became an even monotone, like that of a scientist.

"Tell me what you dream of," Ink said.

"You really don't know?"

Ink crossed his arms. "I really don't."

"All right. The dream I have whenever I fall asleep is about a place called the Night Country. It's a dark, frozen world where the people are forced to live in tunnels, because an evil king has stolen the sun. On the Surface the night is everlasting, and the Undercity is plagued by hunger, famine, sickness, and death. A few of the people in the tunnels have formed a loose resistance movement called the Vermin who fight to overthrow the tyrannical regime, but they're disorganized and poorly armed. And, they have legends about spirits called Visitors, who are sent to the Night Country to reanimate the bodies of the recently dead and help the rebels fight. In the dream, I'm one of those spirits."

"That's one hell of a story," Ink said.

I sighed. "You did say that the Blot rots your brain. I figured that must include some sort of hallucinations, maybe even dementia…"

"Dan."

"I'm sorry. I just want answers, man. I haven't slept in weeks."

"Dan," Ink said again.

"What?"

He reevaluated me with a narrow, beery gaze. "I owe you an apology. I lied earlier. The truth is that I knew a guy once who claimed he had the Blot. That's how I heard about it."

"You did?"

Lying son of a…

Ink folded his hands and nodded. "The stories have been around forever. The people of Country have always had myths about sexually transmitted curses and nightmares visited upon immoral men and women by sex demons. It's not something we hear about in our culture anymore, since sex in America is considered a strictly biological phenomenon, without much of a spiritual component. Do you know the theory of genetic memory?"

"I don't think so," I said.

CORRUPTION

Our conversation was interrupted by a group of men noisily entering the bar. There was a scuffle of removed jackets and raised voices conversing loudly in the front room. I couldn't see the men, but I recognized their voices instantly, and a chill seeped into my blood. They were the same men who had tried to fight Ink, Big Ben, and me on the first night we hung out together.

I thought for sure Ink and I were going to get jumped the second the hooligans stepped into the back room and saw us sitting there, but nothing happened. The bald, tracksuit-wearing thug who Ink had nearly decapitated with his spoon walked in, gave us a dirty look, said something under his breath, then immediately turned around and left.

When they were gone, Ink smiled and said, "I guess they didn't want to watch the BBC."

I glanced over my shoulder at the muted big screen TV mounted on the far wall. Indeed, the usual football match had been changed to an emergency news report about a peaceful student protest that had escalated into a riot somewhere in the east of Country. It showed a raging crowd clashing with the police amidst a cluster of concrete apartment buildings. The camera even briefly focused on one man lying on the ground in a pool of his own blood.

The crowd was protesting a high-level trade agreement between Country and the Russian Federation, meant to line the pockets of a few Russian and German billionaires and their former Soviet-era allies still holding office in Country, all the while further impoverishing Country's poor.

This wouldn't have surprised me much as an American, since our history in America can basically be summed up as "the government helping the rich to gangbang the poor," but in Country, it was what historians call a watershed moment. Country's economy had been steadily growing ever since its ascension to the European

Union after the fall of the Berlin Wall, and was finally poised to break the Eastern European curse of poverty.

This deal, made behind closed doors by a few corrupt individuals operating in the highest hallways of power, was set to threaten all of that.

I wouldn't find out until much later, but three people died in those riots while Ink and I were sitting in Drinks Bar sipping beers and discussing possibly mythical sexual curses.

Ink leaned back in his chair, taking a deep drag off his cigarette, and blew a string of smoke rings up toward the dim lamp above our table. The rings drifted and began circling that tawny, flickering light, falling into its orbit like planets orbiting a star.

Or worm holes orbiting a galaxy, I thought.

"Back to what I was saying about this Blot thing," Ink said. "A guy I knew claimed he had it. He told me a similar story to the one you just told. Only, I didn't believe a word of it. Not at first. But then, over time, I watched him descend further and further into his delusions. He became exhausted. Agitated. Paranoid. He was tired all the time, always had these huge black circles under his eyes, and was always talking about dead cities and crippled kings. I started to believe that the Blot was real."

He does know, I thought.

"I have a theory about this 'Blot.' I formed it after observing my friend suffer and ultimately die from his infection. But let's establish a few things right off the bat. The doctors won't help you, here in Country or anywhere else. They don't know what it is."

"I figured as much," I said.

"These nightmares you've been having – my friend had them, too - they don't sound like dreams to me at all. They sound more like memories. More specifically, someone else's memories that have been implanted in your body by the delivery mechanism of a sexually transmitted bacterium or virus."

"Memories?" I said. The thought had never occurred to me.

"You said you've never heard of genetic memory?" Ink said.

I shook my head. "No, I haven't."

"Genetic memory is the theory that, over the eons, traces of our memories become imbued in our DNA so that future generations of our species can benefit from our experiences. These aren't normal memories that can be recalled consciously. They're extremely long-term, and only available to the subconscious mind, but they guide our instincts, and sometimes, they can resurface in dreams."

"That all sounds like some serious science fiction," I said.

"Maybe," Ink said. "But what if it's not? What if it is real? What if that's exactly what this is, this mystery disease that's infected you and which killed my friend, what's giving you these recurring dreams?"

"Memories from another world, huh. Could be," I said, feeling my heart plummet into my guts.

This guy's not interested in helping me. He just wanted an ear to listen to another one of his conspiracy theories. Whatever Kashka gave me is going to kill me, and there's nothing I can do about it. I should leave.

Ink belabored the point, seemingly unaware of my discomfort. "What if your dreams are simply the resurfacing of genetic memories hidden inside some sexually transmitted infection you were unfortunate enough to catch? What if what you and I know as the Blot was actually *engineered* by someone who didn't want those memories to be forgotten?"

"I dunno, man. Listen, I should get going. I came here because I thought you could help me. Not to listen to some tinfoil conspiracy theory that sounds like it came from a comic book."

I got up, shrugging into my jacket. As I turned to head for the door, Ink said, "Stop. I am helping you, Boy Scout. Sit down."

I did.

Any trace of friendliness had vanished from Ink's voice. "You caught a disease no doctor on Earth can identify, let alone cure. Over the next several months, your mind will rot until you become a sleepless, dreamless zombie, a walking shell that can't do anything but shit, and piss, and masturbate. Then it will be too late. You'll fade until one day, you're just gone. As sure as you were born, this will happen."

"I know," I said, hanging my head.

"That all sounds pretty bleak to me. But what if it's not just any old illness, and there's a reason for it? If someone gave you these memories intentionally, that gives you a purpose. That means you have a goal, a reason to go on fighting."

"What goal? What the hell are you talking about?" I said.

"You have to give it to someone else. That's the only way to buy yourself more time. You must pass it on."

"And how do you know this?" I said.

"Because it happened to my friend. When he was sexually active he led a relatively normal life. Slept at night, minimal marks on his body. Those little black spirals you mentioned came and went, but they'd start to grow when he didn't have sex for a while, only vanishing once he got laid again.

"It wasn't until my friend realized that he was giving the Blot to each new girl he slept with that he stopped. He gave up the game, and that was when the symptoms really got bad. He had nightmares every time he slept, until one day, he stopped sleeping altogether. Those black spots on his genitals spiraled outward until he was covered with them, a single, giant, walking Blotling. He lost his mind. At the end, the last time I saw him, he couldn't even put two words together. Two days later, he was dead."

"Jesus Christ," I said.

Ink slouched, combed his hair with his fingers, and sat up straight again. "Now here I am, talking to you instead of him. It's sad, really. The guy's game was phenomenal. He was my mentor. Taught me everything he knew. You, on the other hand, have got a long way to go to even have a chance at surviving this thing, Boy Scout. And you're running out of time. You don't want to end up like all those other trillions of dead branches on the tree of evolution, do you? No, I don't think you do," Ink said.

"So what should I do?" I said.

Ink drummed his fingers on the table. "You either need to learn to fuck a lot of different women, or you'd better write a nice, heartfelt message to your mom and dad letting them know you're not coming home."

"Would you?" I said.

Ink studied me a long time before responding. "If it was them or me, of course I would. You need to take another look around, Boy Scout. This great moral dilemma you're in isn't one. If you don't learn to play this game, the game is going to kill you. But knowing that won't condemn you. It will liberate you. And in time, you might come to enjoy it, maybe even master it. After all, there is nothing in the universe better than getting what you want."

Goddamn this asshole. Goddamn this piece of shit. I'm not going to subject anyone else to this. I'm not going to hurt people I don't even know. But I have to, or I'm going to die. I can feel it every morning when I wake up exhausted, every night when I lie awake because I don't want to sleep. Ink is right. I don't have a choice. Goddamn him. Ink is right.

And kneeling before that dark altar, I said, "Will you teach me?"

Ink leaned back in his chair, and for the briefest instant as the lamplight fell unevenly on his face, dividing it half into light and half into shadow, I saw the flicker of a golden spiral dancing in his eye.

"Yes. I'll teach you," Ink said.

VI

'Neath all his masks, man is a beast
There comes a point where he will cease
And turn into those howling winds
That drown his demons kept within.

The battle was short as the first
The king's men moaned how they were curs'd
By fallen brothers whose ghosts came
With red slaughter to wake the day.

The Good Knight's last kill tried to run
In distant woods was overcome,
By water's edge the boy gave up,
And got his head crushed with a rock.

When the Knight glanced up from his rage
A third was there, upon the lake
A girl with hair like summer ale
And eyes smould'ring like dragon scales.

"Lady Rusalka[4], forgive me!
Your sacred shape, I did not see!"
Arkadius knelt, begged, and pled.
She'd seen his gilded soul naked.

"The child was not quite innocent,"
The nymph gave her merc'ful judgment.
"Manhood is brotherhood, did you forget?
Make haste,
Correct yourself…
There is still time yet."

[4] *A female water spirit known for her vengeance.*

EPILOGUE

THE UNIVERSE doesn't work in cycles. It works in spirals. What goes around comes around, true; eternal return is also true, that what has come before will come again, and there is nothing new under the sun. But when it comes, it is always a little higher, a little thinner, a little older than before. The rings of the universe are forever moving outward. They never overlap no matter how similar their parallels may seem. We are none of us doomed to go round and round on the same old single, spinning wheel, but challenged to grow outward upon many. Because eternal return isn't a wheel. It is a spiral.

The Night Country was a real place, and it wasn't hard to see why I'd been sent there. Spirals have gravity. You may never be able to find the top of one, but you can always find the bottom.

I awoke to find the Burrow entombed in a cold, drunken silence. No time at all had passed since I'd left. I knew that because I was still on my feet. I caught myself mid-step as I began to lose my balance, like waking up from a dream of falling. It was hell to will my body to move. Queen Rat would sleep for one more torch at least before she awoke and discovered the Glass Book was gone. If I was still in the Burrow when that happened, I was a dead man.

My next stop was Zaea's cell. There was a guard outside dozing at his watch. His eyelid flickered when he heard me coming, but I blotted into him and bashed his head against the cave wall before he could open it completely. I didn't kill him, but he'd be out for at least an hour. I locked his body in the cell next to Zaea's and threw the keys down her privy shaft.

Zaea was sound asleep, curled up in a ball on the floor of her cell. They hadn't given her a bed. There was a bandage over the wound on her head stained with red and yellow fluid. The rawness of her betrayal still stung. Seeing her only made it sting worse. But somehow that pain no longer seemed to matter. I couldn't leave without saying goodbye.

I crept silently to Zaea's bedside, knelt, and gently lifted her right eyelid with the tip of my finger. A golden spiral burned within the stillness of her sleeping eye. I let her eyelid fall and kissed her on the forehead.

"Until next time, Princess. Say a prayer for your father when you wake up. And one for me."

Visitors do not stir or mumble in their sleep; even their breaths and heartbeats are difficult to measure, because the intervals are so long, barely enough to keep a loaner body reanimated. But I could have sworn I saw her lip tremble. I waited there as long as I could, then with a final glance, departed back into that gnawing gloom.

I left Zaea's cell door open. It was the least I could do after all the times she'd helped me.

I was careful to stay close to the walls and peek around every corner as I made my way toward the station platform, but I eventually relaxed. There was no one around. When I reached the Salt Chapel and still hadn't seen a single guard, I knew I was home free.

If anyone found me and learned what I was carrying, I'd be imprisoned, tried, and executed before breakfast. Yet the possibility of getting caught dwindled with each step I took closer to the subway platform, and the maze of the Undersprawl that lay beyond.

The power of my decision, and the thought of the inconceivable power it might bring me, made me feel high.

I wanted the power to control the Blot, to be able to traverse the Spiral at will, like it was said the Crippled King could. If that meant that I had to kill him, I would. If it meant I had to cast the Vermin aside and become his disciple, then I would do that, too. I didn't want to betray my friends. Most of all, I didn't want to do anything that would hurt Zaea. But there was no future for me here in the Burrow, fighting this hopeless fight. I'd have a target painted on my back until the day I died face-down in the snow.

If I could learn to control the Blot, I could save Zaea. I could save Kashka. I could save myself. Maybe I could even save Carly. Or if not, I would become so powerful it wouldn't matter.

Every one of my justifications for betraying them was as empty as the last. The truth was that I was sick of being a failure. The Blot was going to kill me, and I was scared. I was living on borrowed time.

I paused to look inside the Salt Chapel as I passed by. The door was ajar, and the candles lit. I remembered that Gator's memorial service was supposed to be held three torches later.

I opened the door all the way and stepped in. There were two busts of fresh-hewn salt stone standing at the foot of the altar wreathed in piles of white dust and flowers. One of the busts bore Gator's face. The other was Squirrel's.

Maybe he died while I was sleeping, or he's so close the undertaker started working on his headstone, I thought.

Only the bravest Vermin earned grave markers in the fruit orchards of the Last Station. Their busts would stand beneath the weak, drooping boughs of apple and peach trees above the soil where their bodies had been laid to rest. Now Gator and Squirrel would nourish the Burrow for as long as there were people to nourish.

I wanted to thank them, but a voice cut through the silence of the chapel like the snap of a blade.

"Come to ask for forgiveness?" Barn Owl said, stepping out of the shadows behind the door.

I spun around to see the tall, beak-nosed woman rise from the rearmost pew of the church. My fingers snaked under my furs to clutch the Glass Book, but I knew it was too late to hide its awkward, rectangular bulge. "Just to say goodbye. What about you?" I said.

Barn Owl placed one hand on her hip and scowled. "I was waiting, Leech."

"Waiting for who?" I said.

"You, asshole. You're more obvious than a boner in a sweat lodge, y'know that? Did you really think none of us would notice you sneaking off with the queen's new favorite page-turner? You didn't even take a last shot of vodka with us. Now *that*, my young greenboots, is bad form. You're always supposed to have a last drink with the people who would kill and die for you before you turn tail and run," Barn Owl said.

I stood my ground. "If you're planning on killing me, I promise I'm going to take you with me," I said.

Barn Owl relaxed her posture, letting out a chuckle. "Ha! No you ain't. I didn't come here to kill you, Leech. Not even to talk you out of what you're about to do. We all knew you would."

She pointed to the altar, where the Wanderer's floating image swayed in the flickering light of the glowmoss. "You see, unlike some of these other knuckleheads, I actually believe in him. I believe in him so much that I'm willing to let you go, because I know he has a plan. Oh, you've heard of it before. I can read your face clearer than that book you're so indiscreetly hiding beneath your jacket. I know he has a plan for all of us. I think you know it, too. You may have even used to believe it, once. Well, I *still* believe it. And I know his plan is greater than all of us. Greater than you, greater than me, greater than the Vermin and Queen Rat, even greater than the Crippled King."

"Could be," I said.

Barn Owl raised her hands to the ceiling. "We are the fire, Leech. You can spread darkness, or you can spread light. The choice is yours. And if this is what you truly believe in your heart is right, then I have no choice but to help you, because I ain't Him, and I don't know. I only know what I see, and when I see you, I don't see an evil man. Just a lost one."

She dug deep in her coat pocket and pulled out the magic mirror she used to navigate the tunnels of the Burrow, wincing as her bandaged fingers touched cloth. Placing it in the palm of my hand, she said, "Take this. I pray it helps you find your way home."

As Barn Owl brushed past me toward the door, I said, "Why?"

"You really are dumb as shit, aren't you?" Barn Owl said. "I just told you why. Maybe not all our problems can be solved by killing each other. Maybe that's what got us down here in the first place. Sometimes I wonder. What if the Crippled King was just a lost boy like you? What if he wasn't always the genocidal son of a bitch he is now, and all he needed to stay on the right path was the help of someone who saw the good in him? What if the fact that no one did is what caused him to stray?

"Think about it, Leech. That's all I ask of you while you're bending us low and fucking us over. Just think about it. Oh, and by the way, next time you decide to dust a couple of guards, don't stuff the bodies in the fuckin' mop closet. We mop our floors every torch around here."

With that, Barn Owl turned and vanished into the shadows.

I ran.

I exited the Burrow the same way I'd came in, a stairway hidden on the slope of a great, snow-covered valley. A whirlwind of black-bellied clouds swirled over the ghost-white plane of the Surface. I looked up at the hanging umbilicus of the Echelon. A golden paradise awaited me above that smooth, ebony moon. All I had to do was climb.

A distant squawk bit into my eardrums as I trudged down the snowy slope. A hawk was wheeling slowly through the battering gusts of wind overhead. It was the same bird I had seen during the liberation of the prison camp, a snow-white hawk with amber eyes.

He landed on the roof of a ruined house nearby. We stared at each other for a long while, neither of us moving nor making a sound. In his gaze was an invitation that we both knew I would accept. I can't say it was right, but it's what I did.

Mr. Snow squawked once, twice, three times, then took flight, and I followed him to the Amber City.

An hour later, long after I'd gone, another shape emerged from the tunnel mouth. It was a girl with short, whiskey-colored hair. Her head was heavily bandaged and she walked with a limp, carefully retracing a trail of footsteps already being reclaimed by the snow.

End of Book One.

About the Author

Adam Vine was born in Northern California. By day, he is a game writer and designer. He has lived in four countries and visited thirty. His short fiction has appeared in various horror, science fiction, and literary fiction magazines and anthologies. When he is not writing, he is traveling, reading something icky, or teaching himself to play his mandolin. He currently resides in Germany.

Made in the USA
Columbia, SC
27 July 2017